NO STRINGS

LUCY BEXLEY

WHAT READERS ARE SAYING ABOUT LUCY'S BOOKS...

MUST LOVE SILENCE
(A 2021 Goldie Finalist)

Lucy Bexley manages to keep her novel on the light and heartwarming side, with quirky wit, a healthy touch of sarcasm and obvious tenderness towards her characters.
—Rainbow Literary Society, Review by Jude

Must Love Silence is Bexley's debut novel but you would never know that from reading it. She does a fantastic job of offering up two main characters who are both struggling in different ways in a way that feels real. For the time it took me to read this book, I was part of that world. Despite the heavy topics it delves into, the novel has a lot of humor and feels a little like an old-school romantic comedy with plenty of awkward circumstances and clumsy moments that just make the characters even more endearing.
—The Lesbian Review, Cate's Top Books of 2020

Lucy Bexley placed a book in our hands, said "Here you go. It's my first one. I'm really proud of it. I hope you like it." Yeah, we do, Lucy. A lot.

—KJ

Must Love Silence is a wonderful debut novel by Lucy Bexley. It contains everything I love in a fantastic romance: plot, character development, sharp and witty writing, and sensuality. There are some hot sex scenes in here. (fanning myself).

—Lesbian Romance Reader

CHECKING IT TWICE

This is a wonderful heartwarming romance. I adore Lucy's writing.

—Lorraine Rusnack

A really sweet and fun to read novella. I love how Hal and Sacha's characters were written. Both are so charming in their own way. They have good chemistry and they both complement each other. Another good one from Lucy Bexley!

—Christian M.

I really like how Bexley's stories have this humor through them but that they are not over the top. It's the kind that makes you feel warm and sticks a smile on your face. Bexley writes well and puts a surprising amount of depth into the characters, considering this is a novella. I was really impressed with how good even the secondary characters were and that Bexley had the time to make them feel so well formed.

—Lex Kent

THE BRIGHT SIDE

It had just the right about of humor, romance, character development and well….sex.
    —Statum

This group project continues to impress me. I really got a feel for each of the trio of friends. I really want to go to Denver so they can sell me a house, fix it up, and decorate it.
    —Lesbian Romance Reader

JUST MY TYPE

This is a sexy, fun, self-aware read that you won't be able to put down. No matter how you feel about vampires, read this anyway. You'll love it, I promise.
    —Cate Pearce

Cute, quirky, sexy, and hilarious!
    —Riley Scott

I wouldn't hesitate to recommend Just My Type to fans of supernatural romance, and of lesbian supernatural romance in particular. But it strikes me that horror fans might love it, too - and might find themselves wondering, as I am now, what Book 2 in the Just My Type series might look like.
    —TC Parker

Cover Concept: Lucy Bexley

Cover Design: Bryce Oakley

SYNOPSIS

Fun is the one thing **Elsie Webb** takes seriously. Though she'd be having a lot more of it if Haelstrom Media paid her enough to actually get out of debt. She's determined to hold out on contract negotiations for her kids' television show Fangley Heights until she gets what she deserves. There's only one problem, the head of the network just died and left her future more uncertain than ever.

Forty-eight hours and one funeral–that's all **Jones Haelstrom** has to get through before she can return to her life in LA that's as ordered and sparse as an IKEA showroom. When she steps in as CEO of her father's media company, Elsie Webb is her first problem to deal with. Elsie ends up challenging Jones in ways she never could have predicted, starting with an attraction neither can avoid.

As their attraction teeters on the edge of something more both agree to keep it casual. A no-strings agreement and disclosure to HR should be enough to keep things between Jones and Elsie from getting tangled, right?

ALSO BY LUCY BEXLEY

Must Love Silence

The Bright Side

Checking It Twice

Just My Type

Flying First

First Day: A Flying First Short

No Strings

ACKNOWLEDGMENTS

This is by far the longest story I've ever written, so I have even more people to thank. Writing is often a solitary endeavor, but getting the best version of book into the world takes a lesfic village.

To Em, Sam, and Amanda, thank you for making this book much better than I could have on my own.

Dor, thank you for your amazing proof-reading, you saved me for making some downright odd mistakes.

Thanks to my alpha and beta readers: Steph, Bryce, KD, Anita, Angie, Wynnde, Sarah, Sofi, and Susie. Thank you for the care and kindness you showed earlier versions of this book.

G, thanks for all you do so I can write terrible jokes on the internet and also in word documents. It's a dream come true. My cats contributed all typos.

B & S, there a few jokes in here just for you two, as you know one-liners are my love language.

Anna, thanks for encouraging me to write in the first place. I can't believe you're still putting up with me.

Mandi, thank you for your first pass, your final pass and everything in between! Knowing you has greatly improved my life. SC4E.

To all my twitter pals, you make my days brighter and support me at my most absurd. Your friendship is a gift I don't take for granted.

And most of all, thanks to everyone reading this! None of this would be possible without your support.

For everyone who believes that silliness is a virtue.

And for Fozzie, who taught me how to be funny long before I was in on the joke.

But most of all for Em. You restored my faith in this story and myself. I'm not sure if it was witchcraft or extreme kindness, though I suppose both are a kind of magic.

CHAPTER ONE
ELSIE

Was hitting someone with a puppet technically assault? Elsie's mind said yes, but her heart—and hopefully a jury—said no. She didn't want to risk hurting the star of the show, even if he was made of felt. Not to mention, that bundle of fabric and stuffing kept a roof over her head. Elsie grimaced. She didn't really think of Fangley like that—he was a more realized person than half of her colleagues.

The set of her show Fangley Heights was gearing up for a day of filming and Elsie was already nearing her limit.

"Stop trying to control the puppet. Relax. Let *it* control you."

Elsie cringed as Trey's hand came to rest on her shoulder like a small, hot pancake, lingering for a few scorching seconds before it slid off. Trey used his hypnotist's voice, something he'd learned from one of his afternoon acting workshops. Soft and wispy and boring as hell.

Elsie had to admit it was effective. Talking to Trey did make her want to pass out to escape any further interaction with him. His personality was a constant interruption. It was like he couldn't resist talking when she was trying to focus.

Her entire job was to control puppets, and he was trying to make it into some kind of metaphorical, New Age thing instead of what it was: skillful manipulation. These puppets didn't even have strings.

As the nephew of the Haelstrom's second in charge, Trey was the network's golden boy even though Elsie carried the show and frankly, she was reaching her limit with being anyone's second choice. And okay, so maybe there was that one time she had insulted some 'important' sponsors by comparing their conversation to oyster crackers that have been in an old woman's purse since the Great Depression. So dry she was left choking on their dust. But still, people didn't give second chances anymore? Was it too late to stick a stipulation in her contract for next season that Trey's puppet, Smirch, would meet an untimely end? To date, giving Trey's puppet the worst possible name was her proudest accomplishment. Even if it was technically her roommate, Avery, who had come up with it during a particularly intense game of Jenga.

Elsie took a deep breath to keep from laughing at the memory of Avery knocking over the tower in exuberance when the name occurred to them. She checked her monitor as she raised her right arm over her head and above the small wall in front of her. One thing they don't tell you about puppeteering is, it makes your shoulders look great. Like seriously ripped. Well, mostly just the one shoulder, but still they should put that in the drama school brochure. Maybe she could contribute that tidbit so they'd stop asking her for money, which they absolutely knew she didn't have.

"I think if you just loosen your wrist, you could—"

Elsie sliced her gaze at Trey.

His warm whisper washed over her face and she shuddered. With her headset over her ears, she couldn't hear most of what he was saying, a small mercy, but the fact that she could see a bit of sweat on his forehead made his proximity vaguely threatening. What she'd like to do was control him. She'd donate him to Goodwill.

Elsie glanced back down at her monitor. Trey's fingers seared her skin as they wound around her wrist. His new gold watch jangled. She added 'demand a raise' to her running mental list of contract negotiation points. Elsie had a good feeling that all she had to do to get all the stipulations she wanted was to hold out for a few more days. The network would cave, she just knew it.

She took a deep breath and lowered her headset. "Are you trying to derail my entire process?"

"You just looked like you needed my help keeping this little guy steady." Trey reached up to touch Fangley. *Nobody* touched Elsie's puppet. She flicked her wrist so Fangley's hand smacked Trey's forehead before he had the chance. He blinked at her but made no move to call the authorities. So hitting someone annoying with a puppet technically wasn't assault, just as she'd suspected.

Rebecca, the showrunner, poked her head through the studio door and called Trey over. Elsie felt the tension drain out of her. Even Fangley's shoulders relaxed.

Elsie used the momentary peace to ready herself for the scene they were filming that afternoon, the one where Fangley and his cat sidekick, Ratatouille, put on way too much makeup in an attempt to fit in. The beautiful thing about the show was that its connection to reality could be tenuous as long as the bits were engaging. For example, why would a blue-tinted young vampire like Fangley and his Maine Coon sidekick think doing a full clown face of makeup would make them *less* conspicuous? Either way, she was looking forward to the arrival of Gabby, Ratatouille's handler.

The Fangley universe worked on a perfect kind of logic: very little of it.

Fangley Heights was in its third year of production. Most days Elsie couldn't believe her luck. She had picked essentially the most unemployable major, despite her father's desire for her to do something respectable. What he really meant was something with a high earning potential. Her father saw money as a down payment toward happiness, but he always forgot about the mortgage. Elsie had found no correlation between respectability and the size of her bank account. Quite the opposite, actually. Besides, she literally couldn't do math or handle bills. Even calculating tips was beyond her. On the other hand, the idea of saving people made something catch in her chest. So business and medicine were out. Her father wanted her to be employable. She wanted to be happy. But on *Fangley Heights*, most days she was both. Now if only everyone she'd ever met would stop making weird jokes about her being a puppeteer. At the very least bad jokes should be original.

But there wouldn't be a job, puppeteer or otherwise, if she couldn't get next season's agreement worked out. With each contractless day she barreled closer to an uncertain future.

She'd pushed her luck in negotiations, but why shouldn't she be better compensated? Fangley was her intellectual property, even if Haelstrom Media owned the trademark. Though it felt hard to say where everything would land with that in light of Hunter Haelstrom's recent passing. That little vamp went all the way back to a web series she'd done to kill the time she should have spent memorizing Hamlet in grad school. A little something productive to assuage her guilt over wasting time.

Her classmates tried to dismiss children's television as fluff, but this wasn't Punch and Judy hour. *Fangley Heights* had depth. It had whimsy with slightly charred edges. It only barely made sense. It was a show about an orphan vampire being fostered by a family in Brooklyn—a true American story. When Haelstrom Media had reached out to her just before graduation, she couldn't believe her luck. Elsie had felt so sure signing that contract would be her golden ticket, but she was young and naive. She didn't understand sub-clauses and percentages or that one paragraph they always threw in that stipulated media appearance requirements.

Maybe they'd learned their lesson after her season one sponsor disaster. She wished now she'd read that contract, committed every line to memory. Been asked to do a series of complicated crosswords before signing it. But she hadn't, because this was back when she still trusted people to do the right thing. She thought she'd pay off her loans, buy an apartment, and stop worrying about getting by. And yet, they were wrapping up season three and she was still sharing a place with Avery. Treating themselves meant the fancy two-for-one egg roll special.

Elsie was struggling, even though her character was a cultural icon to kids everywhere who were still learning to tie their shoelaces. Fangley was a celebrity. If a puppet could be a celeb. What was she saying? *Of course* a puppet could be famous. Oscar the Grouch? Rizzo? Iconic. Plus, as a nine-year-old vampire desperate to fit in, Fangley was relatable. For the pun-filled *Make-Over-Done* episode, Elsie had spent a solid week working with their local designer and props team on *Drag Fangley*, as she'd been thinking of him. He looked almost frightening this way, just this side of familiar, like a woman in a facemask. A ghoul you could trust.

Elsie studied Fangley and wondered if she should have let the costume department and designers just craft a mask for him. They had made some latex prototypes to mimic a cold cream and blush treatment, but they all looked too much like meringue, the cold cream mask crested in waves. And when Elsie had done a run-through of the scenes with Fangley and the mask, none of his expressions had been visible. Which upped the creep factor considerably past the tolerance of their kindergarten focus group.

The creation of a new Fangley had set them back several weeks and Rebecca warned they were approaching a meeting-with-the-boss level of being behind schedule. All of that was up-in-the-air now with the new boss still being uncertain. But Elsie had a good feeling about today. The "makeup" could be layered on individually to the new version of Fangley; she had the blush and eyelashes lined up on a table behind the wall of the set. Everything was ready to stick on Fangley's ghastly face. They'd be taking a Mr. Potato Head approach. There was probably a merchandising opportunity here, not that she was giving those ideas away to Haelstrom Media for free anymore. Elsie was still waiting to see any income from her point zero five percent share of sales from trademarked Fangley merchandise.

Elsie set about her pre-rehearsal routine. The choreography of puppets was intense. Like synchronized swimming, or one of those two-piece horse costumes. Reliably, Elsie was the ass of their outfit. In this week's episode, Amanda was playing Fangley's next-door neighbor and Trey was playing Fangley's nemesis, the elementary school's suspicious science teacher. A perfect role because it was easy for Elsie and Fangley to get into the mindset of hating him.

Elsie racked her body over the foam roller, extending her back and listening to it creak and pop as she raised her arms over her head. They had an area off to the side of the set for the explicit purpose of working out the kinks that came with contorting their bodies into puppeteering postures. Sometimes it took hours after a shoot for the stiffness in Elsie's torso to fade to tolerable. She brought her hands to the ground, bracing into a wheel shape. There was a whiff of the medieval about modern-day self-care; facial peels, cooking yourself in the sun, stretching your body over a cylinder until it gave way with a series of satisfying cracks. Torture therapy.

Elsie stood slowly, like she was being raised to standing. She punched in her code and freed Fangley from his case. The puppets sitting in a row in their glass enclosures, like little lockers, reminded Elsie of babies in a hospital nursery. Tempting to snatch but constantly monitored.

Elsie set Fangley on the fake stone wall as she considered his outfit. In an increasingly routine bout of interference, the network had insisted on Fangley wearing his black cape even though that made no sense if he was trying to fit in. Everyone knew Fangley preferred to only wear his cape at home, it was a comfort item, like a blanket. But there was concern from 'certain sectors of the market' that kids were forgetting that Fangley was a vampire because the show was doing too good a job of humanizing him. Even though vampires are human, technically. Though in this case, everyone's a puppet.

The door to the fake brownstone creaked open, and out stepped Trey. His conversation with Rebecca must have been brief for him to already be back on set; Elsie hadn't realized they'd finished talking already. So much for her break.

Now she was left to wonder how long Trey had been there, silently observing her? Add that to the list of things it was better to never know. Maybe the network should be more concerned about humanizing Trey.

He hopped down the stairs from the front door to the stage and clicked his heels. In her head, Elsie watched a fantasy of him slipping on a banana peel. Ah, the power of imagination.

"So are we going to do this scene, Els? I've got a good feeling about this afternoon."

"I always come to work, Trey."

"As long as you don't throw a fit about outfits again." He reached for Elsie's shoulder but pulled his hand back as though her arm had been replaced with a bear trap. So, he had the ability to read body language after all.

"Having an opinion isn't throwing a fit. Are you going to throw a fit about your lines?" Trey's secondary character, Myrtle, was slated to be roped in by Fangley to help fix his makeup disaster in time for the spelling bee.

"No self-respecting ten-year-old girl would go along with Fangley's makeover plan."

"As someone who was once a ten-year-old girl, I can confirm that they're usually not very self-respecting."

Elsie breathed a sigh of relief as the director walked onto the set. The official signal that filming was about to start. Only Trey could be less annoying playing an evil puppet named Smirch than as himself.

THEY WERE deep into filming the second scene, the one with Trey's character, when he tripped over Elsie's not-at-all outstretched leg and they had to pause for the day. As they broke and the crew brought Trey ice, Rebecca waved Elsie over to the production control room.

This would be a good opportunity to get Rebecca's advice on her contract woes. Though the way her forehead was doing a Shar-Pei impression gave Elsie pause. Maybe she could see if the props department still had some of that cold cream from *Drag Fangley* on hand.

"So, I've got some bad news." Rebecca gave her a tight smile.

"Okay." *Shit.* "Is everything alright with Fangley?"

"Yes, of course. He's a puppet." Rebecca looked at Elsie like she was ridiculous for caring about the vampire that was literally keeping them both in a job. Millions of people cared about Fangley. He even had his own fan club: The Fangers. Not a name she would have chosen, but the fanbase of five-year-olds were not to be swayed.

"I just got word from the network, and well, you're aware that Hunter Haelstrom passed away last week, right?"

"Yes, it's very unfortunate." Elsie nodded. It was one of those things that was sad in the *royal we* sense but not necessarily upsetting to her personally.

Rebecca shrugged. "He was in his 80s and never once looked me in the eye."

"Okay, so marginally sad. I assume some people are very upset. I didn't really know him, aside from the name on my check. Do you have any idea who's taking over? Have you heard anything?"

"I'm pretty sure the will named his widow. I've only met her once, at the Christmas party two years ago, but I got the sense she wasn't a fan of the work we do here on the Heights. Did you meet her there?"

"Oh, I think I was sick that day." Elsie shrugged. She probably had been sick—sick of absolutely everything going on at work. "Do you think she'll change the show? I mean, she wouldn't, right? The numbers are good and growing each year, but I don't trust Stu for a second not to try to oust us."

Rebecca raised her hands. "I don't have any information. I know these things aren't always logical. We should take every opportunity to make sure she knows how amazing this show is. And I think it's in our best interest to get this season wrapped this week even if it means spending a few nights together. I don't want Stu to see even the tiniest window to give this show to Trey."

"I don't mind pulling all-nighters, but you know I have a no-overnights-with-Trey policy." Elsie shuddered. "Besides, who will get Trey an air cast? He might even lose the leg."

"I've never met anyone who applies soccer foul performances to real life. Once I saw him get a paper cut and fall to the ground asking for stitches."

Elsie caught the gleam in Rebecca's eye. She almost never let loose on Trey. Rebecca was in her 50s and the consummate professional. At work, anyway. Rebecca at Chewy's, the bar down the street, was a delightful person to spend time hating things with.

Elsie wiped a tear of laughter from her eye and took a deep breath. She loved mean Rebecca. Was there anything more soul-nourishing than shit talk? "I'm so sad I missed that. Next time keep the camera running. We can add it to his showreel. Maybe get him some more dramatic roles."

"Noted." Rebecca's face sobered. "I think it's critical for everyone to sign and lock in their contracts. Please tell me you're not still dragging your feet on yours." Rebecca looked at Elsie like she was going to explain why she wasn't mad, just disappointed.

Elsie grimaced.

"I mean it about your contract, Elsie. You need to sign."

"Signing it is me saying it's okay to treat me this way. To underpay me while making a killing off of my ideas." Elsie's last contract draft had been an offer so laughably low that she'd used it to sop up her spilled Lucky Charms milk.

She had *created* the show, and yet every year it felt like she was begging them to pay her enough to buy fresh vegetables. The fact that an apple in Manhattan went for ten dollars was beside the point. Then again, wasn't some money better than no money at all? That's what Avery would tell her. *Just keep us in bubble bath and bubble tea, babe.* Maybe if the show went up a little and met her halfway she could consider maybe, possibly, signing her name on the dotted line. Which was always a solid line, actually.

"I know you wanted to hold out for more money, and I think they're ready to meet you at…" Rebecca glanced at her iPad. "Seven percent below your ask. I'd take it if I were you."

All wavering drained from Elsie. *Seven percent BELOW her ask?* Were they absolutely fucking with her? Last week it was five percent. She planted her feet. Absolutely fuck that. "That's a worse offer than before. How much below Trey's ask are you advising him to take?"

"Even if I had all the details, *which I don't,* you know I can't discuss the specifics of other people's contracts." Rebecca's eyes flitted to the monitor in the control room that showed Trey sitting on the floor holding ice on his ankle and scrolling through his phone.

"Right, because telling me how much I'm being screwed would be grossly unfair to you and the network." Elsie turned to leave. She had an overwhelming desire for this day to end.

Rebecca caught her arm. "Look, just think about it, okay? This show matters so much to all of us. I don't want to see your dream crumble."

But Elsie *had* thought about it. Fangley Heights was her baby. The only thing she'd ever invested herself in fully. But if she could love something she created this much, who was to say she couldn't do it again? She thought about the notebook on her desk, full of half-finished sketches and jokes that brought tears to her eyes. That had always been her barometer for good ideas—what reaction they sparked in her. If she didn't find her own jokes funny, why would anyone else?

Elsie pushed open the door. "Trust me, Rebecca, this is far from my only dream." The door clattered behind her. If drama school had taught her anything, it was the power of a dramatic exit.

CHAPTER TWO
JONES

Jones was late. Her mother, Birdie, loved to say that she herself had never been late a day in her life, because there's no such thing as being late when you run the show, though Jones had a distinct memory of waiting until dusk for Birdie to pick her up after school. Watching the parking lot next to the playground empty until it was just her and Carl, the janitor. (Yes, as a child she'd spent enough time with the school janitor to be on a first-name basis.) Those were the days that Birdie claimed school simply ended earlier than expected.

Jones had inherited a lot of things, but her mother's brazen disregard for others wasn't among them. Jones was late because she didn't want any part of where she was headed. That, and she was currently responsible for another very small human who walked in slow motion. And it was probably even more important for her to be on time now that she was the one in charge of her father's company, however temporarily. She needed to give the impression that it might be permanent, otherwise no one would take her seriously.

After the funeral, Jones' stepmother had booked herself a few days at the spa. It felt so weird to Jones to call someone eleven years younger her stepmother. When Charity asked for time to herself, Jones had wanted to be annoyed, but she understood that Charity was facing a life much different from the one she'd had a week ago. If Birdie had taught her anything, it was that mothers didn't have to be selfless. Sometimes the very act of being selfish, knowing what you needed and taking it, was the thing that made us better to those we care about. So Jones had said she'd stay with her father's child. Well, his other child. Her brother—she needed to get used to saying that. Even if it was just until Charity got back from her mud baths and mourning. Only three days to go, or closer to two depending on what time Charity got back on Saturday for Bentley's birthday. And then Jones could go back to her life. Back to only caring for herself. She'd pick up right where she left off, reviewing the new thousand-dollar snail serum in every A-lister's virtual cart. She could feel the hydrating benefits already.

The city sky gave a roll of thunder. Though it could have been a building being demolished. Both equally common occurrences. Actually, the city probably had more demolition dust storms than actual storms.

Jones glanced down to check on Bentley to make sure she'd remembered his rain jacket but he was gone. Children are like assassins, most dangerous when they're silent. She stopped in the middle of the sidewalk. Other pedestrians on West 42nd streamed around her; one gentleman cross-checked her and knocked her bag to the ground. Apparently Mr. Hockey Moves had places to be, but he could have looked a little less smug about it. Jones shook it off. It wasn't like she was a tourist, even if she technically hadn't lived here in close to two decades. She retrieved her bag then widened her stance to withstand further attempts to trample her as she spun around slowly and scanned her surroundings.

Jones had been in charge for three days and she'd already

lost her brother. She'd never realized panic was a thing she could taste—it sat like battery acid in the back of her throat.

She was looking for a small child dressed like an executive on his yacht. Chinos, boat shoes, one of those little belts with the whales on it—or was it lobsters? Either way, some sort of sea dweller she'd never mess with. One might think this look to be distinctive, but in Midtown it was yuppie camo. When it came to dressing him, she'd done the best with the options available to her. It wasn't just their thirty-seven-year age gap that was making this weird. At over forty, Jones had decided long ago that kids were not in her future. And now, everyone from the cashier at the bodega where she bought milk for her coffee that morning, to the owner of the florist for her father's memorial kept referring to Bentley as her son. Most times, she didn't have the energy to explain the intricacies of their modern family. It was, in a word, a mindfuck.

Jones spotted his tiny figure dressed in an absurdly expensive Day-Glo sweater crouched on the sidewalk half a block back. She released a sharp exhale of relief. What was he—oh god he was picking up a piece of gum. Kids had immune systems of Teflon, right? Or at least city kids did. Honestly, for something Bentley could pick up off of a street in Manhattan, gum was pretty tame and unlikely to be lethal.

She walked back into the rushing stream of oncoming pedestrians and squatted down next to him. "Hey, buddy, can you stay with me?"

He looked up at her with the same slate blue eyes as her own, and it was then that she noticed he was chewing on something. Crunching, really, the sound as one with the jackhammer one avenue over. They really would be putting her immune system theory to the test.

Why would anyone leave a child in her care? Even if she had agreed, a few days was a few days too long.

Jones held out her hand for her brother's, but instead of reaching for it he leaned forward and spit into it. Gum, hard as a flattened penny landed in her palm. This was one for the books. Jones Haelstrom, kneeling on a city street with a palmful of spit and fossilized gum. She threw it into the oncoming traffic like a grenade.

What would Birdie have to say about this? *It's New York, if you're not eccentric there, you're not alive.*

Eccentric and in need of a shower. Oh, right, and really fucking late for this meeting with Haelstrom Media's lawyers.

Jones looked down at her knees. She was in the dress she'd worn to the funeral a few days before. For some reason, she'd expected to go back home to California shortly after the burial, before whatever this new interminable situation was. But what else could she do except offer to stay when Charity said she planned to leave Bentley with his nanny? *You could have gone straight to JFK and boarded a flight home,* Birdie's voice in her head supplied helpfully. Jones had agreed to stay, and now she was stuck like gum to the sidewalk, getting walked all over, while Charity was mummifying herself in a mixture of kelp and clay.

Jones scraped her palm on the concrete and stood.

She grabbed Bentley's hand and tried very hard not to think about why it was sticky.

THE BUILDING'S lobby had a mausoleum quality, all smooth white stone and echoes of ghosts. The double-height ceiling stretched upward, drawing her eye to a banner that hung above the gold elevators. It was a tapestry portrait, faded in the sun, so that the man's tie was now a magenta, but she'd know those icy eyes anywhere. Her father stared back at her like some sort of larger-than-life communist propaganda. Welcoming. Humbling. Deeply unsettling.

He had always considered himself above others.

The security guard glanced at her ID and waved her through. His generic black suit and the clear wire dangling along his neck like an errant curl, brought to mind a secret service agent. Well, even if the security was lax, he at least seemed prepared for secret comms about lunch deliveries. *The Eagle's chicken caesar wrap has landed.*

She knotted her free hand around the strap of her bag. On her other side, Bentley swayed repeatedly against her leg, knocking her off balance in her heels. How could three days create a year's worth of exhaustion? And why the hell was she wearing heels? Right, because she'd only brought one other pair of shoes, and they were her favorite slip-ons, which she loved too much to put them through the marble and meetings and misery of this day. Plus, without her father around, there was no one to get a rise out of by dressing down like she had when she'd interned for him in college.

For the first time in her life, Jones had under-packed. The call that her father had passed came in the middle of the night, and she'd thrown a few things in a carry-on. She figured she'd buy something somber in New York and take the first return flight she could find after a reasonably respectful amount of time. Say, twelve hours after his funeral. She'd definitely planned to be back for work on Monday. And, well, it was *a Monday*. And this was technically work. Only instead of returning to the silly little lifeforce-draining lifestyle articles her editor gave her about green juices puri-fying the soul, she was in a cold Manhattan lobby re-wearing her funeral clothes. Not that Jones would turn down a super fruit soul cleanse herself about now, such was the weakness of her resolve in that moment.

The elevator doors slid shut, and Jones met her own gaze in the mirrored surface. The doors had a slightly wavy effect, like a carnival funhouse where no one exits feeling good about themselves. It was like she was gazing at her future self, and that self was…exhausted. And oddly puffy. If she didn't find a place in New York that sold vegetables instead of bagels, she wouldn't survive the week.

Bentley wriggled his hand free and smashed a few extra buttons. *Perfect.*

They'd be taking the scenic route.

What was a few more minutes? When you're late you're late. And Bentley pressing buttons meant he wasn't eating street gum. Maybe she was starting to understand parents who were chill amid the chaos. She leaned back against the wall, taking some pressure off her feet. These heels were the devil's vise.

Bentley's reflection loomed. He was a captain of chaos, a titan of terror. He could pass for a boy CEO of a startup, heading to a meeting with an angel investor. Jones wished she'd thought to dress down as a power move. His look said *money matters to me but impressing you doesn't,* and frankly, Jones would be trying to channel that energy for the next hour of her life. She *hoped* this meeting didn't take more than an hour. She still needed to figure out dinner, and Bentley kept rejecting her salad options. Even the ones with exciting things like sunflower seeds or blueberries. Kids were impossible.

THE STUDIO WAS STILL BRIGHT, even though it was mostly deserted. A few people lingered near a small set, including a woman wearing a headset and arranging a jumble of stuffed animals.

Behind her, a throat cleared. Every muscle in Jones' neck locked.

"Ms. Haelstrom?"

A man with an egg-shaped head and a wreath of hair extended his hand. When he moved, his head gleamed brightly in the lights. "Stu Winkle, I'm not sure if you remember me. Do you still go by Joanie?"

Jones freed her hand from Bentley's and placed it in Stu's. He very nearly stifled his grimace as she transferred a bit of stickiness. Oh yes, she definitely remembered this guy. When she was a kid, he once offered her candy that was so warm from his pocket, the thought of it still made her gag. By the time she'd interned here during her senior year, his offers had been a lot more suggestive, though equally gross. Still, as much as she might find him distasteful, she couldn't just ignore her father's right-hand man, at least not while he was partially in charge of Haelstrom Media.

"Of course, Stu, good to see you still making people uncomfortable in the workplace. You can call me Jones." He kept shaking her hand until she pulled it from his grasp. Another maneuver she'd borrowed from Bentley.

Stu laughed like he was in on some joke between them. "Come on now, I was just being welcoming."

Jones ignored him. After her years of dealing with Stu and not wanting to annoy her dad, it felt nice to finally speak her mind. She squatted down. "Bentley, how about you go over there and play with the toys?"

Bentley took off running, his little boat shoes squeaking on the floor. Stu reached out a hand as though to pull the boy back.

Jones shot Stu an amused look. "Sorry, I probably should have asked first. Is that okay? I mean I could always bring him to the meeting."

Stu's face sobered at the mention of Bentley in the board-room. "Oh no, this is perfect. Fangley Heights babysits kids after school every day. It's their bread and butter. I'll just fire off a quick text, and someone will be here to watch him in just a minute."

She followed Stu to the door, but when he held it open with half his body blocking it, she stayed back. Jones wasn't exactly large, but she was an adult and there was no way her hips were getting through that space without him "acciden-tally" brushing against her. No thank you. The silence stretched as they both waited for the other to break and move first. Jones nodded at him, and after another moment he pushed the door wide and shuffled through. She'd hold her own door with two broken arms to avoid the feeling she was getting from him. Jones had gotten enough slime on her from the gum incident already. And she'd had enough actual contact on their walk from the train to last her a lifetime. Only the F train could make her miss the 405. At least in LA, accidental contact looked like being rear-ended.

Jones followed Stu through the labyrinth of hallways, her nervous energy ricocheting in her chest like a lightning bug trapped in a jar. Everything looked so different from when she'd interned here all those years ago, Haelstrom Media had moved up in the world both in terms of cultural cache and by two whole floors in this building. She fought the impulse to run and instead slowed to let herself fall a few paces behind. Her eyes scanned the gleaming white floors. She expected to see a trail of slimy footprints in the shape of his loafers, but they just let out a pitiful little dog toy squeak. If only she knew where she was going, she could excuse herself and find a restroom or a quiet corner to take a few deep breaths and center herself. She did a quick safety check for an exit sign and locked eyes with a woman who was watching them with an amused expression on her face.

The woman's gaze drifted over Jones appraisingly. Jones felt the heat of her green eyes like the sun on her skin. So maybe not amused. *But interested?*

Jones looked down at her weird funeral clothes. Okay, interest was unlikely. Maybe she was just sizing Jones up as the new boss. Jones straightened to her best boss height, which was just her real height, but more serious.

Jones watched as the woman raked her fingers through her shoulder-length brown hair, sweeping it to one side so that her curls shot out erratically. It was wavy in an uneven way that reminded Jones of finally letting her hair down at the end of the night. Sweet relief. The freedom of no one left to impress.

Though, if Jones was being honest, the woman had an air of not wanting to impress at all. It was *nice*. And the complete opposite of how she currently felt. So much of her life was people trying to win her over because of her last name and the reputation that came along with it. But this woman had her arms crossed, and she was openly staring. It was straight up subway etiquette. Her ripped coveralls weren't artful, but well worn, almost like the holes hadn't been there when she bought them. How novel. She had them unzipped to the waist with the arms knotted around her midriff, like she'd stopped midway through undressing. Coveralls should not be sexy. Everything about the woman was starting to feel deeply unfair to Jones. Her t-shirt had a weird pattern, black and purple and green. It reminded Jones of a bowling alley. An establishment she'd been invited to exactly once, and she'd promptly sprained her wrist. After that, Birdie had instituted a strict no sports birthday party and bat mitzvah rule, which was fine by her.

Was the OshKosh B'gosh woman on the crew for one of the shows? That would explain the giant hammer she was dragging behind her. It looked impossibly heavy. Jones wasn't a gym person and had no real concept of weight, beyond the fact that her groceries were always too heavy to carry, which was why she got them delivered.

Stu had kept walking, content to let this woman struggle. How irresponsible. Well, that was a potential workplace injury risk Jones wasn't willing to take the liability for. Not on her first day as interim CEO. Plus, if she offered her help, maybe she could do the impossible and make a friend here, instead of just meeting with weird leering men in bespoke suits.

"Can I help you with that?" Jones stepped toward the

woman, before she realized she'd made up her mind. Anything to avoid a lawsuit.

"With what?"

"That, um, hammer? I don't want you to get hurt." That's right. Jones was calm, logical. She had everything under control.

The woman's voice tipped into laughter. "Sure," she said, her eyes flashing and she flicked her wrist.

Shit. Not even an hour in and she was going to need a hospital. She'd never caught anything in her life, and she definitely wasn't going to start with a hammer. Jones ducked and braced for impact. The hammer glanced off her shoulder, and she waited for the pain to come; for her bones to become dust upon impact. Apparently, there would be a lawsuit after all.

And then the hammer bounced. Because Jones, the most gullible woman alive, was so out of her element that she thought the studio would have a mammoth tool lying around instead of some foam prop.

The other woman gave her a sheepish grin. The green in her eyes bloomed. "Oh, shit, sorry. I thought you'd try to catch it. Not…whatever that was." She gestured vaguely up and down Jones' body.

Jones would not blush. She was in charge today. "Why would I try to catch a hammer? It looks like the ones used to drive stakes on a railroad."

The woman shrugged. "I wasn't around when the first railroads were built. But this is television, baby. Nothing here is real."

She'd delivered that last line with an honest-to-God wink. People who could pull off winking had entirely too much power.

Jones felt rage and embarrassment fighting for prominence. And something else just beneath the surface, something that felt a lot like attraction. Since when was a woman throwing something at her a turn-on? *Say something. Anything.*

Jones searched her brain for something quippy. "But *I'm* real." *Ugh, not that.*

Green eyes looked her up and down again before the woman took a step back, then another. "Good to know. Thanks for offering to help. And sorry for hitting on you, you know… with the hammer."

The woman sent Jones a smirk that she felt low in her stomach. Jones was still watching her incredulously as she started walking and crashed full force into the squishy wall of Stu's body. *This could not be her life.*

"Your father never mentioned you were the chivalrous Haelstrom." A crocodile grin split Stu's face. Jones wanted to throw him back into the swamp.

"I'm surprised he mentioned me at all. But sure, I like to lend a hand when I can."

Something rustled behind them and Jones turned to look. She couldn't help it. The woman was pulling her hair back up into a messy bun, which, in turn, was causing her shirt to ride up and show—

"Yes, I can see that. Or a shoulder, in this case. Do you need some ice for that embarrassment?"

Jones fought back the sunburn feeling rising on her cheeks. She only wanted ice if it was a glacier drifting slowly out to sea with her on it. "Are you ready?"

"If you're sure you don't need medical attention, then I'm glad you're still interested in doing business today, since that's why you're here. Right this way." Stu was looking at her like he knew her, which he didn't. He didn't know a single thing.

"Who was that?" She demanded, forcing some authority into her voice. She needed to get this day back on track, now.

"Oh, no one really. Just Elsie, she works on Fangley Heights, that kids show."

"Doesn't that show have the fourth highest ratings on the network?"

"You should know better than to believe everything you read on the internet, Jones. If you wanted the data, you should have asked me for it. Besides, the show could be even more successful without Elsie Webb."

He held the door to the conference room open for her. Never trust a man who holds a door in such a way that you need to brush past him to enter. Stu had perfected that art. Had he learned nothing from his earlier attempt in the studio? Jones grabbed the door handle from him and pulled it so far open its hinges creaked. *There, enough room for everyone.* As she entered the room, she glanced down the polished table to the owlish lawyer sitting at the end. The space was a portrait of everything she'd never wanted. None of this should be her problem. Not the clothes, or the kid, or the embarrassment still flooding her veins from the hallway incident. Her father hadn't trusted her with anything since she'd bombed her internship. Though it wasn't really her fault that she'd refused to take coffee and lunch orders. Her father had accused Jones of being too much Birdie's daughter. Not willing to do what it took to succeed, just looking for a handout. But she wasn't, not really. She just didn't feel much like his daughter either.

Stu pulled out a chair with a dramatic bow, like it was some kind of gallant offering. Jones pulled out the next one over and sat down. This wasn't some restaurant without prices on the menu. He was not going to be in control of this for much longer.

"Sorry to call you in today, Ms. Haelstrom. If these contracts could have waited, believe me, we would have let them." The man extended his hand toward Jones. His grip was bruising. Like he didn't know the difference between a handshake and arm wrestling. "Chuck Westley. I'm your lawyer, well, the network's, professionally speaking."

Chuck and Stu, unreal. "Sure, nice to meet you. Jones is fine."

"So Joanie, like Chuck here was saying, we've gotta hammer out these contracts. No pun intended. The longer the negotiations drag on, the more tempted the talent will be to ask for more. You wouldn't believe how greedy they are. And believe me, we're already giving them plenty. It's children's television for God's sake and these people are confusing it with art."

"Again, it's Jones. Like I mentioned earlier, I did some research last night. It seems like the Children's Entertainment sector is where we make the majority of our money. Especially through merchandising."

"Like *I* said earlier, you can't believe everything you read on the internet." Stu smirked.

Jones sat up straighter. "Okay, so which part of that was incorrect?"

"None of it, I just meant generally speaking. But sure. It's easy to sell puppets and plush toys to five-year-olds. That's hardly an accomplishment." Stu's eyes shone black. A shark in the water. "I was telling you earlier that the show could be more successful. Your father and I were in early talks about a spinoff without Fangley's character. It would focus on Smirch, Trey's character, he's very popular."

Jones hummed noncommittally as she pulled a notebook from her bag and quickly sketched the path they'd taken through the halls. Stu might have escorted her in, but she'd be seeing herself out.

"I think we have a real opportunity here, Trey could be a star, but instead he's stuck listening to Elsie. We're wasting a lot of potential on Fangley Heights."

"Huh. Noted." Jones gave him a close-lipped smile and pulled forward the stack of contracts Chuck had slid toward her. No part of her wanted to review legalese. But who did? Contracts and terms and conditions, you only read them if you had to. And even then, she only skimmed before clicking accept. "So what exactly do you need from me?"

"Just a cursory review so you can sign off on the terms listed. This is really just following protocol. We've been hammering out these details for weeks. Think of yourself as a rubber stamp. Just a name on the line." The lawyer smiled warmly.

"O-kay," she said slowly, fanning through the top pages of the stack like they were a flip book about to reveal their stop-motion secret to her. "I'm not sure why I'd want to think of myself like that. Anything I should know about this contract for Elsie Webb with the red flag on it?"

"Well, Elsie's a bit of a handful. She got us in some hot water at a charity event last year where she refused to confirm Fangley's orientation," Chuck said.

"She got questions about the orientation of a vampire puppet? A child vampire puppet?" Jones was failing to see how Elsie was to blame in this example.

"I don't think it's unreasonable that people want to know what messages their children are getting," Stu said, his voice getting louder with each successive syllable. "But she made a joke of it. Once Elsie makes up her mind about something, there's nothing that can sway her. Everything becomes a moral issue for her. That night she asked the host why so many adults at the gala were sexually interested in puppets. And then later she apologized for kink shaming and recommended Furry conventions to those interested."

Jones held in a laugh, squinting through the glee that story made her feel. She would have paid good money to have been at that event. "And that bothered you all?"

"Of course it did. She lost us a lot of money, but we haven't figured out a way to do Fangley Heights without her. Anyway, we've had some back and forth on her contract negotiations, but I don't think we'll be getting much more pushback." Chuck pushed his glasses up his nose and flashed a look toward Stu.

Well, that sounded ominous. Stu's obvious push for his

nephew Trey was a red flag but unsurprising. In this town flattery and nepotism got you everywhere. But something else felt off about this pressure to sign, too, something lurking beneath the surface of these negotiations. She needed an out with a little time to think, and for once she had one in the form of a probably still sticky little brother. "You know what? I left Bentley hanging out down there, and I don't feel great about that. How about I take these with me and review them tonight?"

"Well, like I said, Joanie—"

Jones cleared her throat and Stu paused as she leveled him with a glare.

"Ahem—Ms. Haelstrom, there's not much for you to review. I've signed off on these terms, and Chuck made them airtight. You giving the okay is just a formality." Stu removed a pen from his pocket and pushed it toward Jones. She slid it back with a single finger. It was unpleasantly warm.

Jones glanced at her map, committing it to memory before snapping her notebook closed. "But a required formality, right? As the current CEO?"

"Interim, but yes. That's technically correct." Chuck nodded.

"Well, the world hinges on technicalities, doesn't it?" Jones lifted the contracts and shuffled them into a neat pile with a few taps on the conference table. The sound was louder than she'd expected, and the nervous look that passed between Chuck and Stu sent a little jolt of power through her. Maybe being temporary CEO of her father's company would have some perks after all. "Okay then. Have your assistant reach out tomorrow, and we can arrange a time for someone to pick these up. I'll leave any changes or clarifications in the margins."

Stu smiled wanly. "Just to be clear, Jones, we really don't have time for changes. Your father felt fine about these. We need to have them wrapped up before Monday, or we'll be in a very precarious position, bargaining wise."

"Well, let's hope no changes are needed then, since I'm not my father and I don't see his signature on these." She dug her heels into the carpet and pushed back from the table, sliding the contracts into her oversized leather purse.

Stu stood quickly, knocking over the bottle of water she hadn't given him a chance to open. "I'll show you out."

"That's not necessary. Just two lefts and a right?" Jones turned and raised her eyebrows at Chuck for confirmation. If she had to look at Stu's slimy face again, she'd need to shower in industrial-strength cleaner.

"You learned your way around pretty fast." Chuck smiled at her, but it was more like a grimace.

"I'm surprised my father never mentioned I'm a quick study. Well then, I'm sure we'll be in touch." She pulled the door closed behind her, wishing she still had that giant hammer to swing.

CHAPTER THREE
ELSIE

Elsie shouldered open the door to the stage, still dragging Fangley's Hammer of Doom behind her. She held in a laugh at the thought of the woman's face as she'd tossed it, her blue eyes going wide as saucers. It was like something out of a cartoon—Elsie's favorite kind of moment. The way she'd braced for impact, ducking into herself as she made absolutely no attempt to catch it. Elsie had never thought tossing something at a woman would be a kind of personality test. But if she'd wanted to extrapolate she'd guess that gorgeous woman was a little unsure of herself. Maybe afraid of conflict? Definitely out of her element and... Oh god, had she just thrown a prop hammer at her new boss?

Elsie thought back to the woman's outfit. All black. Expensive shoes. Definite widow vibes. *Shit.* Of course, Haelstrom's wife would be coming in to take care of things. She might as well kiss her contract goodbye. She'd just leave the hammer on the floor, give Fangley a sweet little forehead kiss, and disappear forever.

A text dinged on her phone and she tucked the hammer under one arm to answer.

Rebecca: *Hey, are you on set?*

Elsie: *Yeah, getting there now, I want to try blocking with Fangley and the hammer. Why?*

Rebecca: *Okay great.*

Rebecca had a talent for ignoring very obvious questions she didn't want to answer in a way that Elsie had always admired.

She glanced up from her phone to see if the puppets' cases were still out on the set, just in time to see a small child swing Fangley over his head like a lasso. Unless that kid was Houdini, someone must have left Fangley's case unlocked.

"Wait, let go of him!"

And the kid, well, he listened, releasing his grip on Fangley's arm and flinging him into the air. Elsie jumped and caught the puppet gently, like the precious gem that he was, cradling him to her chest.

She turned toward the kid. "Where's your adult?" She could feel every beat of her heart throughout her body.

He shrugged and reached for Smirch. Elsie hesitated. She'd never cared much for Smirch. Maybe it served Trey right for faking a catastrophic injury and ruining the rest of their day of filming? He probably had a date to get ready for and just didn't want to work late.

Elsie paused and took the kid in. His blond hair fell into his eyes and he kept blinking it away. His hoodie was the color of the inside of a cantaloupe, glowing beneath the studio lights. She placed a gentle hand on his shoulder and took Smirch. Was the hoodie *cashmere*? She wasn't aware hoodies came in materials other than sweatshirt. Maybe *he* was her new boss.

"Listen, buddy. I understand the impulse to smash Smirch, but believe it or not, we don't want anything bad to happen to him."

Okay, so that was only mostly true but it sounded convincing. Elsie watched his face fall and noticed the faint dark circles under his blue eyes. Without destruction to focus on, he looked ready to pass out. Or cry. She could not deal with either of those outcomes. As he blinked back at her, she racked her brain for ideas.

"Look, I can't let you demolish the puppets, even if some of them deserve it, but let's make a bet. If you can lift this massive hammer I'll teach you how I bring my puppet, Fangley, to life."

His eyes flashed, like the sun breaking through clouds, but he still didn't talk. Despite working for a children's television show, Elsie didn't have much experience with kids. Still, she was pretty sure they talked at this age. He must be about five, Fangley's core demographic. Maybe she could use this time for an impromptu focus group.

She picked up the hammer and feigned tossing it to him and he extended his hands to take it; a refreshing response after earlier.

"Are you sure you can handle this? I don't want it to crush you." She pitched her voice like she was lifting a couch, but his hands stayed outstretched.

He grasped the handle and let out a giggle as the fake wood squished between his fingers. And then he swung the hammer right down onto Smirch's head. Maybe she had more in common with kids than she'd thought.

"Don't let anyone around here see how strong you are, otherwise Rebecca will try to put you to work." Elsie nodded to the control room.

She lost track of time as she taught Bentley—she was still holding out some hope that she'd misheard his name—how to work the puppets. After he'd warmed up, it turned out he spoke just fine. His hands were so small that she ended up getting Ratatouille, Fangley's favorite stray Maine Coon from the corner store. All of the cats in Fangley Heights lived happily in bodegas, as God intended. Ratatouille was softer than the other puppets, more…floppy was probably the technical term.

Elsie was narrating a *Mad Libs* adventure where Ratatouille helped Fangley deliver some Cheerios to an old caterpillar who was really just one of those stick on, grey eyebrows from a Halloween costume—Bentley had some interesting suggestions—when the door to the set banged open.

"Hey, Bentley, are you ready to go?"

The kid glanced up momentarily, then went back to playing as the woman Elsie had seen before in the hallway strode across the set as though she owned it. Right. She probably did. Elsie felt her calm dissipate. Not just a woman, Ms. Haelstrom which meant…it was a very good thing Elsie hadn't abandoned this child. The fact that he turned out to be pretty okay didn't hurt either.

"Ma'am, is he with you?"

The woman's face turned to stone. Elsie probably shouldn't have ma'am-ed her. But rather than being off-putting, her hard expression just made her look like an elegant statue. An elegant statue in heels that Elsie wouldn't mind seeing over her shoulders and…nope. Absolutely not. New, actively grieving boss is so far off-limits she might as well be a special exhibition at the Museum of Modern Art. Not to be touched. Besides, even if Elsie was looking to get involved, which as a rule, she wasn't, work would be the absolute last place she'd seek out a relationship. But since she wasn't interested in entanglements, surely there was no harm in looking. Respectfully.

"We didn't get introduced earlier, I'm—"

"Haelstrom, right?" Elsie tried to keep her expression neutral but she was starting to feel her frustration sour on her tongue.

"Yes, is there a problem?"

"For starters, I've been watching him for twenty minutes, and I'm not a babysitter." Elsie lowered her voice and shot a glance toward Bentley. She wasn't frustrated with him. Luckily, he still seemed lost in his own world with Ratatouille.

"Hm, you could have fooled me."

The comment should have been cutting but Elsie didn't detect any malice behind it. Which made her...curious.

"What do you mean by that?" Elsie felt frustration intensify, but something told her she should hold it back.

"You're good with him. I haven't quite figured that out yet." The woman shot her a tired smile; her eyes were ringed with the same dark circles as Bentley's.

Well, that was not what she'd expected. Elsie wanted to ask more, like what kind of parent hadn't figured out how to talk to their kid? A much wiser part of her remembered that this woman was probably her new boss. Even if she had made the questionable decision of leaving her kid alone on their set to destroy Fangley. "I'm sorry for your loss. We all are." Elsie looked around, suddenly very aware that they were alone on set.

The woman nodded. "Anyway, thanks for letting him play with the toys."

"They're puppets."

"Right, okay."

The woman smiled at Elsie like they were agreeing. Which they absolutely were not. "These puppets aren't toys. They're worth thousands of dollars and integral to this show's success."

"But we sell them everywhere, right? Like toy stores and Target and stuff?"

Ugh, 'we'. There was no 'we' until Haelstrom paid her. Maybe she should ask about her contract now? Or maybe not right on the heels of her bad first-second impression. "No, those are completely different." Elsie wasn't sure why it felt so important for her to make that distinction. The work they did here was real. The puppets weren't easily replaceable. *She* wasn't easily replaceable. "These are *professional puppets.*"

"Okay." The woman gave her an indulgent look.

Smug. Elsie hadn't never cared for smug. "Anyway, like I said, I'm not a babysitter, and I've already stayed later than I wanted to just to be sure he didn't destroy anything on set."

"Got it. Not a babysitter." The woman nodded. "But you work here, right?"

"Yes, I work on Fangley Heights." She gave a sweeping gesture across the sound stage.

"Great. Then just consider it work, bill me for it if you want."

"Fine."

"Bentley, we're leaving." The woman gave Elsie a tight smile as she made her way to the door. She turned back. "Oh, one more thing, are you free this weekend?"

This felt like whiplash. Was this a proposition? Not that Elsie was interested. But she also wasn't *not* interested. Her pulse skittered as she decided to hedge her bets. "I'm not sure, why?"

"Well, I assume you're good with kids."

"Why would you think that?"

"You work on a children's television show. And you and Bentley seem to be getting along."

"Right. Because I have an MFA in theater. I'm good at acting with puppets. Are these kids you mentioned puppets?"

"They're real, I'm afraid. I was wondering if you do birthday parties?"

"No." Elsie clenched her fists, fighting back her indignation.

"Why not?"

"Because I'm not a clown. And also because I make enough money as it is." *Shit.* She shouldn't have said that when she was in the middle of renegotiating her contract. "I mean, I make enough not to clown on the side." Great, because that was so much better.

"Good to know." The woman raised her eyebrows. "Come on, Bentley. I mean it. Time to go home."

Bentley bounded up to her at last. "Did you see I met Fangley?"

Something like shock crossed the woman's face before she spun it into a smile and brought a hand to rest on Bentley's shoulder. She made eye contact with Elsie and raised her eyebrows. Maybe strangers weren't the only people this kid was quiet around.

"I saw that—did you say *thank you* to the nice lady?"

"Thank you!" He smiled at Elsie as he bumped into the other woman's leg knocking her slightly off balance.

"Thanks for hanging out with him."

"Yeah, sure." Elsie smiled but narrowed her eyes at the woman. "Anything for my new pal, Bentley."

***

"I MEAN who just asks a stranger to babysit? I know she's technically my boss, but I do the job I'm paid to do, not cater to some rich woman's whims. He was alone on set when I got there. I might not be an expert on kids, but I feel like *stranger danger* is like, rule number one, you know?" Elsie pulled in a wheezing breath, she really needed to work on cardio. Being able to vent while jogging was essential.

Her feet pounded against the pavement with a persistent rhythm. The sky had gone plum black and the loop through Prospect Park was rapidly fading from beautiful to sinister. Elsie took in the long shadows cast by the streetlights as they fizzed on. Panting and the soft clicks of her dog's nails echoed on the pavement behind her. When she turned to catch Oscar's attention, she caught him looking bored with her rant, which was fair. She was feeling bored with herself these days, too.

Elsie reached back and held out a cookie like she was

passing the baton in a relay race, his dark brown eyes lit up, and his mouth fell open in an easy smile. She wasn't above buying love.

The cookie worked like a turbo boost, and suddenly Oscar was trotting at her side, his soft tan ears bouncing in the night.

Pitties were truly the best of both worlds: great cuddlers and beefy enough that no one really approached her.

They made their way past the Japanese Garden and onto Carroll Street. The exhaustion crept into her limbs as she began to count the tiny landmarks to home. The bodega with the oddly fresh tropical produce, the palm reader, slash cafe, slash notary, and, inexplicably, the perpetually gated shop that sold only religious figurines and hanging plants gone feral, their tendrils slowly creeping their way back outside.

She dropped Oscar's leash as they reached the front of the building, and he bounded ahead, spinning on the stoop to face her. He crouched low, his tail wagging in the air with enough force to clear the cigarette smoke that lingered from one door down. Elsie braced herself for impact just as his big paws planted on her shoulders and he licked her face.

"Gross, Oscar, at least wait for a gal to shower." But she was laughing. She loved these moments with Oscar, the way he'd greet her even though they'd been together for an hour. This run had been exactly what she'd needed after her strange day at work. She still hadn't seen her contract, a fact that was making her increasingly anxious as the days remaining on her current agreement ticked down to the single digits.

"Hark, an intruder!" Her roommate Avery called as they entered the apartment, crouching down to welcome Oscar with open arms. "I told you, Oz, you can't keep bringing home women you meet in the park." Avery lowered their voice conspiratorially. "I know they promise you dinner but they might rob us. Oh wait, that's Elsie. She'll definitely rob us."

Oscar flopped onto his back and wiggled on the rug, his body arcing into a crescent, head nearly touching his back hip. That dog's spine was a slinky. Avery gave Oscar's spotted belly a few solid pats.

Elsie waved to Avery as she toed off her running shoes.

Avery raised their hands overhead like a diver before doing a trust fall over the arm of the couch. Their body made a dull thud against the worn leather cushions.

Wind-chime sounds drifted in from the kitchen—Oscar's tags against his water bowl. The floorboards creaked beneath her feet just how they always did. Elsie loved the sounds of the old apartment they shared. When Avery's uncle had left them the place in Brooklyn, they couldn't believe their luck. Ave had inherited everything from Uncle Bruce as the only other queer person in the family, and thus the rightful heir. In addition to the apartment, they were also the proud owners of a bajillion houseplants and some original mid-century modern furniture.

Elsie had grown to love their shared home, even though she and Avery had done little to improve it. Or even to make it their own aside from filling Bruce's cut crystal bowls with candy instead of decorative stones, and that was about it. Elsie loved this place like she tried to love people, just as they are. She loved the predictability of the hot water never working when she needed it to. That one hallway light that flickered, no matter how many times she replaced it. It was soothing and broken in. The tension eased from her shoulders like the day was a heavy backpack she could finally shrug off.

Oscar returned, leaking water from his mouth onto the floor and soaking her sock as he leaned all of his weight against her knees. She admired his trust in her, nothing about his lean was structurally sound, and yet he knew she wouldn't let him fall.

Avery patted the couch cushion, and the dog leaped away from Elsie. She stumbled while Oscar did three turns on the cushion before settling half on top of Avery.

"Want to talk about it?" Two sets of brown puppy dog eyes locked on her.

"Talk about what?"

"Whatever made you think running was a good idea." Avery shrugged.

"There's nothing to talk about."

"Okay. Want to drink about it?"

Elsie nodded, and Avery padded behind her to the kitchen.

Elsie opened the fridge and pulled out two beers and handed one to Avery. They ran a hand through their hair. It needed a cut, the ocean blue they'd dyed it had almost completely grown out. This was probably the longest Avery's hair had been since they first cut it all off three years ago. They were calling the look *European tennis player slash luxury fragrance model*. Sometimes Ave even wore a jaunty little headband.

"Do you want me to cut your hair this weekend?"

"What's wrong with my hair?"

"Not one thing. It's just getting a little long, and I know you don't want to go back to that barber shop. I won't mess it up."

"You will absolutely mess it up. But I'll probably let you anyway. Let's do it Saturday before roller skating. Now stop deflecting."

"I'm not deflecting, doctor. It's just nothing is going right with work. I still don't have a contract for next season, and now apparently everything is up to Haelstrom's widow who is, like, super young. Well compared to him. She's older than us."

"Oh, so we're talking about the 'nothing' now? Or we aren't?" Avery quirked a perfect eyebrow.

Never in her life did Elsie expect to be jealous of someone's eyebrows. And yet. She glared at Avery's air quotes and sincerely regretted ever explaining how to use them correctly.

"She just left her kid in the studio. And when I talked to her about it, she told me to bill her. Can you believe that? It's like she thinks the whole world works for her."

"But don't you?" Avery raised a hand, deftly deflecting the bottle cap Elsie had flicked in their direction. "I mean, like, technically."

"Okay, fine. *Technically* I work for her. But not like that. And that thought didn't occur to me at the time. Anyway, now I don't know what to do if I don't get this contract. Who would I be without Fangley?"

"You'd be a brilliant and talented actor, slash writer, slash puppet person. He's a stuffed vampire, Els."

Elsie widened her eyes in mock horror. "How could you say that about my monster son?"

"All good things come to an end. You could always create a new character. You have name recognition now."

Elsie reached across Avery and deftly stole a dumpling from the white cardboard container of food that sat on the counter. "Why won't you ever let me mope? Your positivity is overwhelming."

"Fine," Avery said. "If you lose your monster son, the world ends. Cities crumble to the ground. All hope is lost."

"Speaking of monster family members, did your mom get a hold of you? She called my cell looking for you; she said you weren't returning her calls."

"Oh. She was looking for me? Did she dead name me again?"

"Yeah, babe." Elsie reached out to touch Avery's arm.

"Then she didn't really call for me." Avery stood up straighter and took a sip of their beer.

"You're right. I'm sorry, Aves. Should I not tell you when she calls? Or I can just block her number."

Avery waved their hand like they always did as if to say it was nothing. But Elsie knew it was everything. "Let's just forget about Mean Charlene, please."

Elsie nodded. "Want to go back to talking about me?"

"Sure, you narcissist." Avery gave an epic eye roll, but the smile that crossed their face was one of relief.

"You're the worst." Elsie gently shoved their shoulder.

"Strong words from someone I'm treating to day-old Chinese food and mediocre beer."

Elsie popped another dumpling into her mouth and chewed slowly. It was so salty and perfect. It could do with a little sweet chili sauce though. "Should I just sign the contract when I get back and be grateful I have a job?"

She prepared herself for the inevitable deflation she would feel when Avery said yes. She could just see herself walking into Stu's office and signing on for another year of being taken advantage of.

"No," Avery said.

"No?"

Avery shook their head. "Don't sign the contract. They've been taking advantage of you. They co-opted your web series and never properly compensated you. Plus, your agent is worthless."

Elsie laughed despite herself. "You recommended Jason. He's your friend."

"He's the guy who sold me weed in college. We're not friends, I just have his number in my phone in case of an emergency. You said, and I quote, 'Please, Avery, I need to seem like an adult at this meeting and everyone else has an agent.'"

"That's not how I remember it. You vouched for him!" She reached over and poked Avery with her chopstick.

"He's never let *me* down. Anyway, tell me more about this woman who's taking over. She's Haelstrom's widow, right? Maybe she'd be willing to negotiate?"

"Doubtful after how things went today. She barely even thanked me for taking care of her kid."

"What a monster."

"I know! And she kept calling the puppets 'toys'. She just expected someone to entertain him, while I assume she was in some meeting."

Avery brought a hand to their chest. "I am scandalized."

Elsie rolled her eyes. "Fine, I get it, you're making fun of me. But she was awful. So entitled. She asked me if I did birthday parties."

"Hey, that's not a bad idea if you need to make some extra money. I bet parents would pay a lot for a Fangley appearance."

"I'm not doing that. I'm not a clown, and neither is Fangley."

"Right, he's a boy vampire obsessed with social status, and you're his Doctor Frankenstein."

"I prefer 'Victor'. Can you just be on my side? Like for two seconds?"

"I am, babe. I just don't think being on your side means everyone else is terrible. I mean, are most people terrible? Sure are! But the woman you're describing sounds, I don't know, overwhelmed, maybe? In mourning because she just lost her husband? Just consider giving her a break; she might end up being on your side, too."

CHAPTER FOUR
JONES

Jones' knees braced against the top of her suitcase, forcing it closed. The grooves of the hard shell were digging into her skin. She regretted the few outfits she'd acquired while in New York, that were bulging over the sides, like her bag was bloated from a feast. Though nothing about the past week had the celebratory frequency of a feast. Instead, its vibrations had been low and dull.

Her father's funeral had been large and impersonal, like a business seminar. The only adjective his friends seemed to know was 'great'. *Great man. Great leader. Great mind for business.* None of them had ventured to call him a great father, and Jones took comfort in that. She felt no need to refute or pretend. Hunter Haelstrom was indeed great at making money and very bad at making people feel cared for. Maybe not people in general. Maybe just Jones.

Her days as substitute CEO had been oddly contentious. She'd gotten a bit of joy from putting Stu in his place, but not so much that she wanted to stick around and do it again.

Her nights caring for Bentley had been subdued. He was often so quiet, she forgot he was there. Kind of a metaphor for their entire relationship.

Jones could have been a better sister. And she would be. Once Charity arrived home from the spa in a few hours, Jones would head to JFK to catch her flight. Her life would go back to normal. Maybe she could start sending Bentley birthday cards.

Well sending them next year, of course, since today she was here to celebrate Bentley turning six.

Jones inched the zipper around until it snagged on one of her shirts. Damn. She slowly re-opened the case again and tucked in all the rogue material. The next time she zipped it quickly, closing it like she meant it.

A shrill alarm interrupted Jones as she wrestled her suit-case down the stairs, and in a panic she let it clatter down the final few steps. Nothing worse than what happened in baggage claim. The alarm sounded again.

No, not an alarm. Was that...a phone? Did people still have those? Like the ones that plugged into the wall and everything?

Jones considered not answering it, but the ring was too persistent to ignore. A bell tolling just for her. It made the call seem like an emergency. How did people used to live like this? Without being able to set the outside world to silent?

She followed the shrill cries and found the phone on the hallway table behind a vase of glass flowers. A choice, for sure.

The receiver was black and solid, and when she picked it up, it felt heavy enough to brain someone with. Her time in New York was doing weird things to her, her stress levels felt ratcheted up. Though she could think of a few things that might be responsible for that, and one of them was still asleep upstairs.

"Hello?" Jones' voice wavered with uncertainty, like she was calling out to a noise in a dark empty house, hoping for a friendly ghost.

"Charity?" The voice sounded gleeful.

She immediately felt a rush of embarrassment. Of course they were calling for Charity. Jones didn't even know this phone existed, so there was no reason anyone would try to reach her on it. Something pinged in her stomach. She pulled out her cell and texted Charity for her ETA.

"This is Jones, actually." After a pause she added, "Haelstrom."

"Oh right. I thought you'd be long gone by now. It's Stu Winkle. I wanted to discuss some contract issues with Charity. Do you have a number I can reach her at?"

Jones felt her skin prickle. She'd left the meeting with Stu the other day feeling like, if she hadn't resisted, he would have robbed her blind. Or, at the very least, handed the keys to the city over to his nephew Trey. She wasn't about to give him the chance to do that to Charity, who, she assumed, was grieving her husband. Like Jones should be grieving; but that hadn't happened yet. "You can discuss them with me—I have my copies here."

"Ah that's okay. Aren't you heading back to California today? I wouldn't want you to make any decisions that might get overturned once Charity is back."

A wave of defiance washed over Jones. "Actually, I'm more than capable of solving whatever problem there is. Otherwise my father wouldn't have let me take over in the event that Charity wasn't interested in running the company."

"Has she told you she's not interested?"

Jones could feel his hot, excited breath through the phone.

"What were you calling for again?"

"Elsie Webb still hasn't signed her contract. I think we'll be able to phase her out eventually, especially with Trey taking on a much larger role in the upcoming year."

"Trey, as in your nephew? I wasn't aware that we had agreed to him taking on a larger role on Fangley Heights."

"It's just a contingency plan, Joanie. And one your father

likely would have agreed with. Elsie causes more problems than she's worth. It's a kid's show. Everyone involved needs to be beyond reproach."

Jones held back a laugh. Stu thinking of himself as beyond reproach was absurd and yet she believed he did.

"If you're going to be a jackass to me, Stu, let's stick to formalities. Please, call me Ms. Haelstrom."

Stu cleared his throat. "Okay, Jones."

She could hear the sneer in his words. "So, the contract. What's the plan for getting it signed?" Jones asked.

"I was calling to get an extension approved so we can deal with this next week."

"But earlier this week my signing was urgent. What's changed?"

Stu cleared his throat. "I'm in the Hamptons this weekend."

Jones let out a mirthful laugh. "I'll take care of it. Do you have the number for her representation?"

"I really think we're better off doing this next week when I'm back. I know the contracts best and I'm sure Charity would rather extend the deadline so I can deal with any last-minute negotiations myself. This is what I do, Joanie."

That name again. It was overly familiar and yet alienating, because no one called her that. "I don't think so. Please send me the details for her agent and I'll review my copy of her contract. I'll take care of this before my flight. Enjoy your day off."

He audibly sucked in a deep breath like he was about to push back, but Jones ended the call before he could. That was one thing old phones had going for them, the satisfying clack of a hard hang up.

Stu's conniving didn't surprise her much, her father had always surrounded himself with people who would climb over anything and anyone to get to the top. Still, if he was half as smart as he thought he was, he wouldn't be trying to pull that on her. But he wasn't trying to pull that on her, not really. He was trying to manipulate Charity and Jones was just a stand in until her stepmom took over. Jones felt a sudden and surprising surge of protectiveness over Charity. And Elsie. How often was it that successful women got labeled difficult? That men got credit for a woman's good idea because he said it louder and his voice didn't rise at the end of a sentence? She could hear Birdie's voice in her head, *'my, my Jones, if you're not careful you might start to really care'.*

Jones made her way to the kitchen. She'd picked up a mix to make cupcakes the other day, and she started in on that to pass the time. She'd give Stu until the batter was poured to get her the information she needed. In the meantime, she would sneak some tastes of Funfetti and get a head start on that whole being a better sister thing.

Her phone dinged, and Jones wiped the speckled batter from her hands and reached for it. She was a bit surprised that Stu had actually sent the details for Elsie's agent. Little did he know that getting Elsie to sign this contract was the easiest thing she had to do today. Jones could handle getting a simple signature. She was much more worried about overseeing Bentley's birthday party as the lone adult that afternoon. The lack of communication from Charity was starting to spook her.

She thought about calling Susan—Bentley's sometimes nanny—to assist, but just the thought made her feel weak and pathetic. And she was done with being either of those. At least in front of others. If she could handle running Haelstrom Media, surely she could handle hosting a baker's dozen of Bentley's closest playground acquaintances. Even if it did sound like torture, Charity had scheduled this party months ago, and Jones didn't want any part in Bentley feeling let down right now. She simply wished Charity had thought to plan something beyond sending out the invitations. Or that she was already back from the spa and had never left her son with his estranged older sister, but then Jones wouldn't have had the opportunity to eat an obscene amount of cupcake batter. Or learn that Bentley was pretty cool, too.

She pulled up the contact information Stu had sent her. Better get this over with.

THE LINE RANG five times before the call connected. A loud rush of clinking and music made Jones pull the phone away from her ear.

"Dude, where the hell are you?"

She double checked the contact before glancing at the clock. She had the number right: Jason Crouch. It was ten forty-two a.m., and this person sounded, if not wasted, clearly inebriated. Maybe he'd left his phone somewhere. Surely, someone on their most popular show wouldn't work with someone who—

"Brayden, bro, if you don't get here in the next five seconds, I swear I'll tell your girlfriend all about my bachelor party in Vegas."

Somebody had married this guy? Jones cleared her throat. She licked cake batter off her finger and tried not to enjoy this too much, but some people were just more fun to mess with than others. "What happened in Vegas?"

Jason let out a spluttering cough. He must have taken a sip at the exact wrong moment. Jones bit back a smile.

"You're not Brayden."

"Very perceptive. I am not Brayden, but now you've got me curious."

"Shit," he whispered. "Is this Allie? I can explain. Well, I mean, there's nothing to explain because I was just joking."

"You really need to work on your recovery, because that wasn't convincing in the least. Anyway, as much as I'd love to hear all about what you did in Vegas, I'm on a bit of a dead-line. I'm looking for Jason Crouch."

"Great, that's me."

Jones paused, waiting for him to say more, but it seemed it wasn't just lies he was bad at. "Okay, I'm Jones Haelstrom. From Haelstrom Media." She added the last part in hopes of hot-wiring this guy's brain into business mode.

"Right, Haelstrom. That name sounds familiar…"

"It should. I'm calling about Elsie Webb's contract for Fangley Heights. Do you represent her?"

"Last time I checked. Though she did call me the other day and I haven't had a chance to get back to her. Wait, hold on." Cheers swelled in the background.

Jones lined a pan with cupcake wrappers while she listened to Jason order a beer. "'kay, I'm back."

"Is this a bad time?" Jones tried to sound patient.

"Nope." Jason gulped. "I'm just out to breakfast."

"O-kay. As I was saying, I have a contract for the next season of Fangley Heights that I need Elsie to sign today."

"Oh, I thought she already took care of that. I can text her and see what's up."

"I know it's Saturday but she needs to sign today. Other-wise we can't guarantee a contract next season. I'd love to not have to replace her. Unless you have a secret miming career you'd like to tell me about. Spent any time in Paris?"

"Well, I went there once on a class trip—"

"I was joking. Please tell her to arrive by one o'clock. I want this contract signed by five after. I'm hosting an event this afternoon. It's really important that she's on time. Can you please arrange that?"

Referring to a party for a cadre of kindergartners as an event was a bit gratuitous, but what Jason—and Elsie—didn't know couldn't hurt them.

"Yeah, sure." A mashing sound came over the line.

He couldn't have waited one minute before taking a bite?

Jones felt desperate to get off the phone. What happened to professionalism? "Ok great. That was all. I'll text you the address. And remember she has to come before one."

"Got it—see you at one!"

"Well, not you," Jones said, but the line had gone silent, already disconnected. The universal power move of hanging up without saying goodbye.

Oh well. At least everything would be squared away before the party. And then, instead of a diva children's show star, she just had to manage some kids for a few hours until Charity showed up. Easy. Simple. Charity hadn't picked up Jones' calls which hopefully meant she was already on her way. This was completely within her skill set. She fished the cupcake package out of the bin to check the baking time.

THE DOORBELL CHIMED its ostentatious song; it had serious Christmas-caroler energy. Jones checked her watch, not quite two. If it was Charity, she was very late. And if it was Ms. Webb, she was very late too. If she took Jones or her job seriously, she would have bothered to be on time. Even though it seemed much more likely that the agent of disaster Jones had spoken to on the phone had failed to communicate to Elsie. Even if it was Jason's fault, she didn't want Elsie to prove Stu right.

Jones opened the door to a mother on her phone who ushered her kid inside like she was pushing him on a swing. Before she could even call for him, Bentley raced around the corner and slid along the marble floor, windmilling his arms as he crashed into her hip. The woman gave her a queen's wave and mouthed thanks before walking back to her black Mercedes. She'd forgotten how friendly New Yorkers were.

Bentley buzzed with excitement, more animated than Jones had ever seen him. The rest of the kids arrived like a swarm. They buzzed from the entryway down the hall to the TV room. Some seemed to know their way through the house better than she did. They left shoes and coats strewn behind them like they'd been raptured. Three mothers handed her detailed allergy lists, assuring her repeatedly that they weren't really worried, because Susan knew all of this.

Jones had given Susan the weekend off after asking her for her schedule and getting only a shrug. Even thinking of giving someone the weekend off felt strange to her. The whole housekeeper-slash-nanny set up Charity had going made her feel squirmy. She wasn't sure why—Jones had loved her nanny when she was Bentley's age. Susan had explained that she didn't work Wednesdays but still had to get Bentley from school and bring him home. Which, Jones had pointed out, was the opposite of having the day off.

Once the last car had driven away, Jones hurried to the kitchen and fished the flattened box of cupcake mix from the recycling bin. Again. She cross-checked the list of ingredients to confirm she was screwed. One kid couldn't have sugar. Another, gluten. At least there didn't seem to be any peanut allergies. Maybe she could make those kids smoothies instead of cupcakes. If she called them fruit milkshakes, she could probably get away with it.

Forty-five minutes into the party, Jones was defeated by a group of criminal masterminds that couldn't do simple math or tie their shoes, but had totally broken her spirit, and she was ready to throw in the towel. She'd never been this relentless as a child. Or this needy. Every thirty seconds someone needed her to look at some completely unimpressive somersault or answer a question about worms.

She didn't know anything about worms, aside from the way they beached themselves after a rainstorm. Jones was becoming concerned that Elsie's agent might be just as unreliable as he seemed on the phone.

A delicate knock sounded on the door. She'd put a sign up

telling people to just come in and yet every parent insisted on checking her hearing. But all the kids were here. Or at least she hoped so, because one more, and she'd be beaching herself on the sidewalk, too.

Every knock sparked the faintest spark of hope in her chest that Ms. Webb had arrived and Jones could put the contract stress behind her. She needed this week of her not tanking her father's company to be firmly in the books, so she could return to her life in LA triumphant. If only he could see her now…well, he'd probably still be disappointed, but at least she wasn't.

Jones opened the door to a woman whose yoga outfit was straddling formal wear. Even living in LA, she'd never understood paying hundreds of dollars for clothes to sweat in. Then again, maybe once you reached a certain income bracket you didn't sweat anymore. Jones would probably know if she believed in exercise. She'd written a think-piece on that for Pacific Coast Most. Jones dropped her glance down, but the woman hadn't brought a child.

"Can I help you?" Jones asked, carefully pulling the door closed a bit more so that it framed her face and blocked the woman's view.

The woman craned her neck, trying to see in. The shouts from the living room were at a fever pitch.

"Yes, I'm Chester's mom. He called me and asked for a snack."

Jones tried to keep her face blank. Shit. Should she have planned food other than cupcakes? All Bentley ate was three bites of macaroni and a fruit cup. Maybe she should have confiscated phones, like a really hip celebrity party.

"Oh, I didn't realize he'd called you. We have food here. For the party, I mean. Kid food."

"Kid food? Chester has a pretty advanced palate. We might have a future sommelier on our hands." The woman beamed smugly, as if planning her son's future around wine before he stopped eating glue was aspirational and not unhinged. "What will you be serving? He gets cranky if he gets hungry."

So, just like every other person in the world. "Um, pizza. And cupcakes of course."

"He was right to call me," *Ms. Chester's Mom* muttered.

"Why's that? He didn't ask me for anything or mention being hungry."

"He was being polite."

Jones glanced back just in time to see the angel Chester put Bentley in a headlock. Polite, indeed. "Sure."

"He's on a low sugar diet, and he can't have dairy. Please only feed him these. It's very important."

The woman pulled out a bag of something green and nearly translucent. Was this a test? They were as thin as tissue paper and flaked when she touched the bag. Definitely giving off a fish food vibe.

"And these are?"

"Seaweed snacks."

Jones held back a laugh. Fish food vibe, indeed. This poor kid. "Ok, got it. So no cupcakes or other food. Is water ok?"

"He can't free-drink, but he can have some water if you watch him."

Free-drink? She wasn't planning on putting out a bucket of water. Jones felt like she was getting pet sitting instructions.

"Ok, supervised drinking only. Anything else?"

"No, that's it. Please call me if you have any questions. I'll give you my number."

"That's ok. I'll get it from Chester. See you at six."

Jones eased the door shut. What kind of kid would call their mom to ensure they didn't get any sugar? She set Chester's food on the table and took out her phone to order pizza, but not before confirming that the party ended at five instead. *Fuck.*

She took a deep breath. She was nearly through it. Charity would get home and Jones would leave for the airport, and everything in her life would go back to the way it was a week ago.

Now, where the hell was Elsie Webb?

CHAPTER FIVE
ELSIE

The brass knocker shone bright in the mid-afternoon sun. It gleamed against the matte black door, and Elsie had to get close to realize the knocker was in the form of a smug-looking eagle. That was definitely a choice. Below the eagle's grimacing beak was a neatly hand-written note that simply said, "No need to knock, just come on in."

An odd move, even for Brooklyn. The note was fine, really, but it made her uneasy. Elsie would have used an exclamation point or smiley face for maximum friendliness and encouragement. It reminded her a little of the notes she and Avery would put on the outside door when they had parties, though those read, "If you don't know the code, you weren't invited!" Followed by a smiley face, of course.

She pulled out her phone and snapped a picture of the door, making sure to get the address in the frame. She tapped out a message to Avery and attached the photo.

Elsie: *I think I'm about to die in Cobble Hill*

Avery: *There are worse places to die.*

Elsie rolled her eyes and glanced around for other identi-fying markers. There was a garden-level apartment at the brownstone. Its small window was obscured with a pile of newspapers and what looked like a prototype of the first radio. That wasn't a good sign.

Elsie: *Well, I'm dropping a pin. Call all of my friends from soccer if you don't hear from me in 30 minutes*

Avery: *Not the police?*

Elsie: *The police won't do anything. The lesbians on my soccer team are also my apocalypse team*

Avery: *Please go secure your future.*

Elsie: *Tell them to check the basement*

Avery: *What basement are you talking about? Hussy up. I want to go roller skating and kick off emotionally available enby summer tonight.*

Avery: **Hurry* But I'm making hussy up a thing now.*

Elsie's hand hovered above the eagle. Just pushing open the door and walking into the house of Haelstrom felt like a white-girl-in-a-horror-movie move. She was the one volunteering to check the basement when everyone heard a weird sound. That was the part of the film where Elsie would cover her eyes, so she wasn't sure what came next. She was used to her and her friends being eccentric, but rich people really took it to a whole new level.

Then again, who else could the note be for? And did she really want to start this off by knocking and being annoying? She was there to sign her contract. She was there to take charge. Elsie Webb was there to secure her future, just like Avery said. And when she was done, she was going to roller skate and enjoy an ice cream cone like an *adult*. She simply did not have time for the yips.

THE HALLWAY WAS FILLED with a slew of tiny and very expensive shoes. She glanced down at her battered Chucks and surreptitiously wiped them on the entryway rug.

Elsie watched Ms. Haelstrom emerge from the end of the

hall. She was a lot more beautiful when she wasn't bossing Elsie around. And not at all who she would have pictured for Haelstrom's wife. Her honey gold hair was in a high, messy bun, and she was wearing glasses with thick plastic frames she hadn't had on the other day. The front of her blue apron was streaked with flour handprints.

"Oh, it's you. I didn't think you'd show at this point."

Elsie looked herself up and down. "I'm supposed to be here, right?"

She didn't reply right away, and for a terrible moment Elsie thought she might throw up and fire her agent. Though not in that order, hopefully. The woman continued to study Elsie, then took off her glasses and wiped them on the edge of her apron. When she put them back on Elsie could see they were cloudy from the flour that had transferred onto them. Something about it set her at ease.

"Did you come in on your own? Where's your stuff?"

"That's what the sign said to do. And what stuff? I'm here to sign my contract. I think I have a pen somewhere." Elsie began rummaging in her tote bag until she pulled out a purple magic marker triumphantly.

"I think that marker's washability makes it not legally binding."

Elsie's heart stuttered; Haelstrom's glasses and messy hair were activating every librarian fantasy she'd ever had.

"Oh," Elsie grunted. It was more of a sound than a word because she could not currently form a coherent thought. *Perfect timing, brain.*

Elsie felt the warm buzz of the woman's attention flow through her like quickly downed champagne.

"Sorry, for a moment I thought you'd reconsidered your opposition to being a clown." Her voice was low and slightly gravely, like whiskey on ice, but the good kind. Top shelf, artisanal ice. "Didn't Mr. Crouch tell you to be here by one?"

"For starters, I think it's a stretch to call him Mr. Crouch.

Though that would make a great puppet name. Mind if I steal it?" Elsie pulled out her phone and waved it in the air.

"It's all yours."

"Anyway, Monsieur Crouch told me to be here anytime *after* one, kind of open-ended, so, knowing him, I figured I'd show up sooner rather than later."

"Oh yeah, he was a disaster."

Well, at least they agreed on one thing. "Speaking of disasters." Elsie nodded toward the pile of shoes in the hall and raised an eyebrow.

"Today's my brother's birthday party."

"Your brother has some pretty tiny friends."

"Well, yes, he is a child. Bentley, you two met the other day."

Bentley was her brother? Elsie looked at her again, considering this new information. She had assumed the woman standing in front of her was Haelstrom's widow, but that theory suddenly seemed unlikely. "Oh, I didn't realize. I thought you were Mrs. Haelstrom."

Jones' eyes narrowed but a smile played at the corner of her mouth. "Oh, please, Mrs. Haelstrom is my stepmother. Call me Jones."

"Oh, right. Should I call you Ms. Jones?"

"That might be a little odd seeing as Jones is my first name."

Elsie squinted as if it would make this conversation easier to follow. "Ah, okay."

"Jones was my mother's maiden name when she married my father. Hunter's my father. Was my father. Anyway..." Jones waved a hand in front of her as though she was trying to clear smoke.

"So some people have two first names like Adam Scott, but you ended up with two last names."

"Sure." Jones' mouth was a tight line.

"This is going so well," Elsie said with fake cheer. "Let's

see what else I can fumble while I'm here, show you why I'm worth the money you're paying me."

Jones laughed. "Sorry, I'm a little scattered. It's been a trip being back here. I know I'm old enough, but it's supremely weird for people to think my brother is my son. And I'm supposed to be on a flight soon, but I'm thinking that might not happen. Not that that's your problem. Sorry. Again. I've got your contract in the kitchen if you'll follow me."

"I shouldn't have assumed. I hate when people make assumptions about me. We should leave people room to surprise us."

Jones gave Elsie a look she couldn't decipher and then she turned on her bare heel and walked away. Elsie couldn't help but watch; something about the combination of tight jeans and a dress shirt under that messy apron had her feeling like Jones was a gift she wanted to unwrap. *Get it together, Els. She's your boss.*

A shrill scream sounded from the other room. *Right. And this house is full of children.*

Jones cleared her throat, and Elsie looked up in time to see the woman watching over her shoulder with an amused smile on her face. Her grey eyes seemed to flash blue, like clouds parting.

In the kitchen, Jones busied herself with a complicated looking machine. She offered Elsie a slushy glass of water that was so cold it hurt her teeth. She set the glass gently on the marble counter and shivered.

Jones grimaced. "Sorry, is it too cold?"

"Just a bit. What is that thing, a tap to the arctic sea?" Elsie gestured toward the machine on the counter. It looked like a fancy espresso machine and seltzer maker had been fused by a mad scientist.

"It's a new machine, they haven't really caught on yet, but I think they will soon. I was sad I didn't have mine with me, but it turns out they had one in the kitchen."

"I can't believe they had one here. I didn't even know they existed. It's kind of amazing that maybe both you and your dad like bone chilling water. It's an interesting connection, I'm not sure I know anyone else like that."

Jones paused, her glass halfway to her mouth. "You know, I hadn't thought of it like that. Anyway, it's worth every penny because its magic turns water into a kind of—"

"Slurpee?"

"Right, or a frozen margarita without the sugar or alcohol."

"So, just painfully cold with no payoff then?"

"I know, isn't it great? I hope I'm not being rude, but I need to finish frosting these. Your contract is right there." Jones gestured at the far counter with a butter knife covered in frosting.

"As long as I get one when you're done."

She watched Jones' lips part slightly. "Sure, just write that stipulation in the margin."

Elsie made no move to go to the contract. She knew she should control herself and focus on business, but there was something about Jones that made it hard to look away. Without the sharp edges of her heels and glare from the other day, she seemed…soft. She seemed a lot more like the kind of woman Elsie would want to come home to and a lot less like the woman insulting her career.

Elsie cleared her throat. "Anyway, is Bentley's mom, uh, Charity around?" *Good.* A nice, neutral topic.

Jones' brows drew together. "No, she's taking some 'me' time."

Elsie felt the chill in Jones' tone. Not so neutral then. "So you got stuck with the birthday party while she's off at…a spa or something?"

"Something like that. Only instead of the spa, I'm worried she's off eat-pray-loving her way across some island with a one-way ticket and allegedly spotty cell phone reception."

Elsie was starting to get the feeling that nothing here in this house, with this family, was as it seemed.

"Oh, that's—" Elsie wasn't sure how to finish. That's selfish? That's technically abandonment? Jones was still looking down, Elsie was desperate to right this conversation. The dynamics of this family were none of her business.

"Sorry," Jones said. "I shouldn't have said that. It's been a long few days."

"Of course. How many kids are here?" Elsie asked, at last, feeling immense gratitude for her brain pulling a new subject from nowhere, like an endless scarf out of her sleeve.

Jones tilted her head, considering. "Eleven, I think. Twelve with Bentley."

"Do you think they're okay in there?"

Jones looked up from the cupcakes and licked a bit of frosting off her finger. Being in this kitchen was going to give Elsie a heart attack. "I'm sure they're fine."

Elsie glanced toward the door to hide her blush. "I know what 'fine' sounds like, and that's not it."

"I don't hear anything." Jones shrugged.

"Exactly. Maybe we should make sure everyone still has their limbs, and then we can do the contract stuff?" We? What was she thinking? She couldn't just insert herself into this beautiful woman's life and yet...Elsie motioned for Jones to follow and was surprised to feel the slight pressure of Jones' hand on her lower back as they rounded the corner to the living room.

The place looked like a renaissance painting. One of the gnarly ones with demons battling, gnashing teeth, and gore. But beautifully lit. In the middle of the room, two boys were bound together with a golden cord. One of the deep red velvet drapes had been pulled from the window, and the bright sunlight sliced through the room.

"Oh no," Jones whispered. She was so close to Elsie that

her breath was a hot rush across the back of her neck. She suppressed a shiver.

Jones looked wide-eyed and panicked when Elsie glanced over her shoulder at her. She felt an overwhelming desire to shield Jones from the chaos both physically and metaphorically. Elsie knew entertaining kids. She could do this and make up some ground from their rocky start the other day. "It's okay; I've got this."

Elsie clapped her hands. "Okay tiny folks, free the prisoners! It's craft time."

She whispered to Jones, "Can you go get some craft stuff, just whatever you have in the closet?"

Jones raised an eyebrow and shook her head.

"Like glitter, glue, buttons, markers, pipe cleaners, rubber bands, really whatever you have is fine."

Jones nodded but still looked skeptical as she backed out of the room.

Elsie raised her hands in the air; she felt like a ringmaster addressing the crowd. "Who here knows Fangley?"

All around the room, hands shot up.

"Okay good. Fangley couldn't make it today, so he sent me, his best friend. Well, besides Ratatouille. He wanted me to teach you how to make puppets. I really hope no one has stinky feet because I need everyone to take off their right sock."

Elsie bent down and began pulling off the red polka dot sock she had on. She believed socks were an efficient way to express personality.

The kids looked around at each other, a few giggles echoing through the room.

"I mean it; everyone needs to give one to the puppet cause."

Bentley pulled off one of his and waved it over his head, and soon enough the rest of the kids followed suit. Some removed both socks while an alarming number didn't know the difference between left and right. Maybe she should write that into a Fangley episode. Fangley could be following Ratatouille's directions and end up lost in the dark woods of some urban park.

Jones walked back in with a handful of white buttons and some thread. "I couldn't find glue. Wait, they can't ruin their socks, their parents will be mad."

"It's one sock, how much could it cost? Two dollars?"

"With these kids, who knows? Maybe one hundred. Anyway, here's what I found." Jones set what she'd gathered onto the rug next to Elsie.

When Jones' hand brushed Elsie's leg, she shivered. *Focus; that was accidental.* "Could you find better buttons? These are kind of boring."

"I cut these off one of my shirts."

Well, the image *that* brought up for Elsie was *less* boring. Elsie cleared her throat and pushed away the thought of buttons flying off Jones' shirt as she tore it open.

"These are great, actually. Why don't you finish up the cupcakes, and I'll take over here?"

"Be my guest." Jones leaned closer. "For someone who doesn't do birthday parties you sure are saving my life right now." She squeezed Elsie's bicep and then she was gone.

Elsie looked up at a dozen or so expectant faces watching her with rapt attention; her own face aflame.

ELSIE WAS SEWING the final button eye on a tiny striped sock when her phone buzzed. Bentley and a few of his friends had their sock puppets peeking out from behind the remaining red velvet curtain—in terms of window dressing, it was a puppeteer's dream.

Avery: *Where are you? I want to go roller skating.*

Elsie snapped a quick picture of her sock puppet.

Elsie: *I'm saving the day*

Avery: *I knew I should have gone with you. For the last time: puppets are not a form of seduction, Elsbells. If you cancel on me, you're getting the second shower for the rest of the week.*

Elsie made her puppet grimace and sent Avery another photo. Even though the prospect of a week of cold showers didn't seem so bad in that moment.

Elsie: *I'm being a good person, I thought you'd be happy*

Avery: *Wait, is that my sock? I love those red socks, I wear them when I'm meeting new clients!*

Elsie grimaced. Busted.

Elsie: *Call you later Avy Baby*

BY THE TIME the last kid had left, and Jones had explained to some astonishingly angry parents why their children's socks had been mutilated, Elsie felt exhausted. For a brief moment, she wished she could crash on the sofa like Bentley, who was currently face down and snoring softly. But she still had her contract to sign, and Avery would kill her if she didn't meet them for skate night. She shoved her sock puppet in her pocket, thankful for the glittery black nail polish she'd painted her toes with yesterday.

"Thanks for that; it was really nice of you." Jones gave her a tired smile. "I'd be happy to pay you for your time."

Elsie waved her offer away. "Isn't the contract all about paying me for my time? We'll consider that one on the house."

Jones laughed. And she kept laughing. She laughed like she needed it. Like she was clinging to every ounce of humor in Elsie's bland joke. When she caught her breath, she wiped a tear from her eye.

"Not to judge, but I think you might be a little delirious. Can I get you something? More of your pain water?"

Jones shook her head. "I wouldn't have gotten through that without you. You kept me sane even though I'm missing a flight right now. Thanks, Elsie. Let's go over the terms of your contract, so you can get out of here. I've already taken up too much of your time."

Elsie started to protest but caught herself. Maybe Jones was ready for her to leave, Elsie had just kind of inserted herself into their day. "Right, yes, of course." Elsie did come here to sign her contract. And she did need to leave for her plans with Avery. Even if the window for the haircut Elsie promised them had passed. Then why did Jones' words about getting her out drop like an anchor in her stomach? *Because you've overstayed your welcome. And because Jones is trying to leave.*

Once she had the thought, it caught hold. Elsie worked for Jones; she wasn't some friend Elsie was helping out. She wasn't a woman she was trying to impress. Not to mention Jones had just lost her father and probably wasn't looking to be impressed.

Jones slid the contract across the counter. "I took a look and everything seems to be in order, so just review and sign. Sorry that you got roped into an entire afternoon. Though you really did an incredible job with those puppets."

"Yeah, sock puppets are the training wheels of making the real thing." Elsie took the contract from Jones. She scanned the first page. Her name was right, so that was promising.

She flipped to the sign tabs and then back through the pages like they were a word search. She scanned for numbers, but the amount she finally zeroed in on was nowhere near what she'd expected. It wasn't even near the five percent cut she told Jason she'd made her peace with taking.

"Is this a joke? Or is there a zero missing?"

"What do you mean?" Jones stepped behind Elsie to look at the contract. She smelled like vanilla frosting, and Elsie fought to hold onto her frustration. It was hard enough for Elsie to keep her focus around Jones, even when she didn't smell like birthday cake. But just because Jones seemed nice enough didn't mean she wasn't trying to screw Elsie. She just wished it was in the other sense of that word. Jones' shoulder brushed against her, and Elsie steadied the papers in her hands.

"Here." Elsie jabbed at the page with her finger like it was a touchscreen she couldn't get to work. "I was told to expect five percent lower than what I'd negotiated for, which was already bullshit, by the way, but this is closer to ten."

She felt the warmth of Jones' body against her back. It was unprofessional to stand so close to someone. It was making math hard. Okay, math was already hard, but still, Jones' proximity was distracting. Elsie hated it. And also she didn't.

"I thought this was what you'd agreed to, but it seems like this might be your first time seeing that number?"

"I never agreed to this. This offer is worse than the last one I declined. Jason reached out to Stu with what I was willing to take." Elsie turned toward Jones, bringing their faces just inches apart. Jones had a fleck of frosting on her cheek. But all the desire she'd felt earlier had turned to rage. Jones was no different than anyone else on the show, looking to take advantage of her because they assumed she wasn't smart enough to know what was going on.

"Why don't I make some calls and see what's going on? It's clearly some sort of mistake."

"Did you even review my current contract? Is this what *you* think is fair?" Elsie's laugh rang bitterly in her ears. Much more like Fangley's spinster vampire aunt than her usual glee. "This isn't a mistake; it's a tactic. You invite me over here to sign a contract that's been delayed by Haelstrom Media not once, not twice, but three times. It's now the last day for me to sign before my current contract runs out. I'm at your house, on your turf. What part of this doesn't seem calculated?"

Elsie thought she and Jones had been getting along, that maybe she wasn't just like every other person at Haelstrom who didn't value her, but all she'd done was work a birthday party for free.

"Elsie, I didn't know."

"Maybe that's true. But you also didn't check. How much less are you offering me than Trey?"

"I'm not sure. I didn't see the contracts that were already signed."

"The answer should be that I'm being offered more! I created Fangley—I created the entire show. And I write most of the episodes. Without me, this show literally doesn't happen. But you weren't concerned about that. I was so naive. I thought maybe with you taking over for a bit, things would get better. That I'd have a shot at equity." Elsie rushed through the hall lengthening her strides.

"That's not fair. I just—this is a lot, okay? I can fix this." Jones stumbled over her words.

"I'm not sure if you're playing me or if you're getting played too, but I'm done with this. Good luck with your company and trying to continue Fangley Heights without the only person who knows what's going on. I'm done." Elsie's voice rattled with rage.

"Come on, Elsie. I thought you loved the show. What would you do without it?"

The metal of the doorknob was as cold as slushy water against her fingers, as Elsie turned back to face Jones. She pulled her shoulders up to her ears and let them drop. "Maybe I'll do birthday parties."

CHAPTER SIX
JONES

Hi, Birdie." Jones infused her voice with the essence of brightness, like it was a seven dollar bottle of water.

"How's my darling daughter doing?" Birdie sing-songed.

Joyful wasn't a tone Jones was used to from her mother.

"Well, right now I'm wondering when you started referring to me as *your darling daughter*."

"Can't a lady try something new?"

"Okay, mother."

"Don't you dare." Birdie's tone pirouetted to scathing. "It's not too late for me to disown you."

Jones laughed. She picked up the marker Elsie had forgotten the other day and spun it on the table like it could predict her future. "It actually is pretty late for that. We've got a Grey Gardens thing going on. That bond is unbreakable."

"Well, we'd be a lot closer to Grey Gardens if I could get my Brooklyn house back and we lived there together while spending the last of your father's money. Just like when you were a baby, remember? Maybe I could get some work on Broadway."

"I'm not sure there will be much to spend after this week."

"What happened?" Birdie asked.

Jones could almost feel her mother leaning forward over the phone. Birdie Haelstrom relied on gossip the way most people relied on food and water. It made up the bulk of her diet. It sustained her. Her mother had always said the hardest part about leaving her father was that it cut off her access to the good insider info. The kind you won't find in any magazine. Jones had long suspected that Birdie kept her married name just for the social cache, even the thinnest thread tying her to fame was preferable to a full severing.

She weighed whether or not she wanted to tell her mother that the reason she'd stayed was because Charity had never come home Saturday and wasn't answering Jones' calls. Or if she should tell her mother about the situation with Elsie—who, Jones had discovered after a night of poring over each and every contract for Fangley Heights going back to the pilot—had a point. To be ineloquent about it, Elsie was getting screwed by the network, while Fangley Heights and sales of licensed merchandise had been single-handedly keeping Haelstrom Media in the black. Stu's desperation to get Elsie's contract locked in for cheap suddenly made a lot more sense. If they paid Elsie what she really deserved, they might all be out of a job.

She had to tell her mother something, so Jones gave Birdie an executive summary of her last twenty-four hours, leaving out some of the finer points. "My eyes are so tired from reviewing contracts. After Elsie stormed out, I called Stu and made him email me contracts for everyone on the show since it started."

Jones' mind flashed back to Elsie's exit, which had been… impressive. And, if she was being honest, a little sexy. Not many people in Jones' life stood up to her. Or made it clear that they expected better.

"Setting aside why she was at your house in the first place, and why you're still in New York, because those are things we'll come back to later, why didn't you get someone to read them for you? You can pay people to do that."

Jones closed her eyes then opened them slowly. "Are you talking about lawyers? I know how to read."

"Yes, dear, and we're all impressed, but is that something you should still be bragging about? I hope you at least took time this morning for a little spa treatment, even if you did it yourself, because you seem to have some aversion to professionals. Although they really need to make a living too, Jones. It's the right thing to do. Besides, at your age, you really can't flirt with wrinkles."

"I don't need a spa. I need five hours of uninterrupted sleep. I'm forty, not seventy-five."

"You're forty-two, my dear. But if you tell anyone I acknowledged that, I'll deny it."

"Ugh, you're right. I forgot about those last birthdays."

"Wishful thinking. So, Bentley's still not sleeping at night?"

"Yeah. I can't tell if it's getting worse. Last night I woke up to him crying, but he was still sound asleep."

"Have you tried offering him money? It really does wonders."

"I don't think I can bribe a six-year-old to not have nightmares. He just lost his dad, and now his mom is off, probably sipping umbrella drinks in a hammock somewhere." Jones gripped her hair into a tight ponytail and then released it, hoping some of the tension would cascade away with the strands.

"I'm sure she can afford a bed indoors, dear. She's not that wolf boy from the Jungle Book."

JONES LEANED back in her father's chair. She half expected her feet to hover above the ground, but of course, they didn't.

They were planted firmly in this hellish new reality. Her plan to cut executive salaries and adjust Trey's contract down was solid, but that didn't mean anyone would want to agree to it. *They don't have to agree with you for it to happen*, Jones reminded herself for the hundredth time that day. She had no answer for why she was even here on a Monday morning, ready to fight a contract battle on behalf of a woman she barely knew. Except that there was something about Elsie—a spark of passion—that compelled Jones. Elsie standing up for herself shored up her own desire to do the right thing.

Jones had never wanted any of this. Not the pressure of the network or the constant breakneck pace of the television industry. And she certainly didn't want confirmation that she was a disappointment to her father. Her assumptions about that were hard enough. But what she did want, for as long as she was here, was to make things a little better.

It had been an easy enough decision to move to the West Coast with Birdie after the divorce. Not only because she was a child and in reality had no say. She was so much like her mother, or at least all the parts her father had openly despised, which was to say anxious, depressed, occasionally hypomanic. She could still hear his argument that Birdie should just be logical, be grateful for the life he gave her. But Birdie was miserable, and so she left. Well, that and the cheating, but at nine years old, Jones hadn't realized that.

The next few years were chaos until the alimony payments kicked in, but she'd never stopped admiring her mother's leap. Aside from her college years in New York and her brief but disastrous internship for her father, she'd hardly seen him in decades.

And now, she'd let herself be pulled back in out of some misguided sense of obligation. And of course, Charity had split. With each unreturned call, Jones became more sure that none of this was simply a misunderstanding. That pregnant pause when the call crackled and connected only to churn her into voice mail, had already broken Jones' heart for Bentley a dozen times since Saturday. Charity had probably booked her tickets the second Jones confirmed she'd be coming for the funeral. Jones should have seen through it, Charity's spa weekend right after the funeral. If Jones couldn't spot a lie like that, how could she run her father's company? No. Not her father's. If Charity's return was uncertain, Jones needed to start acting like the company was her responsibility. Because it was. And that meant it needed to get a lot more fair immediately.

Jones' head fell back against the soft leather of the headrest, and she closed her eyes. Maybe she could go to sleep and wake up a month ago before any of this happened. *Wishful thinking won't get you anywhere. If you want something you need to make it happen.* Her father's voice echoed in her ears. Spoken like a true boot-strapper who started a television company with nothing but his indomitable American spirit and a small one-million-dollar loan from his father. Wishful thinking probably wasn't necessary when you got to the top by way of a golden elevator. She pictured when she'd heard him say those words in an interview she had found online; he was just a gray suit and cold blue eyes underlined by a vacant smile.

Jones spread out the pages of Elsie Webb's contract on the cherrywood desk in front of her. It was closer to the size of a dining room table. Were men with big desks the white-collar version of those with big trucks? When she'd first come to her father's office last week, she'd found his desk pristine, almost no actual work seemed to be happening here. She'd finally cracked the code to his tablet, her own birthday oddly enough, but even that had only had stock market apps and conservative news sites.

She knew what she had to do. Jones studied the papers in front of her, which were dog eared and scrawled with red ink —she'd borrowed a marker from Bentley. She had the copy of

Trey's contract, also marked up. The side-by-side comparison was stark. He'd been there a year less than Elsie and made twenty-thousand dollars more. His role on the show seemed minimal, or at least auxiliary, while Elsie's seemed integral. She wondered what leverage Stu had used to work out this deal for his nephew, whatever it was it must have been major to force such a disparity.

Outside she heard footsteps stampeding down the hall. A panicked red face she didn't recognize poked through the gap in the door.

"Mrs. Haelstrom?"

"Ms."

"Ms. Haelstrom, we have a problem."

"I think we have a few problems. And you are?"

"I'm Steve, a production assistant on Fangley Heights." The red-faced guy gasped for breath. His hair stood straight up, like a flame reaching toward the sky. "And well, he's missing! Stu sent me to find you."

"Who's missing?"

"The star. Fangley."

"I thought Fangley was a puppet."

"Not just *a* puppet. *The* puppet. He's not in his case." He paused and went even redder.

"Okay, I'm on my way."

As soon as the words left her mouth, Steve bolted. He pushed off her door frame to propel himself down the hall. A missing puppet didn't sound like a good problem to have, but Steve's hair looked like it was on actual fire. Hopefully they had some strategically placed extinguishers around the building.

THE SET WAS pure chaos when Jones arrived with Stu stalking in right behind her. So maybe it was a slightly bigger issue than Jones had imagined. More people than Jones even knew were in the building, milling around the set, breathing heavily into headsets and phones. A few of them who looked a lot like interns, leaned against the walls tapping furiously into their phones. Steve was darting around, looking like someone needed to douse him with a bucket of water.

"Okay." She gave two sharp claps. "Phones down. We don't need this getting out until we get a handle on it. Everyone go get a bagel or an ice cream cone. Stu, can I see you upstairs?"

STU TRIED to lead the way to the conference room, but Jones took a sharp left back into her father's office and settled behind the desk. She was done with his weird power plays.

"I think we should call Charity."

"Be my guest." Jones pushed the phone across her desk toward Stu.

"Actually, I'm calling the police."

"And do what? Fill out a missing person's report? It's a puppet, Stu. Surely the props department has another lying around."

"It's the original Fangley; we don't just have another one sitting on a table."

"That's a little short-sighted. But okay, let's make some calls. How long will it take to make a replacement?"

"It's about principle." Stu shoved his hands into his pockets so hard, Jones was surprised his pants didn't tear. She shook away the image of a male stripper at a bachelorette party she went to last year. Now was not the time to think of that horror show. But really, it never was the time for that, including when it was happening.

"What exactly *is* the principle at stake here?"

"That puppet is worth thousands of dollars. It's not just a prop; it's proprietary and it's *ours*. I don't want some intern putting it up on eBay for a big payday."

"So, to reiterate, the principle you care about is money?"

Stu's nostrils flared. "And, history," he sputtered. "It's part of your father's legacy. I'm sure Charity would understand."

"Please, we both know that the only thing my father cared about was money. You two have that in common. He didn't care about the show or the people who made it. The contracts I read last night made that clear enough." Jones tapped the papers still scattered over the desk. "I guess we don't need to worry about a new Fangley at all if Elsie's not coming back. You really jeopardized her return with that stunt you pulled this weekend."

"Is that Elsie's contract? Did she sign it in blood?" His eyes scanned the red ink covering the page as he reached forward to grab the papers. Jones finished gathering them quickly toward her like a poker player raking in chips.

"She didn't sign it at all, but I did make some comments and addendums."

"The only thing you were responsible for was getting her to agree. If Elsie doesn't sign her contract, we're screwed. In case you didn't know, she is Fangley. She created him and the show."

"That's funny, a few minutes ago, Fangley belonged to the network. You know, the terms seem to reflect how integral she is to its success. But I'm glad you agree that she's irreplaceable, because this contract wasn't reflecting that."

"We agreed to no changes."

"I don't remember agreeing to anything." Jones leaned back in her father's chair. She wanted to put her feet on the desk, stake her claim, but the margin of error where she fell out of her chair instead was just too great.

"Look, it's not my fault she couldn't negotiate better. We pay people what they make themselves worth."

"No, we've been paying her the least we possibly can. But not anymore. I value people, which means Haelstrom Media values people. I couldn't help but notice that Trey's agreement also wasn't equitable—he's making significantly more than Elsie, which isn't right."

"Right, that's what I said. It's business, Jones. Your father had a head for this stuff. You—"

"I, what, exactly? Look, I'm about to scan hers and Trey's paperwork so legal can make some changes."

"There's no way we're changing Trey's. He and I had an agreement."

"Is that how it usually works? You and your nephew agreeing how much he should make? Look, Stu, we can adjust Trey's per episode rate, or you can take a pay cut. Either is fine with me."

Stu's mouth fell open, and Jones could see the gears in his head turning, the exact moment his idea hit. "Wait, if she didn't sign it, then she must have taken Fangley." Stu's face showed the slow dawn of understanding. He slid his phone out of the inside pocket of his suit.

"Put your phone down, Stu. Now. We're not calling the police over a puppet."

"We're calling the police over a theft. This is a breach of contract."

"We're not calling them over that either. Her agreement ran out, remember? So here's what we're going to do: Legal will send me a new contract, then I'm going to reach out to Ms. Webb's representation to review the revised and favorable terms for his client. If he agrees that the new offer looks good, I'll take it to Elsie."

"And what am I supposed to do?"

"Pray she accepts it."

"How about *I* call Jason? If she stole the puppet, I bet we can get her to sign for less, if we promise not to press charges."

"Absolutely not. That's all, Stu. You can go. The days of this company manipulating and bullying people are over."

THE LEAD HAELSTROM lawyer was apoplectic, filled to the brim with litigious rage at Jones' suggestion that they give Elsie a cut of the Fangley merchandise licensing. He stressed that she had agreed to the current percent in her original contract—he should know, he wrote it.

And although everyone agreed that the character was Elsie's, down to the original sketches from her notebook—a stick figure Fangley complete with signature odd-angled fangs and deep dimples—adding a percentage of merchandising now was simply not how things were done. A company should only give money away when they're legally obligated to, or when it's some kind of brand-raising tax write-off. A good deed was only as good as its marketability. Right and wrong didn't usually enter the equation.

When Chuck left to contact the board about Jones' executive capacity, she headed back to her office, or at least the place where she'd left her heels and granola bar, and readied herself for the call she'd been waiting all morning to make.

She liked the way the power of owning the situation felt in her body. Is this how Elsie had felt Saturday when she'd stormed off, so certain she was right? Certain enough that she was willing to risk her job for it. Jones liked the flare of satisfaction she found in doing what was fair.

A FEW HOURS LATER, Jones had a headache, the kind that started behind her eyes and morphed into a halo of white light that was both bright and loud. But they were close to a contract, so the pain was worth it. Jones and Jason, Elsie's agent, felt confident she would sign. Probably. Maybe. The words 'righteous indignation' had been used by him multiple times, though Jones sensed he was bluffing. And possibly didn't even know what those words meant.

Still, she had the feeling that getting Elsie onboard was going to take some serious finesse. By the time she'd wrapped up the meeting with Jason, who was blissfully not at a bar judging by the noise on the line, she had managed to plug Elsie's home address into her phone's GPS. Jones was ready to save the whole damn company.

CHAPTER SEVEN
ELSIE

Fangley sat lifeless on the pillow next to Elsie. The last couple of days she could barely look at him. It was silly, she knew, to feel like she'd let down a puppet, but she couldn't shake her guilt. Avery liked to say that Elsie was the kind of stubborn person that would build a house in the eye of a tornado. Perhaps, but only if there was a good coffee shop within walking distance.

But Elsie didn't feel like that person right now, because here she was, lying in bed on a workday, while the show went on without her. If she was truly stubborn, she would have chained herself to the set like an environmental activist to a tree. Now *those* people knew how to go against the grain.

She wished she didn't know that production would continue without her. She felt a small flicker of hope that maybe it wasn't. The show's dynamic duo was camped out in Elsie's bed. Surely Rebecca and Trey were thrown off by Fangley's empty case. *Shit, Rebecca*. Elsie should text her to apologize. Wasn't apologizing another way of admitting guilt? And Elsie hadn't done anything wrong. You can't steal from yourself.

She'd replayed the voicemail Jones had left her yesterday

morning so many times that the words had lost all meaning. If messages were still left on tapes, it would have worn out by now. Jones had reviewed her contract and 'found some inconsistencies' and wanted to have a discussion about them. Which, of course, as Elsie had been telling her, the inconsistencies were the point. It's not a mistake when it's intentional, then it's just a strategy. At the end of her message, Jones had mentioned holding auditions to cast a new puppeteer to play Fangley as a last resort, but the way she'd said it sounded forced. Like she didn't really mean the threat, or didn't want to mean it. If you're going to threaten someone, your heart really should be in it.

Everyone thinks they're irreplaceable, but life moves forward all the time. The network wouldn't wait for her, just like none of the women she'd tried dating had, with her erratic show schedule. A surprising number of them thought they should be more important to Elsie than her puppet.

You can't be invaluable if you're not even there. At least that line from Jones' message rang true.

When she'd sat on the subway Saturday night with Fangley held close to her chest in a baby carrier, his little legs dangling, Elsie promised herself that she'd move on. And she would, within reason. If the show gave Fangley to Trey, she would burn the place down. Figuratively. But also maybe literally. Now that theft was in her arsenal—or was it kidnapping—why not arson?

A soft knock on her door drew her attention, and she turned to see Avery balancing two bowls of cereal. Elsie flailed a bit until she was able to shove Fangley under her covers, just as the door swung the rest of the way open. She nonchalantly patted down the conspicuous bump beside her.

"I splurged and got your favorite." Avery eyed Elsie's frantic movements, their eyes lingered on her hand beneath the covers where Elsie was attempting to shove Fangley further down. "Am, I um, interrupting something?"

"What? No." Elsie didn't care for the amused smirk on Avery's face. She straightened up to her full seated height, not easy in such a comfortable bed. "I mean I am an adult in my own room, so if you walk in on me masturbating that's kind of on you, buddy."

"So are you masturbating or aren't you? I'd offer to come back, but I know how you feel about soggy cereal." Avery raised an eyebrow and glanced down at the bowls.

"I won't be answering that question on principle." Elsie held her hand out to take the large jade green glass bowl from Avery. It was made for ambrosia salad and Tang Punch and other delicacies from a bygone era, and it was worth more than most of her clothing. Still, it was what they used for cereal and leftovers.

Elsie settled back on the bed, careful not to spill any of the cereal as it sloshed against the rim in angry waves. She fished in her bowl and popped a cotton candy pink marshmallow into her mouth. She enjoyed the way it crunched slightly, like she imagined those green floral foam blocks at the craft store might. "Glad to see you're finally recognizing that breakfast is the most important meal of the day, Avy baby."

"It's one p.m., babe. And the charms, which I see is all you're eating, are 99% sugar—not exactly a meal so much as a one-way ticket to a sugar rush."

"Sure, but breakfast is a state of mind. And time is just a concept. Plus, I think we can both agree I need some luck."

"Well, then you're eating the wrong thing. The marshmallows are the charms. The cereal pieces are the luckies. Most people don't know that." Avery pushed up their glasses and smirked.

How was it possible to adore and want to strangle someone at the same time? Avery lived in that liminal state. They lowered down onto the bed and shot back up immediately as though they'd been bitten. Charms hailed down on

Elsie. Avery's eyes were wide, mouth agape. "Els, please tell me I did not just sit on what I think I did."

"That really depends—what do you think you sat on?"

"Some weird sex toy?" Avery leaned forward tentatively and patted the blanket a few times. "Like a sex…doll?" Avery shuddered.

She loved the way their voice went up at the end, like they were desperate to be wrong.

A few more clovers freed themselves from the confines of the bowl and plummeted to the floor. *Such a waste.* Though Elsie had learned the hard way that the five second rule did not apply to marshmallow cereal.

Elsie wondered idly if she should put Avery out of their misery, but she lived for these misunderstandings. The joys of free comedy. "That's kind of a private question, don't you think?"

Avery stared Elsie down. She tried to hold out, but she'd never won a staring contest in her life. Not to mention the way silence made her skin crawl. She reached an arm under the blankets and pulled Fangley out.

Avery turned away, throwing their free arm over their eyes like the puppet was a cursed object.

"Oh wow, that's worse than I thought." Avery lowered their voice. "And how long have you been having these urges, Ms. Webb?"

Elsie wound her arm back and beamed Avery in the head with Fangley. "Don't be gross. I rescued Fangley from the studio when I went to clear out my dressing room."

Avery narrowed their eyes. "Stole."

"What?"

"You mean you stole him. Haelstrom owns Fangley, right?"

"I mean, technically. And perhaps legally. But he's mine emotionally." Elsie raised a dramatic hand to cover her heart.

"Ah yes, the emotional defense. That always holds up in

court." Avery nodded slowly, pursing their lips. It was *almost* like they weren't being genuine.

"It's always better to ask for forgiveness, not permission."

"Not even remotely true, Els. Do you think we have to worry about the show sending a search and rescue team for him? I don't want a group of hunks dressed in all black crawling across the living room with their defined muscles and…okay, well, maybe I do. Who knows you took him?"

"Just you, buddy. But I'm becoming pretty concerned you're about to turn me in for some abs and tactical gear."

"Relax, unfortunately for my new number one fantasy, I doubt anyone will care that you kidnapped the Fangster," Avery said.

"It just proves they don't know what they're doing. He's a national treasure. His little blue face should be on every oat milk carton in the city!"

"Oat milk?"

"Yeah, the official drink of Brooklyn," Elsie said.

"I love when you're like this."

"Like what?" Elsie asked.

"Feisty. The last few days you've walked around here like a ghost." A frown drifted across Avery's mouth before dissipating.

"I'm in mourning, Aves. I watched my whole career, my future, disappear before my eyes."

"Right, but you made a choice. A bold choice. I mean, you nabbed Fangley in the middle of the night. And you walked away from a show that didn't respect you. It's time to get up off the mat."

"Well, I can't just make a new show with Fangley; they own him. I can't believe I signed that contract three years ago. I gave up everything. If I restart my web series, I'll get sued. Plus, I really alienated Jones the other day."

"Jones is in over her head and obviously didn't know what she was losing when she let you walk out that door. She deserves our sympathy. Her life is probably hell right now with you gone and Fangley missing. Not to mention losing her dad and dealing with family stuff."

"Yeah, that's true. Shit, now I feel bad. I barely asked her about her dad or how she was." Elsie crunched a marshmallow thoughtfully, enjoying the way it dissolved between her teeth. "Should I return him?" She nodded toward Fangley, his little blue arm hanging off the side of her bed made him look lifeless. Elsie could see how Jones could mistake him for a toy. And a replaceable one at that. Just like her.

Avery waved a hand in front of her face. "Earth to Elsie. I mean this lovingly, but you've been obsessed with Fangley for years. Maybe it's time for a new idea. A new character."

"I can't just come up with a new character. Fangley was a moment of genius. A lightning strike. A big bang."

Avery choked on a piece of cereal.

"Don't be gross. He's the best thing I've ever created. I can't just make that happen again. I don't know how."

"Why not? You're Elsie Webb, creator of Fangley Heights. You stand on your principles. You take no prisoners. You can do anything."

"That's a lot of cliches but no need to apologize, I forgive you."

Avery rolled their eyes. "Look, I need to get to work, but by the time I get home I want to see that notebook full of incomprehensible scribbles. Everything starts with trying." Avery grabbed the rainbow notebook on her desk and tossed it at her. She ducked and it hit the wall behind her with a pitiful thud. "And use your lucky marker."

The idea of starting over made Elsie's stomach clench. But beneath the fear, there was the tiniest flicker of excitement. "I'll have to use a spare. I left my best one at Jones' house after she wouldn't let me use it on my contract."

"I mean, that's fair. It is washable. Time for us both to get to work. And remember, I want that notebook to be full or no cartoons tonight."

Avery had always driven a hard bargain.

This time, when Avery threw her second-string purple marker, Elsie was ready. She caught it in her fist and pulled the cap off with her teeth. "Aye, aye, Cap'n!"

CHAPTER EIGHT
JONES

Jones slowed as she approached the brownstone that her phone assured her was the right place with a cheerful and robotic "you have arrived." If Elsie Webb didn't want people showing up at her house, she wouldn't have listed her home address on her contract, right? Right. Unless maybe she was legally required to list it? Jones refused to consider that as she smoothed down the front of her jacket and paced before the chipped terracotta-colored steps.

Besides, Elsie had been to Jones' house. Or the weird quasi-mansion house where Jones was staying. So maybe Elsie had been invited, bordering on being ordered, to show up at Jones' place, but still, fair was fair. It's not creepy; it's business. And Jones Haelstrom was a professional. She had every right to be here, and she was here to make things right. Except exactly none of those facts set Jones at ease. Her mouth was dry, and her palms were sweaty. She shoved her hands into her pockets. *Nobody finds nervous sweat sexy, Haelstrom.*

She was out of her element. So far, her time in New York had been a snarl of missed trains and wrong turns. Her favorite shoes had gum, and something else she refused to examine further, stuck to the bottom. The only thing she'd been able to count on the last two weeks was not one single thing going to plan.

Her life in LA was simple. She had a routine. A little freelance writing, even if it was just inconsequential listicles about celebrity lifestyles. Hint: the secret is always money. How does she look so young? Money. How does he stay in shape? Money. How do they find time to get their pilot's license? Money. How can you get that life? You can't.

But among the articles were a lot of walks to the juice shop and content hours spent tapping idly at her laptop under a big patio umbrella. Probably too many serial killer podcasts to be considered a healthy interest. You know, work. And hobbies. It was all about balance. But she was in charge now. The CEO of Haelstrom Media. Sort of. It occurred to her that she should have gotten some clarity on that before renegotiating the contract that sat in her bag like something radioactive.

Her hands were shaking as she climbed the stairs. Maybe Elsie wouldn't notice her nerves. Jones doubted it. For someone with her head in the clouds, Elsie noticed everything. When she'd shown up on Saturday, Jones had the distinct feeling that Elsie saw right through her. Saw the way her confidence was just a thin blanket she'd wrapped around herself. And when Elsie had exited through Jones' front door, down one sock, she'd seemed completely in control.

As Elsie walked away, Jones had noticed two things: she had the assuredness of a star; and her ass looked great in those jeans. And, well, you couldn't spell assuredness without ass. There was a little rip right below one of Elsie's back pockets that had been playing in Jones' head like a gif. Which was an absolutely unprofessional thought that no amount of guilt was able to clear from her mind.

Jones raised her hand to knock. No matter how gorgeous

Elsie looked, no matter how she tilted her chin and narrowed her eyes and made Jones' knees weak, she, Jones Haelstrom, would remain the picture of professionalism.

The door swung open and Elsie slid into view. Like actually, honest-to-god slid, her feet were gliding across the polished floor, Risky-Business style. She was wearing knee-high socks, an oversized t-shirt, and…that was it actually. Fuck.

Elsie let out a laugh that sounded delighted. "I thought you were my food delivery, or Oscar, but this is even better." She raked her messy brown hair to one side. "What color would you call my hair? Chestnut, maybe? That's what Avery calls it, but it makes me feel like a horse. Like 'her beautiful chestnut braid swayed as she leapt over the jump'. Anyway, nothing against horse girls."

"What are you talking about? Are you feeling okay? Who's Oscar?" Jones reached forward to touch Elsie's forehead before the intimacy of the act made her pull back. Her fingers hummed from the near contact.

Jones paused, studying Elsie. Her green eyes looked slightly glassy, but she didn't look sad. She leaned past Jones and craned her neck to scan the street. Oh. With the height difference the step gave her, Elsie's chest pressed into Jones' shoulder. "You can have some of my snacks, if you want. If they ever get here. Oscar is Avery's dog—they're at work."

"Does Oscar knock on the door often?"

Elsie's laugh avalanched from a chuckle to cackles. Jones hadn't realized she'd made a joke.

Jones clasped her hands together. "Maybe I should come back another time? I was hoping to discuss your contract."

Elsie widened her eyes. She turned around staring into the hallway like she was looking for something. If she had taken Fangley, which was the most obvious option, maybe she was making sure he was out of sight. Jones had already decided to let the minor theft slide. She got the feeling that that puppet was a family to Elsie.

When Elsie looked at Jones again her face was flushed. "You're already here. Why would you need to come back?"

Jones lowered her voice to a whisper. "Because I think you might be stoned?"

"Yeah, but only a little. Come on in."

Jones stood on the porch for another long moment as Elsie disappeared into the house. Jones' feet followed of their own volition, tripping briefly on an empty baby carrier leaned against the wall in the entryway.

Elsie flopped on a leather couch in the living room, her arm around a doll that bore a striking resemblance to the one missing from the studio. There was a cartoon horse on the TV. Is that what had prompted the hair musings?

Jones needed to leave. Now. But instead she settled into a broken-in Eames chair that felt like a bean bag drawing her in. She waited for Elsie to look away from the television, but when she didn't, Jones cleared her throat.

"Okay, like I said, I brought a new contract that I was hoping we could—" Jones shifted in the chair and tried not to tip over. Everything felt off-kilter. Elsie giggled, and something in Jones' chest untwisted.

"Have you ever seen this show? It's totally genius. This horse is—"

"I haven't seen the show. Look, Elsie, if we're not going to go over this contract then I need to leave." Not a single molecule in Jones' body wanted to leave Elsie's presence.

"Why? Don't go, we can hang—" Elsie's phone made a lightsaber sound, and she catapulted off the couch. Her underwear was blue with green polka dots, and that was information Jones absolutely should not have. Just one more image that would be living rent-free in her head.

"Be right back. Snack time." Elsie's eyes flashed as she rubbed her hands together.

She returned a moment later holding a Slurpee and a pack of Twizzlers. So, she really *had* meant snacks. Jones wasn't aware that 7-11 delivered.

"That's a pretty broad definition of food," Jones said.

Elsie held the drink out to her. "Want some?"

There was something about the way Elsie was looking at her that had Jones leaning forward to take a sip before she caught herself. *This is a business meeting, even if she is in her underwear. Your only goals are to get this contract signed and to get out of here without grounds for a lawsuit.*

"Before I forget." Jones opened her bag and retrieved Elsie's contract, setting it on the table. "Your new—and I hope much improved—contract."

There, mission accomplished. Sort of. Time to go.

Elsie looked down, and her eyes widened. She tugged on the hem of her t-shirt with her free hand. Her face flushed adorably, even as she flashed Jones a guilty but pleased smile. "Here, would you hold this for me? You can have some, if you want. It's half coke, half cherry, as God intended. I'll be right back. Turns out it's a little chilly in here without pants. Also, I, um, read better with them on."

Jones stared straight ahead and gripped the drink until her fingers ached. She slid it onto the coffee table and grabbed a handful of gummy bears from the cut crystal dish. The juxtaposition of finery and candy felt quintessentially Elsie. The bowl was something Birdie would love; she had an ashtray just like it.

Elsie was one of those people who was completely themselves from the moment you met them. This was their third meeting, and already Jones felt like she knew her, even if everything she learned just made her want to know more.

Jones was biting into a red bear—she always saved the best flavors for last—as Elsie swept back into the room in tight ripped jeans and a white t-shirt. Jones blinked slowly, trying to stop her full-body perusal. She was not successful.

What had gotten into her? Her body felt as pliant as the bear she'd just demolished.

Elsie's hand grabbed her wrist and Jones gasped. "Did you eat one of those?"

Jones gulped down the candy. "Do these not fall into the realm of snacks? Or, don't tell me—these are props too? Is this the hammer all over again?"

Elsie's brows drew together, like Jones' sentence was a complicated puzzle she couldn't work out.

"Like the hammer at the studio?" Jones prompted. "The one you threw at me."

Elsie giggled. "No, of course not."

The surge of that warm sound through Jones was so unfair.

"Okay, whew. You had me worried there for a second. They would have been pretty tasty for fake candy."

"I mean, they are edibles." Elsie shrugged.

"I know; I just ate one." Jones narrowed her eyes. Elsie was almost nonsensical. She needed to get out of here.

"No, as in weed. As in, I really hope you only ate one and don't sue me. Also, you probably owe Avery some money. They claim they're medicinal for the chronic pain in the ass that is living with me." Elsie's grin was lopsided.

Alarm bells went off in Jones' head. She knew she'd let down her guard too much. "You have candy drugs just sitting out in a *dish?* How could you be so irresponsible?" Her judgment leaked into her voice, sharpening her words.

Elsie either didn't understand her tone, or chose to ignore it. "Jones, relax. You came into my house and ate some bears of your own accord. Neither of us has the upper hand here. Might as well just enjoy the trip." Elsie picked up the Slurpee from the coffee table and pressed it into Jones' hand. "Just out of curiosity, how many did you eat?"

"Two, maybe?"

"Jones. No one eats just two gummy bears. It's simply not

possible, unless all that's left is like the weird pineapple flavor."

"Fine. Four. Maybe five? Do you think I need to go to the hospital?" Jones' heart picked up speed, like a song reaching the chorus. That candy was going to ruin her entire life.

"No, I think you need to relax and watch this show with me." Elsie tilted her head like a puppy hearing no for the first time. "Didn't they taste kind of weird?"

"I guess I thought they tasted a little stale…like they'd been left out on a table."

"Fair enough." Elsie reached forward and then popped a gummy bear into her mouth, swallowing it like a pill.

"What are you doing?" Jones couldn't keep the exasperation out of her voice. Her heart felt like a hummingbird in her chest, but it was too early for her to be feeling anything.

"I'm following you through the looking glass, Alice." Elsie winked and reached for another bear. Jones slapped her hand and for a moment they just stared at each other.

"Aren't you already high?"

"Only a little." Elsie held her index finger and thumb a millimeter apart while she tilted her head adorably.

Jones needed to keep it together. She took a deep breath and shook her head. "No. Someone has to be in charge. Spit it out."

"Aren't you like literally in charge, Jones?" But Elsie reached for a napkin on the coffee table and spit out the bear.

"Shit. I'm going to go to jail." She'd come to an employee's house, taken drugs, and now she was going to have to call an ambulance, and everyone would know. There would be a record. Someone would have to call Charity to come back to the States and remove Bentley from her care. There was no coming back from a mistake like this. Her breathing was a tornado in her own ears.

And Elsie Webb was smiling at her.

"I try not to judge people, but you are not handling this

well. Like, at all. And you're not even high yet, so this is just normal paranoia." Elsie dropped back onto the couch and propped her legs on the coffee table.

"Okay, since you're the expert, what should I do?"

"Could you try being chill for like five to six hours?"

"Hours?" Elsie couldn't be serious. Jones came there to get a contract signed. And sure, she'd been the slightest bit distracted by Elsie's outfit. Or complete lack of outfit, as it were, but this was a business call. Elsie's furrowed brows let Jones know she was taking too long to answer fully. "No, we can't all chill for five hours. I have responsibilities. I have to get Bentley in a few hours."

"Where is Benz?"

"Benz, that's cute. Though I think that's the nickname for Mercedes."

"Is that really the argument you want to have right now? We're wasting valuable pre-buzz time here."

"He's with the downstairs neighbor, Mitch. They were building ships in a bottle or repairing old ham radios or something."

"To recap, you, Ms. Responsible, left your four-year-old brother with the downstairs neighbor? The hoarder guy?"

"He's six now actually."

"Oh, well, okay then. That makes all the difference."

"Mitch is harmless."

"How long have you known him?"

"Like two weeks. He's really nice, quiet."

"Could you call and tell him you have to work late?"

"He doesn't have a phone."

"I mean call Mitch."

"Mitch doesn't have a phone. I'll call Bentley."

"My mistake. It's probably not my place to say, and I'm not judging, but I have noticed in the short time we've known each other, you've left Bentley alone with near strangers twice. First with me at the studio and now with Mitch. At least for me, you have a background check and CORI form on file."

"And what part of that wasn't meant to be a judgment?"

Elsie laughed. "Okay, fair. But I was a latchkey kid, so I know what I'm talking about. Bentley might love doing ships in a bottle in Mitch's storage unit apartment, and he might be a great guy, but I still think anyone watching Bentley should have a phone, for, like, emergencies."

"Well, that's what Bentley has his phone for."

"Of course, how silly of me. You know, the more I hear about this arrangement with Mitch, the more I think I should just get you home for Benz. Want to give him a call while I get us a ride to your place?"

"You're coming?"

"I know they say never go with a hippie to a second location, but this is for your own safety. I don't want you in the back of some Uber when those edibles hit."

SOFT LIGHT GHOSTED ACROSS JONES' eyelids. She blinked slowly, trying to make sense of where she was. Her limbs felt tired, like the couch was holding her back. She considered closing her eyes again, leaning into sleep's embrace, but laughter from the kitchen drew her attention. *Shit, she'd forgotten about Bentley.* But it sure sounded like he was home, so at least she hadn't abandoned him with Mitch. A quick glance at her phone told her it was nearly seven, she'd lost hours of the day. She remembered going to Elsie's apartment after convincing Stu not to call the police. But had she recovered the missing Fangley? Or gotten Elsie's new contract signed? An image of Elsie answering the door in just a t-shirt and underwear flashed in her mind like lightning. Distracting and a little unsettling. She was tempted to count the time between strikes of the image, so she'd know how long she had before she was well and truly screwed.

Jones eased into a reclined seated position, her lower back cracking. She was officially too old for weird sleeping situations. But *why* was she in a weird sleeping situation? She had a vague flash of Elsie's stricken face as Jones had eaten a gummy bear from the oddly nice crystal bowl on the table. *That's right, Sherlock, accidental high.* It had been a good idea for Elsie to chaperone Jones' ride home. Elsie's laugh, almost a cackle, sounded again from down the hall, this time with Bentley's giggle coming in after like a backup singer.

She shot to her feet, back pain be damned. Jones was supposed to be the responsible adult taking care of her brother, while his overwhelmed and arguably far less responsible mother whiled away her time somewhere that was probably sunny and ninety percent sand. But how was Jones any better? Elsie had pointed out that she, too, kept entrusting Bentley to people she didn't know well. And now she'd spent hours sleeping without a care in the world, which had left Elsie to watch Bentley. *Very professional, Jones.*

How could the day have gone so wrong? Jones had gone to the studio to solve a problem. A very specific and eminently solvable problem. Of course, the original issue of Elsie's contract had been quickly usurped by the more pressing issue of the missing puppet. So Jones had taken charge. She'd gone to confront Elsie about allegedly stealing Fangley sometime over the weekend. Probably directly after refusing to sign her contract and storming out on Jones the other night.

Jones knew somehow that Elsie had taken Fangley. Because of course she had. After the way their conversation on Saturday had ended, it was the most plausible explanation. And once she'd fixed Elsie's contract she'd gone to her apartment and *Oh God.* She suddenly remembered the ride here. The way she'd leaned against her in the back seat of the car, head resting on Elsie's shoulder. Elsie leading her into the house, an arm firmly around Jones' waist, like a lifeline tying her to this new reality. A reality where Jones made mistakes and bad decisions and somehow, magically, the world didn't end. She'd gone over there to be the mature rational one, and then she'd drugged herself. She wanted to be frustrated that Elsie had those gummy bears just lying around, but she couldn't bring herself to be. Her body felt light and relaxed. And that was probably the most sleep she'd gotten since the news of her father's death.

She heard another echo of cacophony from the kitchen. Bentley's laughter shot a surge of panic through her. *Right. She was supposed to be taking care of Bentley*, not sleeping off her high and feeling relaxed. Why did she have to keep reminding herself of this? Oh right, the bears. She walked to the kitchen but hesitated before going in. Elsie's voice was animated, she sounded happy. Not at all like she was humoring Bentley. And Bentley's laughter was decadent and unrestrained. Jones had been thinking of him as a serious kid, but maybe she'd missed this secret joy, papered over by loss and radical life changes. Maybe she hadn't really seen him, even though she watched him every day; Jones knew now that she hadn't really *seen* him.

"Ok so the idea behind this one might be a little high concept. So if you don't understand it, just tell me. Deal?"

"Deal," Bentley replied.

Jones glanced around the corner in time to see the two of them bump elbows and then lock pinkies. Had she really been asleep long enough for Bentley and Elsie to develop a secret handshake?

"So the idea is a modernized version of The Brave Little Toaster, which you are about thirty years too young to understand. But it's like all the appliances in the house have a secret life. But in this version, it's all smart devices. So Alexa is the therapist, always listening and trying to help. The robot vacuum is a house cleaner named Krum that always has indigestion, like a tummy ache you might get after eating too much cake."

Bentley nodded seriously.

"The video doorbell would be the neighborhood busybody, always getting in people's business and gossiping about who needs to cut their lawn. The smart lock could be the security guard named Bolt. The thermostat is always trying to make people comfortable but can't make its own decisions and is always overcorrecting. Anyway, I can see I'm losing you, buddy. Basically, they all team up to torment the humans living in their house. Or maybe they're Amelia Bedelias—they have great intentions but always misunderstand the assignment."

Bentley was silent, studying Elsie.

Jones observed them in a kind of suspended state of awe. She didn't want to insert herself and shatter their moment, but she also felt an intense desire to be a part of it, like that space next to Elsie and Benz on the kitchen floor was exactly where she belonged.

"I'm getting that this idea needs more work. I'll revise and get back to you. Want to hear one more?" Elsie asked.

"Yup!" Bentley's head bobbled in his eagerness to nod.

"Okay, so I have an idea for a puppet named Wiggins. What color do you think his hair should be?"

"Blue!" Bentley's eyes were wide as he looked at Elsie, like he was watching Santa on the roof.

"Great choice! Oh, maybe just blue sideburns."

"What's sideburns?"

"It's like hair that grows down the side of your face. Let me draw you a picture." Elsie flipped the page in her notebook.

Jones marveled at Elsie's humor and imagination. It was easier to see Elsie's magic in action when Jones watched her with someone else. Elsie took Bentley seriously and it didn't seem like an act. Jones had seen Elsie write things down in her notebook as Bentley talked. When Elsie liked people, she showed it. Suddenly the warm feeling that passed through Jones in Elsie's apartment earlier made sense. It was an unfamiliar feeling of being home—of being exactly where she wanted to be.

Bentley's giggle echoed around the kitchen like a clinking glass. "That's silly."

"I know. It's perfect. How did you get so good at this?"

Elsie had a notebook in her lap and was holding her marker. Maybe Jones could buy her a nice pen as a thank you…for just being her? Or perhaps a bouquet of purple magic markers would be more Elsie's style. Part of what Jones was starting to appreciate about Elsie was how she didn't care about what she *should* be doing. It had a kind of spark that freed up those around her to be happy, too.

"Sorry to interrupt, what are you two up to?"

Both Elsie and Bentley turned to Jones grinning.

"I'm pitching ideas using a highly scientific method. You've probably never heard of it, because it's a craft secret." Elsie widened her eyes at Bentley. "It's called the *giggle-ometer*. Anything that gets a giggle, gets a check mark. A full belly laugh gets a smiley face. And if you laugh until you cry?" Elsie furrowed her brows, fixing Bentley with a serious expression.

"A gold star!"

Elsie laughed, and Jones felt it all the way down to her toes. Or maybe that was the high still wearing off. Making its way slowly through her body like sand in an hourglass.

"You got it!" Elsie turned her attention to Jones. "Are you hungry? We ordered pizza."

"With pineapple!" Bentley chorused.

"Right, healthy pizza with fruit,"; Elsie said.

Jones crossed her arms. "There's no such things as health—"

Elsie cut her off with a look. "It's fruit salad on a pizza, what more could you want?"

"It's technically only one fruit. A fruit salad is multiple fruits. A menagerie."

"Okay, Mrs. Spelling Bee. Tomatoes are also a fruit. So that's two."

Bentley giggles bubbled up around them.

Jones wanted to argue, but Elsie had her on a technicality.

"Fruit salad pizza sounds great; thank you for doing that." Jones' stomach picked that moment to grumble.

Elsie quirked an eyebrow and smiled at Jones, and Bentley tapped her notebook so she'd continue. And she did. For the first time since Jones arrived, the house felt like a place she could be happy in.

CHAPTER NINE
ELSIE

The doors of the subway car groaned closed like they had trapped an evil spirit, and Elsie settled onto a blissfully empty, and seemingly clean seat. A public transportation miracle.

Jones had kissed her. Once she had appeared in the kitchen doorway, blonde hair rumpled and cheeks flushed like a freshly rescued Sleeping Beauty, Elsie had known she should leave. It was probably weird that she'd stayed for dinner, *and then past dinner*, but she'd gotten lost in sharing her ideas with Bentley and listening to Jones laugh. He had a great head for slapstick comedy, Elsie's speciality. Maybe what was weird was how it didn't feel weird at all, it just felt…nice to be there with them. She suspected the gummy bears were only partially responsible for Jones' epic nap. Elsie had noticed before that exhaustion clung to Jones like fog.

She'd slipped on her shoes, feeling Jones' eyes on her.

Elsie had looked up as she tied her laces, something she only did when she was pretending to be a responsible adult like Mr. Rogers. Women were impressed by double knots, right? "Are you okay?"

"Do you own any normal socks?" Jones asked, a smile pulling at her lips.

Elsie looked down at her feet. Hot pink and covered with sloths. "Define normal."

Jones rolled her eyes but didn't say anything more in response.

When Elsie stepped onto the stoop, Jones leaned in the doorway, thanking her again. The gratitude on her face had stirred something in Elsie. She'd wanted to say it was nothing. Almost said it. But it wasn't nothing, not really.

It was one of the best nights Elsie could remember having in a long time. She replayed watching Jones try and fail to wipe a smear of pizza sauce off her face until Benz stood on his chair and helped her, foregoing a napkin and using the palm of his hand. Elsie had never seen heart eyes outside of a cartoon before, but the way Jones looked at Benz and smiled, all Elsie could see was love. Love for such a simple gesture, that was the key to happiness. Elsie wished life had a replay button, so she could experience those moments again and again with perfect clarity. Memory always degrades, like a VHS stuck in the player, until all that's left is snow.

In the doorway, Elsie had moved toward Jones. For a hug, maybe? When she'd recount the kiss to Avery later that night, this would be an action she couldn't explain. Elsie had felt like the residual energy of the evening between her and Jones had reeled her in. Like she had no choice but to step closer and open her arms to Jones. And even if she'd had a choice, that's the one she would have made.

The warm day had cooled into a chilly night, and Elsie had wanted to step back into the warmth of the house. The thought of shivering on the subway while avoiding eye contact was like an ice bath. Jones stepped into Elsie's arms and they both turned their faces. Elsie had never been one for cheek kisses. This was another thing she couldn't make sense of later. But Jones had turned her head, too. Her mouth was not an innocent bystander. The plausible explanation, of course, was that air cheek kisses seemed very much of Jones' world, which Elsie imagined was full of fancy LA networking events where everyone admired Jones and then she left alone. And Jones' world was something Elsie suddenly wanted to be part of. Her fingers had tingled like they belonged nestled in the crook of Jones' arm as she walked through a crowded room. Jones wasn't all business and confidence, she was a woman who had dropped her life to take care of her brother. A woman who smiled at him like he hung the moon when he wiped sauce off her face with his hand. A woman who didn't shy away from the hard and messy.

Elsie looked up and caught her smiling reflection in the subway car window, framed by a sticker that said 'eat the rich' on one side, and a scratched pentagon smeared over with what she hoped was ketchup on the other. That was life: happiness framed by struggle and absurdity, all of it a little messy. Elsie would have kissed Jones on her forehead if she could have. Laid her down and tucked her into bed. Instead, their lips had met unexpectedly, and Elsie had held it for a second too long before realization set in. A loud alarm in her mind yelling 'bad'. She hopped backward like she was avoiding a wild pitch and stumbled down the top step. Elsie steadied herself on the railing, letting the cold iron beneath her palms ground her.

Jones had looked mortified. Her cheeks glowed in the porch light, making Elsie think of the pizza sauce all over again. She wanted to wipe away Jones' embarrassment with the palm of her hand. That, or keep it forever as something precious. Would that be the only time she'd get to kiss Jones Haelstrom? What she didn't want was for the moment to sour. For awkwardness to creep in.

When Elsie had tuned back in, Jones was apologizing profusely. That combined with her blush gave Elsie the shot of confidence she needed. A little hope was worth a thousand promises. Suddenly, it had seemed very important that she not give Jones the wrong impression.

"Truly, Elsie, I didn't mean to be presumptuous—it was an accident. I'm sorry. I—"

That word accident reverberated between them.

"I don't want you to be sorry unless you regret it. But I'd regret feeling like I took advantage of you. So, maybe next time something intentional? Goodnight, Jones."

Elsie had hopped down the remaining two steps and held her hand up in a still wave like she was putting a stop to the night. She wasn't ready for Jones' reaction. Or maybe she wasn't ready to deal with any of the electric surges traveling through her body. Jones had spent the evening sleeping off a high. It was not the time for Elsie to make a move. If her advances were accepted, she wanted to be sure. And if she was rejected, she wanted to be sure of that, too.

"Hey, Elsie?" Jones' voice was husky, dreamlike.

Elsie's feet had stopped of their own volition, and she'd skidded back a little like she was returning to the safety of first base. Jones leaned out of the door, arms spread wide and braced on the frame, an umpire making a call. "Yeah?" Her heart soared.

"Did you kidnap Fangley?"

"Yup! See you later!"

"Wait! And your contract?" Jones called.

Elsie had forgotten that's why Jones had shown up at her apartment in the first place. Although she had looked over the new terms as they'd waited for the Uber to arrive earlier this afternoon, and the five percent of merchandising in perpetuity alone would be life-changing. It would free her up to create more on the side and even order the fancy dumplings. Elsie had smiled at Jones over her shoulder. "It's good, I'll sign it when I get home."

THE FIRST THING Elsie did when she arrived at the apartment was kiss Oscar right on his big square head. The second thing she did was race Oscar to Avery's room where they dive-bombed onto the bed in tandem. It was a thing of beauty, the way Elsie and Oscar always conspired. The Grouch might technically be Avery's dog, but he was for sure Elsie's partner in crime.

Avery groaned beneath their combined weight, thrashing a bit.

"What the fuck, Elsie? I almost called all your lesbian sports friends and sent them to hunt you down. Oscar was worried."

"Lesbian sports friends? I assume you mean my soccer team, A Little Forward."

"You all are the only ones in the league with a punny name. It's not a trivia team."

"You always forget about My Sister's Keeper, probably because we shut them out every season."

"We're getting off track and I'm not having a sports conversation with you. Where were you?" Avery pulled back the covers and patted the bed next to them.

Elsie toed off her shoes, smiling as they fell to the floor clattering against the hardwood. She settled down next to Avery.

"Jones got high 'accidentally,' so I helped her get home."

"Why did you put accidentally in air quotes? Also, you realize that explanation only raises more questions, right?"

"I regret waking you up."

"Good. That makes two of us." Avery propped themselves up on an elbow, turning toward her.

Elsie avoided Avery's gaze, focusing on the way the light from outside played across the ceiling like lightning bugs. "I'm going to give it another shot, with the show, I mean. That's why Jones was here."

"But why? They tried to screw you over with that contract. What changed your mind?"

"I think I owe it to…Fangley."

Avery pointed at her, the streetlight undulating through the sheer curtains highlighted the delight dancing in their eyes. "You mean you owe it to your new boss lady. Who you have a massive crush on."

"No. A crush? What am I, seventeen?"

"You do! You're full-on smithereens." Avery pulled the pillow from beneath their head and smacked Elsie to punctuate their point.

"Okay, Captain Hook. That's never going to be a thing."

"Never-never?"

Elsie threw the pillow she'd been clutching back at Avery. Near their feet, Oscar grumbled as he attempted to dig a hole to the center of the earth. She wasn't sure how to explain to Avery that Jones had done the right thing when she easily could have not done anything. That Jones had valued her. But she couldn't tell Avery that without them leveling their smithereens accusation again. It had probably been a battle to stand up for Elsie, and Jones had looked proud when she'd set the new contract on the table. Elsie had known before she looked that the agreement was generous, that she'd sign it. And then she'd forgotten it half-read on the coffee table when she'd left with Jones.

"Okay, just a regular crush, got it. So back to the important part, how does one accidentally get stoned?"

Elsie drew in a deep breath, she wouldn't be able to keep Avery from seeing her feelings for Jones for much longer anyway. She could sit silently for three days, and Avery would still divine every thought in her head. *Here goes.* "This part is kind of amazing. So, she came here to give me the better contract she'd negotiated, and then while I was getting dressed, she ate one of your special gummy bears. Actually, more than one. Which you just left out in a dish on the coffee table, by the way. I was trying not to get us sued, even though I think you're technically liable."

"How chivalrous of you, matey. Explain the part about you not being dressed."

"That part isn't important. I was working hard on my ideas when she arrived, and I wasn't in business attire."

"So no pants then?"

Elsie hummed her agreement. "Anyway, I was trying to be responsible. I got her home and made sure she napped while I hung out with Bentley."

"Right, of course. *Not* putting your boss to bed might have been inappropriate. I still can't believe you got her high."

"Allegedly, and it was an accident," Elsie said. "Maybe she didn't get high and was just, like, really tired. Besides, *I* didn't do anything. She shouldn't be walking into people's houses and eating their weed gummies like some modern-day Goldilocks."

"I don't think Goldilocks ate the *bears*, Els."

"You know what I mean. Anyway, the new contract gives me a decent cut of merchandising and maybe I'll finally get to make the lesbian aunt I introduced last season a recurring character."

"I still can't believe they played respectability politics with the long-lost lesbian vampire aunt just because she happened to be poly." Avery sounded exasperated. This was just the kind of thing that set them off, and Elsie loved them for that.

"I know! It makes no sense for her to have a 'life partner' when she's been alive for a hundred regular lives."

"I agree. But right now, I need to know more about your high boss lady. Tell me everything, Baby Bear. What happened when she woke up?" Avery nudged Elsie's shoulder.

"For starters, she's not my anything."

"Ah, but she could be. The world is full of possibilities. Plus, you're a babe, and she's a babe, 'allegedly'."

"You can drop the air quotes. She is most definitely a babe."

They laid awake staring at the ceiling while Elsie recounted the day all the way down to the kiss that almost wasn't, but definitely was. She fell asleep next to Avery, Oscar stretched out like a crocodile between them.

CHAPTER TEN
JONES

Jones watched the all-black Land Rover disappear around the corner. A body bag full of skis on the roof and Bentley buckled securely into his car seat in the back, next to his friend Chester. She closed the front door and turned the lock. She'd held it together long enough to see Bentley off, and doing that had felt like swimming across the ocean. Her limbs were heavy as they sank onto the cold, unforgiving tile floor. Her depression had been looming for the past few days, a storm on the horizon. Jones knew she couldn't outrun it forever, but having a clear goal helped. Her only objective had been to still be standing to see Bentley off.

The trip itself had been a surprise and a gift, something Charity had set up months ago and had forgotten to mention. Or maybe she had figured she'd be back by now. Meanwhile Jones was desperate to hear from Charity. If she would return even a single phone call, Jones might have some structure to work with. She could make a plan. God, she missed making plans for herself and sticking to them. Instead, all Jones had was a single text—a sunset beach photo that could have been from a postcard and the words "need more time".

When Bentley had needed comfort in those first days, he'd

clung to his nanny, Susan, or insisted on visiting Mitch in the garden apartment. When he started coming to Jones at night, it had felt like a small victory, made bittersweet by the reasons for his needing her. His nightmares had her running on empty, even before a bout of her own hypomania robbed her of sleep altogether. The crash was one she could see coming from a long way off—a semi truck veering wildly before jack-knifing.

How could she help Bentley when she couldn't even keep her own moods from hijacking her life. In the past two weeks, she'd called nearly every therapist in the city, looking for an opening with a child grief counselor to no avail. Every child in New York was going through something, it seemed.

It was odd to Jones how infrequently Bentley asked after his mother. He'd probably asked about Elsie and Fangley more in the past few weeks. Jones couldn't blame him, she found Elsie was often on her mind, too. Still, Jones knew she had to tell him something about Charity's prolonged absence, even if that something was that she didn't know anything.

Skiing and a fancy chalet with his friend who's not allowed to free-drink, seemed like just the thing to distract him. If anyone in their house deserved a getaway, it was Bentley. There was no reason Charity should hoard all the vacation. Jones wished she was up for a spa weekend, or a spa month. Maybe she could get her act together enough to do a face mask later—something seaweedy that would make her look like the Creature from the Black Lagoon. Birdie would be horrified at the bruised skin beneath her eyes, she didn't need a face mask to look like an extra in a horror film.

Between extreme bouts of overwhelm from this ready-made life she'd been thrust into, Jones had been nursing a cocktail of frustration and confusion at Charity's actions. Or inactions, really. But Bentley's trip was one good thing. She tried to tap into rage, but her heart wasn't in it. The fact was that Jones liked this new life; she liked the new routine she and Bentley had established. She liked bedtime stories and never-ending questions. She liked having a job where she could affect change and have a say, rather than writing soulless articles with directions for how to obtain the unobtainable. And Elsie. Well, yeah, Elsie. She liked her too.

Jones was mesmerized by Elsie's ability to care deeply about things without letting the weight of that commitment crush her. She did things joyfully, even when she'd come over that first Saturday to sign the contract, she'd taken a detour to help Jones, and more than that she'd seemed happy making sock puppets. For so long, Jones' world had felt fake. She wrote about celebrities and trends that were just the snake oil of the month. With Elsie, nothing felt fake. When she smiled, Jones knew it wasn't because she wanted something. It was because she meant it.

But somehow, none of that stopped this; her depression wasn't directly related to the general state of her life.

AFTER MULTIPLE HOUR-LONG phone calls describing Bentley's nightmares and lack of special dietary needs beyond 'picky child,' she felt confident Chester's family was up to the task.

Jones wasn't aware that Bentley skied—had never thought to ask him—but he directed her to a hall closet. Behind coats and boots and what appeared to be the world's tiniest sword—she'd need to figure out what that was about—she found a pair of Salomon skis, along with the tiniest Burton snowboard she'd ever seen. It reminded her of the longboards that shirtless men used to glide over the boardwalk in Malibu. It was all so miniature, really, down to his bib and mittens, that the entire endeavor seemed untenable as though the mountain might swallow him whole. But she'd packed it up just the same, and Bentley had been ready and waiting for his transport away from her impending storm.

He hadn't run out the door exactly, but he'd definitely speed walked.

And now Jones was alone in the too-big house, the loudest sound her own thoughts and the echo of her father. Jones sank further onto the floor until only the back of her head was propped up by the door and she drifted off to sleep. She'd saved him from this. From her.

WHEN SHE AWOKE it was dark, and her mouth was dry, and her head felt as though it had been hit by something. She moved her neck tentatively, which was a mistake, the muscles were so tight, they sent an ice pick of pain through her back and shoulders. She took her time, unfolding herself as she rose unsteadily to her feet. In the kitchen, she made a frozen seltzer and shook two ibuprofen from the bottle in her bag before hobbling up the stairs to bed.

At some point, her phone alerted her to a text from Elsie. *Just checking in.* Followed by an emoji Jones had never seen before, two ropes looped together. She silenced the ringer. They'd exchanged numbers the night of the fateful gummy bear incident, and had been texting here and there since. Some days, Elsie texted to get Bentley's take on a sketch or idea and Jones' heart felt like it might overflow. The thought of Elsie seeing her like this filled her with dread. She couldn't remember the last time she showered, but she couldn't bear the thought of doing it now. Washing her hair seemed like an impossible amount of work. First the standing, and then the lifting of her arms and the rinsing—it was all too much.

She let her thoughts stray back to Elsie and the other night. Jones had been overcome by the day and possibly under the lingering influence of the spiked gummy bears. That wasn't the only explanation for the way she hadn't pulled away when her lips brushed Elsie's. For the way she froze, and not from discomfort, but from something deep within her that wanted to take the spark of the moment and kindle it into a roaring fire. She had wanted Elsie Webb. Still wanted her.

Jones groaned, rolling over in bed and pulling the duvet over her head. In the privacy of her small, safe space she brought her fingers to her lips and closed her eyes, replaying every moment she could remember. Some were like trying to make sense of smoke signals, blurry and indistinct. Divination filled with snatches of Elsie holding her up, helping her, and Jones *letting* her. The night that she didn't want to be over, had ended with a kiss she didn't want to take back.

But then Elsie had stepped away, dousing the hope that had flickered in Jones' chest. Elsie said no, maybe not strongly, but clearly. She'd hinted at a future time, but Jones knew a brush-off when she heard one. And at forty-two she'd heard plenty. Elsie couldn't be more than thirty. She wore uncomfortable sneakers, like her feet and back weren't constantly kvetching. Jones had nothing to offer her that she couldn't get with less baggage somewhere else.

She'd already let Elsie take care of her too much. It was time Jones got her feet back under her—as soon as she could bear the thought of getting out of bed. She never knew when her depressive episodes would end, just that, most likely, they would. Her lows were like the depths of winter, when it seemed like the cold would never leave her bones, and the days were an endless dreary darkness. But then, while she barely noticed it, the ground began to thaw, and finally in March or April or May the trees would bud, and spring returned.

Jones was cyclical, too. That had always been part of the issue in her past relationships. The issue that most were too polite to give as the reason they found their way to the door and let themselves out of her life.

Even if things were good, Jones couldn't just be happy or stay happy. Her Bipolar II was hard enough for her to deal with on her own, even with the support of medication and a psychiatrist and a therapist and exercise and eight fucking glasses of water a day. She'd learned years ago that it wasn't worth letting someone else into that. No one she'd shared her bed or life with had been able to understand. They wanted to know what was wrong. They wanted something to fix, and then they wanted her to be better.

The in-between times became dreaded, too. Those days when she felt stable when her mood was dictated by the events of her day and not some chemical misfiring. They gave off too much hope, like maybe she'd evened out, but then the longer her happiness went on, the worse it was when she stopped sleeping, to be followed by catatonic days without end; her partners' frustrations would roar back to life. Jones didn't blame them. Or she didn't blame them much.

She had gone her whole life being her own responsibility, why would adulthood be any different? If anything, she finally grew into the adult she'd been since she was nine, when Birdie had left her father and taken Jones with her to California as a sort of alimony insurance. No, that wasn't fair. Birdie loved her in her way. Not as much as she loved herself, but possibly in the same ballpark.

Birdie wasn't the nurturing type. She rejected most ideas of motherhood, preferring to see her daughter as a friend. Once, when Jones was eleven, she'd snuck her into a casino to help her at the tables. The sunglasses that had comprised Jones' disguise had been so large, they'd left a bruise on the bridge of her nose that had taken weeks to fully heal.

AND THEN, on an ordinary weeknight during an anything but ordinary time of her life, Jones had found herself on the business end of being cared for. It had been so perfect and had sneakily become the key that unlocked her grief. Like if she fell, for the first time someone might be willing to catch her.

In one of the most nurturing experiences of her life, she'd woken up from her nap on the couch, draped lovingly in a blanket. A blanket she knew she hadn't pulled over herself. Jones had imposed on Elsie's day, her life, and been met with an unexpected kindness she never would have predicted after their initial meetings. The first day they met when Elsie had claimed not to be good with kids, a glaring untruth Jones had realized after observing her with Benz. Elsie made him laugh, she treated him like he mattered to her, and in the glow of her attention Bentley bloomed.

Jones reached for her phone again. Her mind protested, shoving forward more negative thoughts. Elsie had been humoring her, she'd never wanted to deal with Jones or Bentley. She just wanted her contract fixed, and now she'd gotten that. Although, Jones knew she was the one whose signature it was waiting for so it could go into place. Jones needed to change course before she sunk into the quicksand of self doubt. She put in an order to Empire Kitchen with instructions to leave the delivery on the porch and fell back into a deep sleep.

THE SUN RAYS were an interrogation light when she woke again, she made herself walk downstairs and bring in the bag of food. Jones dumped the chicken teriyaki into a bowl and popped the congealed mass into the microwave before thinking better of it and eating a few desiccated grapes instead.

SHE WAS six hours into *Real Housewives* of Atlantic City, of which she remembered nothing, and three cookies into the second sleeve of Oreos, when Birdie's picture lit up her phone screen. She regretted enabling the setting that made her calls ring even when Jones' phone was silenced. She ignored the interruption and continued staring unseeingly at the TV. The phone rang again followed by a text claiming dire circumstances. When the third call rang through, Jones squeezed her eyes shut and begrudgingly hit accept.

"I wasn't sure if you were avoiding me or dead. And one of those is significantly worse than the other." Birdie said in a rush that made Jones feel like she'd walked straight into a wall of sound.

She turned down her phone volume and wondered which option her mother considered less preferable.

"Hi, Birdie. What can I do for you?"

"You mean besides value me enough to answer my calls?"

Jones grunted. Her eyes still half-closed from the exertion of the conversation. She knew she should pretend nothing was wrong. Seeming fine was the quickest way to end a call. If Birdie sensed any drama, it was like blood in the water, she couldn't stop herself until she tore you open and feasted on your secrets. Jones dug deep for the energy but found her emotional reserves empty. Deflection it was, then. "How's Christopher?"

"Young, tan, and hunky. The other day he cleaned the pool in the tiniest speedo I've seen in years. Safety orange, like a sexy construction-worker-pin-up. Distinctly European. Norms of American masculinity are so constraining for me, personally."

Okay, so, deflecting had been a mistake. Maybe she could try direct, that always seemed to make Birdie uncomfortable enough to cut calls short. Her mother liked to tell a story, and anything that got in the way of that displeased her. "I'm always glad to hear from you, but what makes you call?"

"Christopher and I are hosting a Drag brunch the day after tomorrow, and I need you to overnight me bagels from that place I like on Broadway."

"I don't think they can overnight bagels to California."

"Of course they can, dear. That's why God invented dry ice and big cash tips. Go in there and slip the guy behind the counter enough for a month's rent and anything is possible."

"Tell me more about this brunch," Jones said because apparently she was a glutton for punishment.

"Christopher wants to have his friends over."

"He said that? It was his idea?" None of this was adding up, starting with her mother and a lovely gay maintenance man willingly co-hosting anything. Their social circles weren't even in the same stratosphere.

"Well, I insisted after his roommate Braden picked him up last week. Who knows, maybe one of his friends is interested in being a sugar patch kid for a mature starlet like myself."

Ah, there it was. "You mean sugar baby, and I think you're misunderstanding this situation."

"I've never misunderstood a social situation in my life. Please go now for those bagels and send me proof."

"Like the receipt?"

"Like a photo and the name of the person you tip, so I can track them down if anything's stale. They should do fresh batches. I don't want any end-of-day rocks. My veneers are delicate."

Jones' mind wandered through the narrow twisting aisles of the shop. The ever-present line at the bagel counter. The impatience of everyone behind her. Twenty-two kinds of cream cheese and none of them quite right. You better have had your order memorized like it was seven a.m. at the Starbucks on Wall Street if you didn't want to get jabbed in the ribs by some bubbie's cane. She had a sudden vision of herself getting knocked to the ground in front of the counter and simply never getting up again.

"Jones? It doesn't sound like you're putting on your shoes. I want to hear some hustle."

Jones unmuted the TV, two women were arguing in a nail salon, their Jersey accents brittle as nails after acrylics. "I just stepped outside; can't you tell? Enjoy your brunch." Jones adjusted the blanket, she would absolutely not be bribing any bakers today, or any day.

Getting out of bed had been a failed experiment. Jones ended the call and shoved her phone between the couch cushions before closing her eyes.

CHAPTER ELEVEN
ELSIE

Trey's knee connected with Elsie's rib as he struggled to stand. For the third time in as many hours, she found herself pinned beneath him. His improvising led to tripping, which led to Trey falling on top of Elsie. On her back on a hard floor was a position Elsie only warmed to under very specific circumstances. Circumstances that would never, ever involve Trey.

All she wanted was to do her job. But it seemed Elsie was the only one who cared about getting things right these days. She shoved him the rest of the way off as the toe of his shoe caught her hand. This was officially threatening her livelihood.

"Okay. Enough." Elsie rose to her feet, rolling her head to work out the kinks in her neck until she heard a satisfying pop. "I'm calling this before I crack a rib." Or commit a fireable offense. Well, another fireable offense. She'd already used twenty minutes of her life she'd never get back explaining to him that *bruh* was a word that simply did not exist in the Fangley universe.

Elsie brushed off Fangley, and when she was satisfied

neither of them was too worse for the wear, she turned her glare on Trey.

"I'm allowed to improvise; my contract gives me creative input." Trey crossed his arms. It was hard to look intimidating in a one-piece spandex suit. Elsie knew that from first-hand experience.

"That implies some ability to be creative. Having Smirch end every sentence with 'bruh' and repeatedly tripping over me isn't creative input. It's ineptitude."

Elsie hated being rude, but nothing else got through to Trey. If she showed any weakness he'd bulldoze right over her and put up a tacky luxury condo.

"Did you hear what I said?" Trey's voice stabbed into her thoughts.

"No, I stopped listening."

"I said," Trey paused, straightening to his full height, "maybe you should check our contracts? This isn't just your show. We're a team."

"Sorry for the confusion. I stopped listening because I don't care, not because I wanted you to repeat yourself."

No way in hell were Elsie and Trey a team. Or if they were, it was the kind of team that succumbed to infighting and voted each other off the island. Puppeteering looked fancy-free, but the movements were more akin to figure skating. Precise. Measured. Spatial awareness and dependability were key, and today, for the thousandth time, Trey had demonstrated neither.

She wanted to yell about her own creative input as the literal creator of Fangley Heights. It was the week after their accidental kiss and Jones hadn't been there at all to back her up. This hyper awareness of another person and their absence was a new experience and Elsie wasn't particularly relishing it. She usually had her own back. After walking away from the show, however briefly, she'd felt like she'd forsaken some claim to it. Maybe

Rebecca felt the same way; she hadn't been much help either as she stood quietly off to the side. Like Elsie had let her down. Because she had. She'd jeopardized Rebecca's career along with her own. She'd need to make that up to her. But Rebecca was the queen of reverse staring contests; she could avoid eye contact at all costs. She could probably even avoid it at the optometrist.

Elsie looked over to the main camera, trying to catch Rebecca's eye again. All week she'd continued to produce the show like nothing was amiss. Like filming was always a tangle of missed marks and frustration. Rebecca was staring intently at a sheet of paper. From the way the bright studio lights shone through it, Elsie could tell it was blank. Rebecca never was the best at props. So, she was still avoiding things. *Things* being Elsie.

Elsie had tried to talk to Rebecca the day before, and she'd raised her black phone screen up to her ear and held up a finger like she was on a call. Elsie had pulled out her own phone and called Rebecca. Rebecca startled and yanked the ringing phone away from her ear to check the caller ID. She kept walking and sent Elsie to voicemail. Voicemail. A technology Elsie opposed on moral grounds, like chain emails and paper bills.

Right now, she could really use Rebecca's backup with this whole 'Trey is a creative' thing. Just because his uncle was an executive in the sleaze suite, didn't mean he had two brain cells to rub together. Elsie kept her eyes on Rebecca, who in turn kept her eyes on her blank paper. Maybe she was meditating. She knew Rebecca was right to be upset with her. Elsie had been willing to walk away from the show. A show that was as much Rebecca's as it was hers. If Elsie was on a team with anyone at Fangley Heights, it was Becca. Knowing she was upset with Elsie and that she deserved it sent an ache through her chest. She gently probed her ribs with her fingers to make sure this pain she was feeling wasn't internal bleeding from wrecking-ball Trey. Maybe she should get an MRI.

Elsie turned back to Trey. "We're done for the day. Use the time to figure out the blocking I gave you. This show isn't freestyle."

Trey opened his mouth to reply but Elsie put up a hand.

"And if I never hear you say the word 'bruh' again it will be too soon. Oh, and I'll be making a box for your creative inputs. Let me know your favorite color. I might even bedazzle it."

ELSIE SAW HER OPENING, and beelined across the set. Rebecca startled as Elsie placed a hand on her shoulder. "Can we talk?"

"I really can't right now, Elsie. I have to go over what we got today."

"Rebecca, you and I both know today was shit. This entire week has been shit. Trey can't get through a scene without knocking us both over."

Rebecca put her hand up to her mouth to stifle a laugh, trying to pass it off as a cough. Elsie saw the slightest crack start to form in her icy demeanor. It gave her hope but she'd need to turn up the heat. "I really should see if there's anything salvageable."

"Five minutes, that's all I need." Elsie squeezed Rebecca's shoulder, reassured when she didn't back away. "Please."

Rebecca nodded, and Elsie led the way to her dressing room.

Elsie contorted herself out of the black spandex suit she always wore for filming, gathering her courage to deliver the speech she'd rehearsed. Rebecca took a seat on her chair and tapped her nails on her phone screen.

"Look, I'm really sorry. I shouldn't have done that to you."

Rebecca shrugged but didn't look up. "You did what you had to do for yourself. I get it."

Elsie took a deep breath and then dove into the apology Avery had helped her prepare. "Maybe, but I should have done what was right for us, for the show. And at the very least if I was going to walk off into the sunset in a sexy self-righteous rage, I should have sent you a text. I regret that I didn't. I care about you. What we've built with Fangley Heights means the world to me. I don't expect that you'll forgive me or trust me anytime soon, but I wanted to let you know that you matter to me. The decision I made in the heat of the moment didn't demonstrate that, and I'm sorry if I made you think I didn't care."

Tears shone in Rebecca's eyes. "Well, now you're a jerk for making me cry. I hope you're proud of yourself."

Elsie tilted her head back and forth like she was weighing her options.

"God, you're an asshole." Rebecca laughed.

"I know. I think it's part of my charm, but only a little bit."

"Don't ever walk out on me again. I thought I was going to have to salvage a show with just Trey. And then I'd be in his dressing room right now."

"Actually, is it appropriate for you to be in either of our dressing rooms?" Elsie shimmied her hips as she pulled on her jeans and winked. She ducked as Rebecca threw a plush ear of corn at her. She really needed to return Bob the Cob to the props department.

"It would be a lot more appropriate if you'd stop apologizing to me in only your underwear. This is how rumors start."

"Fine, but one day you're going to need me in my underwear for something job-related and then you'll be sorry."

"I hate you. And I forgive you."

"Thank you. I also wanted to say, next time you want to

ignore me, you should make an actual call or pretend to read a paper that's not blank."

Rebecca gasped. "I really regret not holding onto that corn so I could chuck it at you now."

"I think you mean shuck it at me."

Rebecca scowled unconvincingly. Elsie felt the weight of Rebecca's disappointment ease off her chest, and she drew in a deep breath. She needed to ask her next question before she lost her nerve. "Is what Trey said about his contract giving him creative input on episodes true?"

"I assume so. What does your contract say?"

"I…don't remember. I'm still waiting on the counter-signed copy from Jones Haelstrom. Have you seen her this week?"

Elsie already knew the answer. She'd taken detours past Jones' office on her way to and from the set. Far too many to explain away. The door had remained closed and the lights off.

Why did her life feel like that dark office without Jones' attention? She hadn't had it long enough to get used to it, but Elsie had felt something there. Now that it was gone she missed it. She missed how hard Jones tried, even when she seemed overwhelmed or had been thwarted, she still tried. It was so different from how Elsie approached life, she didn't put her efforts into places that weren't aligned with how she saw the world or wanted it to be. But Jones worked to make things better, and Elsie had been surprised by how effective that was once Jones had decided to fight for her. Even seeing Jones completely out of her depth on Bentley's birthday, but still meticulously decorating cupcakes that would only be demolished, had been a lesson in commitment for Elsie.

"Nope. Maybe she's taking some time off. Or she's spending time on her family's yacht, or whatever rich people do."

Elsie bristled at the way Rebecca's comment seemed to

belittle Jones, but she knew she didn't mean anything by it. "In New York, I think rich people mostly just walk around the Met."

"Yeah, you're right." Rebecca stood from the chair. "Maybe check there?"

"Want anything from the gift shop?"

"Just get things sorted. Oh, and Elsie?" Rebecca paused in the door to her dressing room.

"Yeah?"

"Tell Avery thanks—that was a solid apology."

"Hey! I…can do my own apologies!" Elsie feigned outrage but Rebecca was already laughing so hard she was headed for tears.

ELSIE SLIPPED into her sneakers and grabbed her backpack.

Talking to Rebecca had left her with a sudden and intense desire to review her contract, read each clause and underline the important parts in her purple marker. Without her countersigned copy nothing was really final. They might as well still be in negotiations.

Luckily, this was a problem that could be solved. She knew where Jones lived. She'd been there twice. If Jones could show up at Elsie's apartment unannounced, then she could return the favor. It would be rude not to, really. When Elsie had disappeared, Jones had come looking for her. The thought tumbled around Elsie's chest.

It had been several days since Jones had even responded to a text.

Her last in-person interaction with Jones—saying goodbye at her door and that glancing kiss—had featured in her daydreams. For, well, days. And the dreams she'd had at night didn't end on the porch, they included her walking Jones back inside. There was something there. Something that had taken all of Elsie's strength not to act on the other night.

All of that was absolutely, completely unrelated to why she needed her contract before she could possibly film another second of Fangley Heights. She was being a responsible professional, and responsible professionals followed up on their finalized contracts. And then put them in a special Trapper Keeper for posterity.

So what if she had a crush on Jones? Elsie was probably crammed into that particular boat along with half the world. Jones Haelstrom was one of those rare people whose beauty was somehow matched by her desire to be kind. Not that Jones *was* the kindest, but she cared about being good in a way that made it seem like an active choice. She was so different from the woman Elsie had seen that first day. Elsie was beginning to think Avery was right when they said, *our impressions of people are really a reflection of us. If you want to see yourself more clearly, Elsie, people you dislike are the best mirrors.* Elsie had been considering donating Avery's self-help books to the Little Free Libraries in their neighborhood. It was going to be hard to continue to mock Avery if their wisdom started making sense.

But, if pushed, Elsie could concede that maybe they had a point this one time. Elsie's expectations *had* blocked her view of who Jones actually was. Jones wasn't her father. And then their second meeting had been blurred by the contract misunderstanding. Both interactions had been reflections of Elsie not feeling appreciated at work. Jones was just collateral damage. She really needed to work on being less of a jerk to people who didn't deserve it and more of a jerk to people who did.

The first time Elsie saw Jones, really saw her, was when Elsie had answered the door in her underwear. Jones had tried and failed to avert her eyes. But more than that, she'd gone to bat for Elsie with Stu when she didn't have to. Certainly not after the way Elsie had spoken to her at Bentley's birthday party. It would have been easy enough to blame the failed contract negotiations on Elsie's behavior—her storming out—and use that as leverage to get her to agree to an even worse deal. But Jones had done the opposite of that, and now Elsie wanted to remind herself of just how much more favorable the terms of her new contract were. And if that happened to mean spending more time with Jones, who was Elsie to complain?

So that settled it. She'd pay Jones a visit and see what was going on. Nothing weird about that. And it definitely didn't have anything to do with the little ache she felt each day when she realized Jones hadn't shown up to work. Or returned her messages. One to see how she was feeling (out of line, potentially) and a second to ask a very necessary, inconsequential detail about her contract as a way to hint she hadn't received her countersigned copy. But today, she'd be direct. Besides, she needed to stop finding reasons to walk by the executive offices on her way to set before Stu filed a police report.

Each day Elsie went without a countersigned copy of her contract, she was working without a safety net. She'd been forlornly watching her bank account dwindle like an hour-glass with each subway ride and bagel from the deli. As they approached payday, her nerves were increasing exponentially. She could always switch back to her all Ramen diet, maybe become a cycling enthusiast. But then again, helmets wrecked her hair, matting it like the felted wool toupee worn by Fangley Heights' most ornery Bodega owner, Mr. Snickers. Also, Ramen was out. Her metabolism wasn't what it used to be, and Avery had told her once, hauntingly, that salt made her puffy. What were friends for, if not to tell you devastating truths mere seconds before handing you a glass of wine?

The more Elsie thought about it, the more her annoyance at Jones rose for putting her in this position. Had she changed her mind about the contract terms? Elsie should never be the most professional one in a relationship. That was a given. She pulled out her phone and dialed Jones. As a rule, Elsie hated phone calls—the only thing worse than making one was someone answering. The line rang once and went straight to voicemail. Elsie's mild annoyance ignited, fueled by her frustration from the set.

Instead of recording some bumbling message where she forgot to say her own name, she jabbed the *end* call button as she turned around and headed for the nearest Q stop. If Jones wanted to ignore her she'd have to do it to her face.

THE SUN WAS SHINING as Elsie made her way along the streets of Jones' neighborhood. She'd been too preoccupied before to notice. They were the kind of clean that only money could buy in a city like this. No condoms on the sidewalk. No dog poop in the street. Not a creature stirring near any trash cans. All of which had lids. Elsie knew Jones' family was rich, but she hadn't realized they were lids-on-the-trashcans rich. This was rom-com New York. The place where dreams came true, and fresh-faced assistants from Ohio could find a job in publishing and afford penthouses without familial wealth. She expected Meg Ryan to jump out from behind a dumpster singing a Louis Armstrong song at any moment. Elsie's bad mood slipped away, floating up into the clear blue sky like a loose balloon, off to wreck someone else's day.

A WOMAN EXITED JONES' brownstone as she approached. Her streaked gray hair fell in her face as she adjusted the red plastic bucket filled with cleaning supplies. She jumped as Elsie got closer, her large ring of keys clattering to the stoop.

"Sorry to startle you. Is Jones home? I'm her…Elsie." *Her Elsie? Really?*

"Oh, that's okay, hon. I'm Susan. I'm glad one of Jones' friends is here. She had me worried."

Friends wasn't quite the right word. But *she's my boss and she hasn't talked to me since she got stoned and we kissed* seemed somehow inappropriate for the situation. Elsie knew why *she* was worried but why was Susan? "It's nice to meet you. Why um—"

"I'm glad she called you to help." The woman's face relaxed and a smile slid into place. "She sent me away even though the place is a mess. Maybe you can talk some sense into her. Or at least get her to change her clothes."

Elsie had to stop herself from saying she wasn't there to help. It was just that Jones hadn't answered her texts and with their difference in age, Elsie thought maybe…what? That Jones would prefer a house call? *There's been no response to my missive so I'd better call 'round.* Why would Jones need Elsie's help?

Elsie had a distinct feeling that she should know what was going on. But asking would only give away that she probably shouldn't be there at all. And the thought of leaving before she saw Jones was intolerable. The two times she'd been to Jones' place it had never been a mess. A little disheveled maybe, but clean, neat. Elsie's frustration was like a television she'd muted, still flashing in the background but hard to focus on. She wanted to get inside and make sure Jones was okay. What would Avery make of Elsie's assumption that Jones' lack of response, or absence from work, had anything to do with her? Typical.

Elsie cleared her throat and tried to sound normal. Like her mind wasn't spinning up a hundred scenarios for what was going on with Jones. "I'll give it a try. Where's Bentley?"

"He went on a trip with one of his friends for the week. Skiing, I think?"

"I didn't know six-year-olds could ski."

"I think skiing is more of a lifestyle thing than an age thing."

"Yeah," Elsie said. Was she someone to take care of Jones?

Susan's words didn't make her feel like she wanted to bolt, even though a distant corner of her brain was saying she should leave. "So, you think it's okay if I go in?"

"Sure, someone needs to check on her. Good luck, dear. Try not to get crushed by the avalanche of dishes." Susan handed her a pair of yellow rubber gloves. "You might need these."

"Will do. Thanks, Susan."

The house was dark, the curtains were drawn across every window, and Elsie shivered despite the spring warmth outside. She needed to write more big, creepy houses into the show for Fangley to explore. She called out to Jones half-heartedly. When she got no response, Elsie made her way to the kitchen. Susan hadn't been joking. It smelled like the slightest hint of lemon disinfectant. Elsie imagined Susan spritzing Pledge, like one of those department store women with perfume, as Jones rushed to eject her. Even though it smelled fine, the room looked like the morning after a house party, except none of the dishes or cups were disposable. And there was way more food left over. Bowls full of untouched takeout, half fossilized. Elsie expected to lift one of the forks and have the food come with it like a popsicle.

Something about the mess seemed private. Elsie shouldn't be there. She should lock the door behind her and head straight home. But Susan had seemed worried about Jones. Which made Elsie worried about Jones. And she'd thought Elsie could help. Elsie couldn't just leave if Jones was sick and needed something or someone. If she needed her. Susan had been pretty vague about her concerns.

Huh. Elsie wouldn't have taken Jones for the messy type. Not that messiness was bad. It was neutral. Just because something was different from how Elsie liked it didn't make it inferior. Her own way of doing things didn't have some sort of moral high ground. But Jones had an order about her that radiated organization and discipline. Elsie didn't think it was just Jones' current circumstances, her grief and newfound responsibility for Bentley that she'd hinted at in their text exchanges, or the stress of being in charge that made her seem disciplined in that way.

Jones carried herself as though she belonged in the world. Her clothes were fastidious and all white and oatmeal and tan, like she was confident she could eat a sandwich without spilling. Did Jones eat sandwiches? All evidence in front of her pointed to Jones ordering food and doing the opposite of eating it. Maybe that was her secret. She'd noticed the other day that Jones wore heels so fancy, their soles flashed red. Elsie looked down at her sneakers and carefully slipped them off so she didn't scuff the floor. At least her socks were cute—light blue and covered in little pieces of pie. One was low, but the other came up to her knee, roughly 3.14 times the length of the other. In truth, they *were* a bit annoying, but they were clever. And Elsie could forgive most flaws for cleverness.

Something felt odd about the mess, even for a messy person there was something intense about it. The haphazard stacks of bowls radiated chaos in a way that made Elsie feel at home. Not home like her apartment with Avery but *home* home. Elsie thought about calling out for Jones again. But instead, she rolled up her sleeves and scraped food into the trash, cringing a bit as she did it, even though it was beyond salvageable.

So, that settled it. She'd just do the dishes and leave. Jones wouldn't even know she was there. Elsie decided this was the option that best balanced kindness with the creep factor of being in Jones' kitchen uninvited. *Better to ask for forgiveness.*

Elsie had always loved doing the dishes. The ease of the task, the clear and immediate results. A sink going from full to empty was a job well done. Tangible progress. That, along with vacuuming, made up the chores she was responsible for in her daily life. Avery was a saint who always cleaned the bathroom. They'd never gone so far as to institute a chore chart, or worse, a wheel. For a while, she'd given them both puffy rainbow stickers at the end of every week. But mostly, they had the quiet understanding that Elsie always imagined an equitable marriage might.

It wasn't lost on Elsie that this was the second time she was leaping at an opportunity to help Jones without being asked. Creating one where it didn't exist, even. Elsie wasn't selfish per se. She was self focused. She worked well with others, except Trey. But she tended to keep her circle small, and her chosen family even smaller. She had a personality that attracted a lot of acquaintances and few deep friendships. But she wanted to know Jones. Wanted to scrape her dirty dishes into the trash even if she would be annoyed by the intrusion. Elsie knew she might.

This was a straight-up Snow White move. But even the thought of Jones being frustrated or lecturing her sent a little jolt of anticipation through Elsie. Probably not the time to get aroused. There was plenty of time for sexy lectures later. For now, she'd focus on putting this house in order.

Elsie popped in her earbuds and turned on the audiobook she'd been listening to on commute, a lesbian art heist romance between a dashing museum director and a jaded investigator. She snapped the yellow rubber gloves into place and got to work.

CHAPTER TWELVE
JONES

Jones heard noises in the kitchen. She sighed. Susan just did not know when to quit. It wasn't as though Jones didn't realize the place was bad. And Susan was clearly trying to help because she was paid to do so. Jones hadn't found a way to explain that she deserved to wallow in the mess. That she was embarrassed by it and it made her uncomfortable, but also that was the point. Her environment matched how she felt inside, teetering on the edge of complete disaster. An avalanche of garbage feelings and half-full takeout containers.

Jones toyed with the idea of crawling back into bed, but she'd have to face the mess of her life sooner or later. Bentley would be home in a few days and she couldn't risk Chester's parents reporting her. She hoped they were letting Bentley *free-drink.* She had always been the one to clean up her own messes. Partly because she lived alone, and had for years, and partly because she learned a long time ago that her moods were her responsibility. She couldn't explain her depression or her bouts of mania, so she'd found it was better not to mention them at all.

Jones wasn't sure how long she'd been standing in the

hallway listening to the dishes clink against each other. Was Susan washing them by hand? How strange. Sure, Jones thought she deserved the mess, but she wasn't enough of a masochist to hand wash plates that had been dirty for three days. That's why God invented the dishwasher. She stepped into the doorway and the light from the kitchen stung her eyes.

"Susan, why don't you just use the dishwasher?"

The woman who spun around from the sink was decidedly *not* Susan. Not even a little bit Susan. Jones was suddenly very awake. Awake and ready to flee.

"Hi." Elsie's eyes were wide as she removed an earbud and set it on the windowsill over the sink.

"What are you doing?" Jones cleared her throat, her voice staticky, like a radio station about to be lost in a storm.

"I'm doing the dishes." Elsie smiled and turned back to the sink. She picked up a bowl and scrubbed it. She washed it for a full minute with seemingly no progress. She didn't make eye contact.

Jones had cleaned up after her depression enough times to know the leftover food clung to the bowl with the strength of dried superglue. "Why?"

"I guess because it didn't occur to me to look for a dishwasher? I've never had one of those." Elsie balanced the now clean bowl on top of the overflowing dish rack. Then she fished another dirty one from the sink before glancing around the kitchen. "Also, are you sure you have a dishwasher?"

Jones walked to the counter and tapped the cabinet door that disguised the appliance.

"It's right here, but I meant why are you in my house doing dishes? *How* are you in my house?" Jones tried to sound angry but she heard the awe in her own voice. Elsie was so focused on scrubbing the bowl in her hands. A strand of her dark hair had come loose from her ponytail, and Jones' fingers itched to tuck it back.

"You didn't take my calls." Elsie shrugged then pulled on one of the yellow gloves, letting it snap back into place. "I know it seems like I might travel with these, but I ran into Susan outside, and she lent them to me. I think she was worried about you."

"So you what? Decided to confront me with housekeeping?" Jones' brain sifted through the details, trying to make sense of it all. Elsie at her sink, wearing those ridiculous rubber gloves. The scene in front of her felt comforting—like some sketch from a children's book—and that was the fact her mind was struggling with most. This was an invasion, so why didn't it feel like one? And why wasn't Jones more concerned with how she looked. She could feel the tangles in her hair even without touching it. But all of those things felt too small to matter.

"Actually, I'd just decided to confront you. The housekeeping was sort of by accident."

"You don't need to do that." Jones reached for the bowl Elsie was holding.

"I know." Elsie's response was so soft, Jones almost didn't make it out over the rush of the running water. "But I like doing the dishes, and it seemed easier than waking you up."

"I was awake." Jones lowered her hoodie as if that would help her hear better. She felt exhausted. Maybe that was why the knowledge that she didn't have to rally to deal with the dishes put a lump in her throat. Cleaning after a depressive episode always felt like a punishment for struggling. Sometimes the thought of dealing with the flotsam of messes left by the wave of her low was enough to pull her back under.

Elsie looked her up and down, eyes lingering on her hair. "Okay."

Jones reached up and felt the unruliness there, strands half fallen out of its ponytail. Maybe it wasn't too small to matter after all. She needed a shower, like yesterday.

"You shouldn't see me like this." Jones quickly smoothed her hair and pulled it back in line.

"You're right. Why don't you go shower while I finish these up?"

"No, I meant you should go."

"Jones." Elsie's voice lacked the teasing tone it usually had, but it wasn't pitying either. It was…kind. "When's the last time you went outside? It's lovely today."

"When did I come to your apartment?"

"Okay. You can tell me to leave, and I'll respect that, but hear me out. What if you take a shower?" Elsie held up a hand just as a protest scattered around Jones' mind, pausing at her lips, and she felt a wave of being known. "Before you say no," Elsie continued, "you can put back on the same clothes. And then we take a walk. If you're still miserable after that, you can go back to bed and I'll leave you alone."

"My brain doesn't use sunlight to make serotonin, Elsie. I'm not a plant."

"Wait, you're not?"

Jones held back a smile. Surprising herself that she was still capable of those. A shower didn't sound like the absolute worst thing—right now that alone was progress. And seeing the kitchen clean had lifted a slight weight off her. Like Elsie had excavated some possibility. "Fine. So, if I agree, and that's a big *if*, what's in it for me?"

"Besides my excellent company and bad jokes?" Elsie put a finger to her chin like she was thinking. The rubber gloves lending the gesture a mad-scientist air. "Are you hungry?"

Jones' stomach rumbled. "No."

"Not at all? Not for anything?"

"All I really want when I feel like this is pizza."

"Great—do you know a good place to order from or should I yelp it? I thought the one we had the other night was just okay, and no one should have to suffer mediocre pizza in New York."

Jones crossed her arms. She'd expected a lecture about caring for herself. "You just spent precious time chiseling old takeout from bowls. Aren't you going to tell me I should eat some vegetables?"

"Pizza can have vegetables. They're not mutually exclusive. We can put some fruit on it again, too. Really round out the meal. I'll look up places while you shower, and then we can walk to get it."

Jones mulled it over but didn't respond. Going out into the world seemed just on the reasonable side of overwhelming. If only she didn't have to—

"And I'll do all the talking. You can put your hood up and ignore everyone."

The ghost of a smile crossed Jones' lips. "Ugh, fine. I don't like peppers though."

THE SHOWER HAD HELPED, Jones realized as she slipped on jeans and dabbed some concealer under her eyes. Getting dressed helped too. It was one of the little ways she often tried to trick her brain into functioning. Jeans, a nice shirt, and fancy shoes were sometimes enough to get her out into the world. The costume of an okay person. She wanted to be annoyed with Elsie for having a point, but it was the same advice she often gave herself. Nothing fixed her depression, but sometimes these little things shifted the bricks weighing her down just enough that she could draw in a breath and move a little. She pulled her hoodie back on over her shirt though, just in case she needed to retreat into it later.

Jones climbed down the stairs, half expecting Elsie to have gone, but there she was waiting by the door with a plan and a smile. Their route was already mapped on her phone and Jones eased into autopilot, letting Elsie lead them.

It was a nice day. Even if Jones didn't want it to be. A light breeze was blowing as the sun began its long evening descent. Elsie had told her to pick comfortable shoes, and Jones suspected she'd picked the pizza place based largely on its distance from Jones' house, probably to ensure adequate 'nature is healing' time. *Sneaky.*

On the walk, Elsie pointed out flowers and weird graffiti, and cute dogs. She didn't wait for Jones to answer, didn't push her to talk at all. Elsie seemed content to do the talking for them both.

Elsie stopped them so she could take a picture of a caterpillar on someone's stoop, and it was then that Jones surprised herself by bringing up her dad. She'd had no desire to talk about him or their relationship or anything really, but here in this microcosm of fall, with the kind of woman who notices a caterpillar and makes jokes about it chatting with neighbors after work, she felt herself creaking open.

"I know this may sound strange considering, well, all of this." Jones gestured up and down her body. "But I feel like I'm not sad enough. About losing my father. That's one of the things making me feel the worst. Maybe I'm too broken to grieve. Or maybe our relationship was too broken."

Elsie slipped her phone in her back pocket and stood to look at Jones.

"When we miss someone, it's always the exact right amount. You can't do grief wrong. It's like improv comedy in that way. Or poetry."

"Did you just make that up?"

"I think so."

"Huh, you should consider being a writer or something."

"I'm terrible at spelling though, just atrocious. But seriously, I'm really sorry about your dad—I'm not sure if I've said that. Though to be fair, I was kind of busy being amazing and then an asshole and then back to amazing the last time I saw you."

"Yeah. Mostly amazing. And rightfully frustrated. And thank you, it's been…a lot."

"I bet. What you said makes me think you two were estranged."

"Eh." Jones waved her hands in front of her face like she was clearing a cloud of mosquitoes.

Elsie was familiar with relationships that were best explained as something you tried to keep from eating you alive.

"I think maybe I assumed you were close because of how you're taking care of your brother."

"Yeah, that. Bentley's great, but that wasn't the plan. My step mom, who *is* younger, richer, and prettier than me just kind of bailed after the funeral. She was supposed to be back for his birthday but—"

"What does she say when you talk to her?"

"She doesn't."

Elsie tilted her head. "Say more."

Jones took a steadying breath. "She hasn't called me. I got a text from her so I know she's okay, but I'm just surrounded by this endless black hole of not knowing. I'm trying to care for Bentley, but I'm a stranger. I actually hadn't met him before the viewing."

"Oh, that's...I don't know what to say. Besides sorry I was a jerk to you the first time we met. And the time after that. You're dealing with so much."

Jones laughed. "Oh no, trust me, I get it. If anyone under-stands nursing incandescent rage for the Haelstrom empire, it's me."

"Oh, so you do know a thing about that."

"Indeed. I packed a carry-on for a funeral, and now I'm here indefinitely, contorting my life to fit into this space. Not that there's much contortion, really. My life back home is simple, and this place..." Jones looked around, for what she wasn't sure. "is pretty roomy."

"Right." Elsie looked down, but not before Jones caught

her happy expression flickering for a moment like lights in a storm.

"Did I say something wrong?"

"Oh, um, no. I hadn't put together that you're just kind of visiting. It's none of my business."

"I mean it definitely started that way. But when I think of next week or the week after, I'm here, helping Bentley with his counting and asking him not to repeat your jokes in public."

"Hey, I apologized!"

"Apologies don't remove the phrase *fart attack* from a six-year-old's mind, Elsie."

"A little momento—something to remember me by then."

"I don't think anyone who meets you is able to forget you." Jones hadn't meant to compliment Elsie, at least not so blatantly. Maybe once she had her life more together Elsie would be interested in her. She continued. "Right now, Charity isn't even returning my calls. Things might never go back to normal. Maybe normal is always something in the past that we're trying to get back to, even when we've outgrown it."

Elsie tilted her head. "You sound like a self-help podcast."

"Yeah, but a good one, right?"

"Of course, I'd be sure to hit that subscribe button."

"Great. Please be sure to rate and review. Dead dad podcast is about to take off, maybe Benz will provide sound effects since you apparently encouraged him to practice those."

Elsie knocked her shoulder into Jones', jostling her lovingly. "It's a useful skill! Do you regret not having a better relationship with him?"

"With who? Bentley?"

"No, your dad." Elsie turned toward her. "You don't have to talk about this either, if you'd rather not."

Jones threaded her arm through Elsie's, then kept walking

so they were both facing forward. She wasn't sure if she could process Elsie's kindness in that moment on top of her complicated sadness about her dad. "It's kind of nice to be asked. Is that weird?"

"Not at all," Elsie said.

"I'm not sure regret is the right word because I don't wish I'd done anything differently. I am sad about it. But I just couldn't do it, I couldn't keep trying to be someone he could love. I always felt like I was auditioning for him, trying to prove my worth. I never got the part of *someone he cared about.*"

"If it were up to me you'd get every part." Elsie looked away quickly, and Jones enjoyed watching her cheeks turn red like a brilliant fall tree.

"That's um, really sweet." Jones swallowed down the emotion in her throat. "I worry I'm like him, you know? I mean I'd never even met my brother. Someone who is invested in relationships probably meets their brother before their father's funeral, I'm guessing."

"Sure, customarily. But none of this is standard. And it takes a special kind of person to show up every day, which you have since you met him. Anyone can see that you love him. And more importantly, he can feel it. Don't discount how much you staying has changed things for him."

Jones wiped at her eyes and ducked her head. "Thank you for saying all that. Can we talk about something else before I cry?"

"Crying is always allowed but yes, new topic." Elsie's eyes lit up. "I know we're going to get pizza, but we still have some time before it's ready. How do you feel about Italian ice?"

"That depends—water ices or cream ices?"

"Be still my heart. A woman who knows the difference." Elsie feigned a swoon that would have put Scarlett O'Hara to shame. "Cream ices, of course."

"I feel *good* to *quite good*."

"Great, I know a place right around here."

Elsie took Jones' order for a small rainbow cookie ice and went to wait in line. Jones settled onto a stoop, not even glancing first to determine its cleanliness. Everything she was wearing needed to be washed anyway. She was too busy watching Elsie through the window to notice things like dirt. The young woman behind the counter laughed at something Elsie said and placed a hand on her arm. She looked like she was in her early twenties, blonde hair streaked with pink piled on top of her head. Was that the kind of woman Elsie was into?

Jones felt a spark of something like jealousy. When she was near Elsie she wanted to touch her too, to throw her head back and laugh at everything Elsie said without a care in the world. Just like this other woman was doing right now. She must have felt Jones' eyes on her, because she looked out the window and pulled her hand from Elsie's arm.

A thrill ran through Jones. Which was absurd, right? Of course, it was absurd. She was Elsie's boss. Sort of. Kind of more like a substitute boss just there to show a movie. And she was forty-two, easily a decade older than Elsie, with the baggage to match. The most cynical part of Jones' brain offered that Elsie's kindness was some sort of attempt to gain leverage, but she dismissed it quickly. Blackmail would have been easier. A quick picture of Jones as she stumbled into the kitchen with her dirty clothes and unwashed hair.

Elsie walked toward her, carrying two cups of brightly colored dessert, a proud smile across her face like she was returning from a successful mission. Jones smiled back; she didn't want to bring her down.

"Sorry, I wish I was better company."

Elsie's brows furrowed. "You don't have to be happy or in a good mood to be good company, Jones. Not with me."

"Oh." She felt like she should go on, but what could she say? That Elsie deserved her best and she didn't know how to give that right now. Elsie didn't seem to mind though. She just took a big spoonful of her ice and smiled at Jones, a bit of chocolate at the corner of her mouth.

Before Jones could think about what she was doing, or maybe because Elsie made her feel like she didn't need to think through every possible outcome, looking for things that could go wrong, she reached forward and ran her thumb along the edge of Elsie's bottom lip.

Elsie froze, her mouth dropping open as Jones kissed the chocolate off her own thumb. "Not bad."

"Uh, no. The chocolate toffee bar is really good. Do you want some more?" Elsie seemed to have regained her equilibrium, or at least had gathered herself enough to extend her cup toward Jones with a twinkle in her eye. Elsie winked, grabbing the spoon from Jones' cup and taking a bite. "I always forget how sweet rainbow cookie is. The almond extract is so good."

"Mmhmm."

By the time they'd secured the pizza, Elsie again taking care of all the human interaction, the sun had truly begun to set and dusk clung to the buildings like mist.

As they came up to Jones' brownstone, Elsie lingered on the porch.

"Aren't you going to come in to eat?"

"I wish I could but I probably shouldn't."

"Oh, of course." Jones tried not to let her disappointment show. Elsie had just suffered through an hour of her company. It made sense that she wanted to leave. She hadn't come all this way to…, actually Jones had no idea why Elsie had come over. "I realized I never asked why you were here, which, right now, seems like a very embarrassing oversight."

"Not at all—it doesn't matter. I'm just glad I got to see you."

"Okay." Jones forced a smile.

"Hey." Elsie squeezed Jones' arm. "I really do wish I could stay, but I have to get home to cut Avery's hair. I blew them off the other day because I was too busy making sock puppets with some of my closest six-year-old friends."

Jones raised an eyebrow. Trying to place the name before a light went on. "Is this *the* Avery? The one I owe money for the accidental high? Do you think they'd take pizza as payment?"

"Pizza is actually the main form of currency in our household. But you're good. I do more than enough to make up for a few gummy bears." Elsie winked.

Jones had to resist the urge to pull her forward. Bring their lips together. The thought of Elsie leaving filled her with a sense of dread. In the last hour, she'd felt almost okay. Not great, or really happy, but that hadn't mattered. With Elsie gone, would she just crawl back into bed? Reset her depression clock as she watched the dishes pile up until Bentley's return?

"Well, thanks. Are you sure you have to go? I can't get you to stay for just one slice of pizza or...?" Jones knew she was bordering on desperate.

"Or?" Elsie smiled. "I'm not going to lie. I'm very tempted by the 'or' at the end of your sentence there, Jones, but I promised Ave. And, I know you can make your own decisions, but I think you're in a hard place. I don't want to push anything, or do something you'll regret later."

Warmth and disappointment mixed in Jones' chest. This was still a new feeling, being taken care of, someone else taking the wheel when she was too exhausted. She felt desire and bone-deep relief. "Am I ever going to convince you to take advantage of me, Elsie Webb?"

Elsie leaned in until their lips were nearly brushing, and when she whispered, Jones felt the words shiver through her. "No. But maybe some mutual taking advantage could happen soon. Over dinner?"

"I'd like that, but Bentley will be back soon. My nights are pretty much spoken for." Just saying the words deflated Jones. She was glad to be spending so much time with her brother after missing out on the first years of his life. Really, she was. But Jones also wasn't used to planning her schedule around someone else. Not that she'd had much of a schedule to plan the past few years.

"Are you telling me Bentley doesn't need to eat? I remember him having quite the appetite."

"Oh, are you sure?" No way did Elsie want to have dinner with both of them, it was too much. What was in it for her?

"How about Monday? I could cook here if that's okay."

Jones blinked a few times, letting the offer sink in. "Yeah, that sounds perfect." And Jones was surprised by how much she meant it.

CHAPTER THIRTEEN
ELSIE

S o, let me get this straight. You cleaned her house and then bought her ice cream?"

"I did the dishes, and then we went for a walk. And, I went there in the first place for like…work stuff."

"Work stuff?" Avery asked slowly.

"I needed her to countersign my contract. Plus we went for Italian ices, not ice cream."

"Oh, well, that's very different." Avery turned on the stool in the bathroom, a smirk pulling up one corner of their mouth. "That's new for you—taking care of people you're not dating."

Elsie brushed some stray hairs from Avery's neck, inspecting her work. "I'm literally taking care of you right now."

"The exception that proves the rule." Avery twisted again, and Elsie grabbed their shoulders.

"Stop moving. I will not be liable if I accidentally buzz off your eyebrow, and not in the cool lesbian TikTok way."

"Maybe I could be the start of a new enby TikTok trend."

"Don't even joke about that, Avery. Your eyebrows are

precious. Cosmetic companies have built entire brands around trying to emulate brows like yours."

"They are one of my good features."

"All of your features are good." Elsie placed a finger on Avery's chin and guided their face back toward the mirror. "Now stay still or I will walk out of here mid haircut before you can finish grilling me."

Avery caught Elsie's eye in the mirror. "You know I have an issue with rare meat." Their muscles tensed beneath Elsie's palms until they were statuesque. "Do you think it's maybe a bad idea?"

"No, this haircut will be cute. It's the queer standard. Longer and messy on the top, short on the sides. I'm even trying out a fade this time."

"I don't mean the cut, and I think you know that. She's your boss."

"Temporary CEO, and probably not for very long."

"She has a kid."

The blade of the scissors nipped into the pad of Elsie's finger, and the sharp sting made her stop cutting. "No, she has a brother, just like I do. Hand me a band-aid please." She put her finger in her mouth, soothing where the blades had caught her skin.

"Permission to move?" Avery smirked in the mirror.

"Hilarious. I'm bleeding everywhere. Do you want this in your hair?"

"Okay, fine. I'm just trying to protect my eyebrows. You're not one for idle threats." Avery leaned forward and pulled open the medicine cabinet. They opened a dinosaur band-aid and wrapped Elsie's finger. Pterodactyl this time—her favorite. Elsie had never understood adult's commitment to boring bandaids when there were so many good options. Working with her hands, she had a lot of cause to use them. She liked the ones with animals or characters best. They were like mini-finger puppets. And Avery humored her because she was the one who bought all of their first aid supplies anyway.

"There. Don't forget to wash it when we're done." Avery gave her a serious look. "Even if the kid and the boss thing aren't issues, isn't she quite a bit older?"

"Are you really making age a thing? Your last boyfriend had cardigans older than you."

"That was casual."

"Well, so is this. Sort of. I mean it's not anything. But if it *was* going to be something, it would be casual. I'm good with casual."

Avery laughed. "Since when?"

"Since always. All my relationships are casual."

"Most of your supposed one-night stands led to talks of cohabitation, but if you're suddenly good with casual, then I wish you'd casually clean up the mess you left in the living room yesterday."

"Sit still and stop therapizing me or you're losing an ear, and not in a cool way like a stray cat."

"I think that's a neuter thing, like catch and release."

"Okay, then. That too."

ELSIE RAN a sponge over her bowl from breakfast, missing the rubber gloves Susan had given her the other day as the hot water burned her hands. She'd pick up a few pairs the next time she was at the store. They'd be a good addition to her puppet craft supplies, too. Endless possibilities for demonic chickens. She had her headphones in, and the story she was listening to was getting good. The main characters were recre-ating an art heist and were alone in the museum at night. Elsie was fairly certain they were about to fuck on a bench in front of one of the empty frames. They'd better be planning on erasing the security footage. A robotic voice in her ear interrupted a pretty intense make-out session as it paused her audiobook to announce a new email.

As she rinsed off the suds, Elsie listened to the message.

From: Jones@Haelstrommedia.com

To: Elsie@FangleyHeights.com

Subject: Consent Procedure

Elsie,

In preparation for our dinner arrangement, I wanted to send along this form regarding consensuality through the proper channels. Please review and sign so we can submit to HR. Feel free to run it by your lawyer if you have any concerns.

Sincerely,

Jones Haelstrom

SERIOUSLY? What kind of person signs their entire name at the end of an email? Elsie fumbled for her phone on the kitchen counter, nearly dropping it into the running water. She was both desperate to see the attachment, and the thought of looking at it made her stomach swirl like dishwater disappearing down the drain.

The attached PDF began with a fairly standard non-disclosure. Followed directly by a statement of the 'relationship' between Elsie Haelstrom—well, they'd need to correct that typo—and Jones Haelstrom, which stated they were entering this union freely and of sound mind. The word consensual littered the page in the least sexy way Elsie could imagine. And Elsie loved consent. Her three favorite words in bed were, "is this okay?"

"What are you scowling at?"

Elsie removed her earbud and let it drop to the counter. "I'm not scowling."

Avery held eye contact as they prepared a bowl of

oatmeal. "You're looking at your phone like you're trying to destroy the screen with your heat ray vision."

"It's just this email Jones sent me."

"Oooh, is it something sexy about your not-a-date dinner? Did you figure out what you're going to make?"

"Yes. No. I mean, sort of? It's an HR form to disclose our relationship and say neither of us, meaning *me*, will sue. Oh, and that neither of us is being forced or blackmailed or otherwise coerced into a relaxed dinner, I guess."

"So a sex contract? You're right, Elsie. This does sound very casual. Contracts are the cornerstone of all no-strings sexual agreements."

"Can you not right now? I'm kind of freaking out." Elsie set down her phone and wrapped her fingers around a mug in the sink, holding her hands in the scalding water until it became too much.

"Sorry." Avery's smile slid from their face, and Elsie could imagine them in an office chair adjusting their glasses as they asked her to *say more*. "Look, Els. This doesn't have to mean anything. Jones is the head of the company, and even if that's temporary, she's still everyone's boss, including yours. Being seen as abusing her position would be devastating if she has designs on taking over Haelstrom for good. She probably just wants to be careful so she can make out with you like a teenager after dinner."

Elsie scoffed. Avery was making sense, but she still didn't like what it was adding up to. A form on file made it feel wrong, like she was breaking a rule and not in a fun way because she'd asked permission first. And what was with the formal email out of the blue? Jones could have texted. Did she think Elsie couldn't be trusted? Or that she needed to protect herself from Elsie? Maybe Jones just wanted to protect herself in general, after everything that had happened to her in the past few weeks.

Still, this agreement went against Elsie's very stringent *ask only for forgiveness* policy. She didn't want to say all of that to Avery. How reading the email had made her feel like a dish so dirty it might as well be thrown away. Even if she could explain how she was feeling, that reasoning held water about as well as a shattered glass. She dried her hands again, and when she turned back around, she had composed her face into a smile.

"And how do teenagers make out, Ave?"

"Desperately, not that I'm speaking from much experience."

"You made out with what's-her-name at prom. But not desperately. More methodically, like you were following the steps of a science experiment. And then it exploded all over the kitchen and she ran out crying."

"Wow, okay. Tell me how you really feel."

"I'm just kidding. We've always been better friends, but I was totally happy to help you figure out that you were not into me."

"You're right. Kissing you was horrible."

Avery ducked as Elsie flicked water at them. "So should I just sign this thing? Do we know anyone with a printer?"

"People don't buy printers anymore. But the library on DeKalb has some—I think it's ten cents a page."

"Cool, do we know anyone who has dimes?"

Avery laughed. "So that's it? You're going to sign?"

"I mean, maybe? I'm not sure what it is with Jones presenting me with contracts I haven't agreed to. I feel like I should get a chance to negotiate at least."

"But?"

"But, I don't want Jones to get in trouble. It does feel like we're getting ahead of ourselves though. Shouldn't we make sure we have something to disclose before disclosing it?"

"I know this advice seems out there, but I think you should just talk to her about it. You have her number, right?

And her address. And her email. She literally couldn't make it easier for you to contact her to talk this through."

"I can't believe you're advocating for an honest conversation. I thought you were going to stop bringing work home."

"For the last time, I might be a therapist, but I'm also an adult, being emotionally mature isn't me bringing work home."

CHAPTER FOURTEEN
JONES

Jones sent the email and snapped her laptop shut. Nausea crested over her. She'd started off the day by sending Elsie the consensual relationship agreement to set her own mind at ease. Actually, the consensual relationship disclosure was meant to set *both* their minds at ease, except that now she worried the HR disclosure was too formal and too presumptuous. Jones navigated to her sent messages and looked for a way to undo what she'd done. A second later, the automatic read receipt popped up in her inbox. Jones waited, but no reply came. Her stomach sank. What if, with one PDF attachment, Jones had just ruined her chances with Elsie Webb?

No, that was silly. Elsie would be reasonable, Jones reminded herself. She'd see the value and intention of the agreement. The whole point of it was that nothing was owed. No quid pro quo. No strings. She wanted things with Elsie to go…wherever they'd go naturally. And Jones was pretty sure Elsie wanted the same. A signed agreement was the only way to ensure that, even if it seemed counterintuitive.

The agreement proved that Jones wasn't like her father. She had no desire to use her power or influence to attract a woman. Birdie might call her naive, but Jones wanted to be liked for who she was inside, not her reflection in the outside world. She'd always been a romantic in that way.

She opened her email again to see if Elsie had replied, but closed it before she had a chance to look. The fixation was swirling in her brain, and to indulge it a little would mean indulging it completely. Jones fished her morning pills out of the vial and washed them down with coffee. She had about thirty minutes to chase them with some food if she didn't want the anxiety nausea to become real nausea. Hopefully she'd remember to drink water later. Somewhere over the years not drinking enough water had come to have the same impact on her as a hangover. Brutal.

THE FINAL BUTTON of her dress shirt slipped into place, and Jones adjusted the collar before pulling on her favorite sweater and adjusting everything again. She slipped on her glasses with the large plastic frames and blinked at her reflection. Jones had always used fashion as a barrier between herself and the world, one of the few relevant lessons she'd absorbed from Birdie. Some people had leather jackets and boots, she had sweaters and nerdy glasses.

The thought of facing the office sent anxiety roiling through Jones' body. The way Stu looked at her made her uneasy, and she had the persistent feeling of being watched. The glass walls of her father's office didn't help much with that. But what choice did she have? She was responsible, and responsible people went to work unless they were on their deathbed, a fact she had completely ignored last week without the building falling down. She'd checked her emails when she wrote to Elsie, and the only thing pressing as far as she was concerned was making sure Elsie signed the paperwork before dinner tonight. Ideally, she'd also submit it to the Human Resources department. Maybe it would be an easy day of going over viewership statistics on her computer. And the occasional walk-by of the Fangley Heights set, trying to catch a glimpse of Elsie.

She quartered an apple for herself and started preparing Bentley's cereal. She'd need to get him up soon if they wanted to make it to school on time. Bentley's school was run like a commercial flight. There were no late arrivals, if you missed the final bell, the doors were closed and the building might as well be at cruising altitude.

Mornings were the dreaded time of the day for them both. Getting Benz up for school had been a daily struggle. With the nightmares, he often woke up in the middle of the night and took an hour to get back to sleep. Ushering Bentley into his classroom with dark circles under his eyes felt monstrous. At least she had concealer, the best way to hide distress. Can six-year-olds wear concealer to kindergarten, or does that make things a whole lot worse? Probably the latter Jones decided.

BENTLEY WAS STILL ASLEEP when Jones eased open his door, stopping halfway to avoid the creak. His rosy cheeks peeked out from beneath his blue blanket. He had one arm thrown over his head like a chalk outline at a crime scene.

"Benz, time to get up." She shook him gently.

Bentley remained motionless aside from the steady rise and fall of his small chest.

"Come on, it's time to wake up, or you'll be late for school." Jones was met with a wall of silence. *Fair enough.* She thought of Elsie and how free he'd seemed around her. But Elsie interacted with the world in a way Jones had never been able to, like she was delighted to be there. Jones was uptight and Elsie was...not. She couldn't pull off carefree unless it was a shade of nail polish. But maybe she could be a little less serious, just this once. As an experiment. What would Elsie say?

"If you're not going to get up, I guess I'll have to eat your cereal without you." The thought of pure sugar, those hard marshmallows gritting in her molars made Jones shudder.

But then like magic, Bentley let out a fake snore.

Okay, progress.

"Elsie told me that snoring is bad for kids. I better emergency tickle you until you wake up. Safety first."

A small smile played at his lips and his eyes squeezed shut.

Jones leaned over his small form and fluttered her fingers, making a low buzzing noise with her mouth like an airplane about to land. As soon as she grazed his ribs he squirmed and dissolved into a fit of giggles.

She fell onto the bed next to him and wiped fake sweat off her brow. "That was a close one! You had me worried there."

Bentley curled into Jones' side and her breath caught. She was finally seeing some of the magic that happened between Elsie and Benz, the way he ran to her and threw his arms around her knees before she left like she was a source of strength.

"Jonesy?"

She'd missed when he'd started calling her that—the 'y' rounding her name into sweetness. "Yeah?"

"I don't want to go to school today." Bentley rocked his head, trying to get comfortable on her shoulder, and she wrapped her arm to cradle him.

Jones caught herself before the no passed her lips. When did her automatic answer become negative? Maybe it always had been. She'd adhered to the rules as a child because no one else did. Half the time Birdie made no distinction at all between weekdays and weekends. If Jones hadn't gotten herself up and ready and asked for a ride, school might as well have not existed. Bentley's breath was warm as he cuddled into her, his sharp knees jabbing her ribs.

Maybe just this once, she didn't have to say no. One day where responsibilities took a back seat to everything else—for both of them. The thought was a weight lifting off Jones' chest. They could go to the park or the movies. Was that an option? Did movies play on weekdays? Skipping school without a legitimate reason? She pulled out her phone to look up the policy.

Bentley skipped between Jones and Mitch as they walked through the iron gates of the park. A wagon containing a huge, blue kite shaped like a dragon clattered behind them. Bentley pointed out each scale he'd attached, even though their askew angles made them easy to identify in a field of Mitch's precision. Mitch had been heading out to take Snapper on her maiden voyage just as Jones and Bentley were locking the door for their impromptu adventure.

The morning sunlight bounced off the pond, and Jones was grateful for the sunglasses Benz had insisted they wear so no one would recognize them. She had on a pair of Charity's, white plastic frames that conjured Jackie O. Jones' lipstick-bright smile reflected back at her, doubled in the mirrored lenses of Bentley's aviators. Mitch worked on unfurling the kite while Bentley spun circles on the grass until he staggered into Jones' legs. Snapper was the size of a Great Dane. When everything was tangle-free, Mitch handed Jones the spool of string with a slight deferential bow.

"Why don't you do the honors?"

Jones gripped the string, winding it around her fingers. She'd never flown a kite. How was that possible? Sometimes Jones felt like she'd skipped over childhood and went straight to middle age as a seven year old. She scrolled through her memories, trying to find one where kites were in the air but she'd been much more of a spa kid than a park kid. If you wanted her to explain the benefits of a mud bath, she was your girl.

"You should go first, you worked so hard on it. Not it, *Snapper*." She held the string back toward Mitch.

Mitch studied her and stuck his hands into his pockets. His wispy, white hair matched the cirrus clouds above their heads. "Benz, you're going to teach your sister how to fly a kite; do you think you're ready? Remember what we practiced?"

Bentley stopped spinning. A grin split his face as he staggered forward a few steps and took the string from Jones. He grabbed Jones' fingers with his free hand and showed her the way.

The principle was simple, finding the wind and then watching Snapper dance through the air. He made it look so easy. Bentley's laughter floated through the air.

Jones' phone beeped, reality slicing through the calm day. Stu's number flashed on her screen, she never knew you could add emojis to contacts before she'd seen the crown and squirrel next to Avery's name on Elsie's phone. Even with dread billowing into the pit of her stomach, the little thumbs down brought a smile to her face.

"Hello?"

"Jones, where are you?" Stu's voice sounded cheerful as it rose over the cacophony in the background.

She looked around, suddenly feeling watched."I'm…out." She resisted the urge to explain herself to Stu. She hadn't done anything wrong, and even if she had, she didn't answer to him.

"Hopefully, you're out and on your way to this board meeting."

"What are you talking about? There wasn't a board meeting on my schedule."

"Oh, we must have sent it to Charity by mistake. If you're

not on your way, don't worry about it. I'll cover for you. Besides, it'll probably be over by the time you get here anyway."

"No, I'm headed there now. Stall until I get there or reschedule." Jones watched Mitch and Bentley sailing Snapper among the clouds with ease.

"The meeting's starting now. I'm calling as a courtesy."

A little head's up from Judas. How thoughtful. "Well, then un-start it. Nothing happens until I get there."

CHAPTER FIFTEEN
ELSIE

Jones was leaning against the door to her office, looking every inch a cardboard cut out Elsie would have had in her college dorm for "decoration". She looked like something between a total boss, with her sexy heels and a sweet English teacher, with her dark glasses and honey blonde hair pulled into a thick braid. Elsie clenched her hands into fists to resist her impulse to untie Jones' braid. She imagined combing fingers through it until the silky strands ran wild. Elsie dug her nails into her palm as she trailed her eyes down Jones' body, taking in her thin leather belt that would be perfect for—

A snap echoed in her ears. "You know, when women say 'my eyes are up here' it's usually because people are looking at their boobs, not—" Jones gestured absently down the front of her body.

"What?" Elsie shrugged and feigned surprise. "I like your belt. Where did you get it?" She attempted to divide 7,347 by 4 in her head as she held a straight face. She worked with puppets making fart jokes, Elsie was a professional when it came to not breaking.

"I'll send you a link." A smile ghosted across Jones' lips.

"Yeah, great. Thanks."

"I went by the set a few times today, but I didn't see you there," Jones said, adjusting her glasses with her index finger.

That nerdy gesture had no business being so sexy. Elsie's stomach was gearing up for a back handspring. Jones cleared her throat, but she looked amused.

Elsie blinked her mind back into focus. "Oh yeah, it's a booth day." She reached out and touched the soft cashmere sleeve of Jones' sweater. *Cashmere. That would make great puppet material.*

"What does that mean?" Jones tilted her head.

A small crease formed between Jones' brows that Elsie wanted to reach forward and smooth. Her hands felt drawn to Jones. Elsie shoved them into her pockets to avoid them acting of their own accord. She wasn't exactly clear on the rules at work. She should really reread the HR form that was crunched up in her bag, now that her panic from this morning had somewhat subsided.

Elsie smiled, the thought that Jones could really be interested in this filled her with excitement. "We record audio for the episodes in the sound booth, then during filming our puppets perform a lip sync. Then the dubbed audio gets dropped during post-production."

Jones nodded. "That makes sense, but I wouldn't have thought of that. Of course the puppets don't talk. I guess I assumed you wore a mic while filming."

"That would be a lot to manage, and with the close quarters our mics would pick up other voices and our weird movements. Plus, I'm always babysitting Trey." Elsie sighed and gave Jones a wry smile. "Let's get back to why you were looking for me? I didn't know you were in today. But there were a lot of suits in the building—I felt like I was walking around a Brooks Brothers on Wall Street."

"Oh, there was a board meeting, but it was nothing important, more like a check in on how things are going since my father passed away."

"Ah, that makes sense, I guess. But I didn't see you in your office this morning."

Jones placed a finger on her chin and winked in a way that was not at all smooth. "Hmm, maybe we should go over why you were looking for me in my office?"

"It's on my way to the set."

Jones laughed. "No, it's not."

Okay, fair point. Jones' office was nowhere near the set. "No, it's not." Elsie conceded. "I like to see you sitting at your desk all studious in your sweater and nerdy glasses. It's a nice way to start my day."

"You think my glasses are nerdy?" Jones' eyes went wide in mock surprise but Elsie saw the flicker of a crease next to them.

"With me, nerdy is always a compliment." Elsie assured her. "So, why were *you* looking for me?"

"I wanted to see if we were still on for dinner. I wasn't sure if you were having second thoughts when you didn't reply to my email."

The email. Avery had been right, Elsie should have responded, clarified, cleared the air instead of marching to the library. Instead, she'd shoved the pages into her bag like a failed algebra test.

"I am actually." Elsie glanced up at the sound of footsteps in the hallway, Trey's oozing approach behind Jones.

"Oh, I see." The skin next to Jones' eyes pinched. When had Elsie become attuned to even the slightest shift in Jones' demeanor? Maybe she was just used to studying movements, perfecting them for Fangley. Elsie knew the power of the slightest pull of a facial feature. Though when it came to Fangley, emotions were about as subtle as neon graffiti, whereas Jones' expressions were delicate watercolors, almost imperceptible on their canvas.

Elsie put her hand up to stop Jones. "I think lasagna might be too ambitious. How do you feel about cacio e pepe?"

Jones' brow furrowed, but she didn't press the conversational pivot. "That sounds great."

"Ladies, what are we talking about?"

Jones' shoulders inched toward her ears at Trey's voice, like a turtle trying to withdraw into its shell. But there was no escaping him today.

Elsie squared her shoulders, ready to body block him before he took one step closer to Jones. It was one thing for Trey to be weird to her but Jones should never have to deal with that.

"Dinner." Jones said, her face a blank slate.

"Dinner?" Trey's voice shimmered with glee. "Is this a work thing? You're in luck, because tonight is a rare night where I don't have plans." He put his palm against the wall as he leaned toward Jones, effectively blocking Elsie.

Elsie judo-chopped his hand in her mind. "It's not that kind of dinner."

"What, you won't be eating?" Trey's eyes lit up as he leaned closer to Elsie and lowered his voice to a whisper. "Or maybe what you'll be eating isn't for me?"

"What was that, Trey?" Jones stood up straighter and leveled him with a stare. Boardroom eyes. Elsie felt a little jolt of desire.

"Oh, um, nothing. I was just thinking I'd love to grab dinner with my new boss one night and unwind, maybe renegotiate my contract."

"I'm sure someone from legal would be happy to have dinner with you. I'm not going to get into the habit of working out contract terms myself."

Elsie felt a small spark of hope. If Jones was worried about forming habits, maybe she was changing her mind about leaving. Was that the real reason for the HR form?"

"Was there anything else?" Jones gave Trey a tight smile.

He wilted under Jones' stare. "I actually just remembered I *do* have plans tonight. My uncle wants to go over some things about a meeting he had today with the board. See you ladies tomorrow." He turned on his heels and headed down the hall.

They waited for his footsteps to recede around the corner.

Jones turned to her. "Do I need to worry about him?"

"I find it's best to just ignore him."

Jones laughed. "Already forgotten. Is his character really named Smirch?"

Elsie grinned and leaned into Jones. "Indeed. I'll tell you about that later."

"Deal. Speaking of later, did you sign the form for HR? I can drop both of them off for us before I leave." Jones wrung her hands in front of her, and Elsie was torn between comforting her and keeping a professional distance. She erred on the side of distance.

"No, um, I don't have it on me. Can I bring it tonight?" Elsie felt a rapid of guilt rush through her. She knew she had to sign the agreement before tonight, or maybe Avery had a point, and they could just talk about it later. Just a casual adult conversation that absolutely wasn't terrifying at all.

"Sure, of course. I can just meet with them tomorrow."

"Great, well I should get changed and head to the store."

"Right, okay." Jones' brow furrowed.

"See you tonight." Elsie squeezed Jones' bicep, then followed Trey down the hall.

A bicep squeeze? Smooth. Elsie needed to figure out this relationship-form thing before dinner.

PASTA WAS A SUCCESS. Bentley ate it because Elsie grated enough cheese for it to pass as fancy macaroni. When she pitched it that way to Bentley, Elsie could feel Jones' gaze on her even though she was on the other side of the kitchen pouring two glasses of wine and one of apple juice. Jones smiled and walked over to the table with the drinks. Her eyes caught the light; they looked glossy, like she was holding back tears.

Jones sat next to her, their thighs pressing together. "You're a magician for getting him to eat."

"You can't sell puppet shows about vampires without learning how to frame a pitch." Elsie shrugged. "It really comes in handy."

Elsie did dishes—a task that was becoming familiar to her —while Jones put Bentley to bed. She still avoided the dishwasher, partly to draw the task out and give herself less time to think. Because what came next was a conversation about the form, and Elsie didn't feel ready to ruin the night. She wanted to sign it so she could kiss Jones, but something still held her back. The formality of it felt impersonal. It was nothing like the dance floor proximity that usually kicked off her relationships. Not that this was a relationship. Elsie just wished it didn't feel quite so much like a business arrangement.

She couldn't help but think Avery had a point. Cooking, cutting Bentley's food and chatting with him over dinner didn't feel casual. But it didn't feel like work either. It felt like comfort, like when she and Avery ordered tikka masala and watched *You've Got Mail* for the millionth time. It felt like what Elsie would want to open the door to at the end of the day.

She shut off the water and turned from the sink. If she wanted to stay calm, she needed to stay busy. Elsie scanned the kitchen for something else to do. She'd already put away the leftovers and wiped down the stove and the table, tasks she rarely did at her own apartment. But she wanted things to be easy for Jones; she wanted to be thoughtful in ways she normally wasn't.

When she was sure there was nothing left to do, Elsie touched the folded form in her back pocket, running her index finger along the seam where the paper had become soft after tumbling around in her bag.

A picture on the side of the fridge caught Elsie's attention, and she walked over to examine it. A young girl with hair so blonde it was almost white was being held in the air by a man. They were both smiling in a sea of balloons.

Jones paused in the doorway. "What are you looking at?"

Elsie turned and smiled, running her fingers over the old polaroid. "Is this you?"

Jones stepped behind her. "I never noticed that before. Yeah, that must be me and my dad."

Elsie went from studying the photo to studying Jones. Her mouth had drawn into a tight line before her features relaxed again.

"That was so good." Jones smiled. "I never would have guessed you were a chef."

Okay, so they weren't going to talk more about the picture of Jones and her dad. "I wouldn't go that far. I enjoy cooking, but what I really love is feeding people. It's an act of love with an immediate payoff. With other things in my life, like writing, I might think an idea is good, or a joke is funny, but it will take months for other people's feedback to filter to me. But those sounds you made while eating were a starred review."

Jones smiled softly, the corners of her eyes crinkling skeptically. "Do you always do that?"

"Do what?" Elsie straightened the towel she'd hung on the oven door.

"Say something serious then end it with a joke to deflect a conversation." Jones tilted her head. The effect was sweet, like a puppy trying to make sense of an endearment.

"Have you been taking therapy lessons from Avery?"

"Is Avery a therapist?" Jones took a step toward Elsie.

"Social worker."

"Good to know. Maybe I can call them to get some more

tips. But I'll leave it for now. Can we talk about the email I sent you this morning?"

"You're pretty direct."

"Yes. I was nervous to send it and I feel like it made you uncomfortable, so let's talk about it. I have a few hours before Benz wakes up in the middle of the night, and I'd love it if we had time to get to something other than talking."

Okay, so they were doing this. Elsie's swallow echoed in her ears. "I understand it in theory, but it reminds me of a permission slip. I feel like I'm going to the Natural History Museum or something."

"What kind of field trips did you go on?" Jones opened her eyes wide in mock surprise.

"Very funny. I just meant the whole signing a form thing in order to do—"

"I can see that. A very adult permission slip. But we can go to the museum, if you want. I mean not now, because they're closed, but sometime. I really don't care where we go."

"Okay." Elsie forced a laugh. She could do this. If Jones didn't think the form was a big deal, then maybe it wasn't. She pulled the sheet from her pocket and handed it to Jones. The kitchen light shone through the cheap copier paper from the library as Jones unfolded it. Elsie had needed help printing it and had quickly muttered 'it's research' to the very nice octogenarian behind the reference desk. She had briefly considered just buying a printer but couldn't justify the 300 additional dollars she was sure to spend at Target.

"Thank you. This is to protect both of us, not just me." Jones laid the paper on the marble countertop and leaned over it. She wrinkled her nose as her glasses slipped. "I want this—you, Elsie. And I don't want to spend any of our time together worrying about possible complications."

Elsie twisted a strand of her hair and let it drop once she realized what she was doing. She could hear her mother shouting all the way from Boston for her to just stand still for once. "It just makes it feel kind of serious, you know? Sometimes the women I kiss don't even have last names, or well, they probably have them on some official document somewhere, but not in practice. Anyway, a contract feels a little more serious than that."

Jones let out a quick burst of laughter before schooling her features. "It doesn't have to be. I see you've completed it in purple marker, which I'd like to stress again is not legally binding on contracts. Good thing I have my copy. But also, I want to be clear, we don't have to do anything. We can acknowledge we're attracted to each other and let it end there. I like you, Elsie, and that also means I want you to feel comfortable saying no or walking away and know that that decision won't impact your career at all."

"I do know that. And I don't want to walk away," Elsie said. "I just get a little antsy when things feel serious, I'm not exactly used to that in my relationships."

"This form is the opposite of serious—there are no strings attached. If we decide we want to move forward, we can. This can be one night, or many and nothing that happens will affect our work lives. If it doesn't work out, we can still be friends and colleagues."

"Oh, but will we be sleeping together?" Elsie reached to snatch the form from Jones. "Did you add that stipulation after you sent the email?"

Jones raised her arm in the air, holding the paper just out of reach. "You know what I mean."

"Show me." Elsie made a grab for the paper that put her right in Jones' personal space.

Jones' arm relaxed, and Elsie's fingers wrapped gently around her wrist. Jones' breath was warm and sweet against her mouth.

"Stop talking, please." Jones pressed her finger against Elsie's lips.

Those three words lit something in Elsie. The heat had been simmering all day as she thought about kissing Jones with none of the guilt of their previous encounters lingering in the air. Elsie parted her lips and gently bit Jones' fingertip. She savored the little gasp the bite elicited from Jones. So sexy.

Jones closed the distance between them. The fruity flavor of the wine clung to her lips and Elsie felt lightheaded, like she was drinking an entire bottle of this moment, this kiss. When Jones' tongue trailed along Elsie's bottom lip the flames caught. She backed Jones up until her hips hit the counter. Elsie pressed their bodies together until there was no space between them, until Jones filled all of her senses and heat pooled low in her stomach.

Elsie dug deep and found the willpower to break their kiss. Pressing her forehead to Jones'. Every cell in her body screamed at her for stopping. But Jones needed a contract, and Elsie needed this. "When's the last time you got tested?"

"Is this your idea of sexy talk?" Jones tilted to nip at her neck.

"It is. Think of this as *my* consent form."

"The last time I was tested for STIs was in January at my physical. Nothing to report since then. And you?" Jones' mouth moved up and bit Elsie's ear, her teeth lingering just enough to sting before she soothed the mark with her tongue.

"I'm finding it hard to believe no one's propositioned you in five months." Elsie drew in a shuddering breath.

"I didn't say they hadn't. Just no one I was interested in. But that's not the question I was asking."

Jones' fingers dug into Elsie's hips, and she had to restrain herself from grinding against Jones. From spinning them around and pushing Jones against the counter or maybe lifting her onto it.

"A month ago," Elsie breathed. "Maybe a month and a

half. I can check when Avery and I went to Atlantic City. It was just after that. All good."

"I see. Is that like Vegas, where you don't talk about it?"

"Do you want me to talk about it?" Did Elsie want to talk about it? At this moment, she wanted to do whatever she could to keep Jones pressing against her, her hands wandering like Elsie was a sculpture she was forming.

"Maybe next time. Tonight, I only want to think about you with me." Jones brought their mouths back together, a clash of lips and teeth. The small firework of pain as Jones bit Elsie's lip did nothing to make the sparks in her stomach fizzle out.

Next time. Two words that Elsie was certain would buzz in her head for days to come. Jones was full of surprises. Elsie had a feeling she would need to step up her dirty talk. That could be another thing for next time.

Elsie reached for the button of Jones' tight jeans. Suddenly all she wanted was Jones on the counter and her own knees on the tile floor. Jones pushed her hips forward, and Elsie felt her wetness through her silk underwear. She glanced down and pushed Jones' jeans lower so she could pull the thin material aside.

Jones buried her face against Elsie's shoulder. "Hold on. Elsie, stop."

Jones panting against the sensitive skin of Elsie's neck sent a shiver through her. "Sorry. Too fast? I knew we should have just made out like teenagers, like Avery said."

Jones laughed. "What? No, I think I heard something. And you talked to Avery about this?" Jones' fingers wrapped around Elsie's wrist and pulled upward to remove her hand.

Elsie brought her lips to Jones' neck and slid her fingers into the front pocket of Jones' jeans, mostly to keep them from wandering. "I'm sure it was nothing. Our old building creaks all the time—I'm sure this one does too—"

Elsie's thought was cut off by a howl barreling down the

stairs. Elsie flinched and Jones squeezed her arm, taking a step back. "Sorry, it's just Benz. He's been having these nightmares. It usually takes an hour or two to calm him." A sad smile on her lips.

"Go check. I'll get us some wine."

"Actually…" Jones trailed off, frowning as she looked at the stairs and back to Elsie.

The realization that Jones wanted her to go was like stepping into the shower on one of its birdbath days—the days where the ancient pipes in their building blessed them with just a cool trickle of water while she stood shivering.

"Right, of course. Maybe a rain check on this field trip." Elsie forced a smile. She understood, but that didn't mean her body had gotten the memo.

"Well, we still need to get your form signed." Jones gave her a quick kiss as Bentley cried again. "Sorry, I have to go. Will you lock the bottom lock when you go? And text me when you get home? Actually, use my phone to order an Uber. That way I know who you're riding with *and then* text me when you get home."

Elsie reached up to smooth the worry lines on Jones' forehead. "I'll do both. Good luck."

JONES TOOK the stairs two at a time as Elsie tapped on her phone to order a car. While she waited for the driver to figure out the one-way streets to get to Jones' house, she found the HR form on the edge of the counter. Jones' signature was all sharp spikes of black ink. She picked up the pen next to it and added her name and the date. And then she locked the door behind her.

CHAPTER SIXTEEN
JONES

Jones dabbed vomit from her sweater and tried to ignore the fact that Bentley had eaten something electric blue before bed without her noticing. Nothing should be that bright. If someone had told her five years ago that she'd be cleaning sick off cashmere after a quiet night in, she wouldn't have believed it. Jones had never been wild, she'd gotten sick from drinking exactly once, and it was so long ago that it had involved wine coolers that exact shade of electric blue.

All she managed to do was spread the color. She gave up and stripped off her sweater; it was useless. There were worse fates than ruined cashmere. Like being alone forever. Or being so inept at caring for your kid brother that you inadvertently ruin his life. Jones dropped the garment on top of the pile of Bentley's sheets, then bent down to gather it all up. She was careful to extend her arms, making sure the disgusting bundle stayed away from her chest; there was no reason to ruin her shirt as she made her way down to the laundry room.

Jones tried not to gag as she stuffed the pile of sheets into the washer and fished her sweater back out, dropping it into the waste bin filled with lint and dryer sheets. Her dry cleaning days were becoming a distant memory. She'd learn to appreciate machine washables, now that laundry was a daily ritual.

At least Bentley was asleep again. Whether from his nightmare passing or exhaustion from this stomach bug, Jones wasn't sure. Seeing Bentley sick made her feel useless. And apparently, Jones wasn't okay with feeling useless. She hadn't known how to comfort him, instead she stood at his bedside awkwardly patting his back before crawling in beside him. Jones had pulled Bentley into her lap wishing the whole time that she'd asked Elsie to wait. Or to come upstairs with her. Elsie would have known what to do.

As Jones rocked Bentley, she tried to remember being sick as a kid. Anything to give her a roadmap for how to not mess this up. But her memory of her childhood was a storage room of empty boxes. Birdie wasn't sentimental. Jones had no memory of being comforted or of eating soup in bed, even though movies had taught her those were appropriate things to do. It wasn't that she'd been perfectly healthy—she had simply learned early on that showing weakness or illness was only met with exasperation. When Jones was sick, Birdie acted like she was an employee calling in, causing Birdie's life to be short-staffed, which it kind of was. Jones held Bentley until her arms ached with the effort. Until his breathing evened out. Until she stopped wondering what the right thing was and just focused on making the things she was doing right.

ONCE THE WASHER STARTED ROILING, Jones gathered a mountain of tiny socks from the dryer and headed to the kitchen.

She dropped the pile onto the marble counter. Huh. Most

of the socks were pale pink. Jones swished her hand through them until she found the culprit. A bright red sock puppet from Bentley's birthday. That was Elsie, always showing up and adding color to Jones' life when she least expected it. She held up a set of pink socks before folding them. There was no going back to how they were before. Plus, she was learning to love pink.

Jones' eyes flicked to the counter, and the memory of Elsie's mouth on hers came flooding back. Her kiss had been soft yet demanding, and the warmth of it had swept through Jones. She'd wanted her so badly. The start of the night had been wiped from her mind while she'd cared for Bentley. But now she was alone in the kitchen, clutching a sock that had ruined an entire load of laundry like it was a lifeline. She needed to get it together, stay casual. Instead, she patted her pockets in search of her phone only to find them empty. When had her phone become such a part of her that she didn't even feel it on her person? She spotted it resting on the counter, on top of a small stack of papers. Beneath the paperweight of her device, Elsie had completed and signed the HR form in handwriting that was straight out of a note passed in class. This was handwriting that asked you to a sleep over and told you secrets. Jones' laugh faded, to be replaced by a wave of heat as she pictured it—a slumber party invite from Elsie that ended in no sleep at all.

A selfie from Birdie wearing a feather boa and yellow Elton John glasses flashed on her phone screen. A quiet night in, Jones guessed. Birdie had never tired of playing dress-up, even forty years after her acting days had ended. Nothing from Elsie. Jones pushed down the small sadness she felt when she realized that Elsie hadn't texted to let her know that she'd made it home okay. She could always text *her* instead. Was that casual? Or was it desperate?

She decided to send a quick, breezy apology for their

night getting cut short. If that happened to also assuage her concerns about Elsie being safe, well there was simply nothing she could do about that. *It's not clingy to care about someone's safety. It's nice.* These were the words Jones repeated to herself as she typed her message.

Jones: *Sorry our night got cut short, let's do it again sometime.*

Perfect. So casual. By *sometime*, Jones meant tomorrow, preferably. Or better yet, if Elsie could just turn around and come back, that would be fine too.

Jones put her phone down and busied herself with getting a glass of frozen seltzer. She needed to stop watching the pot if she wanted it to boil. Or in this case, wanted it to vibrate. The metaphor was getting confusing, but the method proved effective.

When she picked it back up, a series of texts accordioned down the screen. Her heart did a little waltz.

Elsie: *I made it home! And yes, let's do that again sooner rather than later.*

The first message was followed by a selfie of Elsie cuddled up next to a very grouchy-looking, tan dog on her couch. Her arm was thrown around him and Elsie was holding one strand of her unruly chestnut brown hair beneath the dog's dark, wet nose like a mustache and another beneath her own nose. It was absurd. It made Jones think of how Elsie's hair had smelled fruity, like a freshly cut pineapple. She looked at the picture again. Jones wanted to blow it up to an eight by ten and have it framed. Maybe it could even replace that weird banner of her father in the office building's lobby.

Elsie: *Let me know if you want another one of me holding today's paper.*

Elsie: *I'm joking, because it's so sweet that you care, and I'm still working on how to handle that.*

Elsie: *That last message was me channeling Avery. Anyway! How's Bentley? How are you?*

The smile on Jones' face was so intense her cheeks ached.

She needed to respond before Elsie thought she'd forgotten about her and the conversation boiled over.

Jones: *Do you even have today's paper? You don't seem like a print subscriber.*

Elsie: *I'm not sure what you're implying. I read widely as a citizen of the world and the great state of New York*

Jones: …

Elsie: *Fine, I like the comics. And one time they reviewed Fangley Heights*

A second later, Jones' phone buzzed again. It was a picture of the comics section with a little heart and the date written in purple marker.

Jones picked up her phone to call Elsie, but her finger froze over the contact. A call seemed both too formal and too intimate. *Intimate, right.* Self-doubt was possibly the most powerful drug. A few hours ago, Elsie had Jones pinned up against the counter and ready to make a lot of questionable decisions. And now Jones was worried about being too intimate. But wasn't the point of the HR agreement to assuage these concerns?

She wished she hadn't asked Elsie to leave. Jones wanted to walk down the stairs with a pile of dirty laundry to find Elsie sitting in the kitchen, maybe drinking a cup of tea with another one next to it for Jones, the steam from both furling together and rising into the air. But there was nothing for Elsie in that fantasy. Just her waiting for Jones or having to deal with things she hadn't signed up for. Jones knew it wasn't fun, or sexy, or low-key to care for a sick kid, even if he was adorable. Everything about that was strings, a whole knot of them. And Jones had promised fun. So instead of saying any of that, she held the offending sock puppet in front of the ruined laundry and sent the photo to Elsie.

Jones: *I have a very serious complaint to file.*

Elsie: *I will pay you one million dollars to delete that photo. I might have sacrificed Avery's socks to the party cause. I told them I was mugged on the way home, and the guy only stole one sock. The dryer mugger*

Jones laughed. Elsie was delightfully absurd, two things she'd never realized were a perfect combination.

Jones: *The dryer mugger?*

Elsie: *Pretty sinister, huh?*

Jones: *This seems like information I might want to hold onto.*

Elsie: *I'm going to bribe Bentley to delete these messages. Also, you didn't answer my questions. How are you and Bentley?*

Jones: *You wouldn't.*

But she knew Elsie would, and Jones had no doubt that Elsie could get her brother to delete the messages and probably all of her apps, too. She quickly saved the photo to her camera roll.

Elsie: *(angel emoji) How are you and Bentley?*

Jones: *We're okay, I think. Benz got sick, but he's sleeping now. I'm…well, I'm exhausted and making roughly one hundred mistakes a minute. I think I'm in over my head with all of this.*

Elsie: *All of what?*

Jones: *I just don't think I'm cut out to care for him.*

Or Haelstrom Media. Jones kept that part to herself. Probably not a good idea to tell Elsie she had absolutely no idea what she was doing professionally either.

She reread her message as Elsie's thought dots undulated on the screen. Jones wished intensely, and not for the first time, that it was possible to unsend a text. Maybe they could both delete this conversation. She knew she shouldn't be telling Elsie all of this. There was nothing casual about being vulnerable. Vulnerability was something she kept locked in a safe. Like her will. Or a gun. It wasn't meant to be taken out unless something had gone very, very wrong.

Elsie's dots had disappeared and Jones felt like something between them had been severed.

Jones: *Sorry, you don't have to respond. I shouldn't have told you all of that. I'm really fine. Just tired.*

Jones' fingers itched to follow that text with another. Something self-deprecating and lighthearted. Anything to pull them back into the realm of casual. But before she could, her phone screen lit up with an incoming call.

Elsie.

CHAPTER SEVENTEEN
ELSIE

E lsie, do you have a moment? You're needed upstairs in the C-Suite." Rebecca was standing next to the camera holding a pink slip of paper. Cute.

They'd just finished a long day of filming that had gone mostly okay. Elsie had been nervous about this episode since she wrote it—she'd been pushing the envelope a bit more with each successive scene she wrote, but she was pretty confident that no one at Haelstrom Media cared enough to read the scripts. Well, besides Bentley, but she wasn't sure where he was at reading-level wise.

"Aye Aye, I'm headed to the Sea Suite on the main deck," Elsie called back, not bothering to cover the microphone near her mouth.

A few PAs around the set cringed. Oops. Elsie pulled off her headset and placed it on top of a box of animatronic corn that a props assistant was holding. "From my ears to yours," she said with a wink.

"C like CEO, you weirdo," Rebecca called back. Elsie caught the tail end of Rebecca's eye roll. "I was trying to avoid saying that Jones Haelstrom needs to see you, but your denseness has forced me to be blunt. On that note, let's call it a day, everyone. We'll reset for the last scene tomorrow. Elsie, you can just leave Fangley there; I'll take care of him."

"I've got it, Rebecca," Trey said as he stepped closer to Elsie and she took an instinctive step back. Her grip on Fangley tightened. Trey's dollar green eyes flashed as he whispered, "Trouble in paradise? I hope you're not about to get fired. Whatever would we do without you?"

Trey's words dripped poison.

"That's literally not how anything works, Trey. She probably wants to compliment the sheer genius of next week's episode. Which I wrote, by the way. Besides, if Ms. Haelstrom was going to fire me, she'd outsource it to your lovely uncle Stu. We both know he's been dreaming of a little Fangley Heights coup."

"Maybe I can bribe Stu to outsource that honor to me. He owes me a favor since he lost our last bet."

"I don't even want to know. And there's no way I'm getting fired today; it's not even Friday."

Elsie really hoped she was right about that. She felt confident she hadn't done anything unfixable for at least the last two to three days. She expected there to be some fallout with the upcoming storylines but those episodes hadn't aired yet. And when they did she'd just ask for forgiveness like she usually did.

Had she taken things too far by calling Jones and pushing her a bit to open up? What if Jones regretted their conversation about losing her father and how much she was struggling to care for Bentley. The Jones she'd been getting to know would never make that a work issue. Plus the retaliation clause in the HR paperwork guaranteed that Jones regretting something wouldn't get her fired. Elsie breathed a sigh of relief. Maybe the form wasn't so bad after all. Okay, no, it was still terrible but she could see the value, objectively. Elsie's thoughts spun like a slot machine as she tried to align good reasons Jones might want to talk to her.

It must be something major if Jones was willing to interrupt filming. Time is money and all that. In this case, Elsie's time was literally Jones' money.

Or maybe she'd gotten wind of the episode set to air next week. It featured the return of Fangley's long-lost lesbian aunt, Misty. She was a vampire with a distinct free love, free blood vibe. For the story, Elsie had dressed her Misty puppet in a free love, rainbow tie-dye caftan, that somehow no one in props or production had commented on. Overall, it was pretty tame, though it did allude to multiple girlfriends and beloveds the aunt had had over the years and implied she had several now. Misty had a locket with all their pictures that folded out like an accordion. Elsie had based it on the wallet picture holder her grandma had years ago, which had contained every single one of Elsie and her brother's school photos from kindergarten through graduation.

In the show, Fangley spent the weekend at Misty's cat-sle in the Catskills. A huge gothic house filled with felines. Ratatouille, Fangley's trusty Maine coon sidekick, came along and made fast friends with the other cats. Elsie loved the episode for many reasons. For starters, it meant Ratatouille's puppeteer Gabby was around more. Plus, Elsie had gotten to help advise on the cat-sle set, and she was so happy with how it turned out. She'd loved working on sets ever since her high school theater days. Carving foam into turrets had a meditative quality.

But what she was most excited about weren't the gags or jokes, but the message; it felt important to her. On its surface, the episode explored jealousy, but at its core, it was about ideas of possession. Clinging to exclusivity versus more open arrangements. How, if you can be open to it, there's always enough love to go around, even if it's not exactly in the way you were taught to anticipate it. The show offered a view of love that wasn't boxed into roles and expectations.

Elsie was proud of the script. And the great work of the

cast and crew. So, so proud. It was cute and quirky and unabashedly queer. Plus, she'd redone the aunt's hair with a long gray wool yarn that she'd combed apart until it floated off her shoulders like a storm cloud. She looked cool as shit. Definitely the kind of mentor Elsie would like to have.

Elsie took her time, reading the names and numbers on every door even though she knew where Jones' office was. She'd never been asked there before, and it reminded her of getting called to the principal's office to apologize for whatever practical joke she'd staged that day—like the time she and her friends had turned the science wing into a Slip 'N Slide when they *accidentally* spilled laundry soap, and then no one could take their chemistry final that day.

She paused a few feet from the office door and smoothed some non-existent wrinkles from her black catsuit. Maybe she should have changed so she wasn't meeting Jones in her office clad in black Lycra like some sort of sexy cat burglar. But changing would have drawn more attention. Besides, the bright orange leggings she'd worn on her commute weren't really more modest. In the end, she decided Jones would appreciate the black spandex suit she and all the other puppeteers wore to fade into the background in case they were caught in a shot.

ELSIE KNOCKED on the open door and waited for Jones to acknowledge her presence. She was standing at the window with her back to Elsie. Elsie had always loved looking down at the city from great heights. How it made the people look like ants and her problems feel like crumbs that could be swept to the ground. It was nice to think that Jones might love that, too.

"Come in," Jones called without turning around.

Elsie took a few tentative steps into the office. She knew Trey was just being a jerk when he mentioned her getting fired, but once that idea was in her head, she hadn't been able to come up with another reason why Jones would request to see her in the middle of the day when she knew they were filming. Every second that Jones didn't acknowledge her presence dimmed her usual optimism.

"Jones? You asked to see me?" Elsie didn't like how tentative her voice sounded; it was a little too high-pitched, like the mouse that lived in Fangley's bedroom. Elsie had a solid poker face, but her voice had always been a serious traitor.

Jones turned slowly, clutching her hand to her chest. "Thank God you're here. I need your help." Her white shirt was splashed with bright red. Elsie continued to scan her, trying to make sense of the image before her. There in her hand was a knife straight through the palm.

Elsie felt woozy, like she was the one bleeding out. She shouldn't have been so slow. She rushed toward Jones and held back a yell. *Be calm.* "What happened? Let me see." Elsie held out her cupped hands like she was going to catch the blood. Her pounding heartbeat thudded in her ears.

Jones reached out her bloody palm toward Elsie, slowly, clutching her wrist with her free hand like it was a wild animal that might escape. Jones' eyes were wide and shining.

"Has anyone called 911?" Elsie should have called 911. That was the *first* thing she should have done. She wasn't a doctor. Her taking a look would just waste precious tim—

Jones' hand smacked on top of Elsie's head and something gooey ran down her scalp. She had a flashback to the sleepover game she and her friends would play, *crack an egg on your head, let the yolk run down.* Goosebumps covered her arms in a Pavlovian response.

Elsie yelped and ducked away from Jones, but she could feel something viscous trickling its way into the collar of her shirt. And Jones was bent in half sobbing. No, not sobbing.

Laughing. What the fuck was happening?

Jones was doubled over with laughter. Tears streaming

down her face that she tried to wipe away before apparently remembering her hands were a murder scene.

Elsie tried to make sense of the woman in front of her but nothing was adding up to make a whole. "Are you okay? Jones, what's going on?"

Jones straightened, her face flushed. "That's payback for hammer time, buddy."

Hammer time? Elsie felt the slots lining up at last, three little hammers leading to the jackpot. The prop hammer she'd thrown at Jones the day they'd met. Elsie touched her fingers to her hair, pulling away from the familiar stickiness of fake blood.

"Are you kidding me? I was scared, Jones. I thought you were hurt!" Her voice was louder than she'd meant for it to be, but her body hadn't realized yet that it could stop panicking. Jones was okay. A jerk? Yes. But hurt? No. Well, not yet.

"You don't think I was scared when you *threw* a hammer at me?" Jones' eyes were twinkling with tears of laughter.

It was hard to argue with that. Elsie had seen the fear on Jones' face when the prop had left her hand and arced between them. She remembered Jones' panicked expression right before she ducked and let it hit her body rather than trying to catch or deflect it. Why hadn't she tried to protect herself at all?

"Have I not apologized for the hammer time incident?"

"You have not. But it seems like you did find time to nick-name it."

Elsie took a step forward, her hand hovering just above Jones' hip. "Even though it was very funny, and obviously made an impression. I'm sorry if it scared you."

Jones placed her hand over Elsie's, bringing her fingers to her hip. "That was barely an apology, but I'm kind of glad to see you're not good at everything."

"What do you mea—hey! I'm very good at apologies."

"Mmm, sure." Jones nodded.

"I can't believe you interrupted filming to prank me. Running a tight ship, I see."

"I have a legitimate reason, too."

"What's that?" Elsie leaned into Jones. The legitimate reason probably wasn't an illicit make-out, but she couldn't help wondering, what if it was?

She liked that Jones had pranked her back. So many of her girlfriends in the past had dismissed Elsie's love of fun as her not being serious. Not that Jones was her girlfriend or anything. But Elsie was serious about fun the way chefs were serious about those little sauces they drizzled on top of plates. Fun was her foundational skill.

Jones pulled away just as their mouths were about to meet, and every part of Elsie groaned inwardly.

She reached in the back pocket of her black jeans and gingerly pulled out a folded sheet of paper, handing it to Elsie. Sticky red finger prints marred the white sheet where Jones had gripped it. "I almost forgot, this is from Bentley."

Elsie pinched the note with her unbloodied hand and unfolded the paper. It was covered by two blue stick figures, one lying on the ground with a knife in its chest. The bottom corner had a sharp-angled heart and a backward letter B. Impressively creepy.

"Is Bentley inviting me to a murder?"

Jones laughed and brought a hand to her chest, as though it had surprised her. "I hope not. But he does have a fencing tournament."

"Oh, so a pre-murder ritual type thing then. That's very thoughtful. Black tie only, I assume?"

"If you come wearing only a black tie, I'm not going to be able to focus on his bouts."

"Fine, I'll leave the black tie at home."

Jones didn't respond right away, just blinked slowly. "Sorry, that was quite the mental image. Anyway." She shook her head slightly. "As I was saying, Bentley has requested your presence at his fencing tournament on Saturday."

"Wait, you're serious? He told me the other night that he did 'swords', but I thought he meant lightsabers or something, because surely no adult would give toddlers swords."

"He's not a toddler. He's six."

"Well, he fell the other day while walking, so it seems like he's still fairly new to it. Another reason why he shouldn't be wielding weapons."

"One of his friends is in his fencing club. I'm sure it's perfectly safe." Jones folded her arms, then thought better of it when some of the fake blood streaked her white dress shirt.

"You know it's just going to be an afternoon of kids poking each other in the butt, right?"

"Are you telling me you want to miss that?"

"Oh no, I definitely want to be there for that. Life is material."

"Okay, good. We'll pick you up at noon?" Jones took a step back, pulling the wet fabric of her shirt away from her body before letting it fall back. "I need to change out of this. Do you mind getting the door?"

Elsie made her way across the office and did a quick scan of the hallway making sure it was empty as she pulled the door closed. By the time she'd turned back around, Jones was standing in a sheer black bra wiping a bit of fake blood from her chest with a tissue. Elsie knew she should look away, but she just couldn't make herself do it. Being in Jones' presence was beginning to feel like elaborate torture meant only to wind her up, never to let her crash down.

Jones cleared her throat. By the time Elsie pulled her gaze back to Jones' face, she was met with a knowing smirk.

Jones held eye contact with Elsie as she grabbed the black t-shirt draped over the back of the white couch in her office and swiftly pulled it on. Elsie felt the moment slip away, her racing mind slowed as her ability for logical thought returned.

Elsie cleared her throat. "I still can't believe that you, Jones Haelstrom, revenge-pranked me. I didn't know you had it in you."

"It surprised me too. Benz helped me come up with the idea. It was really fun. Well, and gross. I'm just glad I remembered to pack an extra shirt."

"Well, that makes one of us." Elsie patted her head and wiped a streak of the sticky red substance onto Jones' face.

Jones' mouth popped open in a surprised O. The mischief dancing in her eyes made Elsie wonder what other things she could do to elicit that reaction from Jones.

Elsie laughed. "That kid is absolutely Machiavellian. You'd better be careful."

"You're telling me. The other day he filled one of the bathroom sinks with dirt and worms to save them from the rain."

"Well, that's just good, humanitarian thinking." Elsie looked around the office, glancing at the clock on the wall. "I should probably head out so I can get cleaned up, too. Before rush hour and all that. I can't wait to take the subway like this."

"Oh no, I didn't think about that. I do love you in that spandex, but I worry you'll get arrested. I finally found the keys to Charity's car, so I can drive you. "

Elsie held back a shiver and Jones' eyes trailed over her. "Honestly, this is the least weird thing most people will see on the MTA today. I'll just go throw on my regular clothes. I'll be fine. People will assume I'm artsy."

"No, really, I can wait. I'd feel better knowing you didn't get arrested."

THEY SAT in bumper-to-bumper bridge traffic surrounded by a symphony of horns and expletives. Jones cringed at every loud interruption. Elsie placed a hand on Jones' knee and gave it a gentle squeeze.

Jones looked over at her, a tight smile crossing her lips. "Doesn't the noise of the city bother you?"

Elsie shrugged. "It's kind of just atmosphere, you know. Like if you're in the woods and birds are chirping, or someone's screaming as they're being chased by a bear. Or whatever else happens in the woods. I'm not very outdoorsy."

"I would hope someone screaming would be concerning any time you hear it."

"It depends what prompts it, I guess."

Elsie flicked her eyes to Jones' lips just as traffic started moving again. Jones eased off the break and merged them back into reality. Elsie enjoyed the flush rising on Jones' cheeks like she would the setting sun lighting up the sky. Maybe Jones was imagining a scenario that might elicit a welcomed scream from Elsie.

IT TOOK NEARLY an hour to make it out of downtown and across the bridge to Brooklyn. Jones kept the radio off, so Elsie filled the car with mindless chatter about episode ideas that excited her. Her imagination whirred to life, and each thought was a bit more outlandish than the last. Jones inserted questions that didn't seem perfunctory—asking about various puppets' hair color and how she made her prototypes.

By the time they pulled up in front of Elsie's building, the fake blood had started to dry in her hair and it felt not unlike when her bangs met Elmer's glue in grade school.

Jones didn't unbuckle when she put the car into park. Elsie's fingers itched to shut off the engine and invite Jones to start something else altogether.

"Did you want to come in?" Elsie asked.

Jones laughed, the fake blood near her mouth cracked like a dry face mask. "That depends. Are you hoping to get me high again?"

"Jones Haelstrom, are you not taking responsibility for your own actions? If you need a reminder, there's a pretty great episode in season one of Fangley Heights all about responsibility. Fangley drinks all the blood in the fridge, and then none is left for his red blood velvet cake."

Jones raised her eyebrows. "No, he eats cake that was made with real blood?"

"Well, 'real' like the kind you slathered me in. We didn't rob a blood bank for the episode or anything like that."

"I see."

"So? Thoughts about…" Elsie trailed off.

"Picking up where we left off the other night?" Jones finished.

"Well, there's that. Or we could just spend some time together. If it helps your decision, I can run in and hide the gummy bears as a preventive measure."

Lines formed around Jones' eyes as she threw her head back and laughed, and Elsie had the fleeting thought that she'd like to map them, discover the secrets each wrinkle had to tell.

"I wish I could, really. But I need to get home for Benz. It's movie night."

Elsie's heart rollercoastered from disappointment of missing out on a night with Jones to joy at her mention of doing something fun with Bentley. She wanted that for them. Loving someone was so much more than taking care of them. "Nice! Which movie?"

"It took me forever to find it and I blame you for that. The Brave Little Toaster. He's been talking about it nonstop since the night we had pizza."

"You should have asked me! I would have been happy to lend it to you, along with my absolute tank of a VHS player."

"I can't believe you have a VHS player, let alone a copy of this movie. Were tapes even a thing when you were a kid?"

"Sort of, but not really. I have a brother who's seven years older than me, and growing up, I loved what he loved. Maybe it was hero worship. Though Avery says that I loved what Eric loved in hopes that it would transfer to him loving me."

"I'm sure he loved you."

Something caught in Elsie's throat and she nodded. "Yeah, in his way. Anyway, I have a bunch of movies I can't throw away. So, The Brave Little Toaster? Get ready to fall in love with Blanky."

Jones' brow furrowed and Elsie shot her a reassuring smile. "Yeah. I still can't get over the fact that you have a VHS player."

"For a while I tried to claim it was a better experience, like people who prefer vinyl to streaming music, but really, I'm just sentimental. And I love that little bit of snow on the screen and the crackle before the movie starts. Anyway, I'm rambling. I should let you go."

Jones looked amused. "Do you want to join us? I could wait while you get cleaned up."

Elsie ran her hands through her hair and then glanced down at the fake blood on her palms. *Damn.* "Do you mean it's not okay for me to show up at your house covered in fake blood because it might scare someone? My, how quickly the rules change."

"Okay, I get it." Jones threw up her hands. "I'm sorry I scared you. Back to the movie though, what do you think? I'm sure Bentley would be thrilled to see you before Saturday. And he won't stop talking about a puppet named Wiggins that he helped you with."

"Share his contact with me?" Elsie pulled out her phone

and snapped a selfie, tilting her head down for maximum blood viewing.

Elsie wanted to go home with Jones. Doing something simple like watching a movie with her and Bentley sounded like heaven. She gave herself a minute to imagine the three of them snuggled on the couch.

Elsie thought of all the times she and her brother had watched Muppet Christmas Carol together, laughing at Rizzo and Gonzo as the intrepid storytellers. It was magical. And some part of her knew she didn't want to take that from Bentley. Or Jones. Those were the moments she held onto, even now when things felt tough with her brother. Their lives had become so different since he'd joined the Army and Elsie had chosen something slightly less traditional.

"It sounds amazing, but I think I'm going to sit this one out. You can count me in for next time."

"Okay." Jones nodded slowly. "Next time."

"Just promise you'll make popcorn. And not in the microwave. On the stove. Oh, and mix in chocolate chips."

"Chocolate chips?"

"It's the only way. Salty and sweet." Elsie unbuckled her seat belt and opened the door. "Oh, and tell me all the parts you two laugh at."

Jones laughed. "Can you text me all that so I remember? You have some very serious feelings about popcorn."

Elsie leaned over the console slowly, holding Jones' gaze. "What can I say? I'm a passionate person. I really want to kiss you, even though I look like a mess."

"I was hoping you might. And it's my mess."

"Well, I can definitely handle being your mess." Elsie winked and closed the distance between them until their lips brushed softly. She pushed her own hair back before reaching to cup Jones' face gently.

When she pulled away, Jones' mouth chased hers and Elsie gave her one last quick kiss. "Enjoy the movie."

Jones' eyes narrowed as she brought her fingers up to brush her cheek where Elsie had just touched. They came away streaked red. She shook her head at Elsie, even as a smile played at her lips.

Elsie wanted to lean forward and kiss her again.

"That was both good and evil. I can't believe the blood still isn't completely dry."

"I told you, salty and sweet. The best combination."

"What if I get pulled over? The police will think I'm running from a crime scene."

Elsie widened her eyes and gave Jones her best innocent smile. "Just explain the situation."

Jones glanced at her face in the rearview mirror, grimacing. "I actually think that would make it worse."

"Huh. I guess you should drive carefully then. And text me when you get home, so I know I don't have to bail you out. In the meantime, I'll check the couch for loose cash, just in case."

Elsie stepped out of the car and eased the door shut. She felt Jones' eyes on her all the way to the stoop.

CHAPTER EIGHTEEN
JONES

Jones pulled up in front of the brownstone. Resisting looking at her phone to see what Elsie had texted her had been torture, but through sheer willpower she'd persevered. She fumbled it as she took it out of the holder. It thudded as it hit the floor. The plastic of the console hurt her arm as she snaked it between the seats in her desperate search. Somewhere in the black lagoon of the car's depths, her phone pinged again. Jones leaned more to the left, and finally her fingers glanced over smooth glass.

After she completed the successful rescue mission, Jones gripped the rogue device with both hands and opened her messages.

In the picture, two pennies, a cheerio, and what Jones hoped was lint were resting in Elsie's palm.

Elsie: *Oscar has already claimed the Cheerio (RIP), but the rest is going straight to your bail fund.*

Jones: *That's too bad, vintage Cheerios are going for a lot of money these days.*

Elsie: *I would never encourage anyone to sue a dog for theft,* but…

Elsie: *You made it home okay?*

Jones: *I did.*

Elsie: *Great—enjoy the movie, don't forget to silence your devices.*

Jones set her phone to airplane mode and made her way inside. She got to work on the popcorn while Susan fed Bentley dinner. Well, first she Googled how to make popcorn on the stove, and when that didn't make much sense, she asked Susan.

Staring at the kernels in the pot gave her plenty of time to process the afternoon. Pranking Elsie had been more fun than she could have imagined. Jones had been nervous that she was abusing her power by summoning Elsie, but once she'd had the idea she couldn't resist. Plus, the fake blood didn't put the company in half the jeopardy that a kiss in her office would; even though there were multiple times Jones had almost closed the distance between them.

She'd been thinking about kissing Elsie ever since they'd been interrupted the other night. Jones knew that in her new reality, Bentley always needed to be her first priority. Her brain understood that but her libido had been slow to catch up. And just maybe her life was expansive enough for two top priorities.

Jones shook the pot of popcorn on the stove, the first kernels bursting like fireworks against the dome of the lid.

The look of shock and delight on Elsie's face as Jones had smeared the fake blood into her hair had been its own gift. A small part of Jones worried that by striking back, she'd start an endless battle. The fact that she could imagine future pranks with Elsie made her flush. The idea of Elsie and the future was glowing so bright in her chest, she knew she couldn't reach for it without getting burned.

Jones hissed as she took the lid off the pot and pieces of popcorn leapt out. She'd have to hunt for them later. Bentley was already settled on the couch in his pajamas. She dressed the popcorn with butter, salt, and one shake of chocolate chips. The idea still seemed dubious.

She made her way to the living room and settled in next to Bentley. She hit play, and as the static cleared and the opening credits rolled, Bentley pressed into her side. Her heart felt as precariously full as the bowl of popcorn on her lap. She lifted her arm carefully so he could snuggle against her. Melted chocolate and salt clung to his fingers, but she'd given up asking him to wipe them despite the white couch. Anyone with kids who purchased a white couch gets what's coming to them.

Her thoughts kept drifting back to the afternoon. She'd had fun at work; she'd done something silly and so unlike herself, and afterward she'd felt almost buoyant. But not out of control. Even as a kid she'd been vigilant against feeling uninhibited. So many times it had been a harbinger of the high before the crash. It wasn't that she feared happiness, exactly. She feared unbridled joy because it was almost always false. And it was heartbreaking that something that felt so good, if a little wild, only indicated the depression that would soon take hold.

So she'd come to view a desire to be silly as a sign that something was off. Safety was feeling measured, calm, in control. But today, she'd felt giddy anticipation, waiting for Elsie in her office, like a balloon ready to take to the sky. She hadn't felt shame afterward, or regret, just a floating lightness. The way Elsie had laughed and looked at Jones like she was proud of her, didn't leave any room in her brain for doubt. Elsie had made a career of not taking things too seriously, of weaving fun and wonder into her daily life. Jones had seen it when she'd talked about her new ideas in the car earlier and when she'd made sock puppets with the kids at the party.

Maybe taking things less seriously was a goal worth aspiring to.

Jones was beginning to wonder if she'd spent so long keeping herself contained for nothing. Maybe with someone who embraced it, letting go wasn't the worst thing in the world; wasn't something that would pull apart her life at the seams.

Bentley let out a soft snore, bringing Jones' focus back to the living room. He was fully slumped against her, his breathing deep and even. She thought about shutting off the movie; it really was more for Bentley than her. But as an adorable electric blanket and intrepid vacuum filled the screen, she found herself reaching for the bowl of popcorn and savoring both the salty and the sweet.

JONES WAS STILL FEELING FORTIFIED the next morning, after she dropped Bentley off at school with the promise that Susan would be there to pick him up later. She'd planned on going into the office, but when she stopped and thought about it she realized that she didn't have any work she needed to take care of there. Her father's team ran all of the day-to-day, which made Jones wonder, not for the first time, how he'd filled his hours.

After parking back at the house and retrieving the book she was reading—the six-hundred page hard back that was to blame for both her eye and wrist strain—she threw it in her big leather purse anyway and set out to explore. She wanted this neighborhood to feel like hers, and the best way to do that was by walking all day and mapping it herself.

The longer Jones went without hearing from Charity—it had been weeks without a word or response—the more she started to think of New York as a kind of home. One Jones wasn't sure she'd want to leave even when the circumstance with Bentley stopped keeping her there.

She passed groups of cute dogs dragging harried dog walkers behind them and many more people than she would have expected for late morning on a weekday. Maybe most people didn't have regular office jobs anymore. She picked up a Rainbow Cookie Italian Ice from Frank's and made her way to the park.

As the cream ice melted to milkshake consistency, Jones tried to focus her attention on the words on the page. She was about halfway through the biography on Judy Garland she'd been reading and the past few chapters had been a bit of a slog. Now the dense paragraphs seemed interminable as excitement pinged through her mind like flies against the inside of the glass. She felt desperate for something to happen but she wasn't sure what. Finally, she closed the book with a satisfying snap and pulled out her phone.

She sent Elsie a message, knowing she was probably working, but maybe instead of bothering her, it would just be something nice for her to find on a break. Like sneaking a note into a lunchbox.

Jones: *Your popcorn hack was a big success.*

Elsie's response popped up right away.

Elsie: *So good, right?*

Jones smiled and laid back on the grass, one hand behind her head. She ignored her anxiety about grass stains and absolutely refused to consider the possibility of other stains. Instead, she focused on the warmth of the sun on her face.

Jones: *I think I ate more than Bentley did. Are you filming today?*

Elsie: *We're supposed to be but Trey had an appointment and is running late. I suspect he stopped for some sort of elaborate coffee. You know what they say, the sun never sets on the Midtown Starbucks line. Are you in your office? Want to sneak out and spend three hours waiting for a cappuccino?*

Jones felt a brief flutter of anxiety in her chest, wings tapping against glass. Days could be valuable without work. Fun was valuable.

Jones: *Tempting. Unfortunately I am laying in the park right now.*

She snapped a picture of her Italian ice cup and sent it along with her message.

Elsie sent a heart emoji, followed by a dagger and a broken heart.

Elsie: *That's shorthand for betrayal, by the way*

Jones: *If you were here, I would have gotten you one.*

Elsie: *Well, if you'd told me you were going I would have blown off work to be there.*

Jones: *Hey, don't blow off work!*

Elsie sent back a selfie, she was wearing her black catsuit and sticking her tongue out. In the background of the empty studio, Rebecca stood in the far corner looking at something on her phone.

Elsie: *You're right. I definitely don't want to miss this. Time is money, etcetera*

Jones: *Exactly.*

Her laugh was loud in the nearly empty park, and a woman pushing a stroller looked over at her as she walked by. *Don't mind me all alone grinning at my phone,* Jones thought. *I'm just experiencing something like happiness.*

Elsie: *Okay, I've thought of how you can make it up to me. But it won't be easy*

Jones: *I'm listening. Or, well, reading.*

Elsie: *Thanks for clarifying*

Three dots appeared, and a second later, Elsie sent a wink face, before dots appeared again. They came and went on the screen until Jones' anticipation had her hopping up from the ground and pacing.

Elsie: *How do you feel about roller skating?*

Jones: *Slightly terrified but open to it.*

Elsie: *I can work with that. Send me your shoe size and your next availability for a free evening. I would offer an afternoon, but I'm not sure I could get the time off work*

Jones: *Let's plan for Friday. Do you have any recommendations for puppets? Bentley's been asking for one like Fangley.*

Elsie: *Always. Does he want me to make him one?*

Jones: *I'm sure he'd love that but I was thinking I'd check out a toy store too. Maybe Leap Frog. Do you need anything?*

Elsie: *That's a good store. Don't buy a Fangley puppet, I'll make him a real one, but they should have other monster puppets to choose from*

Jones remembered Elsie's strong feelings about the Fangley toy puppets at stores. It was sweet that she was willing to make Benz an original.

Jones: *Okay, I'll pick you out something as a thank you, any ideas?*

Elsie: *Surprise me*

JONES' arms went numb as she carried the bags back home. So, she'd gone a little overboard in the toy store. She'd even found a puppet making set. It was probably much more rudimentary than what Elsie used, but Jones thought it could be fun for her and Bentley to do. Maybe they could make the Wiggins puppet he wouldn't stop talking about and give it to Elsie.

While she was out, she'd pulled a few strings and arranged a sleepover for Bentley on Friday.

BY THE TIME she stepped off at Elsie's subway stop two days later, her limbs were buzzing with excitement. The skirt of her dress flitted around her knees. Maybe not the most practical roller skating outfit. But if Jones was going to make a fool of herself in front of Elsie, which was *highly* likely, she was going to look hot enough to cancel that out.

Elsie was waiting out on the sidewalk in front of her

building talking to someone about her age. Jones paused a few feet away and waited for a natural break in their conversation. She wasn't trying to eavesdrop, but she wasn't trying not to either. She was Birdie's daughter after all.

"Avery, you're not invited because it's a date."

"Do you think *she* knows it's a date?"

Elsie sighed so loudly, the sound made its way to Jones, and she took that as her cue to interrupt.

"I did know it was a date, actually. I don't agree to go roller skating with just anyone."

Elsie's face lit up as her eyes traced a smoldering path down Jones' body. "I thought you didn't agree to go roller skating at all."

"Same thing. Am I late?" Jones leaned in to give Elsie a hug then lingered close; she smelled like pineapple, fresh and happy.

"Not at all. You can't really be late for roller skating at the park. You are, however, dressed inappropriately."

Jones looked down at her light-weight black dress. And then she took in Elsie's very short jean shorts and striped knee-high socks. The kind of socks that made Jones think of all the places Elsie's legs would look great draped over. She did her best to swallow down her desire. "This is very easy to move in."

Elsie's eyes flashed, and the reaction was so brief that Jones might have missed it if she'd been able to look anywhere else. "Good to know."

The person next to Elsie cleared their throat.

"Right, sorry. Jones, this is Avery, my roommate and best person. Avery, this is Jones, my…" As Elsie trailed off her cheeks flushed pink.

"Just Jones," she interjected, jumping in before Elsie fell off the verbal tightrope she was walking. "Nice to meet you, Avery. I've heard a lot about you. Is it really okay for me to use your skates?"

"Oh yeah, I've only tried them once, and it was kind of a disaster, because *someone* was too busy making puppets with children to catch me when I fell." Avery winked and swept their hair back from their face.

Jones grimaced. "Sorry about that. Though she did save the birthday with those sock puppets. Do you want to come skating?"

Avery laughed. "Thank you for offering! I was giving Elsie a hard time but I actually have a date tonight."

"Hey!" Elsie glared at them. "If you have a date tonight, why were you making me feel bad for not inviting you?"

"I'm not responsible for how you feel." Avery crossed their arms. "I just thought it would have been nice to be invited. Plus giving you a hard time is my gold medal sport."

Jones felt like she was watching ping pong with the speed of their verbal volleys.

Elsie widened her eyes at Avery. "You're a little responsible for how I feel after—"

Avery made a show of glancing at their bare wrist. "Look at the time! I should probably get going. Make sure she catches you." Avery smiled at Jones before narrowing their eyes at Elsie. "Text you later, Els."

THEY WALKED the few blocks to the park, then found a bench. Jones sat and loosened the laces on her skates but Elsie held up her hand.

"Those socks are way too thin."

Before Jones could fully register what was happening, Elsie was kneeling before her and rummaging in her bag. She pulled out a pair of purple tie-dye socks triumphantly. She handed them to Jones but stayed kneeling in front of her. It was hard to focus with Elsie on her knees like that, when all Jones had been thinking about was...how tonight would hopefully lead them back to this position with fewer dogs and strangers around.

"So do you want to put them on?"

Jones started. "Oh, right, of course."

She pulled the purple socks all the way up to just above her knees. Elsie adjusted each one, the light touch of her fingers ghosting across the back of Jones' knee. She drew in a sharp breath. Elsie drew back and smiled before reaching forward and gently grasping Jones' right foot. "Is it okay if I help with your skates? It can be a little tricky to get the laces right."

Elsie caring for her was kindling a soft glow in Jones' chest. It was simple, adjusting laces, bringing socks. But it was more than that—Elsie had thought ahead, thought about her. Jones felt like she was living in some sort of Brooklyn fairytale, where she was about to be gifted with a glass skate and a key to the meticulously distressed dive bar down the block. She laughed at the thought, which she only realized when Elsie's brows furrowed.

"Sorry, help would be great. I was just thinking that you're like the Prince Charming of Crown Heights."

"*Finally.* I've been waiting years for someone to greet me with my proper title." Elsie gave a mock bow before reaching for the skate and easing it onto Jones' foot. "Let's get going before we lose the sun and you turn into a pumpkin."

"I thought only the carriage turned into a pumpkin."

"Fine, if you're willing to risk pumpkin feet, so be it."

Elsie's fingers wrapped around hers, and she let herself be pulled from the bench. Elsie leaned forward and put a wireless earbud in Jones' ear before stepping back and placing the other one in her own ear. Then she fiddled with her phone.

"I made us a Friday Night at Hot Skates playlist. I hope you like 90s boy bands."

Jones laughed. "I mean who doesn't?" Every little thing

Elsie did amazed her. Jones felt a bit guilty that she hadn't expected Elsie to plan or to have things so…together.

"Exactly. Ready?"

When Elsie started to pull away, Jones interlaced their fingers again. "I think I'm going to be pretty bad at this."

Elsie smiled. "Doing things you're bad at is the best."

Jones gave Elsie a questioning look. "I don't understand."

"Because there are no expectations—you get to surprise yourself." Elsie was grinning with conviction. "That's how I feel when I'm writing scenes, a rush of surprised pride that my brain could create something so strange and magical."

BY THE TIME they got back to Elsie's apartment, Jones had a skinned knee, her shins were filled with molten lava, and she felt very, very happy. She was humming a song from Elsie's playlist, the one Elsie had serenaded her with—something about tearing up her heart.

While Elsie took Oscar out, Jones wandered to the dark living room. She ran her hand up the lamp until she found the switch, bathing the couch in a soft glow.

The door rattled, and she turned to watch Elsie walk in, her hips swaying in her tiny jean shorts. Jones' mouth went dry. She tried to swallow then coughed a bit instead.

"I'll get us some water. Can you stay for a bit?"

"Yeah, I can stay as long as you want me to." Jones' cheeks flushed, her mind speed skating through her thoughts. She tried not to trip over how much she wanted Elsie.

Though so far that evening, tripping hadn't been a total bust. Earlier, Jones' skate had hit a rock propelling her sideways and into Elsie's arms. There in the park their bodies were flush together just for a few seconds, but even now she could feel Elsie everywhere—arms tight around her waist, the warmth of her chest as Jones leaned to catch her breath.

Elsie returned with her water, and it was all Jones could

do to take a quick gulp before she was moving toward Elsie, bringing their lips together and walking her back toward the couch. "I was hoping to finish what we started the other night."

Elsie's fingers grazed her hips then ran under the hem of her dress. It had definitely been the right call to wear it.

Jones brought her hands to Elsie's ass and squeezed. She broke their kiss and whispered, "I've been wanting to do that all night. Those shorts are not fair."

"I wasn't aware we were playing fair." Elsie leaned forward, and Jones shivered in anticipation of soft lips on her neck. Instead she felt the sharp sting of Elsie nipping her ear.

"I've been wanting your legs thrown over my shoulders. And I want you to keep those ridiculous socks on."

"Interesting. Isn't keeping my socks on breaking a cardinal rule of sex?"

"Not my rules. Not when you look like that. Besides, I don't think we're going to make it to bed." Jones walked forward, her body pressing into Elsie until she gave way and fell back on the couch.

She wasn't used to being so bold, and she half wanted to ask Elsie how she was doing. But she liked this feeling she had with Elsie, like maybe she'd be bad at it, but she was more likely to surprise herself. And tonight she wanted to surprise them both.

"In my head I was planning to kneel, but I'm not sure my skinned knee would forgive me."

Elsie's eyes opened wide. "I'm so sorry. I forgot about your scrape—let me go get stuff to clean it."

"No."

"No?"

"Maybe later. Lay back."

Elsie complied, turning her body so her head came to rest on the arm of the couch. Across the room, Jones could hear Oscar's slight snoring on his bed, but she was getting better at focusing with distractions. Jones slid her hands up from Elsie's knees, over her thighs, until her fingertips slid under the frayed hem of Elsie's shorts. She skimmed below the pockets that were just poking out from beneath the frayed edges, until she reached the hem of Elsie's underwear. When Elsie's hips lifted, all the anxiety left Jones' mind. She reached for the buttons and pulled them open quickly, enjoying the soft sound they made. She hadn't thought about button fly jeans in a long time and was suddenly deeply grateful for them. What a perfect innovation. Or was it a throwback to the original design? Jones could research that later.

She slid the scraps of fabric down until Elsie was able to kick her feet and fling them somewhere. Jones knelt between Elsie's legs. She felt the heat of Elsie's sex on her own thighs.

"Come here," Elsie whispered.

Jones crawled up her body, hovering above her until Elsie threaded her fingers into Jones' hair and pulled her down roughly. Elsie's hips pressed up into Jones and desire flooded her.

"So, my legs slung over your shoulders, huh?" Elsie raised an eyebrow.

Jones wished her glass of water was closer by. Her own confidence felt like borrowed skates she was trying to remain upright on, whereas Elsie had the natural ease of perfect balance.

"Mmhmm." Jones got out at last.

"Show me."

Jones kissed her again, running her tongue along Elsie's lips before pushing inside. Elsie met her kiss and deepened it. She pushed up Elsie's shirt and started to make her way down her body. Pausing to kiss her breasts, pulling a nipple into her mouth through the thin fabric of Elsie's bra. It was neon pink and see-through, and Jones felt a bit self-conscious of her own plain black set.

She pushed the thought from her mind as she pressed

open mouthed kisses to Elsie's stomach and then the sharp planes of her hips. Her body was so unlike Jones'. Elsie's stomach was taut while Jones' had softened. She loved her body, but Elsie's felt like something she wanted to worship. And so she did. She used her free hand to slide Elsie's underwear down and eased herself between her legs.

Elsie adjusted the pillow beneath her head.

"Comfortable?"

"I want to watch you."

The pulsing between Jones' thighs became insistent. She kissed the inside of Elsie's hip, right where her leg met her sex and then slid Elsie's knee over her shoulder. Elsie's sock-clad foot rested on Jones' back. Elsie bent her leg to pull Jones in, and she took her cue.

Jones used the tip of her tongue to part Elsie's folds. Her mouth brushed against Elsie's clit and she reveled in the way her hips jumped slightly at the contact.

"You're so wet," Jones mumbled.

"Yes, well, someone very sexy was telling me all the things they've been wanting to do to me."

"She sounds great. And very smart. Maybe a genius." Jones ran her tongue from Elsie's opening back to her clit and focused her attention on drawing ever tightening circles around it. Elsie's hands tangled in Jones' hair, putting a slight pressure on the back of Jones' head. Jones smiled against her and pulled Elsie's clit between her lips and sucked gently.

"Fuck Jones," Elsie managed between gasps. Gasps that spurred Jones on.

Elsie's incoherence gave her a thrill of encouragement, a little reminder that she knew what she was doing after all. Sex was muscle memory, just like riding, well, a woman.

"Tell me what you want, Els."

"Inside. I need you inside," Elsie said on a sigh.

She looked up at Elsie, still sucking gently on her clit and danced her fingers down, dipping one into her and then another. Elsie's hips bucked and Jones found a rhythm, curling her fingers each time she came close to pulling out, and when she did Elsie let out a slight whimper between her moans.

"Fuck, Jones. Don't stop. I'm going to—"

Elsie's gentle grip on Jones' hair turned into fists pulling frantically. It was just the right side of painful to send Jones' own wetness rushing to her awareness. She shifted, pressing her thighs together to relieve some of the mounting pressure. All it did was make her want more. More of Elsie, more of whatever it was they were doing. Below her, Elsie's muscles went taut and she stilled, her walls gripping Jones' fingers as she pressed herself against Jones' mouth.

"Fuck," Elsie said between gasps.

Jones stilled her tongue but kept steady pressure on Elsie's clit as she came back down from her orgasm.

When Elsie's breathing evened out, she shifted up onto her elbows. Her green eyes gazing down at Jones. "Come back now, please."

Jones pulled away just enough to nip the inside of Elsie's thigh before settling into her outstretched arms. Elsie cupped her chin and kissed Jones deeply. Jones opened her mouth when Elsie's tongue ran insistently along her bottom lip.

When their mouths broke contact, Jones noticed the faintest dimple on Elsie's left cheek. "I could get used to this," she mumbled, pressing her forehead against Jones' shoulder.

"What?" Jones kissed the top of her head, breathing in the pineapple scent of her shampoo.

"The taste of me on you."

CHAPTER NINETEEN
ELSIE

The body on top of Elsie's stirred, and she spent a few moments before opening her eyes to remember the night before. Jones had fucked her on the couch and then again in her bed, both times she'd had her socks on. She would forevermore consider them lucky. Jones seemed different the past few days, more relaxed, like she wasn't sitting on the edge of her seat, ready to bolt at the first chance she got. She was still the same person but it was like her personality had gotten a massage. She laughed freely, even when she'd fallen while skating.

Elsie's heart had plummeted when Jones' skate hit a dip in the path and she stumbled forward, releasing her grip on Elsie's hand. She had held Jones' injured knee between her palms, wishing she'd remembered safety gear. Wishing she would have bought safety gear, actually. All Elsie could think as she was clearing away the small rocks from the cut, was that Jones needed to be spared any pain. Elsie much preferred the unsteady skating moments when Jones stumbled into her arms.

Though her performance later in the night made Elsie think Jones wasn't too bothered by her skinned knee. And last night was a masterpiece. Jones, a maestro whose fingers deftly shifted from fast to slow and back again, Elsie's body alive with every note. When her body had tensed, readying itself to leap over the edge, Jones' fingers had slowed, becoming deliciously deliberate.

Elsie had asked. And then she'd begged. But Jones just hummed kisses against Elsie's neck, whispering, 'be patient, you'll like it'.

When Elsie's moans turned to gasps and then to noises she didn't recognize from herself, Jones picked up the pace of her fingers again.

Elsie's nails dug into her shoulder followed by the soft percussion of Jones' sharp inhale.

When she came at last, the sensation didn't burst like a firework that was there one moment and gone the next, leaving only smoke behind. The orgasm Jones conducted was more like a comet trailing slowly across the sky. Elsie traced the arc of it. Shooting stars might be things you wished on, but comets were worth remembering.

All Elsie had managed was a choked 'keep fucking me— don't let me come down.' And Jones had done as she was told.

AFTER ROUND THREE OR FOUR, Elsie had dragged Jones into the shower and kneeled before her. She'd gingerly washed Jones' cut before not so gingerly going down on her from that position. Or staying down, since she hadn't had to go anywhere.

Her hair had been full of shampoo and Jones' fingers had threaded into the long strands, moving gently. Elsie wasn't sure she'd ever gotten a head massage while giving head before, but she'd never be able to go to the hair salon again without thinking of Jones' hands on her.

Elsie's thoughts returned to the present as Jones rolled off of her and Elsie suppressed a whine. All she wanted was to be pressed back down under Jones' warm weight. The lightness of Elsie's body felt disorienting, like the room had lost gravity without the anchor of Jones. *Surely there was a metaphor there for a suppressed desire to be held down. To be less flighty. To be the kind of person friends called in a crisis.*

She reached to pull Jones back to her, but Jones was already getting out of bed. She stretched her arms over her head, and Elsie took in the most glorious morning view she'd ever seen. Jones' blonde hair was sleep-wild as she raked it back from her face, and her body was bare, just a few scattered freckles and the faintest spider web of stretch marks above her hips. Elsie had kissed those marks last night, let her tongue map them as Jones writhed on her fingers.

"Come back to bed." Elsie pulled the sheets up over her chest, her bare skin growing cold in the absence of Jones' warmth.

Jones leaned over the bed and kissed her. "I wish I could. I have to pick up Benz and get him ready for his fencing thing."

"Fencing thing? Is that the official term?"

Jones smiled. "Mmhmm."

"Rich people are so fancy."

"It's a burden, to be sure. Are you still coming?"

"Of course, I'd never miss an opportunity to see kindergartners duel."

"Right." Jones laughed. "If you're free after, maybe you could come for dinner?"

"That sounds perfect." Elsie raised herself up on her elbows. "Do you want breakfast?"

"Sure, I'm going to run to the bathroom."

Elsie hopped up and dashed to the kitchen, returning a few minutes later with food just as Jones finished pulling on her dress.

"Et voila." Elsie held out the paper-towel-wrapped bundle dramatically.

"Thank you." Jones took it gingerly. "What is this?"

"A balanced meal. Pop-Tarts, strawberry, of course, topped with peanut butter."

Jones laughed. "I haven't thought about Pop-Tarts in forever. Thank you. Benz would be jealous. Maybe next time I can make you breakfast."

Elsie's heart sped up at those two magic words: next time.

THE FENCING *thing* wasn't at a rec center or high school gym as Elsie had expected and dressed for. She wondered if she could borrow a blazer to dress up her jeans and shirt. She passed three men in salmon-colored polos before she reached the main hall in the country club. She hadn't been aware any of the Burroughs *had* a country club. She imagined Fangley and Ratatouille sneaking in here, posing as waiters for some very fancy gala, and ruining everyone's carefully constructed life by chasing a rat across the dining room.

The great hall had gleaming wood floors unmarred by sneaker scuffs, and a vaulted pine ceiling that felt almost Scandinavian. She half expected to find saunas nearby. After a few minutes, she spotted Jones standing next to Benz, who was dressed all in white like a little mummy. He was slicing the air with his sword, in flagrant violation of probably a dozen safety codes. The sword was thin and flimsy, when he jabbed it into the ground it bowed slightly before snapping back into shape. She was fairly sure that it was called a foil, based on the Wikipedia article she'd read in the car on the way over.

Bentley ran to Elsie as she approached, dropping his sword and throwing his arms around her legs. She'd expected his outfit to be canvas but it felt more like some kind of high tech armor. "Ready for the wars, buddy?"

"Yup!" Bentley was already running back to the cavalry of

other kids who were also dangerously armed. Though, she'd take her chances with them over the rows of nearly identical parents who appeared to have traveled there fresh from a photo shoot for *Yacht Life Magazine*. Their topsiders squeaking like dog toys against the polished wood floor—broad navy and white stripes should be limited to maritime activities—wearing them this far from the ocean should set off some alarm, like an ankle monitor, and they should immediately be pushed into the nearest body of water, even if you had to fill a kiddie pool to do it.

Other kids filtered in and Elsie recognized a few from Bentley's party. The warm greetings she received made her feel like a very niche celebrity, which she kind of was.

Once she got past the wall of white jeans, Elsie spotted Jones sitting on a rough-hewn pine bench. She wasn't aware that rec centers were built like Swedish spas, but rich people did love luxury wood. Why cut down a forest here at home when you could increase the devastation by shipping lumber half-way around the world?

Jones looked wholesome in her oatmeal colored sweater and dark jeans. Elsie made her way over slowly, taking time to savor how lucky she was to be the person Jones was expecting.

Elsie took a seat on the bench and bumped her shoulder into Jones in greeting.

She watched the flush on Jones' face creep slowly toward her ears.

"Stop looking at me like that," Jones whispered.

"Like what?"

"Like you're seeing me naked."

"Okay." Elsie slid so close to Jones that their shoulders brushed together. "But the last time I saw you, you *were* naked. My mind needs time to adjust."

Jones shook her head but she was smiling. "I'm glad you made it."

"Mmhmm. I'm worried I'm not sartorially appropriate—I didn't realize the dress code was *yacht casual* for this event."

Jones squeezed Elsie's thigh, her fingers grazing bare skin through the rip in her jeans. A tasteful rip, thank you very much. One that the manufacturing company thought increased the value of these pants by a full twenty dollars. "I guess we both wanted to be brave and go for a pattern."

Elsie was wearing a patterned button down shirt that she'd stolen from Avery. It was navy blue with outlines of pink brontosauruses.

She glanced at Jones' sweater. "Cable knit isn't a pattern, Jonesy."

"What did you call me?"

"Shh, I think they're starting. Ready to watch some kids poke each other in the butt?"

"I just hope he doesn't get hurt."

"Hey, it's okay." Elsie rested her hand briefly on Jones' knee. "He's going to totally poke some butt out there."

"What?"

"You know, like kick."

"Okay, I'm cutting you off from butt jokes for the rest of the day."

"Harsh but fair."

Two kids walked to the center circle and gave each other formal bows before drawing their swords. Bentley was up third so they suffered through parents foaming at the mouth while kids treated their swords like pool noodles. The ref, for his part, treated it with the grace of a rec team soccer coach, just waiting for the orange slices to be brought out.

Elsie was surprised with how seriously Bentley seemed to take his bout. He shuffled his feet and struck out with precision. It was honestly a little unsettling.

"You should hide the knives," she whispered in Jones' ear.

Jones' hand found the rip in her jeans again, and Elsie's heart rapped. She hadn't expected these easy touches. She sensed Jones was vigilant in all situations, not even brushing by someone in an elevator.

WHEN THE RINGLEADER had had enough, he seemed to randomly pick a winner. Bentley grinned as his arm was pulled up into the air. The decision was immediately disputed by a woman in heels so sharp they were ice picking the wood. She advocated for her son to get a higher score, while her son did an impressive barrel roll off the mat and headed for the snack table.

Bentley followed and picked up a small treat. Elsie leaned into Jones.

"Are those cucumber sandwiches? For children?"

"Vegetables are good, right?"

"Wait, did you bring those sandwiches?"

Jones shoved her shoulder, and Elsie tipped sideways at the unexpected contact. "No, I brought orange slices."

"That kid is eating with his pinkie extended. I think we need to get out of here before they Stepford us."

A mane of blonde hair leaned between them interrupting their conversation. The gold strands sparking against Elsie's shirt. Elsie turned to look at the face attached to the French manicure gripping her shoulder, and her cheek brushed the stranger's. She was one thousand percent too close. The woman's face was one she'd never be able to pick out of a Ralph Lauren line up.

"Are you Bentley's moms? We're used to seeing Susan."

Susan? As in Bentley's nanny? Elsie felt a pang of sympathy for Bentley. If her mom had felt up to it, she would come to every single thing Elsie did. Even the high school plays where she only helped with set design or was on tech crew doing lighting.

"Oh no, we're not." Jones' eyes had gone wide. "I'm his sister and Elsie's…his biggest fan." Jones' voice was brimming with false cheer like she was trying to talk someone out of giving her a ticket before flipping them off behind their back.

A palm trailed possessively to Elsie's lower back. She turned to give Jones a reassuring smile as she savored the touch, but she noticed Jones' hands folded in her lap. A nail trailed along Elsie's spine, and she jerked away. Turning to glare at the woman. *What the hell was going on?*

With the way the woman behind them had her hand on Elsie's lower back, she didn't seem to be the queer police.

Elsie gave the woman a polite smile and scooted forward. The woman's eyes flicked to Elsie's mouth in such an exaggerated way, it was like a cartoon gesture. She should use it for the show.

This woman and her husband were probably in the market for a unicorn. She wasn't in stripes, at least. That was a bridge too far.

Jones wrapped an arm around Elsie and pulled her close. Elsie almost missed the look Jones shot the woman and she reveled in the glow of Jones' affection. She felt safe and wanted; and more than a little smug.

Elsie knew she wasn't Bentley's parent but it still stung how quick Jones had been to deny it. Which was ridiculous. Elsie was starting to feel like Bentley was hers, in the same way she loved Fangley, a sort of fierce protectiveness mixed with wonder and hope for the future. It didn't hurt that Benz was also hilarious and always up for a caper. If only she could place him in a clear case to keep him safe between shenanigans.

When Elsie turned back to the mat, the second bout was in full swing. Bentley was on the ground and Jones was already on her feet. Elsie caught her wrist even though her own heart was in her throat. Would it be inappropriate to snap the other kid's sword over her knee like a stick? Maybe not appropriate but pretty funny. She imagined it bending and snapping back into place, the medieval equivalent of a trick candle.

"Give him a second." Elsie could feel Jones' pulse beneath her fingertips. "Did you see what happened?"

"That little sociopath hit Bentley in the face. He almost skewered his eye." Jones' voice shook a bit.

"Hey!" A woman shot off the bench from the row behind them. "That little sociopath has a name, and it's Bradson."

Elsie turned to the woman, even her nails looked expensive where they dug into her palms. "Sorry, do his friends call him Bradson or does he prefer Brad the Impaler?"

The woman let out a huff and sat back down.

Jones' soft chuckle tickled Elsie's ear. "Thanks for that. I never know how to deal with insufferable people."

"Oh really? I much prefer confrontation to that woman who hit on me. Thanks for shutting her down. Hey, look." Elsie nodded to the mat where Bentley got to his feet to a subdued round of golf claps. He stumbled a bit but whether from being knocked down or the stiff white suit he was wearing was unclear.

The ref raised Benz's arm in victory and when he slid up his helmet he was grinning. Elsie hadn't realized he could smile so big.

CHAPTER TWENTY
JONES

Jones had underestimated the power of a six-year-old wingman. Before they'd even made it to the exit, Bentley had persuaded Elsie to come home with them. He rattled off an increasingly intricate series of plans that lined up like dominoes promising to cascade late into the evening. Elsie declined a duel but agreed to working on "their TV show" together before dinner, which they negotiated would be dinosaur shaped chicken nuggets and broccoli.

Jones got the front door open, and Bentley rushed into the house, kneecapping her in the process with his épée—a word she and Elsie learned an hour ago from a pretty rude woman.

Bentley turned, calling after Elsie to meet him in the living room before skittering up the stairs.

"Sorry," Elsie whispered. "Is this okay? I didn't mean to invite myself over."

"You didn't; Bentley did." Jones bumped Elsie with her hip. "And I'm glad you're here. You should probably get in there before—"

Bentley called instructions from the top of the stairs, and Elsie snapped to attention, her eyes widening. "I don't want to keep the genius waiting. We'll try not to destroy too much to make our puppets."

Jones laughed but Elsie's face stayed serious. "Why would you destroy things? Just use the puppet making set I got at Leap Frog the other day."

"Okay, we'll use that as a base." Elsie grinned and kissed Jones on the cheek. "And don't worry, I almost never need to destroy things to make puppets."

"How frequently is 'almost never'?" Jones asked.

Elsie shrugged.

She loved Elsie's serious face. Jones had never met anyone who took fun as seriously as Elsie. Fun was her mission each day, her reason for being. Joy glowed within Elsie and it elevated everything around her. "Okay, just don't ruin anything essential, like the fridge or my shoes."

"Got it. We'll raid your closet but leave your shoes alone."

And just like that, Jones was left with a shoulder squeeze as Elsie dashed up the stairs after Bentley. Maybe she'd read a book.

LAUGHTER FILLED the house as Jones sat at the table looking up recipes to pitch to Bentley for the week ahead. When she finished, she wandered into the living room to see what the creative minds were up to, but the vibe shifted when she crossed the threshold, like an unexpected wind sweeping through a nice day—heads lowered and voices turned to whispers. It was strange to be both happy about something and a little hurt by it.

Back at the kitchen table she opened the autobiography she was slowly working her way through. The Judy Garland bio she'd finished a few days ago had delivered on drama and devastation. Maybe that was the secret; If you wanted your story to be interesting, it was better to let someone else tell it. So far this new book was about as exciting as waiting in line at the DMV. A weird concept, the DMV, so much red tape and waiting to do something you didn't want to do in the first place, like it was confusing itself with Space Mountain.

Her phone pinged, and she let out a sigh as she lifted her eyes from the page. One paragraph in and she was feeling drowsy. Pharmacies should sell this book next to the bottles of melatonin.

Elsie: *Wish you were here—Benz wants to surprise you with a show before dinner*

Jones: *Oh, whew, I thought I was too uncool to join the creature feature.*

Elsie: *Remove the 'un' and you're on the mark. Curtains at 6:30, black tie optional*

She glanced at the time on her phone, only forty-five minutes to go. Surely she could hold her eyes open and soldier on through these pages until then. On second thought, she'd set an alarm just in case.

"CLOSE YOUR EYES!" Bentley said through giggles.

"Okay, they're closed."

And good thing they were, because a moment later, his own hands ungracefully clapped over Jones' eyes.

"Now they're double closed!"

Bentley sounded absolutely gleeful. Jones imagined this was how he sounded on Christmas morning. Or how he might have sounded on his birthday, if she'd done a better job.

She cleared her throat, pushing down the feeling of failure; even though it was fading, it still stretched like a shadow at certain moments.

"What's your show called?" Jones asked.

"Homo Alone," Elsie said at the same time Bentley said, "The House has AIs."

"Elsie!" Jones shot her a warning look.

A laugh burst from Elsie, she was clearly enjoying herself and enjoying messing with Jones. "Sorry, Bentley's right. The working title is now, *The House has AIs*, pronounced eyes, of course."

"Of course." Jones tried to nod, but Bentley's hands were holding her head in place.

In her right ear there was a blast of Bentley humming the Fangley Heights theme song. It stampeded through her brain.

"Okay, it's showtime!" Elsie's voice rang out from across the room.

Jones tilted to the side as the cushions shifted rapidly. Bentley leapt off the couch, landing on the floor with a soft thud.

"Open your eyes," they said in unison.

Jones blinked the scene in front of her into focus. They'd constructed an old-time puppet show set out of a cardboard box and…Jones turned to look at the window, the darkening sky visible through the glass that had once been covered by a red curtain she now hoped wasn't glued to the cardboard set.

A disc shaped puppet came into view. It appeared to be two glow-in-the-dark frisbees rubber-banded together—the overall effect reminded her of a clamshell. Purple magic marker eyes were drawn on the top disc. It was impressive how they'd scoured the house and discovered enough supplies to MacGyver several puppets while seemingly leaving most of the set Jones had bought untouched.

Bentley made a vrooming sound from behind the box stage, and then he groaned loudly.

A phone screen lit up near the top of the set with an arm just visible next to the curtain. "What's wrong, Krum?" Elsie's voice was somewhere between British and robotic; it reminded her of the lady who lives inside her GPS.

"Indigestion. I think they've been eating hot chips again."

"Let me check the pantry inventory." AI Elsie followed this with a series of beeps. The phone screen flashed on again.

"Just as you suspected. The household is now out of Flamin' Hot Cheese Crumbles. Shall I order more?"

The frisbees made a jerking movement forward while groaning. "Please, no more!"

Whistling started and a balloon with bright blue sideburns drawn on it floated onto the set. "L.C., please turn on the lights." Elsie had lowered her voice, like she had gone over to the dark side. It was the perfect blend of silly and gruff.

Jones laughed, adjusting her elbows where she leaned forward on her knees.

"Of course, Wiggins, one moment." Elsie's voice was back to its AI accent. At the top of the set, her phone's flashlight came on and illuminated the scene.

Bentley's small hand gripped an elaborate construction paper living room set, complete with a bright green couch and coffee table with a bowl on top that Jones strongly suspected was filled with gummy bears. At least no one would be eating those ones by mistake.

By the time they got to the end of their show, Krum had accidentally eaten Wiggins' pants, revealing some incredible heart boxer shorts stuck to what looked like chopsticks. This, of course, had led to worse indigestion. Jones' own stomach ached from laughing.

THE NEXT FEW days were perfect. Her routine in New York was becoming so regular that she could go through most mornings on cruise control. Wake up, shower, make breakfast, wake Bentley, do whatever witchcraft got them both out of the house on time. Repeat. The weekend was similar, except at point-five speed and with no real bras.

There were days she still missed her place in LA, but not the job she was on indefinite hiatus from. She missed the sunlight and her candles and the pillows that didn't hurt her neck when she slept. She could just get those things here, though. Even if she didn't have natural sunshine, store-bought was fine. She slipped her phone from her pocket and added items to her cart until she had everything she missed most from home. Then she clicked *buy*. And just like that, her old life would show up at her door in three to five business days.

Everything she missed was just stuff, something easily replaceable. When she thought of LA, she thought of smoothies and her favorite pair of shoes. Small things she could get anywhere. How different her life in New York was; everything that mattered to her here was unwieldy and messy and irreplaceable and perfect.

New York was Bentley laughing as he tied his own shoes together as a prank. It was also Elsie slipping a note into Jones' purse telling her to have a Fangtabulous day, the purple magic marker bleeding into the napkin it was written on, giving the entire message a sinister undertone. The marker always made her think of how Elsie had filled out their no strings HR agreement. Jones didn't regret the arrangement, but she liked that her ties to New York were weaving themselves into something worth keeping. It was imperfect and messy in a thousand different ways, and she thought she might want it to be hers for real.

CHAPTER TWENTY-ONE
ELSIE

Elsie reminded herself not to skip. Like actually told her legs to tell her feet to knock it off. Maybe it was the change in the air—a crispness that meant cute coats and perfect boots and seasonally appropriate lattes. Or maybe it was just three nights in a row with Jones. Three nights of increasingly elaborate ploys to get Bentley to try new things that didn't end in cheese. And last night, when Bentley wanted Elsie to read his goodnight story, and they'd all laughed at her monster voices until tears blurred their eyes. The glow of their attention had made her feel like a star. She felt part of something. And maybe that wasn't a good reason to feel a little in love. Maybe no reasons made sense to feel a little in love. It was just a state of being. It just was. She could feel their lives zipping together like a warm coat. She was verging on the type of pathetic she usually made fun of Avery for.

This time with Jones felt like the start of something. And with each day it was a little harder for Elsie to remember that it wasn't. Because what she was doing with Jones was explicitly not anything. It was designed to end without complication. And she had agreed to that. A fact that she had been kicking herself for since the moment she'd signed the form for HR. She'd been working up the courage to tell Jones how she felt but hadn't quite found it yet. In the meantime, she was soaking up her and Bentley's attention like it was the last truly nice day of the year.

Elsie was pulling on her street clothes after a long day on set when her phone danced across the vanity in her dressing room. A picture of Jones with her hair tangled from sleep lit up the screen. She liked her buttoned up, but she loved Jones a little undone.

"Hey you."

"Hey yourself. So I know we had plans tonight, but I need to go meet a therapist I found for Bentley, and I'm not sure how long it will take. Susan has the afternoon off for an appointment, and I hate to ask you to do this, because I know you're not a babysitter—"

"Jones, just send me the address. I'll go pick up Bentley."

And that was how Elsie found herself leaning against the iron gate outside Bentley's school, milkshakes at the ready, hoping a six-year-old wouldn't stand her up for their date. Babysitter or not, she had big plans for their afternoon.

"Elsie!" Bentley's voice reached her like a siren.

"Benz! Jones had an adult thing, is it okay if we hang out for a bit?"

In lieu of a response, Bentley reached up for a foam cup. "For me?"

"Against my better judgment, I got you a Superman one. I didn't even know they made Superman shakes."

Bentley took a sip and smiled at her with lips already ghosted with blue.

"So, how do you feel about taking an adventure?"

Bentley nodded, free hand twisting into the hem of Elsie's jacket.

She gestured with her arm like she was setting the scene. "We'll travel under the city to the most magical place on earth, The New York Public Library. It's a castle filled with treasures."

Bentley was nodding animatedly, sipping his milkshake. Elsie said a silent prayer he wasn't lactose intolerant, though with the amount of mac and cheese this kid housed, he was probably fifty percent dairy at this point.

"What do you say?" Elsie swung her backpack off one shoulder and undid the clasp. She fished around until her fingers landed on her book, and she pulled it out with a flourish. "Can you help me restore this mass market paperback to its rightful place on the shelves of the grandest library in all the land?"

"Yeah! Can we get my sword?" Bentley's eyes shone with excitement.

"I wish, buddy. They allow a lot of things on the subway, but last time I checked, swords were still frowned upon."

An intense rush hour commute later, the pair stepped off into the bright sunshine of Bryant Park, leaves skittering over their shoes.

"Is that a castle?" Bentley looked mystified.

"Even better, it's a public institution."

Bentley gave her a puzzled look.

"Okay, it's a castle. But that's a secret. Do you want to hear the story?"

"Tell me!"

"Once upon a time, more than a hundred years ago, three different kingdoms joined together, consolidating their riches to establish this regal place. They brought in the greatest craftsmen from all over to create its beauty. They mined the earth for the stone with the right properties to protect the treasures inside. There was no other building like it in the surrounding lands.

"The king of the land was a man named Teddy, who was

very much into water buffalo for some reason. But then he was challenged by a man named Taft who defeated him in battle, and his symbol was the great lion.

"There was a Great Sadness sweeping through the land and the lions were named Patience and Fortitude—to lead us through the dark times." Elsie led Bentley to a statue of one of the giant cats and hoisted him up so he could reach out and touch it.

Elsie let out an oof as she set Bentley back down and opened the heavy door to usher him inside. He was about twenty pounds heavier than she'd expected, but not everyone could be a svelte two pounds like Fangley.

"You see, this was a castle for the people, and it shared the greatest resource in the world—knowledge. Follow me." She watched with joy as his eyes went wide.

"Okay," Elsie whispered, placing a hand between his shoulders to gently guide him out of the doorway. "I need you to take this token and slide it into that slot. It's the key that grants us magical entry, now that we're not delinquent with the sacred items it bestowed upon us for the binding period of a fortnight."

Bentley tilted his head to the side. "But it's a book."

"That's right, this place only deals in the riches of the written word."

"You're weird." Bentley scrunched up his face and giggled. "Why are you whispering?"

"Because I've been entrusted to guard these secrets, and now I'm giving them to you. Can you handle that responsibility?"

Bentley nodded solemnly. The book landed in the returns with a satisfying *thunk*, and Bentley craned his neck to stare at the ceiling in the lobby, as tall as a Rockefeller Christmas tree. "It's like Dad's work."

Elsie thought of the lobby at the studio, with its white marble that always felt so cloying. Something so grand that didn't feel expansive or wonderful; there it just felt big for the sake of being big. "Yeah you're right, but I think this might have a few more secrets.

"In the beginning, everyone that worked here got magic shoes to keep them safe on the impenetrable marble floors that even the strongest dragon couldn't break through.

"This room here is full of ancient tomes from far away lands. Beneath this golden ceiling, maps bigger than you of places long forgotten hang on the walls or are tucked away in secret drawers. They reveal how the world was charted. A lot of those explorers were wrong and only thought they discovered things. Anyway, let's continue on.

"Here you'll uncover books of elixirs with yellowed pages —you'll be old enough to concoct those one day.

"Okay let's pass under this enchanted archway so we can continue our quest. Are you ready to keep climbing so we can ascend to the tower?"

Bentley's hand tightened in Elsie's. She cleared her throat.

"We're about to pass beneath skies filled with Gods. Let's try to hold our breath. Along with the Gods there are great inventions, everything used to be written by hand until a magical machine was created that printed out pages so everyone could have them. Well, not everyone, that took a long time, and even now not everyone has equal access to information. But still, this was the start of something that changed the course of history." Elsie was wheezing by the end of that spiel; her lung capacity was not suited for architectural tours.

She pushed open the swinging door to reveal the Rose Reading Room. "Some of the books are so old and fragile, they're kept in special time capsule cases so they don't turn to dust in your hands. Do you see how the ceiling touches the sky? You can even see the clouds up there."

"Wow," Bentley whispered. He dropped her hand as he spun around.

Elsie watched him like he was a precious treasure. "I know. It's huge, but we can't run in here." Elsie pointed toward the ceiling. "Let's go to the balcony to survey the land. There used to be a system of tubes that sent books all around the library."

"Really?"

"Yeah, but now they use conveyor belts. Let's see if we can find the kid's section. It will be filled with books, and you can borrow as many as you want. I mean as long as they will fit in this bag. We need to make it home before darkness falls on the kingdom."

"You took a six-year-old to the library? Of your own free will?" Jones laid back on the bed, her glasses perched on her nose. The look was stern and sexy and was making Elsie feel all kinds of ways.

"Yeah." Elsie grinned. "The library's the best. It's like an amusement park for the written word."

She and Bentley had had a great time—when they'd gotten back to the house he'd rushed downstairs to tell Mitch about his adventure.

"I'm just trying to understand what prompted you to get on a train at rush hour when you could have just gone to the park."

"Fine, I was already planning to go to the library today because I had an overdue book. But I also thought maybe he'd never been there. We found him some new books to read before bed."

Jones let out a surprised laugh. "That makes more sense. It wouldn't have occurred to me to take him to the library for fun, but he's talking about it like he went to Disneyland. And the new books are great—I literally couldn't say *goodnight* to the moon one more time."

Elsie crossed her arms and leveled Jones with a serious look. "I say *goodnight* to the moon every night."

"Of course you do." Jones nodded indulgently. "I wish I would have known you were going. I would have had you pick something out for me. This book is really boring."

Jones' wrist bent under the weight as she held up her doorstop of a book. Elsie was surprised it didn't injure her.

"What is that? An encyclopedia?"

"Do they even print those anymore?"

"Maybe?" Elsie said slowly.

"It's not an encyclopedia. That would probably be more interesting with a clearer narrative arc."

Elsie leaned over Jones and snagged the thick hardcover from her. She bench-pressed the hundred-pound book over her head and looked up at the cover. "That's because it's a book about...the life of a business man?"

"It's an autobiography, and he wasn't just successful in business, he was also an inventor."

"Well, then he could have invented a more interesting life story. You've got to abandon this book. There's no shame in a DNF."

"A DNF? Is that some sort of sex thing?"

Elsie laughed. "I hope not. It means *did not finish*. If a book's not for you, you can just stop reading it."

"But I've already read a third of it."

"And that's exactly why you should stop reading it. You've invested too much time already, it's a sunk cost. You know you can check something off your to-do list by simply deciding not to do it, right?"

Jones started to nod, then shook her head and scrunched up her nose. "No, actually, I'd never thought of it that way."

"Okay, well that's a tip for you, I guess. I'll keep this book in case I need to bludgeon an intruder, and you can take one of the books I got at the library."

"How do you do that?"

"Do what?" Elsie tilted her head like a confused puppy, which she knew from the internet was extremely adorable.

"You're both serious and silly." Jones didn't look amused, but she didn't look bothered by it either. She seemed thoughtful. If Elsie gazed into her gray eyes long enough, she was sure she could see the thoughts swirling in her head like a whirlpool. Jones shook her head. "You're doing this thing that I think is to take care of me, but it's wrapped up like a joke. Like you're supporting me through teasing."

Elsie nodded. She loved watching Jones try to work things out, especially things about her. Jones' eyes trailed over Elsie like the answer was hidden on her face. "Was there a question in there, Jones?"

"No, it's good. It's wonderful. You surprise me. I know this sounds sappy, but when I expect you to crack a joke, you pull me in tight, and it's only then that I realize it's exactly what I needed. I just…like it. I'm not sure I'm making sense."

Elsie's heart did a little cymbal crash at Jones' words. Her feelings rushed the stage, holding cell phones aloft, begging for an encore. She had to clear her throat before she could respond, and even then her voice was rough with emotion. "You're making sense. I was wondering, is it okay if we just read tonight, is that weird?"

Jones brushed a strand of hair away from Elsie's face and gave her a soft smile. "Not at all. I'm pretty exhausted, even though I know you have ways of keeping me up. I'd love to just read before bed with you. Though I'm a little surprised that's what you want to do."

"Really? Because I can't keep my hands off you?"

"It's more that I usually want your hands on me. But no. I just didn't have you pegged as a big reader. The library trip surprised me, too." Jones winced. "I didn't mean that like it sounded. I meant for it to be more neutral."

"It's okay. I'd be insulted, but I actually get that a lot. Reading doesn't have some sort of moral value, so I don't take it personally. Though it can make you a better person because when you see things from a different perspective than your own, it creates empathy. Reading creative things inspires me to be creative, so I read as much as I can. Usually on the subway and before bed. And now I think I'm boring you. In conclusion, I'm not sure you need to see the world as a boring business guy anymore."

Jones made a grabbing motion with her hands. "You're right. Book me, please."

Elsie pulled a novel with a bright blue illustrated cover out of her bag. "Okay, before you say no, I know this book is really good."

Jones narrowed her eyes. "If you haven't read it, how do you know?"

"Because I've read everything Arden Abbott has written. This one is about a radio host who gives love advice to callers. Sometimes her advice is great, but other times it's bitter or very bad. Her show is called Love Bites, like the title."

"Okay, that feels like a very 90s, Reality Bites reference. If you think it will be good I'll try it." Jones tapped on the cover of the book. "Why does this woman's neck have puncture wounds?"

"Oh right, so a few more things. The radio show host is obsessed with vampires. Possibly like someone *you* know. So, the title has a double meaning, I guess." Elsie smirked.

Jones groaned, and Elsie picked up a pillow and threw it at her. "You just spent days reading a boring book some guy wrote about himself. Romance novels are smart and funny. The most brilliant minds in the world are writing and reading romances."

"Is that true?"

Elsie shrugged and pulled another novel out of her bag. "It sure seems true."

• • •

ONCE THEY'D SETTLED IN, Elsie's focus was interrupted by Jones' laughter. "Oh, this is a disaster already. I love it. The host, Amy, just gave terrible advice to this woman who happens to be her next-door neighbor. The woman's partner cheated, so Amy told her to throw all of their stuff outside, and then, when Amy got home, she couldn't get in her apartment, because it was blocked by clothes and books and an entertainment center. Big *Real Housewives* energy. I love it."

Elsie leaned over and kissed Jones' cheek. "Sounds like a pretty classic meet-cute. But ours was better."

CHAPTER TWENTY-TWO
JONES

A few days later Jones woke exhausted and sore, and very, very happy. It was situational happiness, an Elsie-induced mood. So many of Jones' days were dictated by things outside of her control, although assuredly in her head. So strange that her own mind was the one thing in her life that she couldn't bend to her will. No amount of money or negotiating or flirting made her brain behave the way she wanted it to.

And it had not been behaving. It spun improbable future scenarios and resolutely refused to leave this safe space next to Elsie and face the day. Jones had been trying to get a read on how things were going at the work and the general climate. She wanted to know how much needed to change. But the staff responded to questions like they were witnesses testifying to congress, no one would deliver a definitive answer for fear that their words might be held against them later if and when power shifted.

Last night, she'd lain awake long after a naked Elsie had fallen asleep beside her. As she listened to the soft rush of Elsie's breathing, Jones wondered if each new day drew her time in New York closer to its end, or if it simply added another foundational pillar to the life she seemed to be building here. She was starting to think she wanted one life much more than the other.

A soft strand of Elsie's hair tickled Jones' ribs, pulling her attention away from her swirling thoughts and back to the present. Jones had been waiting for Elsie to wake up and now that she had she was making her presence known. She sighed as Elsie's warm hand splayed across Jones' hip to hold her steady. Elsie's hair trailed down her stomach, then her legs; Jones traced her path like a full body shiver until Elsie placed an open-mouthed kiss on the inside of Jones' thigh, erasing all other sensations from her consciousness.

Jones wanted to stay in bed all day. It was so nice to have a reason to not want to get up rather than to not have a reason to get out of bed. But it was Thursday, and that meant work and—

Elsie parted Jones with her tongue and Jones could have sworn she heard her own groan reverberate in Elsie's chest. Jones bit her lip. She really needed the rest of the house to remain asleep.

"Fuck." Jones gasped.

Elsie hummed against her clit and reached up to palm Jones' breast. Jones didn't want reality to shatter this moment, but when she thought of being irresponsible her heart raced. This was fun, but she really didn't need to make things harder for herself at work. Stu's snide comments here and there about her dating life made Jones think that he was well aware of this 'no strings' agreement she had with Elsie. At least she was pretty sure it was the thought of being irresponsible that had her heart thudding like that, and not whatever magic Elsie was currently working with her mouth.

She reached down and stroked her fingers through Elsie's messy brown hair. "Els, it's a school day."

"Shit, sorry." Elsie lifted her head, biting her lower lip as she winked at Jones.

The movement shifted the blankets so that they covered Elsie's head like a cloak. The scene was almost unbearably cute.

She looked guilty and adorable, like she had ruined her dinner by eating Italian Ice, and she wasn't sorry at all. That look unwound something in Jones, loosened the ties of her reserve and made her feel bold. There was nothing soft about the flash of hunger in Elsie's eyes. And this time, Jones was sure her heart rate had nothing to do with nerves.

She relaxed back onto the pillow. "Don't be sorry, be quick." Jones placed a hand on Elsie's shoulder, and she took her cue. The look in her eyes as she lowered herself back between Jones' legs said she loved a challenge.

Elsie's tongue made precise contact with Jones' clit, winding her higher. It felt like only seconds to Jones before her thighs were shaking against Elsie's shoulders as her orgasm began to barrel down on her. Elsie entered Jones with two fingers, confident, and fast, and exactly how she liked it.

She came hard with her fingers in Elsie's hair and a scream clutched in the back of her throat. When she came back down, Elsie's soft breaths were marking time against her hip.

Jones leaned up on her elbows, sweeping her hair off her forehead and trying not to think about how disheveled she probably looked. "Come here."

Elsie crawled up her body in a way that made Jones wonder what she had done to get so lucky. Being around Elsie made her feel blessed. And not just because the sex was good, even though it was. To say Elsie had talented hands was an understatement. They were her livelihood after all. But it was all the other moments that felt perfect. Elsie had seen her at her lowest, washing her dishes and getting them ice cream instead of looking at Jones with pity. Elsie didn't look at Jones like she was someone that needed to be fixed. She looked at

Jones like she was perfect exactly how she was. And Jones was starting to believe it.

When Elsie was around, Jones didn't feel like a burden, because Elsie made her feel like a gift.

Elsie's mouth trailed over hers and she tasted herself on Elsie's lips. She was trying to work out a way to taste Elsie and still get everyone to work and school on time, when Elsie's light touch on her forehead drew her attention.

"You look so serious. Where did you go just now?"

"Oh, I have a very serious plan. But—" Jones paused.

"But what?" Elsie was half on top of Jones, and her hips pressed against Jones' leg with impatience.

"I think you might need to join me in the shower."

"Hmm, that seems like a real hardship. I guess I better get it over with." Elsie hopped up like she hadn't spent most of the night fucking Jones instead of sleeping.

Jones eased out of bed, her eyes on Elsie's ass as she disappeared into the bathroom.

Elsie sat on the counter as Jones did her makeup. "Do you want me to drop you at your place so you can finish getting ready?"

"I *am* ready." Elsie ran her hand through her wet hair. "We're just recording audio today, not that Fangley cares if I wear makeup." She traced her finger along the faint dark circles under her eyes. "He'd actually be into these, I think."

"Do you want moisturizer? I have this great stuff for my laugh lines." Jones rummaged in the drawer looking for the red pot of face cream.

"Laugh lines?" Elsie squinted at her.

"Yeah, around my eyes." Jones tapped the spot next to her temple, even though she didn't really want Elsie closely inspecting her wrinkles.

"Oh, I love those. But I do agree that you need more of them."

"That's not what I meant and you kn—"

Elsie reached forward and tickled Jones, making her squirm. "I'll need to work on that." She kissed Jones' cheek and hopped down from the counter. "I'll get Benz breakfast while you finish getting ready." Elsie took a few steps toward the door, then stopped. "Actually, is that okay? I don't want to cross any boundaries. If you don't want Bentley to know I stayed, I understand. I know we're not really telling anyone about us."

Elsie's smile was forced, not reaching her eyes. And Jones' heart sank. Did Elsie think she was a secret because Jones didn't want people to know? She would shout about Elsie from the rooftops if it wouldn't make Elsie's life harder.

Jones stepped forward and pressed her lips to Elsie's. "I'm sure he'd love it if you got his breakfast. I want you here. I know we're keeping things under wraps at work, but that's just so we don't have to deal with anyone's bullshit. You don't need people making assumptions about you or the show just because we're together."

Together. Why had she said it like that? Maybe because fucking sounded crass and in no way captured the way Jones wanted to pull Elsie to her every time she was near.

"Right, okay," Elsie said on a sigh that sounded relieved. "That's what I thought."

THE MILE-LONG DROP-OFF line at Bentley's school meant they were running late. Elsie's fingers tapped relentlessly against the console, until Jones smothered them with her own hand.

Jones covered Elsie's hand with her own. "Relax. I'll let you out in front. We'll be there in five minutes."

"Sorry, you're right." Elsie relaxed back in the passenger's seat. "Trey's been taking every opportunity to undermine me lately, and it's affecting me more than I realized."

"You have the talent of a hundred Treys." Jones squeezed her fingers, urging Elsie to turn her hand over. "Fangley Heights is your show. All Trey has is jealousy."

Elsie blew out a breath and laced her fingers through Jones'. "Okay, thank you."

When they pulled up in front of the studio, Elsie leaned over and gave Jones a quick kiss. She pulled back suddenly, her eyes going wide. "Shit, Jones. I'm sorry. No PDAs."

Jones' pulse was racing in her chest, but the look on Elsie's face was breaking her heart. Her head said to reassure her. And something much lower and more insistent reminded her that it would be hours before she could kiss Elsie again. And so, before she could reason herself out of it, Jones clutched the front of Elsie's shirt pulling her forward until their lips met and the city continued to twirl all around them.

CHAPTER TWENTY-THREE
ELSIE

The soft whoosh of Avery skidding to a halt in front of her open door broke Elsie's concentration. Two fuzzy grey eyebrows sat on her desk like geriatric caterpillars, she'd been just about to sew them on the latest puppet she was creating. She'd been chipping away at new ideas and builds for Serious Mayhem, the new production company she hoped to maybe launch one day. It was a new dream, but a powerful one. Her post-Fangley project was still untitled, but at least it had legs now, *literally*. She leaned the puppet into a sitting positioning propped up by her open laptop. As she straightened up on her stool, her neck and shoulders protested. Making puppets wasn't all fun and games. Sometimes it was a mild inconvenience, and once she'd even needed stitches from a sewing machine with a homicidal agenda.

"Hey." Avery rapped gently on the doorframe. "Are we still on for dinner?"

Elsie lowered the magnifying glasses she was wearing for the stitching details and blinked. She took in Avery, their plaid shirt and suspenders landing somewhere between a lumberjack and an accountant counting logs. A little Paul Bunyan with a pocket protector. "Definitely!"

"You know those glasses make you look like the smart dwarf."

"Wow, that's rude. They're all intelligent in their own way. They have forest smarts." Elsie held back her laugh.

Avery laughed. "Forest smarts?"

"Yeah like street smarts, but for people who don't live in the city." Elsie crossed her arms over her chest, feigning serious offense.

"What are you working on there? It looks kind of involved." Avery squinted at the mess on Elsie's desk.

"I had an idea for a puppet with these Eugene Levy-esque eyebrows, except I want to put them on a track, so over the course of a scene I can make them migrate across the puppet's face." Elsie held up the mechanism like a sliding lock that she'd been working on.

"Well, I am speechless. Your brain creates things that most people would never be able to imagine."

Elsie laughed. "Thanks, I think. So, dinner? Want me to order us something?"

"No, I can pick it up on my way home."

"Home? As in where you are right now?" Elsie raised an eyebrow then stretched her arms over her head.

Avery patted the tote bag on their shoulder. "Oscar and I are going to drop some books off at the library. Do you need me to return any for you?"

"Nope, I'm good." Elsie's cheeks heated as she awaited Avery's gentle call out. Because Avery's call outs were always gentle even when the truth of them stung so much it took the breath from her lungs. They were gentle, especially when they stung. She knew she'd been spending a lot of time with Jones and Bentley, but she hadn't told Avery about her one-on-one time with Bentley.

"So if I look around the apartment, I won't find any overdue books with your name on them? Like in the fridge, maybe? Or, I don't know, under a couch cushion covered in crumbs?"

"First, that happened *one time* and *you know* that books and snacks go together. And second, you will not, because I returned them." Elsie drew in a breath. It wasn't a big deal. Everything was still casual. "Jones got caught up with a thing, so I picked Bentley up from school and took him to the main branch."

"I need you to say that all again, but slowly," Avery said with the methodical cadence of a podcast host.

"Jones went to meet with a possible therapist for Benz, so I hung out with him for a bit. I decided to take him to the library since I had books to return there anyway."

"I'm so glad she's finding him a therapist. I know so many people aren't taking on new patients right now. So Jones was busy and you took him on an errand?"

"I mean, sort of. It wasn't a big deal. He'd never been, so I walked through it with him and told him some embellished history." Elsie looked down, not wanting to meet Avery's gaze. She knew they'd make a big deal out of this.

"I can't believe you took someone to your sacred space." Avery took a step into the room, like they were trying to cut off the exit if Elsie decided to bolt.

Elsie sighed. It was a true burden to know another human so well. "It's not my sacred space. It's a public institution. Anyone can go there."

Avery did that annoying thing where they let the silence hang until Elsie could feel the pressure of needing to speak, anything to release the tension filling her up like a balloon about to burst.

"So I like the library, and I wanted to show it to Benz. It doesn't have to mean anything."

"I agree that it doesn't have to. But we should also acknowledge that to you it does."

"Avery, I love you, but I don't want to do this. Can't we just get burritos and watch an anime movie like cultured adults?"

Avery glanced past Elsie toward the window. "It's still light out, babe, we have time for all of the above. Tell me—how's the *strings* part of that *no strings* arrangement going? Are you about to trip and fall?"

Oscar lumbered into view and laid down on top of Avery's brown leather Oxfords.

"Look, Ave, I know that what I have with Jones is casual, but that doesn't mean I can't take it seriously. I love spending time with her, and I think Bentley's great, too."

"Taking it seriously is the opposite of casual. What does Jones say about all of this when you two discuss it?"

"Well, if we were to discuss it she'd probably say—"

Avery held up a hand and stepped forward like a crossing guard determined to halt traffic using just their palm and epic stink eye. "You haven't discussed it?"

"We don't need to discuss it. I signed the papers and so did she. I know it doesn't mean anything." Even as the words left her mouth, Elsie's feelings thrashed inside her, the truth of them twisting like a knife in her gut.

"Okay, but *do* you?"

Was that a tear glimmering in Avery's eye? Elsie really needed to make some less perceptive friends.

"Please don't look at me like that."

"Like what?" Avery asked.

"Like you're method acting a Dickensian street urchin," Elsie said. "You don't need to feel bad for me. I know what I signed up for. Quite literally—I wrote my name on the line using an actual pen."

"Impressive. I'm only bringing this up because I care about you. I think Jones is great, you know that. And I love seeing you happy. And you have been happy, Els."

"I know. It's just been…nice. Like when we agreed to keep

things simple, it took the pressure off. I feel like I get to be my whole self. Not some watered down version of my personality because I'm worried about coming off as normal or serious enough to date someone. When I'm with Jones—with both her and Bentley, really—I feel like I fit without having to contort myself."

"I want that for you. Everyone deserves to be their full self."

Oscar let out a loud snore.

"Yes, even you, Oz," Avery said, crouching down to scratch his ears. "Promise me you'll talk to Jones about it? Just to make sure you're still on the same page. She could go back to LA at any time, right?"

LA, two letters that took the wind right out of Elsie's sails. Jones had another home, another life. Maybe Elsie was the thing she was just playing at.

Elsie shook her head. She needed to redirect Avery before they got her to agree to anything else. "Can you get me guac on my burrito?"

Avery tilted their head, narrowing their eyes at Elsie. It was a look that said, 'I don't love what you're doing, but I'll allow it.'

"Guac is extra."

"Fine, will you pretty please get me guac on my burrito?" She gave Avery a sickly sweet smile, blinking rapidly a few times for good measure.

"I will. And Els?"

"Yeah?"

"Benz is a really cute nickname and I know you don't give those out lightly. They're lucky to have you." Avery smiled and adjusted the tote bag on their shoulder.

Elsie shrugged even as the heat rushed to her cheeks. She felt like the lucky one. "I don't know about that."

"That's okay." They picked up Oscar's leash and took a step back into the hall. "I do."

CHAPTER TWENTY-FOUR
JONES

Jones' mascara clattered onto the bathroom counter. She picked up a cotton ball and began to wipe away the raccoon eyes her shaky hand had given her. Elsie would be there any minute to pick up Jones for their dinner date, but her bodily reaction didn't seem to be nerves. When Jones leaned against the sink, a bone-deep exhaustion settled into her. She thought about curling up on the floor, pulling the bathmat over her shoulders and calling it a night. She pushed off the sink and heaved herself back into a standing position. It had been a few days since she last saw Elsie and Jones missed her. She really, really didn't want her bad mood to ruin their time together. Elsie was too important to let this relationship fall apart like all her others had.

She smiled at herself in the mirror. If she squinted, her streaks of mascara almost looked like the tough face paint football players wore, manly makeup. She wet the washcloth and scrubbed it over her eyes, which were now red and irritated and even more tired than when she'd started this cosmetic renovation project twenty minutes ago.

She applied a bit of concealer to even out the places where she'd washed her face a little too vigorously and pulled the dress from the back of the bathroom door. Elsie had told her to dress casual but like, "somebody-might-take-your-picture casual not overdue-laundry-day-in-college casual". Jones wasn't sure what either of those things meant. She'd chosen a simple dress; it was cotton, the most casual of all the fabrics.

The doorbell rang as she threaded her arms through the straps. Rather than struggle with the zipper, which might bring her to tears—dress zippers being notoriously nasty foes—she headed for the door to let Elsie in. Let her vanquish the gnashing teeth on this hidden seam. Jones took a steadying breath and wished she'd put on more makeup to hide behind. It was a fine balance between the protective properties of concealer and the frustration of a perfect winged eyeliner application.

She could do this. She just had to get through a few hours, and then she could be back home and crash. Plus, she'd be with Elsie. Elsie always made her feel better. Deep down, Jones had been wondering if that was something she was coming to rely on about Elsie, like the way some people relied on an aspirin to take their headache away.

Elsie couldn't be a simple way to mask her problems. Then again, wasn't that the entire point of their *no strings* arrangement? Casual pain relief? Well, that was grim.

Elsie knocked, and Jones startled backward before yanking the door open. Her heart rocketed off her ribs.

Jones leaned an arm against the doorway. "Hi." There, that was good. A normal, casual greeting. Elsie's eyes ran over her, and Jones enjoyed the sensation. Elsie's admiration felt like a barely there touch, tickling along the skin of Jones' clavicle.

"Hi yourself." Elsie took a step into the hallway, leaving a warm kiss on Jones' cheek.

Yes, she could definitely get through the night with Elsie at her side. Maybe after a few hours together she might even feel better, having kept her depression at bay. Jones knew she shouldn't think like that. It was too much pressure to put on another person, and completely unrealistic. Still, the scent of Elsie's pineapple shampoo zinged through her senses like a natural sugar rush.

Jones eased the door closed and turned to Elsie. "The babysitter is on her way."

"Oh, great. You look fabulous." Elsie's gaze ticked over Jones again.

"Thanks. I wasn't sure what you meant by *casual*. Can you zip me up?"

Jones turned, and Elsie's fingers found their way to the skin on either side of her spine. "Maybe we should just take this off?"

Jones couldn't hold back a wistful sigh.

Elsie's fingers paused at the base of her spine. "What's going on with you?"

"Nothing. Your suggestion sounded nice to my tired brain. But dinner will be good, where are we going?"

"Coriander. It's a new restaurant, only ten tables, very tiny and hard to get into. All the food is vegan. I pulled a few favors with the hostess. She used to date Avery."

"Oh."

"Does that not sound good? Do you, um, not like vegetables?"

Jones swatted at Elsie. "You know I like vegetables."

"Right, delivered on a bed of pizza."

"This place just sounds kind of aggressively cool."

"You're aggressively cool."

"No, I'm an aggressively exhausted forty-two-year-old who was up most of the night with a six-year-old."

Elsie's hands slid from Jones back, her dress still open, as she stepped around to face her.

Jones sighed and closed her eyes. "I'm sorry, just give me a minute. I'll pull myself together."

"Hey, are you okay?"

Jones blinked her eyes open and nodded so hard that her dangling earrings moved like wind chimes. "Yes, absolutely." She wanted to look anywhere but at Elsie so she could blink away the tears she felt gathering on the horizon.

Elsie was silent, but the way she was holding eye contact made Jones feel naked in a way that had nothing to do with clothes.

Alarm bells went off in her head. Telling people she was dating that she was feeling down for no reason, and that they couldn't fix it with a nice dinner or funny joke usually led to disaster. But Elsie had seen her at her lowest, well maybe not lowest, but definitely a lower tier, and she hadn't run. Elsie had shown up *more* after she saw Jones gripped by depression, and that sparked a hope that just maybe Elsie was different than anyone else Jones had known. Still, she should give her an out tonight or just rally and push herself through hours of good food and an even better date. Leaving the house sounded like actual torture, but surely for Elsie she could.

Elsie had now been watching her for a long time as she struggled through her thoughts, so long that it was probably getting awkward for anyone not in Jones' head.

Okay, here goes. Jones dropped her voice to a whisper. "I'm not really okay actually."

Elsie nodded and reached out to give Jones' hand a soft squeeze. "Did something happen?"

Jones shook her head, noting that Elsie didn't seem annoyed or disappointed, just interested with the slightest hint of concern.

"Just my regular downward spiral." Jones took a steadying breath, time to push through. "We can leave in a few minutes. Bentley's already asleep, so, as soon as the babysitter gets here, we're good. She's running a little late. But let the record show that I am ready." Jones raised her arms and did a slow twirl, using the moments she faced away from Elsie to run a finger under her eyes, careful to preserve her makeup.

She was dressed, her makeup was done, and there was no way in hell she was going to let Elsie down. Elsie, who looked so cute in her silk blouse and ripped jeans; who'd gone out of her way to get a reservation to a restaurant that sounded exclusive. Exclusive and horrible to Jones right now, but still.

"What are you thinking?"

"I'm really looking forward to dinner." Jones forced brightness into her voice, but it came off like unflattering fluorescents.

"No, you're not." Elsie smiled, intertwining her fingers with Jones'.

The warmth of Elsie's hand in hers felt reassuring, like if she needed to let go, she might not fall too far.

Jones sighed. "Okay, *you're* looking forward to dinner, and *I'm* looking forward to spending time with you."

"I can barely stand vegetables and I had salad two days ago. Let's stay in. Does that sound better?" Elsie kissed Jones' hand then let it go so she could walk past her toward the kitchen.

She rushed to catch up. "We have to go out. I don't want to let you down. Plus you went to all that trouble to find a healthy place."

Elsie turned and reached for Jones' hand again. "Jones, listen to me, please. Dinner was just a pretense. I was looking forward to spending time with you."

"Right, but not like this." Jones wiped at her eyes again, which were defiantly filling with tears faster than her blinks could bail them out. She felt like a mess.

"No, exactly like this." Elsie smiled. "Except."

Jones' whole body tensed as she waited for the inevitable. *Except what?* She wanted to ask and didn't want to ever know. Did Elsie need to be reassured that Jones was happy to see her because her greeting hadn't been excited enough? Did she need Jones to be fixed now that Elsie was there? Jones took a deep breath. Her stomach muscles steeled themselves for the gut punch of rejection. When she spoke, her throat was desert dry. "Except?"

"Except...your dress is very sexy but it doesn't look that comfortable. Do you want to change? If you leave your phone with the contact pulled up, I can call the babysitter and cancel."

"Really?" Jones was crying harder now, and there was nothing she could do to stop it. "You're sure?"

"I'm sure." Elsie reached forward and ran her thumb along Jones' cheek, wiping away a tear. "Are you hungry?"

"Not really. Maybe."

"Okay.

JONES CAME BACK DOWN after washing her face. She felt uncertain about being so vulnerable. Her eyes were underscored with dark circles and the little lines that makeup usually hid well enough, but something inside her wanted Elsie to see. Maybe to give her another chance to turn back. Before she invested too much. Before they both did.

Elsie was in the kitchen spreading peanut butter on a Pop-Tart. "Sorry, I've been running all day so I made toast. Are those my clothes?"

Jones looked down at the loose sweatpants and baggy Haters Gonna Hate t-shirt with Statler and Waldorf. "Yes."

"And here I thought the dress was sexy. This is another level completely, Jones Haelstrom." Elsie took a step toward her and gave her a quick kiss. When Jones licked her lips after Elsie pulled away, she tasted peanut butter, and a second later her stomach let out a mortifying grumble.

"Yours are already in the toaster." Elsie took a bite of her food, chewing like she was contemplating something. Or maybe she was just dealing with the glue of peanut butter.

Jones felt her eyes roaming everywhere. "Unless you want mine?"

Jones wasn't sure where Elsie had found Pop-Tarts because they definitely weren't on her shopping list. "Did you…bring Pop-Tarts to my house?"

"You're welcome." Elsie grinned, holding hers out for Jones to take a bite.

Jones finished chewing and uncemented her tongue from the roof of her mouth. The sweet jam with the warm pastry really wasn't bad, but Elsie was still someone she was trying to impress. Jones wondered if that feeling like she was one wrong step from falling off the side of the earth and losing everything would ever go away. "You shouldn't have to eat that when you had a nice dinner planned. I'll cook something."

"Are you kidding? If I opened a restaurant, I'd serve these for every meal," Elsie said with a smile that seemed sincere. Maybe it was. How long had Jones been searching for ulterior motives behind every glance that came her way?

Better safe than sorry, Jones moved toward the counter, ready to fix the situation. There had to be some way she could salvage the evening.

Elsie intercepted Jones with a light hand on her hip, the touch spread warmth throughout her, just as comforting as the pajamas she was currently wrapped in. "I can't believe any part of you feels like cooking right now. I can order us Thai food. Let's watch a movie or something."

Jones nodded, stepping into Elsie's touch and wrapping her arms around her.

"Thank you."

"There's nothing to thank me for. I just want to spend time with you if you're up for it. We can watch a movie and not talk and crash at nine, and it will still be the highlight of my week. Or if you don't want company, I can head out and text you when I get home safely."

Jones felt a small smile pull at her lips. "You should always text me when you get home safely, but I think I'd feel better knowing you're safe here tonight."

"Me too. This is where I want to be."

Behind them the toaster popped up and Elsie tightened her arms around Jones when she jumped at the noise. For the first time all day she felt safe.

JONES HARDLY REMEMBERED the opening credits. She woke to Elsie wrapping an arm around her back and placing another beneath her knees.

She stirred and protested. "You can't carry me. You'll hurt your back."

"Maybe, but it would be worth it," Elsie whispered against Jones' ear as she scooped her up.

CHAPTER TWENTY-FIVE
ELSIE

Hey, I'm going to go put Benz to bed, and then I was thinking we could open the wine you brought?" Jones stood in the doorway of her kitchen the next night in a half-tucked flannel shirt that looked like it would tear if you tried to wear it in the woods, which is to say, Elsie liked it very much.

"Sure, sounds good."

"Say goodnight to Elsie," Jones said, nudging Bentley.

"Good night," Benz growled in a new monster voice he'd been practicing for the past few days. It was really coming along. Elsie had been trying to figure out if there was a character she could use it for.

Jones' soft steps accompanied Bentley's clatter up the stairs. Elsie waited until they'd crested the top before pulling out her phone. She opened up her text thread with Avery, grimacing when she realized she hadn't replied to their last few messages, even though she knew she had, at least in her heart.

Elsie: *Sorry, I thought I wrote back. I'm going to stay over at Jones' tonight. Can we do a dinner date later this week?*

Avery: *Sure, I already made vegan mac and cheese.*

Elsie rolled her eyes.

Elsie: *We've been over this. It's only Mac if you use noodles, and because I know you I know you used steamed cauliflower*

Avery: *Cauliflower is versatile, it's been expanding its horizons for years. It's a personal inspiration of mine.*

Elsie: *Cauliflower is depressing, but I can't have another argument with you about your vegetable delusions. Whether you're emotionally prepared to admit it or not, what you made is steamed vegetables with cashew cheese sauce, you'll probably be hungry in an hour*

Avery: *What I made is delicious. And I'll be asleep in an hour. Do you think you'll be home tomorrow night? Oscar's been sleeping in your bed.*

Elsie laughed. Oscar was an angel boy who would never. Unless…

Elsie: *No he has not, unless you're also sleeping in my bed*

Avery: Shrug emoji. *I guess you'll have to come back sometime and see.*

She shook her head.

Elsie: *Oh the drama. I was home this morning, you were just out, it's not my fault you were too busy to be home*

Avery: *It's called having a job with regular hours.*

Elsie: *I know, such a strange choice you're making*

Avery: *Okay, go have a good night. I'll harass you next time I see you. Just don't forget about the viewing party.*

Elsie's stomach dropped. The episode airing at the end of the week was the one she was most proud of. She'd been looking for ways to work more queer issues and families into Fangley Heights in a way that would get past the network. She wanted it to be an if you know, you know situation.

Hopefully queer families would feel recognized, and everyone else would let it go right over their heads, and somewhere in all of that, kids would learn through osmosis that many kinds of lives are valid. Still, she was nervous about how it would be received. Avery had been planning the watch party since the day Elsie told them the episode was being filmed.

Elsie: *I wouldn't miss it for anything*

She powered off her phone screen and set it face down on the table, where it would probably stay until tomorrow morning. She loved that about being with Jones. How it made her disconnect, because the main person she wanted to talk to was right there. Speaking of—Jones would probably be down any minute. Elsie went to the counter and pulled out wine glasses. Then she unbuttoned the top button of her shirt, and then two more for good measure. She glanced down at the sliver of her neon pink bra on display. Definitely too much, she wanted Jones to want her, but Elsie did have some pride.

ANOTHER FIFTEEN MINUTES PASSED, and Elsie had officially run out of the backs of cereal box mazes to complete. Some were harder than they looked.

At the top of the stairs, Elsie turned left instead of right. The door to Bentley's room was slightly ajar, and the light from inside had the soft glow of a lava lamp. She pushed it open as quietly as she could, glad she'd taken the time to fix the squeaking hinge yesterday after she'd noticed Jones wincing every time it let out its siren screech. Elsie really didn't want to undo all of Jones' hard work getting Benz to sleep, especially since he'd been up a lot the past few nights, meaning everyone was running on very little sleep and not for fun reasons, like writing bad jokes or other things she liked to do in bed.

Inside, she found exactly what she suspected, except the complete opposite. Bentley sat up straight against the headboard, flipping through a book in his lap. Next to him Jones was curled up on her side, breathing deeply.

"She went to bed in my bed," Benz explained helpfully.

Elsie tiptoed over. She slid Jones' glasses from her face

where they sat at an angle like a teeter-totter. Elsie set them on Benz's nightstand right beneath a Fangley nightlight that definitely hadn't been there before. Was that new merchandise? Was it weird that she wanted one? Fangley looked ethereal and just a bit creepy with the light glowing in his blue cheeks. It was exquisite.

"Okay, bud, time for you to get some sleep too. Do you have enough space?"

"Yeah," he said in a whisper fit for the stage.

Elsie held a finger up to her lips. "Do you need anything? Water?"

He widened his eyes and shook his head. She walked around and held up the covers for him to wiggle under, then pushed his hair back from his forehead.

"Sleep well. If you need anything, come down the hall and get me, okay?"

Bentley nodded once and then squeezed his eyes shut like he was making a birthday wish for some REM cycles.

Elsie backed her way across the room and shut the door quietly behind her. She pulled the door to Jones' room half closed as she stripped. Elsie pulled on a Muppets t-shirt she'd left the other day and resisted the urge to leave her pants in a tangle on the floor. Instead, she folded them and set them on the dresser. Elsie crawled into Jones' bed, falling asleep wrapped in the scent of her.

ELSIE WAS GETTING USED to spending the night at Jones' house; she was just at that point where the disorientation of waking up in a new place tipped into the familiar. Meaning, she could find her way to the bathroom without turning on the lights or banging her shin on the bed frame. As she returned and slid beneath the covers, Jones turned over and pulled Elsie in. Being wrapped in someone's arms wasn't something that she'd ever thought could be so intimate, but there was a closeness that came from Jones instinctually reaching for her that made Elsie feel like she was exactly where she was meant to be.

"Hey," Elsie said, her voice still blurry with sleep. "When did you come to bed?"

"Around three when I woke up feeling like I'd been stuffed into a suitcase."

"Well, a twin bed is a pretty tight fit for two people, even if one of them is fun-sized."

Jones let out a gruff laugh, it was the kind of laugh Elsie wanted to hear every time she walked into a room. "I think he's ninety percent knees and elbows."

"Yeah, that checks out."

"Anyway." Jones' arm tightened around Elsie's waist, and she rested her chin on Elsie's shoulder with a gentle pressure. "I'm so sorry about last night."

"Why?" Elsie tried to turn to look at Jones, but she couldn't make the angle.

"I let you down again."

"Don't you think I should be the judge of that?"

"I suppose so, but I was looking forward to our night together. I don't want you to think I'm boring. I mean I am, but you shouldn't think so."

"You didn't let me down. And one gal's boring is another gal's bliss. You were so sweet sleeping next to Bentley, who was wide awake by the way. It felt like walking into a theater to catch a really cute movie playing."

"And how long was this movie you watched?" Jones slid her fingers beneath Elsie's shirt and up along her ribs until she squirmed away, then Jones pulled her in tight again.

"It was more of a gif, really," Elsie gasped. "I looked briefly and respectfully; I swear."

"Mmmhmm. Don't those play endlessly? And isn't it pronounced jif?"

"Oh, you don't want to be that person, just go with the status quo here."

"So, what did you want to do today?"

"Smooth." Elsie turned toward Jones. "I don't have much planned." Elsie gulped. "I want to start building some buzz on social media for the episode that airs this week."

"What episode is that?"

"Oh, Fangley goes to visit his aunt. It subtly explores queer relationships." Elsie tried to use her most nonchalant voice, but unfortunately it was chock-full of chalant.

"On a kids' show?"

"Why not?" Elsie took a steadying breath, readying herself for the speech she'd given a hundred times at work. "Heterosexual relationships are shown all the time."

"Good point. I can text a few people to help with the promo if you want."

Elsie was hit by a breeze of relief. "That would be amazing." Her nerves dissipated, only to be replaced with a completely different set of butterflies as Jones' fingers slid over her stomach and downward.

CHAPTER TWENTY-SIX
JONES

J ones knew the knocks on the door could only be one person. Unique as a fingerprint, the beat radiated both authority and impatience. Jones stiffened.

Elsie jumped up from where she sat next to Jones on the couch, unaware their night was over.

"I think that's dinner."

It wasn't. Jones scanned through the possibilities, but short of shoving Elsie out the back door, she didn't see any. She followed Elsie silently down the hallway.

BIRDIE STOOD in the doorway in a white pantsuit and gold stiletto heels. Elsie's cheerful 'hello' pitched down halfway through the greeting, and Jones could hear the smile falling from her face.

Birdie craned her head around Elsie, a look of smug amusement tugged at her face, or at least the parts not botoxed within an inch of their life. "I'm glad you're no longer answering your own door. I always found it ghoulish. What if I was an intruder? You could be murdered already."

Jones raised an eyebrow. "You technically are an intruder."

"I guess it's a good thing I'm murder-proof, otherwise we'd be in trouble." Elsie winked at Jones.

Jones appreciated how Elsie approached everything like improv—every interaction was a yes, and…even the ones that should be a hard *no*.

"Yes, well." Birdie cleared her throat and nodded toward something at her feet. "Dear, will you bring my bags in for me? I'm afraid my daughter is forgetting her manners."

Bags? As in multiple. Not that the number of bags Birdie traveled with directly correlated to the amount of time she was planning to spend somewhere. Her outfit changes rivaled those in her acting days—the whole world her stage.

Elsie snapped her mouth shut before opening it again. "Oh wow, you're Jones' mo—"

"Please hurry dear, before the chimney soot of this wasteland sinks into them." Birdie gestured toward the door. "I hear that white suede is *so* hard to clean, and I'm not ready to throw the lot out."

"I doubt it's chimney soot." Jones rolled her eyes. "We're in Brooklyn, not 1866 London."

Birdie scoffed. "The city should end at Manhattan. It's the last best place."

"No, that's Montana," Elsie said.

Jones' fingers brushed Elsie's wrist, but she shook off the grasp. "It's okay, I'm happy to help." Elsie's voice was fluorescent bright—it reminded Jones of how she spoke to Trey on the set of Fangley Heights, cheer smothering absolute rage.

"She's not the help," Jones whispered sharply to Birdie.

Jones watched silently, feeling stunned as Elsie hauled two armfuls of bags off the porch and into the hall. Jones should be helping. But helping would mean this was really happening, and Jones wasn't ready to face the reality that Birdie had swooped in.

Birdie reached for Elsie. For a horrifying second, Jones braced for them to shake hands. Birdie had a terrible handshake, limp and boneless. Something green fluttered in Birdie's palm. Elsie shoved her hands into her pockets and retreated a few steps. A fucking tip. Jones had to do something. She'd explain that Elsie wasn't a bellhop, and even if she was, five dollars was not a big enough tip for anyone to deal with Birdie's baggage.

"It's so nice to meet you." Elsie's voice had faded to a dull gray.

"Yes." Birdie replied, but her gaze locked on Jones. The smile melted from Elsie's face, and Jones saw her do that thing where she dropped her shoulders to calm herself before smiling again.

Elsie stepped next to Jones and for a brief moment, and she hoped desperately that Elsie wouldn't touch her. As soon as the thought materialized, Jones felt terrible. It was a selfish desire that had nothing to do with Elsie and everything to do with how much she dreaded the possibility of a debate with her mother about Elsie's age.

Elsie stopped short, likely reacting to the miasma of tense energy radiating off her, but Jones still felt a pang of rejection although she knew she had no right to.

Jones steeled herself before reaching out and touching Elsie's arm.

"Where's the boy?" Birdie asked.

"You mean Bentley? He's upstairs, I think." Elsie looked at Jones who nodded her confirmation.

"Well, if you aren't certain, shouldn't you check on him?" Birdie tilted her head.

"I—sure. I bet he'd love to say hello to you." Elsie said in a way that implied the opposite and headed toward the stairs.

Jones took a step after her before hesitating.

"Oh, that won't be necessary," Birdie replied, flashing her teeth.

Elsie paused briefly on the second step but kept walking without acknowledging Birdie's comment. "I'll be upstairs with Benz."

"Come on, Dear. I can't believe how long I've been here, and no one's offered me wine." Birdie waved her hand like she was clearing smoke from the air.

"You just walked in the door."

"Exactly."

In the kitchen, Birdie settled onto one of the low-backed leather chairs that bordered the island. She crossed her legs like a textbook illustration from finishing school.

"So how are things?"

"It depends. Which *things* are you referring to?" Jones turned to search the kitchen wine rack for something to match the vintage of Birdie's taste buds. That it allowed her to not make eye contact with her mother when she answered was simply a happy accident. Jones had worked hard to get past her extreme desire to avoid conflict with Birdie. She might have faltered at first, but she wasn't going to backslide completely. And maybe Birdie really *was* just curious about how Jones was.

"Things, you know, like with the estate. Have you figured out the division of assets?" Birdie scratched a nail on the marble countertop, its black surface flecked with what Jones feared was real gold. Birdie seemed intent on mining it.

Right, *those* things. "Things are the same as last time you asked. Dad and Charity didn't have a prenup, so everything is jointly theirs. His will left pretty much everything to her." Jones slid the glass of wine across the counter.

Birdie took a deep sniff, followed by a small sip that she swished like a mouthwash enthusiast. She slid the glass back across the counter. "This is fine, I'll drink it." Birdie nodded to the glass that was still half full.

"That wasn't a tasting portion," Jones said. "That was a full glass."

"Well, haven't you become *quite* the optimist? A full glass doesn't have any empty space at the top," Birdie replied with a tight smile.

"Aren't you a vision of optimism?" Jones sing-songed.

Birdie fixed Jones with a stare as she took a healthy drink from the now topped-off wine glass. "I wish you wouldn't call him *Dad*."

"Yes, you've made that clear. And I never addressed him as *Dad* to his face. It's shorthand, like when I call you *Mom*."

"Yes, well, I'd also prefer you didn't do that. I thought you were going to fight the division of assets."

"No," Jones said slowly. "You told me to fight it, and I said that I see no reason to."

"Well, you should at least be compensated for raising her child. Come up with an hourly rate and send her a bill." Birdie opened her purse and pulled out her phone.

"Birdie. I'm spending time with my brother. Life isn't about money."

"Well, that's because you're living it wrong."

Jones crossed her arms, trying to resist shrinking into herself. "What are you doing here, Birdie?"

"Can't I come to check in on my only daughter?"

"You can, but I'm not sure why you'd start now."

THE DOORBELL GONGED through the hall. Jones had forgotten about dinner, but her stomach growled in a Pavlovian response.

"I'll be right back."

Birdie caught Jones' wrist as she attempted to side-step her mother. "Isn't your girl going to get it?"

"It's not like that. She's not my—"

"Where's your bracelet? And why aren't your nails done? Your arms are bare like you've been doing some sort of hard labor."

Elsie's footsteps thundered down the stairs. "I've got it!" she called.

Oh no. The last thing Jones wanted was for Elsie to inadvertently do Birdie's bidding.

Birdie raised one manicured eyebrow and handed her now empty glass back to Jones. "Let's try something a little nicer this time. Nothing with a colorful label, and the cork should be as old as I am."

"Oh, so crumbling into the bottle then."

Jones was saved from Birdie's response by Elsie's cheerful bop into the room—it still seemed forced, but yet, Jones had never been more relieved to see anyone.

CHAPTER TWENTY-SEVEN
ELSIE

The movie flickered on the television screen with the strobe light cadence of a thriller. Someone was about to get very dead. Beside Elsie, Avery had abandoned her in her time of fear and was sunk into the old leather couch like it was swallowing them whole. They let out a snore that was only heightened by the terrible heavy breathing coming from the heroine crouching behind a tree.

Elsie and the actress let out a relieved breath in unison as both of their phones rang. Finally, a reason to pause the traumatic movie Avery had chosen to 'unwind'. It was probably easier to 'love' scary movies when you slept through their most terrifying parts. Elsie was officially diagnosing Avery with cinematic narcolepsy.

Jones' name flashed on the screen of her phone and Elsie felt relief mixed with mild annoyance, like a cocktail with just a touch of too much bitters. She wanted to clear up how they'd left things and she'd been worried about Jones, worried about the shift in her when Birdie arrived.

"Hey, hold on one sec." Elsie pinched the phone between her shoulder and ear. She patted her hip twice so Oscar would follow her to the door. Might as well get him out one last time before bed. "Okay, sorry," she said as she clipped on Oscar's leash, and they eased out the door and into the cool fall air of the city night.

"That's okay," Jones said in a whisper that made Elsie pull the phone away from her ear and squint at the volume. Yup up all the way, as usual.

Elsie softened her voice. She wanted to convey to Jones that she was there for her, that she could meet Jones where she was, even if her own feelings were hurt. Elsie wasn't sure when she'd become that person, but she didn't hate it. She knew Avery would be insufferable about her *personal growth*. "Is everything okay? Are you hiding?"

"What? No. Why would I be hiding?"

If the situation were reversed, Elsie might be hiding from Birdie. Not because she couldn't handle her, but mostly because she didn't really want to, which was why she'd taken off in such a rush, leaving Jones to hold her own.

"Why wouldn't you be hiding? Anything could be lurking out there. Or inside."

"That's comforting, thanks." Jones' laugh was breathy and forced. "I was calling to apologize for earlier."

"Oh, which part?" Elsie paused while Oscar thoroughly inspected a fire hydrant.

"All of the parts?"

Jones' voice had a cute little whine to it. Elsie considered not letting her off the hook just so she could hear it a little longer. Though that whine would be much more enjoyable in other situations.

"Yeah, it wasn't great. You kind of rushed me out the door there. But I know you were thrown off by your mom just sort of appearing out of nowhere. Did you have an inkling she was coming? Or, like, the equivalent of a storm tracking device for her northeast trajectory." Elsie tried her best to sound understanding, and keep her tone light, even though the memory of Jones pressing Elsie's jacket into her arms still stung.

"Birdie failed to mention it when she called me yesterday, but she never likes to show her hand. She says she's here to go to a charity event, but I suspect it's actually to strong-arm me. She's been wanting me to push for more money from my father's estate, but it all goes to Charity. The person, not the cause."

"Of course, although between us, she looked pretty frail. I think you could take her."

Jones laughed. "Yeah, but she's scrappy. She often finds a way to get what she wants."

"Why give when you can take? How are you doing with everything with your dad? I know we haven't talked about it much." It was difficult for Elsie to witness how fraught Jones' relationship with her mother was, too. Though she knew that didn't compare to how hard it was for Jones. Elsie could feel how overwhelmed she was radiating through the phone.

"I haven't wanted to talk about it. I still don't, really. In the beginning, right after the funeral, it felt like I heard from everyone I'd ever met, but I was too overwhelmed to process anything. By the time I got some breathing room, my whole life had changed. I was caring for Bentley and all the calls dried up. And then you came into my life and things brightened."

Elsie's heart felt like it was glowing even as it ached for Jones. "I didn't realize that. If you ever want to talk about anything, I'm here."

A cab sped by and laid on its horn.

"Speaking of *here*, where are you?" Jones' voice sounded skeptical.

"Wow, what a smooth change of conversation, Jones." Elsie laughed, her hurt dissolving at the way Jones had opened up and at her efforts to right what happened earlier. "I'm leading Oscar on his nightly olfactory tour of the block."

"I see. So not somewhere private?" Jones asked with what sounded like mock innocence.

"Everywhere in the city is a little private—there's so much going on that no one really cares what any one person is doing. Do we need privacy?"

"I guess I was hoping for a photo to keep me company since you're not here tonight."

Elsie stopped in her tracks. "Jones Haelstrom! What would HR say?"

"If I had to guess, I think they'd probably wonder why you were sending them such a sexy photo. As soon as they got done drooling over it."

"I didn't get the feeling that Cathy was into me."

"Babe, I think everyone is into you."

Elsie felt the smile building in her chest before it broke across her face. *Babe.* Jones had never called her anything sweet before. Four letters that made her feel more cared for than any long declaration.

"I'm sure a photo can be arranged," Elsie said in her best business tone.

"Please don't get naked on the street."

Elsie laughed. "You're no fun. Okay maybe later then. How late will you be up?"

"I'm actually headed to bed now," Jones said through a yawn that made Elsie want to curl up next to her. "Maybe something to wake up to, I expect my circadian rhythm to be thrown off without you sleeping naked next to me."

"So, it's the naked part that's essential then?"

Jones laughed. "I like it best when you surprise me. Goodnight, Els."

"Night, babe."

Elsie slipped the phone back into her pocket and finished the twenty minute lap around the block while Oscar sniffed each curiosity with the professional dedication of a sommelier.

. . .

AVERY STIRRED when Elsie shut off the television, switching the room into darkness.

"Hey," they said groggily. "Did the movie end?"

"Yup! It's done!"

Avery reached for the remote. "Did you love it?"

"I definitely loved the end of it." Elsie smiled innocently.

"Is that because it ended?"

"You know what they say, *all's well that ends.* Get some sleep Avy-baby, I've got a photoshoot to orchestrate."

Avery hesitated before widening their eyes. "Oh. Jones is a lucky woman. Wear your torn to hell Guns N' Roses shirt."

"Not my sexy Nickelodeon shirt?"

"Actually, that's perfect for you."

CHAPTER TWENTY-EIGHT
JONES

Jones had been joking when she told Elsie her circadian rhythm would be messed up without Elsie in her bed, but her body seemed to take it as an order. She'd tossed and turned until dawn streamed around the edges of the curtain, and despite frequently checking her phone through the early hours, no photo from Elsie had arrived. As soon as the light came, she shot out of bed like she was being freed from being grounded. Jones ambled down the stairs to seek refuge in coffee and absolutely not check her phone. Elsie was probably still asleep anyway.

She was steaming milk for her coffee when her phone shimmied across the marble countertop. Jones reached for it so quickly that she almost fumbled it to the floor. She caught it at the last second and took a deep breath, and held it savoring the anticipation like something sweet melting in her mouth.

She exhaled and swiped up, and there was Elsie looking like the perfect mix of ridiculous and sexy. The photo had the blurry effect of a Glamour Shot. Elsie was kneeling on her bed, hair in a high side ponytail. Jones used her thumb and forefinger to zoom in because yes, Elsie had absolutely crimped her hair. She wore a loose t-shirt that fell off one shoulder, revealing a smooth expanse of skin uninterrupted by any bra strap. The overall effect was *hottest girl in an 80s music video,* and it stirred that desperate teenage crush feeling in Jones that she hadn't realized had been hibernating.

As she stared at the picture, Jones grinned so hard her cheeks hurt.

Jones' phone dinged again, and she realized she had no sense of how long she'd been transfixed by the photo.

Elsie: *Sorry that took so long—I had to sleep with my hair braided so the ponytail looked perfect. Worth it, right?*

Jones: *Very, very worth it. I think I know what I want for my birthday.*

Elsie: *Is it the latest Cindy Lauper album?*

Jones: *What can I say? Girls just wanna have fun.*

Something behind her creaked, and Jones spun to see Birdie seating herself at the kitchen counter.

Jones' phone flashed with Elsie's next reply and she reluctantly turned it facedown. She'd save the joy of Elsie's response like dessert for after what was sure to be a distasteful conversation with her mother. Birdie woke up in the morning like the dawn was a personal attack on her well-being.

"How did you sleep?"

"The bed might as well have been a futon."

Jones pictured the California king mattress on the sleek frame in the second guest room. It wasn't worth fighting about. Perhaps Birdie was used to sleeping on clouds.

"Were you hoping for some coffee?"

"Yes, I thought your girl might be up and making it when I came down at six. Otherwise, I wouldn't have bothered getting dressed."

Birdie's covering was half-open and getting dressed was a very generous description for the thin silk between her naked body and the rest of the room. Jones closed her eyes and took one of those centering breaths that all the meditation apps swore by. Nothing. She still felt pissed. "Elsie? No, she didn't stay over. And she doesn't work for me."

"Oh." Birdie's lips pulled into something between a grin and grimace. A *grinace*. She had a smear of red on her canine, either from eating her enemies or from the lipstick she wore to bed. Or maybe she'd put it on when she woke up. *You can't face the day until you put on your face.* Jones had worn blush and a "tasteful" hint of mascara for her kindergarten class photos.

"Well, I mean she does work for Haelstrom Media on Fangley Heights. It's a puppet show." Jones knew she was rambling. She stopped talking and focused on measuring coffee grounds into the espresso machine, spilling half on the counter. "She's, we're—nice. I mean she's nice and we're dating."

"Well, well, well." Birdie's face lit up.

"You cannot give me more than one 'well' before I'm sufficiently caffeinated."

"You're so much like your father. Finding a pretty young thing at the office." Birdie's thin wrist poked out from the sleeve of her robe as she adjusted a tennis bracelet, the diamonds so big a ball boy might be tempted to retrieve them.

Jones felt the rage gather behind her eyes like a migraine. "Are you kidding me? You're literally trying to date your pool boy. Who's gay, by the way. In case the drag queen brunch didn't tip you off."

"Lots of men like to be glamorous. Maybe he's poly." Birdie's silk caftan slid down her thin arms as she shrugged.

"Where did you learn that word?"

"I'm on the internet."

If Birdie's eyebrows hadn't been frozen in a constant state

of surprise for the last decade, Jones was sure she'd be raising them in self-satisfaction. Jones wanted to argue, but instead Birdie's earlier words played through her head. Her relationship with Elsie was different from her father's latest marriage. Wasn't it? It was surely different from his marriage to Birdie, fifteen years his junior, a new actress on one of his shows.

An actress wooed by the powerful executive. Such a cliche that Jones had slipped into it without meaning to. Could Jones really blame Birdie for chasing her pool boy? Maybe these bad decisions were in her blood.

But Elsie wasn't a bad decision. She was kind and caring and sexy as hell. And when Jones was around her, she wanted to be the best version of herself. Not that Elsie made her the best version of herself and without her, that would go away. But being near Elsie made Jones want to grow. She wanted to tend to herself, which wasn't something that had ever occurred to her to do before.

But how was she different from Birdie chasing her pool boy or her father marrying a series of increasingly younger women until his latest was younger than Jones herself? It was a romantic Benjamin Button situation.

Not that she had chased Elsie. Jones hadn't used her power over Elsie to seduce her. Right? Jones replayed their first kiss. She'd gone to Elsie's with a contract and Elsie had brought her home and cared for her.

Jones' insecurity came barreling back. What if Elsie had cared for her because she needed the job and Jones was the one to sign her contract? But Elsie's interest hadn't faded once the contract was signed. And she'd even gone along with the HR agreement.

"I'm just not sure what's in it for her."

Jones flinched. She glanced at her mother.

Birdie was smiling, coral lipstick imprinted on the mug before her. "She's not even trying to be famous; she hides behind that set pretending to be a little vampire boy."

"So you *have* watched her show?"

Birdie picked up her phone. "It's on the *internet*. I might have skipped around in a few episodes last night."

"And?"

"And what?"

"What did you think?"

"I think a pretty girl like that should be willing to show her face."

Jones let Birdie's words sink in. She was right, in a way—Elsie wasn't trying to be famous, she was happy doing what she loved. She'd signed the HR form and she was still here. Probably texting Jones right now, perhaps wondering where she'd disappeared to. Or maybe even sending some outtakes from her photoshoot. The thought sent a shiver of anticipation down Jones' spine. *No, Elsie definitely wasn't taking advantage of her.*

CHAPTER TWENTY-NINE
ELSIE

O kay." Avery clapped their hands together and surveyed the coffee table. "We've got popcorn, seltzer, chocolate, wine, and egg rolls. What else do we need?"

"We're watching a twenty-two-minute episode, Ave, not setting out on the Oregon Trail."

"We're watching *the* episode." Avery turned to Jones, who was snuggled next to Elsie on the couch. "Did she tell you that she tried for over a year to get Rebecca to green-light this script? That it's the one she's most proud of?"

"Interestingly enough, Elsie did not mention any of that to me."

Elsie shrugged. She could feel both Jones' and Avery's eyes on her, and she didn't like the sense of collusion she was picking up between them.

"I'm proud of all of my work. You both know it's not my style to go overboard about things."

Avery barked out a laugh, and Elsie could feel Jones chuckling beside her.

"Elsie, when I got my Master's Degree you hired skywriters."

"Skywriter," Elsie said.

Avery tilted their head. "What?"

"It was just one." Elsie shrugged.

"Okay," Avery said slowly. "You hired a skywriter and got me business cards that said 'the doctor is in'."

Jones put a hand to her chest, like she was trying to steady herself enough to talk through her laughter. "Overboard is your middle name, Els. It's one of the things people love about you. After Bentley showed a slight interest in puppets after his birthday, you built him a craft chest. I had to confiscate the hot glue gun, by the way."

Elsie huffed, feigning indignation. "People should be encouraged! And as for the glue gun incident, I have apologized, but I stand by my initial assessment that Elmer's is not going to get the job done. That kid is going to end up with a chest full of haunted-looking puppets with no eyes."

Her protestations set off a new round of laughter. Elsie knew she could be a lot when she wanted to encourage someone or celebrate their achievements, but she didn't usually extend that philosophy to herself.

"You're right." Jones' arm was warm as it wrapped around Elsie's waist. "No one needs haunted puppets. It's just a watch party. Let us celebrate you."

As much as she loved Jones' house, she really liked having Jones in her space. Elsie took a fistful of popcorn, throwing a piece into the air before leaning her head back to catch it in her mouth. It was a party trick that also happened to buy her a few seconds to blink away the tears she felt brimming in her eyes.

The episode had aired earlier that day, so they were streaming it. On the bright side, that meant no commercials. But it also meant that a lot of people got to watch it before Elsie did.

She stuffed the rest of the popcorn she had into her mouth

to buy more time, but when she finally spoke her voice sounded scratchy. "Okay, fine, support me."

"Yes!" Avery jumped onto the couch, and a second later Oscar jumped up, too. "Okay, Oscar, it's showtime."

Elsie tossed Oscar a piece of popcorn as Avery pulled up the episode.

She managed to feed Oscar two more pieces before Avery slapped her hand away. "Fine, but now he knows who loves him more."

"Right, me, because I don't want him to get sick. Everyone ready?"

Jones' fingers dug into Elsie's hip, pulling her tighter. "Ready," they said in unison.

ELSIE DIDN'T WATCH the finished episodes often. When she'd watched the pilot, it had made her squirm, like she was a fly trapped against the window—desperately needing to get out but not smart enough to fly the other way. She'd watched all the way through with Avery who'd asked her to sit still one hundred times with the patience of someone herding cats.

It was strange to hear her voice and movements so disconnected from herself. When she was recording, she knew she was there, felt present with every action, but watching it back, it could have been anyone. Had she really lilted up at the end of that sentence? Why did she move her wrist like that? And why the hell couldn't Trey hit a single mark? The opening scene looked like Smirch's audio was poorly dubbed.

When the episode ended, she felt lightheaded and wondered if she'd been holding her breath. A small part of her wanted to cry for her creation, for the payoff of believing in herself.

Jones and Avery had laughed throughout, and every few minutes Jones would run her fingers up and down Elsie's back. It had felt like love.

"I knew you were talented, Elsie, but I didn't expect to be moved by a children's show."

"What you were getting at was so much deeper than simple jealousy." Avery nodded. "It was so well done. And I can't believe how many sex jokes Fangley's aunt made. Did Rebecca not catch them?"

Elsie shook her head, but Jones was already leaning forward. "What do you mean by 'many'? I only caught one and it was mild."

Avery smiled. "Well, when Misty has that dinner party and everyone puts their keys in the cauldron on the front entryway, that's a sex party thing."

Elsie coughed. "Or it's a way for people to not drive after drinking. Who can say!"

Jones' eyes were wide, like she was trying to calculate something in her head. "Okay, that's okay. Kids won't really get that."

"Right." Avery nodded, a devilish smile sneaking across their face. "The jokes are for the parents."

Elsie hopped up from the couch. A distraction was needed. That or an escape. She felt uncomfortable with the dissection of the scenes, even though she was thrilled with how the episode had turned out. "Anyone need a refill? No? Okay, I'll be back."

As she made her way into the kitchen, Jones' phone began to ring. When she returned, Jones planted a quick kiss on her cheek before rushing out the door with the phone still pressed to her ear.

"Did something happen to Bentley?"

"I don't think so." Avery's face had drained of some of its color. "From what I gathered it was a very loud man. Lou, maybe? Jones seemed more annoyed than anything."

"Shit. Could it have been *Stu*?"

"Oh, maybe. I didn't realize people were still calling themselves that. It's like guys going by Dick."

"Well, he's definitely a Dick. I hope everything's okay; he works for Haelstrom Media and does what he can to make Jones' professional life a headache." Elsie's heart sank. She didn't feel ready to let go of the buoyant pride she'd been feeling, but it was slipping through her fingers, being replaced by the heavy stone of dread as she ran through possible reasons for Stu's call to Jones. "You don't think it's about the episode, do you?"

"Nah, those people have more important things to focus on than pan- and poly puppets. Plus, it aired a few hours ago."

"You might be underestimating the scorn people feel for women who don't play by society's rules, but I hope you're right. It's just a little show. Pan and Polly would make really cute puppet names though."

Avery took Elsie and Oscar for a walk around nine, claiming that they all needed to get some fresh air. Elsie suspected Avery was trying to trick her into not looking at her phone every thirty seconds. She'd only sent Jones one text asking if she'd gotten home okay, but it had gone unanswered. She wanted desperately to ask what Stu wanted and why it was more important than saying goodbye to Elsie, but she reminded herself that Jones didn't owe her anything. They were casual. Jones had had her sign a contract to that effect.

The feelings Elsie had were just lust, that and she'd been confusing spending time with Jones and Bentley as *belonging* —as being a family. But she was a guest. A fun, silly guest who was not to be taken seriously.

A text from her agent buzzed on her screen as Elsie and Avery rounded the corner of their street. Oscar was dragging behind them. He treated walks in temperatures above seventy degrees like they were absolute torture.

Elsie tilted her phone screen toward Avery.

"What do you think Mr. Crouch wants?"

"Maybe he's finally reaching out to apologize for the contract thing."

Avery laughed. "I doubt it, but I love that you dream."

Elsie opened the message.

Jason: *NY Radio wants to profile you tomorrow. Can you be charming before noon?*

Elsie rolled her eyes and typed a middle finger emoji before deleting it. Jason was annoying, but this opportunity was huge. Maybe she was finally getting the recognition she dreamed of for making an offbeat and progressive show.

Elsie: *Charming is my default state. What time and where?*

Jason sent her the details. The three dots of a followup message appeared and disappeared several times, and with each undulation Elsie felt her heart rate climb.

Elsie: *What else?*

Jason: *You probably know that you're trending and have been for a few hours. Well, not you, but #MistressMisty, which I think has something to do with your show, because I keep seeing you tagged.*

Elsie pulled up the social media app on her phone. She'd had notifications turned off, and when she tapped the alerts, she thought her phone might explode. There was no way she could get through the hundreds and climbing, so she clicked on a few. She gathered that the queer community was rallying around Misty. One post said, "Never thought I'd have so much in common with a puppet but we're both swingers with yarn for hair. Finally some REPRESENTATION."

Avery's elbow hit her arm, and she turned her phone screen to them. "Damn, you're blowing up."

CHAPTER THIRTY
JONES

The battery icon flashed red across the phone's screen. Jones promised herself that if she had to answer one more call from someone pretending to be concerned for children's welfare because of a TV show, that she was within her rights to lose it. Once the phone died, she might bury it beneath the tree out front next to Blankets, her beloved childhood hamster.

At least Birdie had absconded with her pool boy after Jones had stood firm on her refusal to fight her father's will. Dealing with her mother on top of all of this would have done Jones in.

The calls had been coming from all over the country. School boards, Parent Teacher Associations, Church Groups, Neighborhood Watch leaders. It was like they were all working off the same script. They were telemarketers gone feral. Once Parents for Propriety had posted her phone number on their website and launched their *God hates Fangs* campaign, her day had gone from dumpster fire to apocalypse. How they even got her number was beyond her.

She knew what these people wanted, it was the same thing the board of Haelstrom Media wanted—an apology that passed blame to Elsie. They wanted the episode pulled. And all of that would be so easy if it weren't impossible. Jones couldn't do that to Elsie. She definitely couldn't take down a show Elsie was so proud of.

Jones' phone rang again, and she tried to summon the courage to be frustrated with Elsie, but she couldn't. And Jones knew she had to keep taking these calls to control the narrative. If she could do that, she could protect Elsie.

Jones hit the accept button. "Hello, this is Jones Hael—"

The woman on the other end was shouting before Jones even finished saying her name, so she set the phone on the counter while she waited for her to pause long enough to imply that a response was required. There was no need to turn on speakerphone when the person on the other end was yelling like they were a peewee football coach.

She knew she needed to call Elsie back, but she wasn't sure what to say. Jones wasn't sure what she *could* say before she talked to the board tomorrow. She didn't want to make a promise to Elsie that she couldn't keep.

But surely Elsie could have predicted this backlash—Elsie had been in children's television for years, and this was hardly the first boycott of a popular show. Surely the script was run by others. Jones knew, because she'd spent the early morning hours researching how past scandals were handled. Always the same mix of blame and apology. Certain sectors of the population could consistently be counted on to go wild when children were shown anything other than heterosexuality. Onesies saying, "Women want me, diapers fear me" were fine for boys but somehow seen as an issue if put on a baby girl. It wasn't the sexualization of kids these parents had a problem with at all. It was the implication that their kids might not live up to their heterosexual ideals. The hypocrisy made Jones' head do that thing where she could feel her pulse behind her left eye, like her skull was a balloon being over-inflated.

The only thing Elsie was to blame for was making a good show that she believed in. That was the thing that bothered Jones the most, and she knew it bothered Stu and the network, too. Though that might be more about him wanting Fangley Heights for Trey. The episode was good. It was smart and funny, and Elsie's fingerprints were all over it. Not to mention Jones loved those fingerprints. Loved Elsie's hands, in general. Jones shook her head. Fielding phone calls from people calling you Satan wasn't the best time to think about sex. Or maybe it was.

Jones relocated her phone on the windowsill above the sink and thought about nudging it into the sudsy water. It would be a mercy. Telecommunication euthanasia.

She'd been doing more dishes by hand as a way to clear her mind—Elsie was right, it was kind of meditative. Plus, she now had a lot of clean dishes. She put in her headphones and winced as the woman on the other line screeched into her ear about traumatizing her child. Jones turned the volume way down and made a noncommittal noise before grabbing a coffee mug and the sponge.

Elsie had texted and called, but Jones hadn't had a moment to herself. And what could she say? Middle-aged people are pissed because you implied sex can be for pleasure and not just to make baby vampire puppets? Jones would laugh at the absurdity of it all if laughing wouldn't make her head explode.

And she realized she could do just that. She could end the conversation by not having it. She hit the red end button while the head of some church group she'd never heard of was in the middle of a spittle-fueled—she assumed from the pops on the microphone—tirade on sheltering children to protect their purity. For people so vociferously concerned about the innocence of children, they sure spent a lot of time thinking about children and sex.

She'd only washed half a plate, finger-painted with something she hoped was ketchup, before her headphones chirped as a very posh sounding AI read out a text from Stu.

"Did you green-light this interview? I thought we agreed on no press. Get her under control now."

Jones clicked the link in the text. Had Elsie mentioned an interview? She didn't think so, but it wasn't as if Jones had returned her calls. The piece was on NY Public Radio's site. Not the biggest deal, but definitely a Grande-sized one. Jones' heart slingshotted at the photo of Elsie laughing behind the microphone. As she read the synopsis, Jones' thrill for Elsie getting recognition plummeted to concern for the fallout that would inevitably land on her.

Elsie Webb talks with NYPR's Jira Levi-Anderson about puppets, sex, and breaking barriers in Children's television.

Jones hit play and scrubbed past the introductions and summary of Fangley Heights.

JIRA: *So Elsie, can you tell us if you're working on any new projects? What's next for you, assuming Parents for Propriety get their wish and Fangley Heights gets canceled? Oh my gosh, this is actual cancel culture in action.*

Elsie: *I try not to throw that phrase around, because people taking issue with creators for harm they've caused is valid. But I don't think I'm in that boat, and I hope the show doesn't get pulled. Haelstrom Media has been so supportive of the stories I want to tell. Jones Haelstrom in particular has a great vision for the future.*

Jira: *You're a bit of a visionary yourself.*

Elsie: *Well, I don't know about that, Jira. But there's nothing wrong with celebrating queer stories and ways of being. But that said, I have been working on some new ideas I'm really excited about. One is still in the planning stages, so I'm holding that one close. But I can say that I had an idea for these two characters, Throg and Wiggins. They share an apartment in Manhattan.*

They're roommates because New York City rent is impossible, but everyone thinks they're fucking.

Jira: *Well, are they?*

Elsie: *I mean, just hand stuff.*

Jones sucked in a deep breath. She closed her eyes, picturing Elsie's face as she delivered that joke. Her emerald eyes would be glittering. Jones felt a small smile sneaking across her lips despite her best efforts to keep her face blank. Laughter wracked her body before she knew it was coming. Tears clouded her vision. After all of the calls she'd gotten, it was refreshing to hear NYPR say nice things about the show, and for Elsie not to take the controversy so seriously.

There was a moment of silence before the interviewer cackled. It took her a few seconds to catch her breath.

Jira: *Sorry, that brought tears to my eyes.*

Elsie: *I was going to say 'just butt stuff', but I've heard this is a family program.*

Jira made a sound like she was choking on water. There was a silence on the show before Elsie spoke again.

Elsie: *Why don't I say a little bit about the characters while Jira catches her breath? Throg is an insurance adjuster. I guess I'd describe his build as lumpy. He's a monster who favors pocket protectors. Wiggins is a barista who likes nursing injured bugs back to health, mostly spiders and the occasional beetle. He often mistakes leaves and bits of trash for bugs, but he's doing his best. It's kind of an odd couple scenario.*

Jira: *Thanks for that Elsie. I think I can breathe again. Your humor should come with a warning. And an inhaler. I'm sure I speak for our audience, too, when I say that I can't wait to see your new idea come to life. I'm sure our listeners would love to know who your influences are.*

Elsie: *I mean Kermit the Frog, for sure. But also less celebrated characters like Rizzo the Rat and the Fraggles.*

Jira: *You are too much. I was thinking more along the lines of human influences.*

Jones could practically see Jira putting her hand on Elsie's arm as she said that.

Elsie: *Right, of course. Well besides Henson, there's Frank Oz, and definitely Fran Brill. I like to think I'm influenced by everything around me.*

Jira: *And the world is influenced by you. Thanks so much for joining us on Chat Lab, where we discuss all things shifting the narrative in popular culture.*

Elsie: *Thanks for having me.*

Jira: *I've been chatting with Elsie Webb, whose show Fangley Heights, has been outraging some while bolstering others with its queer undertones, and overtones. We'll return in a moment with what shows and events you can't miss this week.*

A commercial for a fundraiser came on, and Jones stopped the show. She braced herself for another irate text. Of course when asked about her influences, Elsie would name puppets she loved and admired, not people. It so perfectly captured what she loved about Elsie.

And sure enough Jones' phone dinged again.

Stu: *DID YOU CATCH THE SEX JOKES?*

Shit. Jones had been too busy enjoying the sound of Elsie's voice to consider how this interview might strengthen the public's case against Fangley Heights. Well, besides the fact that Elsie mentioning her name definitely wouldn't *decrease* the number of angry calls she was fielding. Jones had a lot to process, not the least of which were Elsie's apparent plans for a new show. And she really should work through some of it before talking to Elsie.

She picked up her phone to power it down, and its black screen showed only her own reflection, blissfully unresponsive at last.

CHAPTER THIRTY-ONE
ELSIE

G ive me that before I throw it in your beer." Avery swiped Elsie's phone from her hand just as she'd hit the call button. They glared at the screen and then made meaningful eye contact with Elsie as they powered down the phone and shoved it into their pocket.

"Is threat therapy a new thing you're trying? Is that Freud?" Elsie's protest was half-hearted.

Avery was right. Elsie had been obsessing over her phone the entire time Avery had been at the bar to celebrate her interview. Which had gone amazingly well, if her social media notifications were any indication. She felt like everyone in the world was trying to get her attention right now, except Jones. And instead of getting excited about all of the exposure Fangley Heights was getting—#PuppetPride was trending, and her follower numbers were ballooning into the tens of thousands—all she felt was apprehensive. The two voicemails she'd left for Jones were pitiful, bordering on embarrassing.

Elsie was just lucky Avery hadn't been able to see the texts she'd sent in between her calls. What Elsie disliked most about the whole thing was how little this behavior felt like her. It wasn't like her to chase someone, especially when she hadn't done anything wrong.

Even the queer community getting really into Fangley Heights and rallying behind her creative freedom wasn't enough to hold her attention.

Her hand absently reached for where her phone had been all night on the bar top, and Avery seamlessly slid her drink into the empty space in front of her.

"Sorry, habit," she said with a shrug.

Elsie lifted her glass and saluted Avery. Where would she be without them to save her from herself?

"You still haven't heard from Jones?"

Elsie shook her head. "No. I keep feeling like I should apologize, but the backlash is absurd. It doesn't matter to me."

"It is absurd, but it's also real," Avery said. "So it probably matters to Jones, because I would guess that she's dealing with the brunt of it. Did you see her quoted on social media?"

"Yeah, she said she was proud of the show." Elsie sighed. "And Jones matters to me, so if we apply the principles of physics, the backlash also matters to me."

"That's not physics, Els. How many times did you fail that class?" Avery smirked.

Elsie closed her eyes. "Twice."

"Exactly. Your sentiment is right though. She might be overwhelmed. Plus won't you talk to her tomorrow at work?"

"I assume she'll be there for the meeting." Elsie took another long pull of her drink.

She'd gotten a voicemail from Stu earlier requesting her presence tomorrow to discuss "the current state of things." He'd spoken like he was inviting her to a summit and not what was closer to the principal's office. She knew enough of what was coming to dread it. She'd either lose her job or her dignity tomorrow. At least tonight she could be happy, or at least try to be.

The bar Avery had picked was a careful study of seediness. Like one of those pioneer village recreations, every detail was studied and intentional, from the sticky floor to the stale popcorn and waxy bartop Elsie was leaving half moon shapes in with her thumbnail. The jukebox in the corner was filled with classic country, with a few blues albums spliced in, and a dartboard with absolutely lethal projectiles drew a small crowd across the room. The bartender, who had been serving them seven dollar Budweisers all night, had a mustache that matched the one her dad had had most of her childhood. Though her father would have never paid seven dollars for a beer that was less than a dollar at the liquor store a few doors down. Someone should really open a bar that just sold Forties and all the seating was on a stoop. Actually that probably existed.

Avery slapped her arm, and Elsie startled. "I just got invited to a Fangley Heights watch party tomorrow. Some of my queer friends from grad school are getting together to watch old episodes. I think one of them is writing a paper on queer motifs in your work and their power to be seminal."

"Really? They know it's a kid's show, right? And my motifs are mainly, like, fart jokes."

"Don't dismiss yourself, Els. The world could be such a different place if we taught kids to love and accept themselves, even if they don't fit into one of the two predefined boxes."

Elsie nodded. "That means a lot coming from you. When I frame my work as silly, it lowers the stakes and that makes it feel less scary to me. What if people start noticing and then I make something…not good?"

"What if they start noticing and you change the world? Tanner Tavish, that queer media influencer, tweeted that she watched yesterday's episode with her niece and that the show is subversive, brilliant, and gayyyyyyyy."

"Well if Tanner said it. How many y's did she put on gay?"

"At least eight."

"The more y's, the closer to God."

"Elsie. Listen to me, this is a big deal. Of course I knew you were fabulous before all these other people, but after the dust settles here, you're going to be an icon. Maybe Tavish will profile you for Queerty."

"I don't want to be an icon."

Avery narrowed their eyes.

Damn, they always saw right through her. Elsie sighed. "Fine, of course I want to be queer royalty or whatever, but right now I just really want Jones to call me back. I've gotten a few media requests, people want me to respond to that press release Parents for Propriety put out saying they're going to boycott the show because it encourages sex and devil worship. Though none of them seem to have an issue with vampires, so I'm not sure what logic they're clinging to."

"I guess they've never seen a Disney movie."

Elsie laughed until her beer went up her nose, and then she cried a little. "Right? Sorry for depicting a happy and fulfilled older woman. I can see why that would be threatening to moms in their thirties."

"Probably don't say that if you make a statement."

Elsie wiped condensation from her beer and reached for her phone, coming up empty-handed since Avery had moved it. "Do you think she's mad at me?"

"You didn't do anything wrong, and besides, since when do you care if someone is mad at you?"

Since *now*, Elsie thought, but didn't say. Avery was right, caring about this wasn't normal for her and Elsie didn't particularly like that it did matter to her. This was a new feeling, a nervous anticipation that someone she liked wasn't happy with her. Even if she hadn't done anything wrong, her worry that she'd disappointed Jones had been enough to deflate her high from the radio show. "You're right, I'm sure it's nothing. She probably is just overwhelmed."

"Oh good, you're back! The Elsie Webb I know has never cared about what anyone expected from her regardless of the consequences for others."

"Wow, you make me sound like a real catch."

Avery grabbed her hand; their eyes gleamed with the earnestness of someone who had had one too many drinks. "You are."

Elsie slid both of their glasses away. "I think it's time to switch to Temples."

"If you mean Shirley, I'm in. Can I have your cherries?" Avery asked hopefully.

"I love you, but absolutely not."

"Okay fine. But I do mean it. I admire that about you—how you're able to be true to yourself. I've always wanted to be more like that."

"What do you mean? You're working every day to be true to yourself, Ave."

"Yeah, I am. But you inspired me to come out."

"How many of these have you had?" Elsie peered at the contents of Avery's glass.

"Don't do that. I mean it. I knew you'd support me fiercely, no matter what reactions other people had. The way you move through the world matters, Els. It opens up doors for people. And it made me feel brave enough to be who I am. The work you do on Fangley Heights matters, too. Don't let some angry PTA mob or dude in a suit make you doubt yourself."

Elsie had to blink quickly to clear the tears in her eyes. "I had no idea that I made you feel safe enough to come out."

"Yeah, do you remember that speech class we had in junior year?"

Elsie nodded.

"Well, you decided to do a speech laying out your evidence for Heta Wilson being queer based on an analysis of her film roles. Do you remember your closing line?"

Elsie laughed and affected a serious tone, "In conclusion, it takes one to know one."

"Exactly. I thought steam was going to come out of Miss Harken's ears. But I sat there listening to you and I felt a wave of clarity. I'd known that the categories presented didn't feel good to me. But I didn't feel any more like a boy than I did a girl. Remember how I used to get changed for gym class in that storage closet between the two locker rooms? When you said that line, something just clicked for me. I'd been wondering for a long time, but I felt like I didn't know enough to be sure. But at that moment I thought, *I am* one, *and that's the only qualification I'll ever need to be sure that I'm nonbinary.*"

"You were the one you'd been waiting for. I love that."

"Exactly, I stopped waiting for some external confirmation. That night I came out to you, and you said okay and asked if I wanted to go get Slurpees."

"That sounds like me." Elsie laughed, but it quickly trailed into nothing. "But this is my job, you know? And it's Jones' job. These parents are coming with their pitchforks. Maybe I should just apologize and end this so I can take more chances again in the future."

"If you're sorry for something you did or regret your actions, then by all means apologize. But if you're only apologizing to appease others, others whose opinions you don't even care about, then why bother? No one wants an empty apology. They're going to expect changed behavior."

"You're right. I have nothing to apologize for at all."

"I know I am. Do you think Jones wants you to say you're sorry?"

"She hasn't said that. Though she hasn't said anything to me. How did it all go so wrong? It feels like just yesterday we were eating snacks and celebrating the episode."

"That *was* yesterday, babe."

CHAPTER THIRTY-TWO
JONES

Jones' phone screen lasered into her eyes as she grabbed it to shut off her alarm. It should be illegal to be woken up before six a.m. unless it's for something good like coffee or sex. At least this day could deliver on the coffee part. Her phone showed twenty-two missed calls and she tapped to expand the list. Only one was from Elsie, and that made her heart sink for a reason she wasn't sure she was ready to examine. She was surprised by Elsie's restraint, even with Jones' radio silence, Elsie had simply asked for a call back. If the world was on fire, Elsie would probably calmly walk across the room for a pitcher of water. Jones felt a blip of frustration that Elsie didn't seem more concerned about the current situation the studio was in. But that wasn't fair, Jones was used to the frantic energy that traveled with insecurity—one hundred missed calls and texts. Elsie had asked for what she wanted and Jones had ignored it, hadn't called her back. She might have felt like she was fighting for her life, but really she was fielding phone calls.

Still, her message was a nice break from the apoplectic tenor of Stu's voicemails, all of which ended without a goodbye.

The rest of the calls were a mix of diatribes from representatives of 'concerned parent groups' and outright threats to Haelstrom Media and Fangley Heights for promoting *Satan's sexual agenda*. Elsie would appreciate that phrase, maybe she could even work it into a plot.

But when Jones opened her messages, she hesitated. She didn't want to tell Elsie that everything was going to be fine when she really wasn't sure. It was probably better if they didn't talk until the meeting this morning.

Seeing Charity's message among them stole her breath for a second. Of course, during this crisis would be when she resurfaces. She left Charity's message for last. If she was finally returning the countless calls Jones had left her over the past weeks, the news was probably big. She wanted to focus on every detail. And Jones wasn't sure how much more big news her brain had room for. She'd at least need to fortify with caffeine. And a few painkillers to calm the pounding in her head. She rolled out of bed and made her way to the kitchen.

Jones' coffee mug sat steaming before her as her curiosity won out. She hit play and a burst of staticky silence greeted her. Charity's voice came through choppy, like a radio station about to be lost. Jones listened to it three times but couldn't make out anything coherent. Maybe Charity was coming back and maybe she wasn't. Either way, leaving Bentley had stopped feeling like an option for Jones a while ago. Like Elsie had said, Jones hadn't just stayed, she'd shown up. She was finally understanding what Elsie meant by that.

Jones still wasn't sure what staying meant for her. She could buy a place in New York and keep working for Haelstrom. The second part of that thought turned her stomach. The only Haelstrom she wanted to work for was herself, not her father's ghost. But at least staying in New York could mean a real shot with Elsie.

Those logistics could all wait. At present she needed a

plan to save Elsie's job before Charity got back and fired her. For the next few days, Jones was still in charge, as long Charity hadn't called Stu, too. If she had, Jones might as well go back to bed. But instead she got dressed and handed over the guard of the house to Susan on her way out.

The phone rang harshly over the stereo as Jones dodged another kamikaze cab driver on the bridge and waited for Susan to pick up. Her knuckles were white on the wheel. She just needed to hold on tight until she could fix everything. Simple.

"Hi, did you forget something?" Susan had a particular talent for never sounding annoyed.

"I just forgot to tell you that Benz likes peanut butter with his apple slices. I put some in a little container in the fridge."

"Yes, I know. That's how I always pack his lunch."

"Okay, right." Jones pictured Benz sitting at the kitchen counter where he'd been when she left. "And he has a permission slip in the green folder in his backpack. I signed it so that needs to go—"

"To Mrs. Anderson. I'll make sure she gets it. You don't have to worry; I'll take care of it."

Jones felt completely made of worry, a sort of buzzing unease swarming her senses, but Susan was right. If anyone was the expert on caring for Bentley, it was Susan.

Jones ended the call and spent the rest of her drive stress singing Adele. A fairly good use of time.

Stu was waiting for Jones in the building lobby with a cup of coffee that may or may not be poisoned, and a smile that definitely was. Her headache ticked behind her eyes as she took the cup and brought it to her mouth. Not bad.

Overwhelmed didn't even begin to cover how she was feeling. Her heart was doing its honest best to beat its way out of her chest. Stu doing something nice almost brought tears to her eyes. God, she was a mess.

Stu's voice boomed. "I'm glad you got here early so we can strategize. I know we're on the same page about this. Our first priority has to be to fix this and stop the decline of the share price. We need to shift the blame away from Haelstrom Media. It's the classic defense of a few bad apples, or in this case just one rotten one."

Stu threaded his arm around her and led them to the elevator bank. Jones' stomach turned and it was only partly because her blood was now half caffeine. They were assuredly not on the same page. She wasn't confident they were even in the same book. But Stu had more experience with this than her. Even more than he wanted to punish Elsie, Jones hoped that he wanted to protect the company. They made their way upstairs and to the boardroom.

"So what's the plan?" Jones had a few ideas, but none of them seemed like good options.

Stu took a seat at the head of the table. "We need a charm offensive. I've put a call into Trey's friend Anthony. He works at Pip in the Morn. Elsie will be the first interview on tomorrow's show."

"Is another interview really the way to go here?" Jones asked.

"It is, because we'll be writing her answers," Stu said, giving Jones a smug smile. "I'll submit a list of approved topics to Anthony to pass on by this afternoon. PR is already working on those, and they're writing a list of talking points to all of those topics. Elsie will have to stick to those exactly. And keep quiet until she has a chance to apologize tomorrow."

"There's no way she's going to apologize." And Jones wasn't convinced she wanted her to. Elsie loved Fangley Heights.

"She will if you ask her to, Jones." Stu smiled sweetly.

"I'm not sure that's going to be enough. And I'm not sure I can ask her to." Jones' chest tightened as she thought about it.

"She needs to take this seriously; we all have a lot at stake. If she won't agree to an apology, we'll incentivize her. We're within our rights to call on the morality clause in her contract."

Jones shook her head. "She hasn't breached that. Surely, we reviewed the episode as is our standard practice and nothing in it went against our policy."

"Not the episode. The clause covers her public statements. She made jokes in the interview that are unbecoming to the Haelstrom brand. And she retweeted something that I found offensive."

"My father did a million things worse than Elsie's off-hand joke."

"Look, I didn't want to do this, but Elsie's not the only one whose reputation is on the line here." A smirk slithered across Stu's face.

Jones' stomach iced over. "What does that mean?"

He slid forward a manila envelope that Jones hadn't noticed before. "Your relationship isn't as secret as you thought."

Jones narrowed her eyes. "We disclosed it to HR."

"The public doesn't care about that. All they will see is that you let your girlfriend put out an offensive show. Even if you weren't involved in the approval, they'll still think you exerted your influence. They'll question your judgment and so will the board. You're in charge, after all."

"What's in the envelope?"

"Just open it."

Jones picked it up and ran her finger along the seam. She slid out the photographs and even though her hands were shaking, it was clear what they were. Photos of her and Elsie arriving at work in the same car. The second photo was of her and Elsie kissing. The final one was zoomed in on just their faces, lips pressed together, a smile ghosting across her own mouth. She wanted to frame it. She also wanted to tear it apart.

Jones knew it had been a risk to start things with Elsie. She'd been naive to think their relationship wouldn't have consequences.

Stu cleared his throat. She wished he'd pretend to be a little less pleased.

"As you can see, this is also personal for you. Even if Elsie doesn't take the episode blowback seriously, I'd think she cares enough about you to walk this back and do the interview tomorrow. But you need to help convince her. It's your reputation on the line here."

Jones wanted to scream, because Stu was right. Who knew what the fallout would be if these photos were released. Maybe she'd lose her job or her credibility, who knew how that would impact what columns she got to write once all this CEO business was over. She might be compared to her father with his taste for young actresses looking for a leg up, like Birdie had suggested the other day. Or maybe Charity would question her judgment and not want Jones around Bentley anymore. That seemed like the worst consequence of all. Even if these fears were unlikely, their claws sunk into Jones' mind and wouldn't let go.

"Where did you get these?" Jones demanded.

Stu reached out to take the photos back. "I'm not at liberty to say."

"But they said they'd release them if what? Elsie didn't apologize?"

"That was strongly implied."

"Okay." Jones released her grip on the photos.

"Okay?"

"I'll get her to apologize." It was the right choice to protect both her and Elsie, but still, she hated herself for it.

CHAPTER THIRTY-THREE
ELSIE

Elsie's first mistake had been her fourth beer the night before. Her second mistake was clicking accept to the meeting invite for nine a.m. that she'd seen on her way home from the bar. Work email should be blocked after hours, or at least require you to re-type your password to prove you really do want to check that message from your boss at 12:03 a.m. But Elsie's email had no such requirements; it let her traipse into her inbox and click accept any old time of day. And now she was here, on this loud street, in the too bright morning sun, elbowing her way through a gaggle of middle-aged women blocking the door to Haelstrom Media.

Nothing good was waiting for Elsie in that stale conference room, she was sure of it. She had half a mind to turn around and head back to her apartment. She could curl up with Oscar on the couch if Avery hadn't taken the dog to work with them. Or she could use the day to put the finishing touches on the prototype puppets she'd been making for her new show idea. She was getting close, even if the robovac puppet had proven harder to master than she'd anticipated.

A woman clenching a poster board and a Starbucks cup in her fists backed into Elsie, crunching her foot beneath a sensible sneaker. People really should have back-up cameras, or come equipped with those beeping noises trucks had. Elsie took a few steps back from the group, their light pink t-shirts with P4P emblazoned on them in what was definitely Comic Sans made them look like a wad of bubble gum. Parents for Propriety sure didn't care about the propriety of their own acronym.

Maybe she could give them something to think about and make this day enjoyable after all.

"Excuse me." Elsie angled her shoulder to slice into the space between two of the women, but they closed ranks and she bounced backward.

The door to the building opened, and the women began to buzz. A bewildered grip Elsie recognized from around the studio stopped before them.

"Do you work for Fangley Heights?" A woman called out. Her ponytail was so high and tight that it looked like some invisible force was trying to lift her off the ground. Hair that intense probably meant she had leadership qualities and was responsible for this outburst. Elsie assumed she was in charge.

The guy nodded, his floppy blonde hair falling into his eyes. The women began to chant in unison. There was something witchy about hearing a group of women chant their frustration. In theory, Elsie didn't hate it, but the words that flowed out of their mouths set her blood to boil. They reminded Elsie of the weird sisters in MacBeth with their double double toil and trouble.

"Keep Fangley Heights wholesome, like it was made for your son!"

The women chanted over and over until it became nonsensical. Though admittedly, it didn't make much sense to begin with. The laziness of the rhyme frustrated Elsie. That, and the fact that it was unnecessarily gendered. But then again, so much of the world was unnecessarily gendered, like socks and Bandaids. Also a true missed opportunity on their part to rhyme Fangley Heights with dykes.

Elsie stepped through the crowd and shooed the grip—Kevin, maybe?—away. There was no reason for him to deal with their abuse; no one seemed to have any issues with the camera set up. The women turned to yell after him, and Elsie used the distraction to head for the door. She knew she shouldn't engage. She only had a few minutes to get upstairs if she wanted to be on time for what was sure to be a lovely chat with Stu and Jones. Elsie had trouble picturing Jones in that room, in opposition to her. One of the women called her name and Elsie let her hand drop from the door. Surely she could be a few minutes late for a good cause, especially if she was about to get fired.

"What?" Elsie's words burned in her mouth. She'd been winding up for this fight as she tossed and turned all night, but still she knew she shouldn't have it. Arguing with parents, even if they were manhandling her, wouldn't help her case with the network.

"You work for Fangley Heights."

"I created it. And honestly, if the best you can do is that terrible rhyme about being wholesome then I guess you haven't been watching many episodes. Where's your creative spirit? Here's one for you—you might like to protest, too bad you don't know best." *Okay, so much for not arguing.*

The woman stepped back as though slapped.

"Do you approve of satanic orgies?"

"No." Elsie paused, pretending to consider the question deeply. "I only approve Lof regular ones. Next question." The woman's mouth gaped open, and Elsie tried not to laugh.

"Are you considering an apology?" Another woman called out.

"Yes, Fangley and I have considered it, and we're ready to accept your apology." Elsie was gaining confidence in her replies. Her nerves had evaporated and she felt like she could stand on the street all day.

She pointed to a woman a few steps back from the rest. "Yes, you with the absurd velvet scrunchie."

The woman reached up and patted her bun. "I was wondering how you can justify promoting monsters to children?"

"Are you talking about puppets or the mayor of New York City? Because he paid the Network for that Fangley commercial for the city."

The momentum of Elsie's body shifted sharply as a hand wrapped around her wrist and slingshotted her backward before she had a chance to call on the next member of the angry mob.

"What are you doing?" A familiar voice hissed in her ear.

Jones. She had missed Jones, even though in that moment Elsie got the distinct sense that Jones hadn't missed her.

"What?" she asked innocently.

"Stop talking." Jones' grip tightened on her wrist, and Elsie...well, she didn't hate it, even though she knew Jones meant it to discourage her behavior.

"I'm addressing their concerns."

"Inside. Now." Jones turned on her heel and walked back into the building pulling Elsie along with her.

Once Elsie was able to gain control of their momentum, she dug in her heels, halting them just before the elevators. Whatever this was, this thing between her and Jones, Elsie wanted to figure it out down here and not in that fish tank conference room, surrounded by men who maybe wanted to see them fail.

"Jones, wait, just talk to me."

"You're already late."

"You're the boss; just write me a hall pass or whatever." Elsie's, albeit terrible, attempt at levity was met with the artic blue of Jones' gaze.

Didn't her eyes used to seem warmer?

"Okay fine, can you at least explain why you didn't call me back?"

"No." Jones dropped Elsie's wrist and brushed her palm on her light gray pants.

That felt…not great. Elsie had heard of being brushed off, but this made her feel like something dirty. Like a crumb being swept away.

"Why not? The least you can do is tell me it's over and you—"

"No, I can't explain it. I wanted to call you back, and also I couldn't do that at all. Look, we can't do this here." Jones said through gritted teeth.

She walked to a corner of the lobby and stepped to the other side of an imposing and inappropriately tropical potted tree. Elsie followed her. It was an absolutely terrible hiding place and Elsie loved that Jones had picked it. She searched her mind for a joke to keep herself from crying.

"This is like a cartoon hiding spot. This tree is skinnier than my arm." Elsie forced a laugh. "Remind me to write this into an episode."

"Do you have a better idea? And if we can't fix this there won't be more episodes."

Jones winced as she said the last part, and Elsie felt the sting of the threat as though she'd been slapped.

"Why wouldn't there be any more episodes?" Elsie had realized her and Jones' jobs could be on the line, but it hadn't sunk in that it would mean no more Fangley Heights.

"This is what we called you in to talk about. We're getting a lot of pressure from Parents for Propriety to issue an apology and take some sort of disciplinary action."

"Apology for what, specifically?" Elsie wanted to get Jones' opinion of what she'd done wrong.

"The episode, Elsie. The implication that happy, well-adjusted people can have multiple partners. I know it's absurd, but we both have a lot on the line here."

"I hate this. Just because they don't like it doesn't make it not true. And that wasn't even really what the episode was about."

"I know that." Jones pushed up her glasses to her forehead and rubbed at her eyes.

"Do you agree with them?"

"Well the board does. And so does Stu." Jones dropped her hands to her sides, and Elsie caught her wrist.

"I don't care what they think. They'd agree with anything if they thought it would get them on a lifeboat. I want to know if you agree. Really agree."

"It doesn't matter what I think. This has become a real problem for us."

"It matters to me, Jones. Did you even defend me or the show?"

Jones sighed. "How would that look?"

"I don't know. Maybe like you *cared* about me."

"That's not fair. You know I care about you. *Present tense.* But it can't be like that here. It has to be professional."

"You can be professional and still care about people and have their back."

"No, Elsie. We signed that form for a reason. I can't give you special treatment."

Jones' voice was almost robotic, like she was a machine powering down to avoid engaging with Elsie and Elsie hated it. "I know you care about the rules, Jones, but all rules are just suggestions. And in this case they're your suggestions. You make the rules, so you can just unmake them."

"I can't do this right now. We're late, and now we're going to walk in together. I need you to hear what they have to say and be agreeable. This is for both of us. And for the show."

Elsie watched Jones walk to the elevators and disappear behind the golden doors.

. . .

THE VOICES in the conference room went silent as Elsie approached. And she knew they'd been discussing her in a way they weren't comfortable with her hearing.

"Have a seat, Miss Webb."

Elsie sat in the absurdly comfortable conference chair as she waited for the torture to commence. She poured herself a glass of water that she proceeded to choke on. Not a great omen when the simplest thing proves impossible.

Elsie steeled herself for what came next. She expected the demand of an apology. She held back her laughter when Stu offered to provide her with a script. As a white, male executive, Elsie imagined Stu had absolutely no experience apologizing.

His utter glee at the situation bled through his carefully professional mask like it was cheap makeup.

"I just don't think I can apologize when I have nothing to apologize for."

"Apologize for the hurt you've caused."

"What hurt? Parents for Propriety are a small group, not the majority of Fangley Heights fans. Have you seen the support online? Especially from the queer community. Here —" Elsie slid her phone from her pocket and pulled up the app.

Stu didn't reach for the phone when Elsie offered it. She stared at it until the screen went back to black.

"None of that matters. Parents for Propriety are making a lot of noise. They're controlling the narrative. But we have a plan to take it back. We've been able to book you on a morning show tomorrow so you can apologize and reframe the themes of the episode."

"I'm not going on a show to apologize."

"Actually you are. We're exercising the media appearance clause in your contract. You'll be representing the show and the network on Pip in the Morn tomorrow, not your own opinions."

Was there an uglier sentence in the English language? Pip in the Morn was the kind of mindless drivel for people who wanted to feel informed but didn't have the focus to read gossip magazines. "And if I refuse?"

"We can terminate your contract," Stu said. "We already have grounds to terminate it for violating the morality clause."

"That clause is a sham."

"Not anymore. We're taking this seriously, Elsie. You should too."

"When you take ridiculous people seriously, other people start to think they have a point."

"Maybe they do. Look, Elsie, we can't do this all day. Everything's already scheduled." Stu looked at Jones. "Do you want to tell her or should I?"

"Tell me what?" Elsie looked at Jones who seemed to be studying the cuff of her shirtsleeve as though it held the secrets to the universe.

"Maybe it's better if we just show you." Stu slid a manila folder across the table toward Elsie.

She ran her fingers over the front before opening it slowly. She felt like whatever was behind the cover was poised for a jump scare. Inside the folder was a glossy photo, a little grainy but clearly Elsie and Jones in front of the Haelstrom Media building, kissing.

Elsie remembered the kiss, it had been a quick peck that she'd wanted to last longer. And she'd gotten her wish after all, because here it was in this photo, forever.

"Where did you get this?" Elsie asked.

"Someone sent it anonymously," Stu said, smiling.

Elsie's skin crawled. "So not from someone in the media? It's not professional."

"What do you mean?" Jones asked.

"Well the zoom sucks, and the focus is a bit off." Elsie tapped the picture. "This was taken by someone who takes a lot of blurry candid photos."

"Professional or not, this is bad. For both of us," Jones said.

"Why?" Elsie reached out toward Jones who leaned further back in her chair and away from Elsie. Usually it was touching the stove that burned, not reaching for it. Elsie pulled her hand back. "Jones, the entire point of the HR contract was to protect us, right? We're not doing anything wrong."

"Whoever took this photo doesn't care if our relationship was consensual and disclosed. And neither will Parents for Propriety." Jones' voice was steady but she still didn't make eye contact.

Elsie shook her head in disbelief. "Just because people don't approve of what we're doing doesn't mean we did something wrong. We can choose not to care what people think."

Stu tapped the table. "Haelstrom Media cares what people think, Ms. Webb. We rely on what they think of our shows to stay in business. Your apology tomorrow could keep things from getting a lot worse."

Elsie sat silent, looking at the photo. They looked happy, their fingers intertwined as they kissed through their smiles.

"Please, Elsie. Think about the future," Jones said.

She jumped at the sound of Jones' voice, even though it was almost a whisper. There were tears in Jones' blue-gray eyes that made Elsie think of raindrops falling into a stormy ocean. Suddenly Jones' fear crashed over Elsie. She didn't have to agree in order to want to protect Jones, to save her from whatever she was feeling right now. Even if Elsie didn't like it, she could do this for Jones. She cared about Jones, and Jones cared about this.

"Fine." Elsie stood up. She needed this conversation to end.

"Fine?" Stu sounded triumphant. "So you'll do the appearance tomorrow and stick to the talking points we've emailed you?"

"When did you email me?"

"While we were talking," Stu said.

Elsie didn't look at Stu; she kept eyes fixed on Jones. "Yes, I'll stick to the talking points."

Stu folded his hands on the table in front of him. "Great, so for tomorrow—"

"Just let me know where and when, unless you already did that too." Elsie let the door to the conference room fall shut behind her with a dissatisfying soft whoosh. She couldn't help but feel like that was the door closing on whatever she and Jones had, too.

———

ELSIE UNLOCKED the apartment and promptly laid face down in the entryway as Oscar scrambled over her, trying to find skin to slobber on.

"Well this is a bit dramatic, even for you." Avery's voice curled up at the end in an amused lilt. It had the effect of pulling the corners of Elsie's mouth up, too. She had to apologize, so what? There were worse things than apologizing when you didn't mean it. Entire relationships were built on apologies like that. Only, those definitely weren't the kind of relationships Elsie wanted. She wanted kind honesty. She wanted integrity. She wanted a partner who supported all her progressive puppet show dreams. Maybe her mistake hadn't been the episode, but that she mistook Jones for that person, that partner. And now all she had was an insincere script to memorize by tomorrow morning.

The talk in the conference room had made her feel like a

child, like her parents were forcing her to apologize to her brother for cutting the heads off his GI Joes. Again.

"The drama is proportional," Elsie mumbled against the wood floor. Oscar took her words as encouragement to pounce. He planted a paw into her kidney and when she jerked in pain they both yelped.

"So it was as bad as you thought it would be?"

"No. It was worse."

Avery bent over her, their green eyes looming very close to her face. "Ah, there you are. So I take it the meeting didn't go well."

"Very observant." Elsie held out her hand and let Avery heave her up. If Avery offered to carry her for the rest of the week, she'd say okay at this point.

"Was Jones there? Did they fire you?"

"Yes, but she might as well not have been. And no, but I kind of wish they had."

"Elsbells, tell me what happened."

"I have to go on Pip in the Morn tomorrow to apologize for the episode." Pip's name felt like a pit caught in her throat.

Avery shrugged. "At least she's hot."

"So not the point."

"Okay, okay." Avery raised their hands in a defensive motion. "She also asks good questions. I'm sure she'll be open to whatever you have to say."

"Well, she'd be the only one. I have a script I'm supposed to stick to. Jones definitely didn't have my back. If she's going to have me give up my integrity to appease closed-minded people I might as well go all in. Maybe I should recommend a corporate sponsor for Fangley Heights; we could do product tie-ins for margarine and defense contractors."

"Look, I know you don't want to do it, but—"

Elsie interjected. "No buts, only asses."

"Is that the attitude you had with Haelstrom when you wanted Jones to support you?"

"Why are you asking it like that?" Elsie narrowed her eyes.

"Like what?" Avery asked.

"Like if only I'd smiled more, or been more agreeable, things would have gone my way."

Avery shook their head. "That's not fair."

Elsie slumped back onto the floor. "I know. I'm sorry. Can we please get dumplings before this conversation goes any further? I hit hungry five minutes ago."

"Oh great, so now we're basically at the start of the apocalypse."

"Order now please. I want those potato ones. And sweet chili sauce. A lot. Like more than they think one person can eat."

"Fine, but this is why you have heartburn," Avery said. "And also why your sugar is so high. Why is it always dumplings that you want?"

"Dumplings are the answer to all things," Elsie said. "Sick? Get dumplings. Want to celebrate? Dumplings. Watching your life burn down around you? That calls for at least two kinds of dumplings."

"Fine, but I'm picking the kinds."

Elsie growled as Avery pulled out their phone.

They'd relocated to the leather couch, Oscar dividing the space between them, waiting for one of them to make a fatal mistake with their chopsticks so he could gobble up a dumpling.

Elsie tried to speak through a mouthful of dough and savory sweet potato filling, but Avery glared at her. She made a show of chewing very slowly before speaking again. A dumpling only buys so much time before cold reality returns.

"I knew the plan was always for Jones to go back to California. I mean we didn't talk about it, but I knew. This isn't her life; it's a side quest. And I know we said no strings, and that our relationship wouldn't impact work life, but I guess I assumed that also meant work wouldn't impact our relationship. I feel like I deserved the benefit of the doubt and her support."

"You do. You deserve all of the love and support. But—"

"No buts, Avery, I'm a tits gal myself. How many times do we have to go over this?"

"I love you, but please don't ever say that in public." Avery made a show of shuddering, and one of their dumplings rolled off the couch. Oscar lunged after it like it was a jumper and he was Spiderman. The dumpling never hit the floor.

"Did you see how fast he was? Now, if only he moved like that when I called his name at the park."

"It's all about the right motivation. Back to what I was saying—you deserve support. And," Avery paused for emphasis, "so does Jones." They held up their hand.

"I didn't even say anything."

"Yeah, but I could tell from your breathing that you wanted to interrupt. All I'm trying to say is that Jones is in a hard position, too. I'm sure she's facing the brunt of viewers' and sponsors' frustrations about the episode."

"Ah!" Elsie held up her index finger to stop Avery.

"I know their complaints are BS, Els. But you know that Jones still has to deal with them, so whether they're founded or not, for her they are very real right now. And I bet she's grappling with how to be fair to you without you both losing your careers."

"Yeah, I guess you're right. Ugh, I should have been nicer. I was really hurt that she didn't return my messages, but I don't think I really thought about how this would affect Jones. She must have had a hellish time. She's probably still having it, actually." Elsie pinched the last dumpling out of her cardboard container and tossed it in the air. Oscar's jaws snapped like an alligator as he gobbled it down. Two for two.

"That—right there—is why he begs, Elsie!"

"Relax, it was a dumpling. And my life is devoid of joy right now. I need everyone on my side that I can possibly win over."

They were silent for a minute; the only sound was Oscar's hopeful pants as he looked back and forth between them like he was watching a tennis match.

"I should have just walked away in the first place. When my contract expired."

Avery shook their head. "No, I think walking away was a mistake."

"But you said you supported me!"

"I did. I do. I'd support you shaving your head, but that doesn't mean I think it would look good."

"Damn, Avery." Elsie picked up a couch pillow and swung it toward them. "That's really hurtful. I can't believe you don't think I could pull off a buzz cut."

Avery blocked the pillow and tossed it aside. "Elsie, my love, take this seriously."

"Okay," Elsie cleared her throat. Avery always knew how to cut through her defenses. "Do you think I can still hang out with Bentley once Jones goes back to her life?"

Avery furrowed their brow. "Maybe this *is* her life."

"What do you mean?" Elsie asked, sitting up straighter.

"I don't know Jones that well, but I've seen the way she looks at you. And you've told me all about Bentley. If she had to decide, I think this would be the life Jones wants to come back to," Avery said with a shrug.

Elsie narrowed her eyes. "So you're saying I should play nice?"

"Yes, Elsie, I'm saying you should play nice if you can find a way to do it without compromising your integrity."

CHAPTER THIRTY-FOUR
JONES

The sound of glass shattering came from somewhere downstairs, followed by a crash. It sounded like someone, or something, was in the kitchen. From the general tenor of the destruction, they were either an inebriated raccoon or the world's worst home invader. A perfect start to what promised to be a terrible day.

Jones rolled out of bed and pulled on jeans she'd left crumpled by her nightstand, too defeated the day before to walk to the hamper. Dirty jeans weren't her first choice, but confronting someone in her underwear seemed impolite. She padded quietly down the hall to Benz's room. He was under the covers, cheeks flushed with sleep. She pulled his bedroom door shut, wishing there was a lock on the outside. Though if there was one, that would raise some weird questions.

Daylight was breaking, and the sky she glimpsed through the windows was murky like tea with just a splash of milk. Maybe the burglar just wanted breakfast. If you believed fairy tales, home invaders were often motivated by wanting breakfast. And sometimes a nap, which was very relatable.

Jones could go for some breakfast right now, or at least coffee.

She tiptoed down the stairs and toward the kitchen, willing the old floorboards not to creak. Something heavy clattered in the kitchen below and Jones looked down at her empty hands. She needed a weapon if she wanted to appear menacing. She looked around the hallway for anything she could grab. The mirror on the wall was impractical, if she could even get her arms around it, she knew it would be too heavy to carry. The old phone on the hallway table looked promising but she couldn't risk the noise. Where was one of her beloved biographies when she actually needed it. The element of surprise was her only advantage.

Jones grabbed a long, thin package leaning against the wall. What had even been in it? Wrapping paper? A sword? She had no memory of either, though both would be more effective than this cocoon of packaging for the confrontation she was about to have. The cardboard box was long and empty, but maybe if she held it like it was heavy it might be convincing.

Nope, she was definitely going to die.

A slight woman sat on the counter. She was busy wrangling her dyed blonde hair into a high messy bun on her head. When she finished, it looked like some kind of street bird had built a nest there. Jones squinted against the bright pink of the intruder's leggings. A loud crunch interrupted her examination and Jones let the box fall to her feet. To add insult to injury, the intruder was eating the fruit Jones had been saving for breakfast. Maybe that was a blessing in disguise since it freed her up to eat Pop-Tarts instead.

The woman turned and smiled, and Jones knew her immediately. Her body tensed, wanting to fight and freeze simultaneously. Charity's eyes traveled to the floor, taking in the box now splayed open at Jones' side. It had nothing left to give.

"What were you going to do? Ship me back? I thought

you'd be glad to see me." Charity punctuated her sentence with another loud bite of her apple.

"I was saving that." Jones nodded to the apple. The rest of her thoughts were still scrambling to assemble themselves, but her thoughts on Granny Smith apples were a constant no thank you.

Charity's cheeks puckered in. "Do you want it? I don't love the green ones—they're always too sour." She held out the half eaten fruit to Jones.

How strange, no one had ever offered her an apple that they'd taken a bite out of. Something about the gesture made her think of Elsie, and that was accompanied by a small pang in her chest. She shook her head. Charity took another bite and grimaced.

Jones waited for her to finish chewing. "I don't think you're here to talk about apples."

"You're right, I'm not. I'm here to talk about what happens next. Don't take this the wrong way, but you look like hell."

"And you look like a woman who's just spent weeks on a beach while I took care of things."

"I spent weeks sobbing in empty hotel rooms, but you're right that there were beaches nearby."

Weeks sobbing? Jones had imagined Charity having the time of her life. Clinging to the last bits of youth that she thought she had lost forever. She'd pictured her with umbrella drinks and tanning oil applied by the sure hands of someone else. In none of these imaginings was Charity sad.

"Why didn't you call?"

"I did, like twenty times yesterday—straight to voicemail. I thought maybe you were giving me a taste of my own medicine."

"Nope, I'm just living in a nightmare."

"Because gross. And also, your voicemail is full. I didn't even know that was a thing that could happen."

Jones laughed. "Yeah, that's fair. Yesterday was a disaster, and my phone dying was the only mercy. We're having some backlash about an episode of a show. But I was asking why you haven't called at all."

Charity spoke again. "I saw the news. And look, I'm sorry…for everything and so grateful for you. You saved me when I needed help. I'm not sure where I'd be without you. Where Bentley would be. I need to come back, I know that, but I can't face it alone. Hunter took care of so much, even if it was just the management of our lives and not the actual doing. I don't want to let Bentley down, but I don't think I'm the kind of person he needs. He needs someone smart. Someone who doesn't run away when things get tough. Someone made better by the pain of others."

Emotion stuck its sharp edges into Jones' throat, planting itself there like an apple seed. "No one can be everything. You're his mother. I don't think that's something anyone else can give him. I've made a lot of mistakes recently. Like a lot. But one thing I learned is that trying matters so much more than the end result. You just have to be here. You just have to try."

As the words came out of Jones' mouth they clicked like pieces of a puzzle, filling the empty spaces in her. They were exactly what she herself had needed to hear, too. She'd made a mistake asking Elsie to apologize. It was the wrong decision. But maybe it wasn't too late to make a different one. She just needed to show up. She needed to try.

Jones had had money her whole life. She'd never had love. And one was a lot more overwhelming to grapple with than the other.

What was left of Charity's apple thudded into the sink, and she dragged her fingers down the thighs of her yoga pants. Charity looked up at Jones, blinking tears from her eyes. "Will you help me?"

Jones cleared the emotion from her throat. "I've been helping you." Was Charity asking what Jones thought she was? Could she really have a life here with Bentley? With Elsie?

"No, you've been saving me. Bentley needs you, and I think I might need you, too. I know I've already asked for so much and I should have been more available. But when I woke up and Hunter was motionless beside me, my heart was chucked clean out of my chest. One deft twist of the knife, and my life as I knew it was over." Charity's eyes glistened in the sunlight now streaming through the window above the sink.

"Charity, I'm so sorry. I had no idea what it was like for you. I made assumptions about you and my father, and I was wrong."

Charity held her hand up. It had the slightest tremor as she started to speak. "I need to say this. I know you think I married Hunter for money. I don't blame you for that. Everyone thinks that. Hell, he probably thought that. And they were right. I married him because he represented the kind of future I felt sure I wanted at twenty-three. Maybe it's untraditional, but after I married Hunter I fell in love with him. And I didn't just grow to like him. He lit up my world. He made me laugh, and he made me feel safe. I was happy." Charity wiped away tears, which were falling more freely now.

"I wanted to find a way to give him more than he gave me. When I got pregnant with Bentley, I felt like I was finally giving him a gift to match all that he gave me. To give him another child, he loved you, you know." Charity pointed to the polaroid of Jones on the fridge. "And he knew he messed up, this was another chance for him… But I think I confused his happiness with mine. Or I forgot to consider mine as something separate. Right now, Bentley reminds me so much of all I lost. I know that's terrible and unfair, but it's also true."

Charity had wrapped her arms around herself and her fingertips left pale circles where she gripped her arms.

Charity blurred in front of her as Jones blinked tears from her eyes. "I'm so sorry. And I really have loved getting this time with Bentley. It's been so special to me."

"I love Bentley. But I'm not sure how to love him without Hunter. Please stay."

Charity's words knocked the air out of Jones. So much of what Charity said made Jones think of Birdie and all the ways she cared for Jones but didn't quite love her. Or couldn't show up fully. "I just—I've made a bit of a mess of things here."

Charity tilted her head to the side. "Messes are made to be cleaned up."

Jones let out a choked laugh. "You just say that because you have a housekeeper."

"Maybe. But let me be your housekeeper. Let's get it in order." Charity rubbed her hands together.

Jones began talking, slowly at first and then the words rushed out. Every way she'd let Elsie down, every wrong decision she'd made and time she hadn't been brave enough, every way Jones was sure she wasn't good enough for Elsie.

When Jones stopped talking, Charity held out her arms. It was strange for Jones to be beckoned closer by her stepmother who was starting to feel a bit like a younger sister. But Jones took Charity's outstretched hands anyway, letting them hold her in place and slow her spinning mind.

"If you care about her, nothing else matters. Fuck what other people think. You can marry for all sorts of reasons—opportunity, practicality, strategy, desperation, or because you genuinely love someone. I think that last one is rarer than people think. If you have a chance at that, you have to chase it, Jones. And in this case chasing it means not going anywhere. Don't go to California. Don't bail because work is difficult.

People love to get mad, because people love attention. Your father never believed me, but there's a lot more to life than Haelstrom Media. Show her you're there, even when she's not necessarily asking you to be. Just, you know, not in a stalker way."

Jones looked around for her keys, her mind a marquee flashing Elsie's name. "I think I need to go. She's giving an interview this morning that I helped push her into. I know she doesn't want to do it, but we gave her no choice. I can't let her apologize for creating something she believes in. Something that's good and means so much to people. I might as well have told her she needs to apologize for herself. For being."

"So go, apologize. Do you want some coffee? I can probably figure out the espresso machine." Charity released Jones' hands and jumped down from the counter. Her bare feet made a soft thud on the kitchen tiles.

Jones glanced at the clock. She'd barely have time to make it if she left now. "No time!" Jones rushed to the door and pulled her blazer off a hook swinging it over her shoulders as she shoved her bare feet into her shoes.

Charity's voice followed her out the door. "Nothing is guaranteed, Jones. You need to set yourself up for happiness now. Go get your girl."

CHAPTER THIRTY-FIVE
ELSIE

Elsie paced in her dressing room. It was both nicer and larger than the one she had at Fangley Heights, and that somehow felt appropriate. The talking points from the studio were clutched in her hands as she reviewed them one last time. Yes, she apologizes for the episode. No, she hadn't meant to encourage polygamy. Yes, she could promise it would never happen again. The last one was easy, seeing as no matter what, she was pretty sure she wouldn't have a job by tomorrow.

CONTRITION was written at the bottom of the page in Jones' handwriting, only shakier, like she'd been freezing when she wrote it. Still, it was underlined. Twice.

Elsie looked at herself in the mirror. She never wore makeup for work, well not until recently when she thought she might see Jones. But now, blush stood out on her cheeks against the foundation and whatever else the makeup artist had shellacked on. She looked a little like the version of Fangley wearing cold cream, only her eyes appeared a little more vacant.

She let her mouth fall open in the mirror before closing it. She might as well be a puppet, with the way Haelstrom

Media was pulling the strings. She glanced down at her suit; it was much more feminine than she'd like, but she and Fangley wore costumes all the time. This was just that. Sort of. Except even Fangley had more freedom to be himself than Elsie did right now. How pitiful that she envied a puppet, even if he was the coolest puppet in the room.

Elsie imagined Fangley giving a speech written by Stu Winkle about the importance of listening to your parents. She shuddered. Elsie plucked at the pearls on her neck before settling them beneath the collar of her royal blue blouse. She was in tuxedo slacks that were tailored for women in such an extreme way that they almost seemed like mockery. The front pockets were sewn shut, naturally, so she tucked her notes back into her waistband. The corner of the paper bit the soft skin of her hip. The sting of it made her think of Jones, how she loved to kiss Elsie there until she'd left a mark.

But now Jones wanted Elsie to apologize, like her work didn't mean everything to her. Like it wasn't an expression of who she was.

Was this who Jones wanted her to be? Someone who apologized for the things they believed in just to appease the loudest person in the room or to save some money? Elsie knew that thought wasn't fair, but she couldn't stop her mind from going there. She felt adored when Jones looked at her. Not the past few days perhaps, but generally. But maybe the person who'd repeat these talking points was the kind of person Jones wanted long-term. Not just for some no strings fling while she was in New York, but for real. Could Elsie be that person?

Avery's words from last night came rushing back to her. Maybe Jones would pick this life, pick Elsie. So maybe she should pick Jones, too. Show her that she mattered more to Elsie than being right. She reread the scripted questions and responses. She could do this.

Elsie reached into her tote bag, her hand like one of those

arcade claw games, grasping for her purple marker three times before extracting it successfully. She drew a dumpling on her palm. Dumplings were the answer to all things. Once she got through this interview, she'd order some. And they reminded her of Avery and their wise words. It was actually getting pretty annoying how wise they were.

Elsie shook her head. Eyes on the doughy, fried prize, Elsie.

Suddenly this interview seemed like the bridge between who Elsie was and a life with Jones.

Elsie's palms were sweaty as she opened the door and took the first step toward her future.

THE BRIGHT LIGHTS of the morning show studio burned Elsie's eyes. It was only a few blocks from where they filmed Fangley Heights, but everything felt foreign. The huge crew swarmed around the show's host, and Elsie stepped back into the shadows off stage to avoid detection. It was no use though, she was immediately engulfed in makeup brushes and a voluminous cloud of hair spray.

Pip in the Morn. Aggressively British, though Elsie had always suspected Pip's accent was fake, and she was secretly Karen from Ohio. Just like half of New York City's residents. Nothing against Karens or Ohio, except that she'd had bad experiences with both in the past.

"Okay." A woman leaned in so close that the microphone of her headset brushed Elsie's cheek. "When Pip says 'recent controversy' that's your cue to get ready. But do not step out on stage. After the cue, Annie will do a final touch up. And when Pip says, 'and here to discuss Fangley Heights' recent controversial episode is the show's creator, Elsie Webb'— that's you—you'll walk out on stage!"

Elsie tried not to roll her eyes. Where would she be without headset lady to tell her that she created Fangley

Heights? She definitely hadn't picked that up when she was, you know, actually creating the show years ago. Instead of reacting, she ran her fingers over the outline of the paper in her waistband and nodded. Today would be an exercise in not reacting how she wanted to. She might as well start now. Elsie needed to push down all shakiness and get through this segment for Jones. It would only be five minutes. She could do five minutes.

"Okay, so, when you walk out, look at Pip first like you're happy to see her. Then look directly at the camera and audience with a smile and a wave. Got that? Pip gets your attention first, then everything else. She doesn't like to be ignored!"

A morning show television host probably never dealt with being ignored. At least Pip had picked the right field.

"Got it. Pip, then the camera."

"Great! Once you sit down, you'll do a brief greeting. Ask Pip how she's doing, and then she'll segue into the questions. These are the questions that your agent and studio cleared. Do you know your talking points? Is there anything you want to rehearse?"

"Nope, I've got it." Elsie cleared her throat, itchy with her impending lies. She looked around for a bottle of water. She'd probably get some on set in one of those primary color coffee mugs shows like this love to use as merchandise tie-ins.

"Great, okay! Whatever happens, try not to let her rattle you. We have a full show today, and we can't let your interview go off the rails. Just stick to your talking points and try not to elaborate too much. And try to have fun out there; you look like you're about to attend a funeral."

Well, you all dressed me. A shiver ran through Elsie. This was a firing squad, not a casual conversation. At least firing squads were quick.

"Here, let's loosen you up a bit; no need to be so serious." Elsie expected the woman to attempt a shoulder massage and felt a wave of relief when her fingers ran along the collar of Elsie's shirt, opening the top button and then another. And finally one more. Her conservative outfit had just gotten a whole lot sexier.

It was weird to have someone unbuttoning her blouse professionally, though the woman didn't seem to mind as she ran her hands over Elsie's shoulders smoothing her blazer.

The host's voice boomed over the speakers. "And here to discuss Fangley Heights' recent controversial episode is the show's creator, Elsie Webb."

Finally she was getting the credit she'd always dreamed of for the show. If only it wasn't to shove her off the lifeboat.

Elsie felt a little push against her lower back, like she was a swing being propelled forward. Next thing she knew, she was stumbling onto the soundstage as a crowd of tourists roared. Real New Yorkers wouldn't be caught dead showing this much enthusiasm. If you held up a card that said applause on the subway, a man in a Yankees cap would rip it from your hands and break it over his knee.

Elsie took another step across the soundstage. She wasn't used to wearing heels. She felt like she was walking on stilts, woefully unprepared for the act she was about to perform. She wanted to put her arms out for balance but resisted. Pip then crowd, Pip then crowd. Elsie's eyes locked with Jones' and she struggled to keep the surprise off her face. Jones was standing off to the side of the soundstage and somehow Elsie had missed her arrival.

She lowered herself onto the couch, running her hands over the light gray fabric. All she had to do was stick to the script. She could worry about her integrity later.

"My, it's hard to imagine someone as adorable as you making something so raunchy. Though, I suppose that's half the fun." Pip winked. Her eyes were the blue of sour candy.

Elsie's mouth was dry; the carefully rehearsed words were in her throat. "Excuse me?"

Pip threw her head back and laughed. Her hair didn't move at all. This show really was all about the hair spray. "I'm talking about the episode—all those women at the castle. Or was it cat-sle? I mean, I think we can all understand why women throw themselves at you."

Wasn't this supposed to be scripted? Elsie's fingers itched to grab the paper from her waistband and review Jones' notes. She needed to get this back on track. Pip was looking at her like she wanted to devour her, and Elsie didn't think it was in a professional, hard-hitting interview type way. "The show isn't about me. It's a fictional show about a young vampire living in Brooklyn."

"Right. In the episode that's come under fire from concerned parent groups, Fangley is visiting his aunt who lives in the mountains with her menagerie of girlfriends."

"I'm sorry, Pip, was there a question in there?" There, that was nice and professional. Back on track.

Pip brought her head to her desk as she laughed like Elsie had said something hilarious instead of uncomfortably seeking clarification. "Well, many people, including Parents for Propriety, believe that Fangley's aunt is *you*, and the episode is *your* agenda."

"My agenda for what? Puppets? Would I love to be an ancient, lesbian vampire with a lot of charisma? Of course, who wouldn't? Is that my reality? Sadly, no."

This time Pip flailed in her laughter, latching onto Elsie's arm with nails that felt like talons. Elsie's joke had been, at best, moderately funny. "If you figure out the secret to being an ancient lesbian vampire, be sure to take me with you to your castle."

Holy shit. Pip in the Morn was flirting with her. This was not going according to plan.

Elsie sat silently as Pip wiped tears from her eyes with her index finger, drawing a careful line, like she was afraid of messing up her makeup. With the way nothing smeared, Elsie assumed she was covered in spray paint. Pip slapped at Elsie's arm, letting her hand linger.

"Goodness, you're so bad." Pip drew out the bad, her accent a parody of propriety.

Elsie scanned the side of the set for help, but all she got was hairspray lady smiling and giving her a thumbs up. "What can I say? I get paid to write jokes for children."

"Sure, but back to the episode in question. A lot of people felt like you were pushing a very specific agenda, one of free love and homosexuality. That maybe Fangley's aunt was a way to indoctrinate young people to your way of thinking."

"First, I want to clarify that Fangley's aunt doesn't identify as a homosexual and neither do I. That word is largely pathologies."

Pip leaned in, her chin resting on her fist. "I'm learning so much already. I knew you'd be educational."

Elsie reacted only by blinking SOS in Morse code. "Fangley's aunt is a puppet, and the only agenda I have is to encourage children to be creative and understanding. To be themselves, whatever that means. I want them to see their questions and identities reflected back to them. Whether that's about sharing toys or—"

"Sharing partners?"

Elsie's eyes searched the crowd for Jones or a producer or a concerned audience member. Any adult who could put a stop to whatever was happening here. She could feel indignation rising in her like a wave. She tried to remember the script. Maybe she could stack up those words until she had a breaker wall.

"Most kindergartners don't have partners, at least not that I'm aware of. If anyone's over-sexualizing the show it's Parents for Propriety."

A smattering of applause broke out in the audience.

"Well, us artists know that all art is about the desires of the creator at its core. Are you really arguing that the show you created and star in doesn't reflect your views on polyamory?"

Did Pip whatever-the-hell-her-last-name-was consider her morning show *art*? Maybe she made clay mugs in her spare time. "Well, I do believe in self-expression and acceptance."

"And boy do you know how to express yourself." Pip winked at her, and for a nerve-wracking moment Elsie thought Pip's fake eyelashes might dislodge and flutter onto the absurdly large desk in front of her.

Elsie took a steadying breath. Time to get to her talking points. Or rather the studio's talking points. Thinking of them as Jones' still didn't feel right, even if they were in her handwriting. "Fangley Heights reflects my views in terms of being a good person and respecting others. I believe those should be universal values. But the audience also brings their own interpretation, and that's what happened here. However, I do want to say that I take responsibility—"

"Hold that thought! We're about to take a quick break. I'm going to ask our adorable guest to stick around for a few more minutes, so we can get to the bottom of why everyone's so mad at her. We'll be right back after this."

THE CAMERA WOMAN signaled that they were out, and a makeup artist rushed toward Elsie like she was a first responder. Elsie was about to be forcefully saved with concealer. If only they could find a way to hide her completely.

She was frustrated that the moment she was getting back on script, and doing what Jones needed her to do, Elsie was thwarted by Pip and her commercial break.

She looked around for Jones, but she was deep in conversation with Stu and neither looked happy. Elsie wasn't surprised to see Stu there, he probably wanted to be the first to report her screw-ups.

Jones looked disheveled; she had a t-shirt on under her

pristine blazer, but Elsie couldn't quite make out what was on the shirt. She was dressed like she'd thrown on whatever she could reach before evacuating. Elsie loved her like that. Stu's hand hovered above Jones' lower back like he was testing to see if a burner on the stove was hot. Elsie made her best attempt at shooting flames from her eyes directly into his palm. He dropped his hand back to his side, evidently he realized if he touched her he'd get burned.

The thought made Elsie laugh, which caused the makeup artist to reprimand her with a quick, "Stop moving or you'll lose an eye."

Pip was at her desk reviewing notes, probably for the next segment. Elsie hadn't seen a teleprompter anywhere, which surprised her, and was probably why Pip was completely off script. Maybe she had a touch more freedom in her ridiculous show than Elsie had thought.

"We're back in sixty, everyone!" A booming voice called as the countdown back from the commercial break began.

Before she knew it, the crowd was being prompted to applaud. For what, Elsie wasn't sure. Maybe just the fact that anyone was still watching this absurd interview?

Elsie could feel Pip's attention return to her as though she'd walked through a cloud of gnats, gross and mildly annoying. Everything in her body screamed that she should run. But Elsie still hadn't gotten through the talking points. In fact, she'd probably only done more damage with her responses so far. And she needed to prove to Jones that she could prioritize what mattered to her.

"So Elsie, I'd be remiss if I didn't ask you this—do you regret the episode? Do you feel like you took things too far?"

"Those are two very different questions."

"Mmm, how so?" Pip leaned forward across her desk, presenting Elsie with an eyeful of her cleavage.

Okay, this was it—the moment for Elsie to prove to Jones she could put her and the studio first. She took a steadying breath and opened her mouth to recite her pre-planned answer. But before she did, she looked out at the audience. There was a kid in the front row wearing a Fangley shirt, a football helmet, and a tutu. They looked awesome and excited to be there. Elsie watched as the Fangster raised the Fangley puppet on their arm and had it wave to her. Screw it. She couldn't pretend to be ashamed of a show she was so proud of. A show that made a little kid dress up to be in this audience so early in the morning.

What she should have said was, 'I am so sorry for the stress I've caused the families that watch Fangley Heights. The plot was an oversight, and we never meant to encourage hedonism or polygamy. Our entire cast and crew, as well as Haelstrom Media, is committed to making sure nothing like this ever happens again. We'll be establishing a parental review board for script approval.'

But what she actually said was, "It was a good episode. I find the reaction to the content by so-called grown-ups regretful. And obviously things went too far for some members of the audience. Particularly the adult members who belong to witch-hunt organizations masquerading as concerned parent groups. They're concerned their kids could be queer, and instead of sitting with why that frightens them, they're attacking a TV program that teaches their kids to love themselves no matter what. Maybe those parents are the ones who need to watch the show and learn to be decent."

"Okay, so you have some feelings about this. But from a business perspective, isn't upsetting your key demographic— or the parents of your key demographic—a pretty catastrophic issue for the future of the show?"

Okay, so, no more Mrs. Nice Pip.

"That's not for me to decide. Either Fangley Heights will stay on the air or it won't, but I'm not interested in pretending that, if I had behaved a little better, these people wouldn't have come after me as a queer woman."

"So you think the negative attention being directed at the show is personal?"

Elsie's mind flashed to the photos of her and Jones kissing that had been sent to the office. The implicit threat that had arrived alongside them in that manila envelope. We know what you are.

Elsie paused as she scanned the soundstage for Jones. When she found her, Jones' eyes were wide and her face pale. That could have been the glare of the lights that gave all-white skin that wasn't heavily made up the pallor of glow-in-the-dark stars.

"I think—"

"Okay, that's all the time we have! Thanks for joining us, Elsie. You can catch Fangley Heights on HMN Wednesdays at 4pm—get in while the getting's good! Or at least for as long as it's on the air. And be sure to stay tuned! When we return it'll be time for everyone's favorite segment, Pip Pip Hooray! where I celebrate my new favorite things! You don't want to miss the best new juicer in town. Vitamin C is the new vitamin for me!"

"And we're out!" A male voice called from behind the camera.

Elsie slumped back against the couch, feeling like she'd just crossed the West Side Highway on foot.

ELSIE LOOKED around for the best place to throw up in this dressing room. She'd messed up that interview, and with it she'd thrown away her chance with Jones. Why couldn't she have just recited her talking points? If she didn't like the question asked, she should have just answered the one she wished had been asked, like a politician.

She sank into her black swivel chair and put her head between her knees. That's her career then. She thought about Fangley trapped in his case at the set. Did she have time to get back there before her access was cut off? Surely Stu and Jones were racing to the studio now to do damage control. Maybe liquidate all Fangley merchandise. Elsie would never see that little blue ghoul again, all because she'd let Pip get under her skin. She had a feeling Pip was actually trying to get under her skirt. At least she'd dodged that bullet. Her stomach rolled just thinking about it. Not that Pip wasn't attractive physically, she just had an ugly personality.

Elsie slipped out of her heels, then began pulling on her Converse. If she left now, maybe she could run to the studio. A thump on the door startled her, and Elsie half expected whoever it was to splinter through the wood like the Kool Aid Man. She swore when she shot up, hitting her head on the vanity in the process.

Elsie froze. Maybe she hadn't dodged Pip's advances after all.

CHAPTER THIRTY-SIX
JONES

The show had already started when Jones had gotten there, and they wouldn't let her backstage. So she stood to the side of the set, watching anxiously. Hoping she wasn't too late. When Elsie walked out she looked gorgeous, even though her smile was fake—it looked brittle, like if it broke it would cut her.

Beneath her blazer, Elsie's Dr. Teeth shirt that she'd slept in hung loosely. She tucked the hem into the waistband of her jeans, hoping she could pull off relaxed cool instead of sleepwalking zombie.

Jones did her best to tune Stu out and listen to Elsie's interview, but every time he went to touch her, rage threatened to erupt. Mercifully he seemed to pick up on that and settled instead for giving her a long list of various reasons why they should fire Elsie anyway, regardless of what she said today. Jones shouldn't have been surprised that he'd shown up as well.

"Jones, you dated her, surely you've learned she can't be trusted."

Jones wasn't a violent person, but in that moment her fingers flexed, and she wondered what it would be like to slap Stu and have that broadcast to every living room in America, or be memorialized forever as a GIF—the ultimate form of modern self-expression. Elsie would probably love that, Jones becoming a meme.

She turned to Stu and drew in a deep do-not-fuck-with-me breath. "Quite the opposite actually, not that it's any of your business. If you could see past the politics and money, you'd know that Elsie has more integrity than all of us put together. And sure, sometimes she comes out swinging when she'd be better off writing a strongly worded letter, but she believes in things. And she fights for what she believes in. That's a lot more than I can say for you. Or for me, lately."

"What's gotten into you?" Stu's voice rose in pitch and he seemed alarmed.

"I realized there are more important things than Haelstrom Media. I don't care what it means for profits or how many billable hours it takes the lawyers, regardless of the outcome today, we're reverting the rights for Fangley Heights to Elsie."

"You don't have the authority to do that." Stu's eyes looked black despite the bright lights of the soundstage.

Fireworks of applause exploded in the air around her. Jones looked up in time to see Elsie exiting the stage. She made her way to follow but was stopped by an increasingly beefy succession of security guards. She needed a diversion.

An arm wound through hers, and Jones felt a scream rising in her throat. She was only mildly relieved to see it was Pip and not Stu trying to steer her away from the crowd.

"I was hoping I'd get a moment alone with you. That Elsie is a real firecracker. Sorry I didn't stick to the script we agreed on, but it was more interesting this way. Better television. You understand, right?"

Jones nodded, barely listening. Her brain was a neon sign flashing *Elsie*. Everything else was grayscale. "Can you get me back to see her?"

"Of course." Pip's hand slid to Jones' lower back as her other hand rose in the air and snapped.

Jones startled. A split second later, a scared looking young man appeared at her side, his wide eyes radiating hope for the opportunity of a task.

"Evan, show Ms. Haelstrom to the dressing rooms."

He nodded quickly, his chest puffing out just the slightest bit. "Right this way."

Jones followed him backstage as he wound around a few corners. "The dressing rooms are all down here, just past the lounge."

"Amazing. Thanks Evan," Jones said.

"It's Anthony, actually."

She furrowed her brow. "Oh, I thought Pip said…"

"Yeah, to Pip we're all Evan," Anthony said with a laugh.

"Right, well, thanks!"

God, was she like that? Did she see people as interchangeable? Jones might be in her own world sometimes, but she was never bad enough to call everyone Evan. The thought flew out of her head as she picked up speed, scanning the doors for Elsie's name.

This hallway was way too long. As Jones ran, the distance between her and Elsie stretched. Her heartbeat echoed in her ears like a drum solo. People stepped in front of her and stopped dead—couldn't they see she was about to miss her chance at happiness? Couldn't they hear the desperation in her footfalls? Or at least her labored breathing? She needed to get to Elsie before she took off and Jones was left on the wrong side of the door forever.

SHE DIDN'T SO MUCH KNOCK on the door to Elsie's dressing room, as she let her body collapse into it with a thud. When the door opened, she stumbled over the threshold. She reached for something to save her and found Elsie. She was wrapped safely in Elsie's arms before she even realized she wasn't still falling.

"Hi." Jones' breath was shaky, but it wasn't from her run or her near fall. Elsie smelled like pineapple, and Jones could still picture Pip's fingers running along Elsie's forearm. Forearms that had framed her head in their tenderest moments. Apparently, she felt some sort of way about Elsie's forearms.

"I'm sorry." Elsie brought her hands up to cup Jones' face, and she caught a flash of purple.

Elsie was sorry? Jones struggled to imagine a situation in which Elsie had *less* to be sorry for. She'd come here to throw herself at Elsie's feet and Elsie had already beaten her to an apology.

Jones grabbed Elsie's hand and turned it palm up, squinting at the smeared squiggly purple lines. "What's this?"

"Just a reminder to myself. To try to be good, and not let you down out there. And that if I could just get through that, everything would be fine. Obviously it wasn't very effective. And it looks like I left a little behind on Pip's white couch."

"Ah, it serves her right after her performance." Jones swallowed hard and interlaced her fingers with Elsie's, hoping that a bit of that secret message would rub off on her, like she could absorb some of Elsie's goodness and her courage. "But you? You have nothing to be sorry for. You were perfect out there."

Elsie squeezed Jones' hand and seemed to sniff back a tear. "I'm so relieved. I was sure I'd ruined this by letting you down."

She pulled Elsie closer and pressed their foreheads together. "You didn't ruin anything, but I almost did. I was wrong to put you in that situation. I made the wrong call."

Elsie shook her head and let a quiet laugh escape. "It's not like I've been making a lot of great decisions lately. I love the show and the episode and Fangley, but I know I made things worse. For the network but also for you. Sometimes I double down when I should just sit down."

Jones pulled back a bit, catching Elsie's gaze. "That sounds like an Avery line."

"Hey, I can have my own insights."

Jones narrowed her eyes at Elsie.

"Okay fine, that was a paraphrase of an Avery line. But still…"

Jones laughed. For the first time in days she felt something other than stress flowing through her.

"I'm so sorry." Elsie continued, her warm hand finding Jones'. "Did I mess everything up?"

"No, I mean yes, technically, but I'm really proud of you." Jones ran her thumb gently back and forth across Elsie's palm. "I watched the Fangley episode again last night. And it's so smart and funny and compassionate. And that part when she reassures Ratatouille that being a city cat doesn't make him less of a feline. Followed by the Feline Fine song—I laughed until I cried, and then I just cried." Jones paused and looked at Elsie for a moment.

"Really? You cried?"

"I did. The whole message is that love is the point, not how you get there or what it looks like. Misty might not meet society's expectations, but she's happy. And trying to meet those expectations would rob her of who she is. What's more moving than that?"

Elsie's smile made Jones feel light-headed with relief. She wanted to be worthy of that smile forever.

"Yes, that's exactly it!" Elsie's smile grew wider. "Her beliefs make her who she is."

Jones glanced away, trying to hold onto her composure. She hated what she'd asked Elsie to do. It had been selfish, she'd let business get in the way of what really mattered to her. "And that's what I did to you with this ridiculous interview. We tried to control you and make you someone else, and doing that stripped away all the special things."

Elsie's thumb traced across Jones' cheek until their eyes locked. "I love that about you. How you're able to look at something again and come to a new conclusion. I can cling to my views even when being flexible is the better option for everyone."

Jones tried to focus on what Elsie was saying, but all she could hear was that one word. Love. That's what Elsie *loved* about her. That word fluttered through Jones' chest as it tried to make its way to her own lips. Because she did love Elsie, and the possibility of their lives together lit something in her when she didn't realize there was anything left to glow. Instead all Jones said was, "love," her voice rising at the end like it was a question and not the statement that would lead to the rest of her life.

Elsie's eyes widened. "I didn't mean to say that, but I think I said it because I do mean it." She paused and cleared her throat. "I've fallen for you, Jones. And for the possibility of more. I want to go to Bentley's sword fights."

Jones smiled as the word settled in her chest like a bird in its nest. She brought her forehead to rest against Elsie's again. "They're called fencing bouts. At least I'm pretty sure they're called that."

"And I want to teach him how to tie his shoes."

"He knows how to do that."

"Fine, then I can teach him how to double knot them or tie a tie."

Jones' laugh was effervescent in her chest. "Okay, both of those are still up for grabs, but—"

Elsie cupped Jones' cheek and looked into her eyes. "I know this isn't what we agreed to, this isn't *no strings*, but I want to see where this goes. I know my time on the show is done. So we won't have the HR agreement to hide behind." Elsie bit her lip. "What do you think?"

Jones smiled and closed the space between them. "Sign me up."

THE CHAOS of midtown engulfed them as Elsie and Jones left Pip in the Morn's studio hand in hand.

Jones felt so free, holding onto Elsie like that. She stopped walking and turned to her, leaning close. Elsie kissed her hard then. She kissed Jones like she was making a thousand promises. And Jones accepted each one as she melted into her. Elsie wouldn't let her fall. Elsie's hands wove into her hair, and Jones cried out when her fingers caught.

"My, Jones, what big tangles you have."

"I might have rushed here before I had a chance to brush my hair. Or get dressed properly."

"Did you oversleep? Because I had to be up at four a.m. for this. *And* I showered."

"No, I was defending the house against an intruder."

"Oh God." Elsie cupped Jones' face and studied it like she was looking for bruises.

A pedestrian bumped into Jones, pushing her even closer to Elsie.

"I should clarify. I presumed it was an intruder, but it turned out to be Charity."

"Wait, Charity's back? Tell me everything."

"Geez, Elsie, buy a girl breakfast first, I'm starving."

"I know just the place."

Jones tightened her grip on Elsie's hand, nothing was going to make her let go of this moment. "As long as it's your apartment, it's perfect."

CHAPTER THIRTY-SEVEN
ELSIE

Are you sure about this?" Elsie paused with her finger on the button in the elevator, because the moment she pressed it, things would blow up.

"I'm sure. The original Fangley should be yours, even if the board won't relinquish the rights for the show to you." Jones adjusted the black ski mask she'd just finished pulling over her head.

Elsie hadn't previously considered that someone could look attractive in a ski mask, but Jones had her glasses on under hers and her two French braids poked out on the bottom. It was a little like getting a peek at a present through the wrapping paper. Her feistiness, and the whole breaking-the-law thing weren't hurting either. Elsie's fingers itched to tear the mask off and kiss her. To feel Jones' soft lips against hers. To breathe in that little gasp of surprise she always made when Elsie deepened their kiss.

"You know, black ski masks are basically a neon sign that we're up to no good."

"I thought you'd like them—we're like the robbers in Home Alone."

"Oh, right. I keep forgetting you and Benz watched that

last week. Your entire plan is starting to make sense, even though it's a lot more Kevin than the robbers. The robbers were not the hero of that story."

"Hey, it's a good plan. And we are literally about to rob someone. Besides, you've seen the security at this building. A booby trap on the studio door will buy us precious minutes if they come around. Once that bucket of marbles spills on the floor, it's over for them. Now, let go of that button and put on your ski mask."

Elsie did as she was told. The mask was soft and smelled a little like Jones' purse—spearmint and perfume. "I am glad you went with marbles. I know from first-hand experience that no one likes to be covered in fake blood." Elsie shuddered. "It scarred me for life."

"It wasn't that bad."

Elsie leaned in close. "The worst part was washing it off alone."

"Stop trying to get me out of my very high tech heist outfit. And I never said anything about fake blood—maybe I splurged for the real deal."

"I sure hope not." Elsie knelt to tie her shoe. No need to trip herself when she'd probably fall over one of Jones' obstacles.

Jones looked perfect in a pair of black leggings and a black zip up hoodie she'd borrowed from Elsie. She reminded Elsie of when she did tech for theater in high school, and she had a brief flash of wishing she'd known Jones then. Each day it felt like Jones became a little more herself, more willing to take risks and sign on to Elsie's questionable plans. As a thank you for her help tonight, Elsie was going to take Jones to an all night diner and buy her chocolate chip pancakes.

The elevator dinged and Elsie cringed. She looked both ways before exiting onto the floor for Haelstrom Media. It was time for *Operation Puppet Heist* to commence.

They stuck close to the wall as they made their way to the

studio. Elsie's arm strained as she tried to carry a red bucket of marbles without them rattling.

"Where's Benz tonight? He didn't want in on this?" Elsie whispered.

She doubted anyone would be around tonight besides the single night guard Gerry, who liked to spend his shifts playing Nintendo in a utility closet near the dressing rooms. Elsie had spent several evenings absolutely destroying him in Mario Kart.

"He's busy having a movie night with Charity. You'll be pleased that he's decided *The Brave Little Toaster* is the movie everyone must watch."

"Well, that's correct. I knew he was a smart kid."

Once they were inside the studio, Elsie held the ladder Jones had stashed there earlier. Jones climbed up to booby trap the door with a dubious combination of the bucket of marbles and a ruler. If it worked, they'd probably commit manslaughter in addition to getting away. She laughed a bit at the thought, and the ladder shook.

"Hey, focus." Jones turned her head to peer at Elsie. "I don't want to get arrested."

"How can you get arrested when you run the place? Also, Gerry is not going to arrest us."

"Remember, I stepped down after your interview, when it became clear the board had always intended to fire you no matter what you said. Charity is now officially in charge."

"Do you think the whole thing was just Stu's plan to give Fangley Heights to Trey?"

"Well, it won't be Fangley Heights without you."

Jones slid the bucket to rest on the ruler wedged between the door and the jamb. It teetered as Elsie and Jones locked eyes. "Moment of truth."

Jones pulled her hands away slowly as their contraption settled. The whole thing was resting on the triangle shaped door hinge. "For both of us I guess. I still can't believe you gave it all up."

Jones took Elsie's hand as she climbed down the ladder. She hopped off the last rung and into Elsie's arms. "I don't think I'm giving anything up. Now, let's go get your vampire puppet kid."

They made their way to the puppet cases, and Elsie blinked away the sweat that dripped into her eyes behind her ski mask as she keyed in the code. A beep, and an angry red light blinked back at her. Yikes.

"Want me to try?" Jones was standing over Elsie holding her cellphone flashlight aloft.

Behind the plexiglass barrier, Fangley looked frozen in a block of ice. "It's not like I'm getting the code wrong. They must have changed it."

"Okay. I have an idea." Jones nodded once, then walked away, leaving Elsie in darkness as the bright light of her phone disappeared.

Jones returned a moment later with a hammer.

"Where did you get that?"

"From the props room; it was right next to the fake one you threw at me."

"I love you, but you've got to get over that."

"Never." Jones winked and then brought the hammer down on the keypad with a crunch.

"What the hell, Jones!"

Jones smiled. "What? They upped the security on these cases after the last time you—"

Elsie raised her hands. "Okay, okay, no need to point hammers."

Somewhere nearby, an alarm wailed like an infant. Appropriate, because this felt like baby snatching, down to the empty carrier at their feet.

Jones continued to hit the keypad until it came away enough for her to pry the case open with the claw end of the hammer. Elsie reached her hand through the opening and pulled Fangley through the gap. A real child would not have survived such a maneuver, but her felt son was resilient.

Jones grabbed Fangley and tossed him into the baby carrier. "Okay, run!"

The pieces clicked into place just as Jones reached the door. The plan was for them to sneak out through the back but—

An earth-shattering clatter filled the space as Jones pulled the door open and marbles hailed down. Jones spun toward Elsie in a panic and immediately began to stumble. Elsie rushed forward to catch Jones only to have her feet go out from under her just as she got close. She had to hand it to Benz, the marbles were a good plan.

Beneath her, Jones groaned and Elsie lifted up on her elbows to gain her footing.

Jones' smoky gray eyes stared up at her, the rest of her face obscured by the mask. She reached up and ran a finger over Elsie's lower lip. "How do you smell so good while doing crime?"

Elsie laughed. "I'm worried you have a concussion. We have to hurry, unless you want to get caught in more ways than one."

Jones huffed and let Elsie pull her to her feet.

The alarm was growing in intensity as they made their way to the elevators. Elsie smashed her hand on the button but nothing happened.

Jones was busy buckling Fangley into the baby carrier.

"Jones! We don't have time for that. The elevator's not working. The buttons won't light up."

"Oh shit. Maybe they locked them down," Jones said.

"Is that even legal?"

"I'm not sure we're experts on what's legal right now."

"Touche. So, stairs?" Elsie reached for Jones' free hand, and they raced to the stairs.

By the time they burst through the emergency exit, they were breathing hard and Fangley was dangling from the carrier by one leg. Elsie ripped off her ski mask—she didn't want to draw attention. Though anything goes when it's cold in New York. She took the carrier from Jones and tucked Fangley back inside.

"So what now?" Jones asked as she pulled off her own ski mask. Her hair was fuzzy from the hat, and if Jones' hair was disheveled, Elsie could only imagine the nest on top of her own head.

"Now we calmly get the hell out of here."

"Okay." Jones pulled out her phone and started tapping on the screen.

"What are you doing?"

"Our Uber is eleven minutes away. I mean what is the point of even living in the city if it's not ready at a moment's notice."

Elsie let out a laugh that echoed into the side alley. "You're thinking of cabs, babe. I guess you're going to have to slum it on public transportation this time, my dear."

WHEN THEY STEPPED into the Diner-saur forty minutes later, Jones' glasses fogged so badly she had to clean them before they could make their way to an empty booth.

Two menus were slid in front of them as a waitress with a lavender-gray updo cocked a hip against their table. "What'ill it be to drink, hun?"

The woman was about Elsie's age and seemed to be immersed in the character of *diner waitress*. When Jones ordered a green tea, Fran—according to her name tag—licked the tip of her pencil before jotting something down on her order pad. The entire act was exquisite.

"And I'll have a vanilla milkshake—we're celebrating." Elsie shot Fran a smile.

"Anything for the baby?"

Elsie glanced down at the carrier in the booth next to Jones.

"Just a high chair and some water, thanks."

Jones' eyes widened, and she watched Fran walk away, hips swinging like a pendulum. Then she turned to Elsie. "You're going to put Fangley in a highchair? Won't they think we're odd? What if they call the police?"

"We're at a diner after eleven p.m. Everyone's a little odd here, Jones. No one here wants to deal with the police, I promise."

Elsie watched Jones, waiting for her to immerse herself in the ten-page menu before she dared to reach into her pocket. Nerves were jumping around in her stomach like it was a mosh pit. Her fingers wrapped around the thing she was looking for, and she gingerly slid the item from her pocket.

"I, um, have something for you."

"Oh, you do?" Jones narrowed her eyes. "What is it?"

"Just close your eyes and hold out your hand."

Jones crossed her arms. "No way am I falling for that again after Bentley gave me the worm you two found on the porch that way."

"I promise this isn't a worm, but it was a joint effort with Benz."

"Okay, fine. I guess I can't complain after I've flipped through a menu I can only hope was covered with syrup."

Elsie laughed as Jones pinched her fingers together as to test their adhesiveness.

"Okay, ready?"

Jones' chest rose with a theatrical deep breath. "Ready." She scrunched her eyes closed and held out her hand.

Elsie placed the gift in the center of Jones' palm. It was nothing. It was everything.

"Okay, open your eyes."

Jones held up the brightly colored string—mostly green and black because that's what Bentley had.

"Is this a friendship bracelet? Are you breaking up with me in, like, the nicest way ever?"

"No, well yes, I mean…"

Jones laughed. "I like your thread choices."

"Not threads, strings. Now that you're staying, I thought maybe we could have some."

"Running a heist together didn't feel like enough of a commitment for you?"

"I know it's silly." Elsie bit her lip, color rushing to her face.

"No," Jones said, sliding the bracelet over her wrist and pulling it tight before grabbing Elsie's hand and squeezing it. "It's perfect."

THE SWEET EPILOGUE
ELSIE

The metal door creaked shut behind Elsie, punctuated by a definitive slam. She was late, and now everyone was aware of that. She glanced around trying to spot Jones and Charity. Off stage, someone flicked a switch and doused the auditorium in black. The utter darkness swallowed Elsie like water, making her movements unsteady and less predictable. She greeted the back of a metal chair with her hip and bit back a curse. Somewhere to her left a flashlight illuminated, and then she saw a campfire version of Jones' face lit spookily from below.

She shuffled her way down the row. She only stumbled once, and Jones' arms wrapped around her waist and pulled Elsie onto her lap. Maybe running late had its perks.

She and Rebecca had been in the writers' room all day, which is what Elsie was calling her living room until their show got picked up. Until then, she was figuring out how to have a true creative partner in Rebecca. Someone whose jokes she would listen to with an open mind; Avery was calling it her *how-to-play-nice-with-others* phase. Elsie was still insisting on consulting with Bentley fairly regularly. In addition to a writing credit, he was also paid in books and ice cream.

She might have made it on time if she hadn't had to stop at the candy store near Times Square, where she'd been stuck in line between a tour bus worth of children.

Elsie slid over to her own seat and waved to Charity. Now that her eyes had adjusted, the dark was more murky than anything. "Did you get a chance to see Bentley in his costume before the show?"

"No, he was nervous and wouldn't let me or Charity backstage."

"I'm sure he'll make an excellent Audrey II. We worked hard on his costumes."

"I know you did. The seedling one is so cute." Jones squeezed Elsie's hand.

"It's diabolical, babe." Instead of letting go, Elsie laced their fingers together and pulled Jones' hand onto her lap. She ran her thumb over Jones' ring finger. She felt her own stage fright rise up in her throat, though she was still several hours away from her big moment.

A light above the stage flickered on, and the show began.

THEY WAITED in the hallway outside the auditorium for Bentley. Elsie was buzzing with nerves and trying very hard to focus on what Jones was saying. Usually, she'd soak up Haelstrom Media drama like a pancake soaks up syrup, but all she could think was that she hoped she'd done enough to make tonight perfect.

"So we got the initial ratings back for Fangley's Friends and it's not great. Anemic, really. Your writing really was the lifeblood of the show, Els."

"Jones Haelstrom, did you just make a vampire joke? Have I accomplished my mission to make you silly?" Elsie grinned. This, right here, was happiness.

"No? At least I don't think I did." Jones furrowed her

brows. "Oh, lifeblood! My comedy is more Freudian slip than anything."

"Okay fine, tell me more about Trey failing." Elsie hoped gossip about her former co-worker would distract her from her nerves about what was to come later that night.

"In the Smirch-led episodes Trey's writing seems almost lifeless. Fangley Heights reruns are outpacing Fangley's Friends viewership two-to-one."

"You've gotta stop sweet talking me while we're in public. Did he ever admit to taking that picture of us? That's the only way I can make sense of it never getting out."

"He didn't, but I did get Stu to give me the copies. I'm thinking of having the closeup of us kissing framed."

"You are so romantic," Elsie said. "Want to ditch Benz? I thought we could grab dinner, maybe take a walk in the park."

"He's coming out now. We'll just say goodbye—I think he and Charity have an after-party to go to at some trampoline place."

"Oh that could be fun!"

Jones shook her head. "Babe, I wasn't suggesting we join."

Bentley ran down the linoleum tiled hall in his green spandex suit, like a cute little CGI-monster waiting to happen. He careened into Elsie and then reached out an arm for Jones too.

Elsie ruffled his hair. "You were great, buddy. How did the costumes feel?"

"The big one was a little heavy but Chester said I looked really scary." Bentley widened his eyes.

Elsie held her hand out for a high five. "Yeah you did! Oh, I almost forgot. I made these for us." She fished the two thin sheets out of her pocket and handed one to Benz.

"What are those?" Jones asked.

"It's an Audrey tatt-II, just temporary, sadly." She showed Jones the monstrous Venus fly trap she'd drawn.

"This is so cool! Mom, did you see?" Bentley called.

Charity broke off her conversation with Chester's mom and stepped toward them. "That's great, honey. Maybe Elsie and Jones can help you with it when you stay with them tomorrow."

Elsie loved when Benz slept over at Jones' new place, and she knew Jones did, too. But things had been nice with Charity back in the picture. Jones seemed more at ease. More able to enjoy being Bentley's big sister, another new experience for her.

When they parted ways, Elsie led Jones back to Prospect Park. The spring air was still warm around them, even though dusk was approaching.

"There, perfect. I'm starving." Elsie all but ran to the pretzel kart parked just inside the entrance.

Jones appeared beside her a moment later. "You know, when you said dinner, I thought you meant indoors and like an actual meal."

"Have you met me? Besides, these are fresh. Do you want salted? Or sweet? I think they have cinnamon sugar. Please just don't say plain."

"Is there another dinner in our future?"

Elsie shrugged.

Jones sighed. "Fine, I'll take sweet."

"You can have some of my salt one too, if you want."

Pretzels in hand they made their way to a bench, scattering grains of rock salt like breadcrumbs. Inside, Elsie's stomach was doing flips, and she prayed she didn't lose the pretzel. She really was hungry.

She took as many bites as she could, until her nerves got the best of her and she couldn't wait another moment to enact step one of her plan: happiness.

Next to her, Jones was glowing, backlit by the setting sun. Elsie got off the bench and knelt in front of her.

"What are you doing?"

Okay, this was it. "I'm—"

"Did you lose something?" Jones started to stand, and Elsie felt the moment slipping away.

"Nope, your shoe is untied."

"Oh." Jones settled back on the bench.

Elsie grabbed the laces of Jones' shoe and gave them a tug before Jones had a chance to examine them and see that they were still very much tied.

"Do you remember when I brought you roller skating here?"

"Of course I do. You tied my skates and held my hand. I think that was the moment I really started falling for you."

"Me, too." Elsie drew in a deep breath and released Jones' foot back to the ground. "I knew that you were special. That I loved who I was when I was around you, who we were together. That night was a glimpse of how good things could be."

"Elsie, what is this?"

She reached into her jacket and grabbed the velvet box like it was made of glass. She eased it from her pocket, having to angle her hand now that it was gripping the box.

"Elsie." Jones' voice had a hint of panic as her hand came to rest on Elsie's shoulder.

"This is me saying I don't want to go a day without you giving me a hard time for buying you a pretzel from a cart instead of a fancy dinner. I want to spend the rest of my life moving boring biographies that you actually hate reading into new apartments for us. I want to spend years canceling the plans we made with other people so we can stay home and eat takeout. I want to sign one more contract that defines our relationship forever. I'm even willing to submit it to HR. I want—"

Jones' hands were on Elsie's face now. "I want that too. All of it except the HR thing. They'd probably be confused because neither of us work there anymore."

Elsie leaned back and brought the ring box between them, cracking it open.

Jones laughed, which was exactly the reaction Elsie had been hoping for.

"Did you get me a diamond gummy bear instead of an engagement ring?"

Elsie tilted the box back and forth, grateful for the street lights that had blinked on a few moments before. "Isn't it beautiful how it catches the light?"

"Will I ever live down the gummy bear thing?" Jones reached for the box, and Elsie let her take it. She ran her fingertip over the bear. "Is that actually real?"

"I think you should bite it and find out."

"Oh Els, that's only for gold, babe."

Elsie snatched the bear from the box and bit off its head with a loud crack.

"Oh my god, don't break your mouth. I'm very fond of it."

Elsie grinned and licked the sweetness from her lips. "Rock candy."

She raised herself and settled back on the bench next to Jones. Elsie reached into the inner pocket of her blazer and produced a ring pinched between her thumb and index finger. It was simple, a gold band with a single diamond sitting on top like a little moon.

Jones' hands wove into Elsie's hair and she let herself be pulled forward. She could feel the tears running down her cheeks as Jones whispered *yes* over and over again. When their lips came together, their kiss was the perfect mix of salty and sweet.

THE SALTY EPILOGUE
ELSIE

Sign up for my mailing list to get a bonus epilogue! This free bonus is an explicit scene between Elsie and Jones full of steam and just a dash of silliness. Get the bonus scene at https://BookHip.com/LWLCXMF or visit www.lucybexley.com for more details.

Thanks for reading!

THANK YOU!

Thank you for reading my book! The support of readers is what keeps me writing.

If you'd like to keep up with my releases and other news, you can sign up for my mailing list at www.lucybexley.com or follow me on twitter @bexley_lucy.

As an indie author reviews are critical to helping new readers discover my books. A review on Amazon and/or Goodreads is greatly appreciated, if you're so inclined!

ABOUT THE AUTHOR

Lucy Bexley writes romcoms where queer women trip over things and fall... in love with each other. Her stories balance laughter and love with real-world struggles such as anxiety and addiction. Lucy lives in Boston with her partner, pets, and several cases of seltzer. She's the author of six sapphic romances including Must Love Silence and The Bright Side. When she's not writing jokes in a Word doc, she's writing them on Twitter.

www.lucybexley.com